MARAUDERS

Starship Hope Book Two

T.S. VALMOND

The Starship Hope: Marauders

T.S. Valmond

PRINT ISBN: 9781999501297

EBOOK ISBN: 9781999501280

Cover Design by: Goerz Designs

for my crew,
Stacey and Allison

We've done the impossible, and that makes us mighty.

— MALCOLM REYNOLDS

CHAPTER 1

Captain's Personal Log: 4327.9.2

The faces of the dead fill my dreams.

I'm back on Zelenia, walking my dog, Victor. He's impatient to be at the park near our home where he can run free. We pass by the houses of several neighbors. They smile and wave until they recognize me. Then their smiles fade, and their arms fall to their sides as we pass.

They know the truth. I see their hands balling into fists, murmuring amongst themselves as they come after me. The nice old man who helped me with my groceries picks up a shovel and joins the growing mob. The kind, young couple across the street each grab a broom and rake before they also follow me, yelling out curses and threats.

I try to run, but the pavement comes up with my running shoes, weighing me down until I can't move anymore. I look around for help. There are no friendly faces. Victor escapes my fumbling grasp on his leash and runs to sit beside my father. His expression is easy to read. The lines on his brown face are sharp with disappointment, his eyebrows drawing together as he shakes his head back and forth.

The throngs of angry neighbors and friends overtake me before I wake up, gasping.

"Your time will come."

My father's words are a whisper in my mind as I force air into my lungs and reach for the wooden box on my nightstand. I pull out the metal tin and stare at the nanodots inside. I count them— seven in all. I've only taken one on the day my world was destroyed. Then, as my breath comes less shallow than before, I know I'm okay. I put the tin back into my wooden box of secrets and close it again.

I'm not sure how long I'll last like this.

CHAPTER 2

Stars can't be brilliant without a curtain of darkness.

Captain Dana Pinet pulled back her elbow, sweat dripping into her eyes. She held her arm extended palm out, fingers curled, waiting for the next strike. Dana made slight adjustments to her stance, shifting the weight between her feet before she used her body's momentum to propel her forward.

She missed kicking Commander Wade Chance's head by millimeters.

He lunged at her, lifting her from the waist, the impact of the forward motion dropping them both to the yellow mat under their bare feet. Dana struggled to take in a breath underneath him. Wade didn't give her long to recover. He straddled her, one leg on either side of her waist, his arms keeping her pinned to the mat. Dana used a scissor kick to buck him off, and it took another quick kick to his chest to force him back and off her. She scrambled to her feet again, ready for the next advance. Wade wasn't normally so predictable, charging again from the same direction. At the last moment, Dana dodged to one side while extending her right leg to trip him. He fell facedown onto the mat.

Before she could enjoy the view from above him, he rolled up onto his feet. Face to face again, she had to duck to dodge his left swing. She blocked several open-handed hits with her arms, but he hit like a hammer, even with his palms. Dana stumbled backward, grasping for balance. Wade took the advantage, using his entire body to plow her back onto the floor. In a practiced maneuver, he slid behind her, keeping most of his weight on her hips, wrapped his right arm tight around her neck, and held. She pulled at his arm, but it might as well have been a steel pipe. Trapped, with no way up, she couldn't take in a full breath. Stars swam in her eyes before her hand slapped twice against his arm in surrender.

He released her in an instant. She gasped for breath for a moment, coughing when the air came in too fast. Then she stumbled to her feet.

Wade circled her, preparing for another charge. "You all right?"

Dana wanted to wipe that triumphant smirk off his face. She cleared her throat before speaking. "I'm fine. Don't look so disappointed."

"What can I say? I'm glad you're out of practice. You almost had me."

He wiped at the sweat streaming down his face with the bottom of his shirt, revealing the toned stomach underneath. Dana glanced away from him, letting her eyes settle on the matted wall behind him. She rolled her shoulders as a bead of sweat made a trail down her back. Her arms and legs burned with exertion.

Their morning runs had turned into morning workouts, and earlier that week, Wade had taken his first swing at her. He'd taunted her to the mat until she'd flung herself at him to shut him up. They'd both ended the workout sopping wet and with exhausted smiles on their faces.

This morning they'd run for ten minutes before sparring again. They were both fresh and energized this time, and Dana planned to nail him to the mat. Wade was lean and strong, with lightning-fast reflexes, but he lacked the strategic thought that had kept her out of his grasp for the better part of an hour. The only reason he'd gotten her the last time was because she could feel herself tiring.

"How many fingers am I holding up?" Wade asked, flashing three fingers at her and wiggling them.

"Why?" She stopped circling and stood still.

"You look like you took a major beating. Besides, I don't want the captain to pass out in front of the crew. It's bad for morale."

Her unwavering charge at his chest, head down, cut off Wade's laughter. He tried to dodge, but she anticipated the movement. Wade had all of his weight balanced on his right front foot, and she corrected her course in time to bash him in the side. He groaned before he hit the ground. She used her legs to pin down his arms. He wiggled and squirmed but couldn't get free. Instead, he managed to get his legs underneath him and lift her off the ground. With his hands released, he forced her back to the mat. The thud as she hit made him hesitate, but she groaned, proving she had some breath left.

He wrapped his arms and legs around her until she couldn't move, pinning her to the mat. "Such a cheater, plowing into my ribcage," he said, still holding her tight.

Dana wasn't ready to give up, but as she struggled, he only tightened his physical hold on her body like a snake. She placed her hand flat to the floor and slapped it twice, releasing Wade's hold on her. She didn't bother getting up, but turned her head to face him when he lay down on the mat beside her.

"Not bad. Better than the first time."

Dana wiped the back of her hand over her forehead. "I can't wait to knock that smug smile off your face."

"You and how many more?"

"I don't want to bring someone else in on this, but if you don't start letting me win, I might have to."

"Don't be a poor loser. I'm sure you'll be better next time. Maybe stretch a little more."

She punched him in the shoulder.

"What did you do that for?" he howled.

It was Dana's turn to smirk. She knew he'd never hit her back, and it hadn't hurt him as much as he complained.

They both fell into a comfortable silence, not filling it with frivolous conversation as they stretched out their sore muscles. Dana winced when she reached her left arm over her head.

Wade's expression changed, his eyebrows drawing together in genuine concern. "Sorry about that."

He was biting his lower lip in the way he did when he felt guilty about something. She hated that face. She'd seen it before, back when they used to date. Maybe that was why she wanted to plant him face-first into the mat.

"Don't," she said.

"What?"

"Don't do that." Dana waved a hand in the air around his face. "Don't act like you've broken me."

Wade's face tightened, and he looked like he was gritting his teeth.

"I'm fine," she insisted.

Dana waved a hand in the air again, this time as if encompassing the room and everything in it. Needing to fill the now-awkward silence with conversation, she leaped on the first thing that came to her mind.

"Have I mentioned that every time I watch my mother's vid message, I cry at the sight of my dog?"

Wade's eyes came up and met hers for an instant longer than she could take without looking away. "Really?"

Dana laughed at herself, but the same sadness gripped her chest even now. She swallowed back the emotion, willing herself not to cry.

"When I watch my mother talking about her day, we're as close as ever. Then..." Dana's voice hitched as she fought back tears. "She mentions Viktor, and she shows him sitting by the door. I break every time. Seems wrong to be mourning my dog more than my mother."

"It doesn't surprise me. She was larger than life. The woman was shameless. Fearless." He huffed out a laugh. "Remember the officer's ball? She came with you and stole the entire night, as I recall."

Dana could picture her mother that night, dressed in one of her new evening gowns, twirling in front of the dignitaries and political figures of the time as if she were their queen. They loved her, and even a few of the husbands got angry jabs from their wives when she passed by them.

"She knew how to light up a room."

"Yeah. You have it, too, but you wield yours a little different. You command a room where she entertains it."

Dana had never thought of her and her mother sharing anything other than DNA. She was most often compared to her father. Even after months of mourning him, her mother couldn't seem to bond with Dana the way she could with everyone else.

"You cry for your dog because Viktor lived, ate, and ran with you," Wade continued. "He was your constant companion, and an innocent. He didn't understand why you left or how little time he had. Your mother would have lived out her last days to the fullest, you know that. Oh, I'm sorry," he said when he caught her crying.

He lifted his hand to touch her, but then dropped it as if she were on fire. It only made it worse. Rebellious tears sprang into her eyes and he reached out a hand again, this time to hold her shoulder.

"I think that's it. Viktor didn't understand, and somehow that's worse." Dana wiped an angry hand over her face, but she didn't shrug him off. "Enough," she said, more to herself than to Wade.

Wade cleared his throat. "While we're on the subject of vids, I need your help with something."

Dana latched onto the change of subject like a life raft.

"What's wrong? What happened?"

Wade shook his head. "It's what's not happening."

Dana waited for him to continue. It sounded personal,

and she gave him the time and space to share when he was ready, as he'd done for her. They'd come so far in such a short time. She would never have dreamed just a few weeks ago that they'd be here, talking about their grief like old friends.

"I shouldn't be bothering you with this, but I'm worried about Maggie."

Dana kept her eyes from widening and pressed her lips together to hide her surprise. The last thing she wanted to talk about with Wade was Maggie. His boisterous reporter girlfriend was his business. Maggie was a woman used to getting what she wanted, and Dana wasn't sure she trusted her. She told herself it wasn't just that she always seemed to have unblemished skin and perfect hair. Or the fact she'd brought more shoes with her onto the *Hope* than any one woman in space deserved.

She banked the jealousy creeping through her and focused on Wade. He was her friend now, and she would be there for him. She waved him on with both hands. "I get it. You need a female opinion. Let's have it."

"That's it. You'll tell me if I'm being an insensitive tool."

"Most likely, but I'm listening."

He grinned and gave her an exaggerated eye roll before he continued. "She hasn't been the same since we received our messages."

"Everyone's been unsettled by those videos. They were essentially carrying voices from the grave," Dana said, thinking of her own sleepless nights, the nightmares she'd been having.

"True, but at least you're talking about yours."

"Maggie isn't?"

"No. She won't tell me anything about what's in her

message. Worse, if I come in and catch her watching it, she'll turn it off. Then she'll pretend like I didn't just see her crying over whoever sent the message."

"That doesn't seem suspicious. Have you shared your message with her?"

Wade tensed as his face grimaced.

"Not really. We've talked about it, though. It's from my mom. Dad doesn't say much of anything, but I can't exactly show her the vid."

"Why not?"

It was Wade's turn to clam up. His cheeks reddened, and he shook his head, as if deciding about something. "She... says some things about you that Maggie wouldn't appreciate."

"About me?"

Wade stood up, then gave Dana a hand to her feet. It was even harder to bank her curiosity after that statement. She wanted to know more––needed to know more.

Wade must have read her expression because he raised an eyebrow. "Put it this way, if Maggie saw it, she'd be unhappy."

"Has she met your mother?"

"Yes, several times," Wade said before looking down at the floor.

Dana cleared her throat. "I see your point. Well... maybe that's why she's been holding back. Because you haven't shared yours."

Wade bit his full lower lip while he thought about it. "No, I don't think that's it. We've talked about mine at length. She hasn't asked to see it, and she's satisfied with my summarizing it. With hers, there's nothing. She won't even say if it's from a family member or a friend." He ran a hand through his brown curls. She'd seen that tick before when he was anxious. "I wish she'd say something about it like you have. You and I have no problem talking about our messages. What's on hers that she doesn't want me to see?"

Dana was pondering the same question. Maggie was hiding something. Something so big she didn't want her boyfriend to know. Though it fed into her suspicions of the woman, this wasn't the time to tell Wade that.

"I can't answer that. But you obviously care for her as much as she cares for you. There's no reason to push her. Be there for her when she's ready."

The words were out of her mouth before she'd thought about them. Dana leaned down, putting her hands to the floor attempting to hide her face as she changed the subject.

"You could invite her to come workout with you in the mornings. Maybe that will get her talking. She'll be too exhausted to resist."

"Yeah, right," he scoffed. "Have you met Maggie? She doesn't wake up until noon, and she works until midnight. Besides... she doesn't exactly know I meet up with you every morning."

His words caught up to her brain a second later, and she took a step back from him. "Wait, what?"

His mouth opened to answer when a loud *boom*, followed by the rocking of the room, brought them to their knees. They both scrambled to get back to their feet, running for the comms a moment later. Dana put her hand over the panel and spoke.

"Status? Are we under attack?"

"No, it originated inside the ship."

Something rocked the ship a second time. A wave of electricity ripped through the panel to her hand, coursing up her arm. She flew backward hard against Wade, who'd been right behind her, and crashed onto the mat several feet away. They peeled themselves off the floor and crawled for the door. Wade reached it first. Dana watched him grip its edges through blurred vision, trying to force the sealed doors apart. He was beating on the door and calling for help when dizziness overtook her.

She shook her head in a feeble attempt to force back the blackness creeping along the edges of her vision but failed.

CHAPTER 3

Dana opened her eyes, trying to make sense of her surroundings, but everything was so dark, she couldn't make them out. Panic filled her when she realized she couldn't see.

She must have screamed, because suddenly heavy hands grabbed at her. She slapped at them. The annoying humming in her ears blocked all sound from getting through, even her own voice.

Then she felt the soothing touch of fingers on the side of her face. The figure leaned closer, and she could barely make out Wade's features. She wasn't blind, her eyes were beginning to adjust to the dark. Dana stopped hitting at the hands and relaxed into them.

His mouth opened and closed in wide, exaggerated movements. He wanted to kiss her? That had to be it. He'd turned off the lights and lit the candles. She arched her back and lifted her chin toward him. He was so handsome. She remembered the feel of his kisses as her eyes fluttered closed, awaiting the warmth of his mouth on hers.

Then his firm hands shook her. Her eyes went to his shadowed face again. Something had made his features so severe. Why was he so angry? No... not angry... worried. What had she done to cause that facial expression? Did it have something to do with the dark?

The room was still tilting and spinning as Dana reached out a hand to rest it on the side of his face. She wanted to make the dizziness stop and after a long span of silence the room's gyrations slowed. Wade smiled down at her, his mouth moving again. What was he saying?

Even with the buzzing gone, it was like listening through water. Dana reached up to rub her ears, finding they were wet. Had they been swimming? She tried to look at her brown hand, but it was invisible in the dark. The skin of her hand hurt as if it had been burned, and she couldn't see why. The buzzing in her ears was still too loud. Her hand went to her mouth where Wade hadn't kissed her, then to her face.

"Dana, can you hear me?" Wade's voice filtered in through the buzzing. He still sounded too far away.

"My ears are ringing," Dana said as she tried to sit up. "What happened?"

His hand was heavy against her chest, forcing her back down. "Not yet. You're hurt. Let me find something to help."

The haze in her mind was parting, and she was beginning to remember where she was. Dana lay still, her back against the mat on the exercise room floor, assessing her injuries. It was taking her mind longer than it should have to replay the last things she remembered. They'd been sparring a few moments ago... had he knocked her out? No... they'd both been on their feet near the door. They'd been talking about Maggie...

Her face burned as she realized she'd almost reached up and kissed him in her semi-conscious delusion moments ago. She was thankful the dark hid her embarrassment.

Wade gave her just enough time to revel in her embarrassment before he returned with a round, palm-sized flashlight. He set the flashlight down, face up between them, as he worked. He held a couple tubes in one hand and blue bandages in the other. Wade rubbed medicinal cream from one tube over her hand, then wrapped it before moving along to tend to the wounds she hadn't yet noticed further up her arm. Only when he'd finished did he ease her into a sitting position.

"How long was I out?"

"A few minutes," he said, passing her an open water tube. "What's the last thing you remember?"

She sipped the cool liquid, easing the scratch of her dry throat. "A loud boom."

"Do you remember me speaking to Cliff over the comms?"

"No, what did he say?"

"That the cause was internal. Then an electrical surge took out the comms with your hand still on it. Blew us both back onto the mat. We shook it off. We were both headed back to the door for help, but when I turned around, you'd passed out."

"Did anyone hear you?"

"No, and if it took out the communications system and the doors, the damage must be pretty extensive."

"So, we're stuck here for now." Dana looked up. The nearest crawling tubes were three men high. The ceiling was even further up. They'd never reach an exit conduit in a room designed for intense climbing and jumping.

"I've already assessed the room," Wade told her. "There's no way out of here without help, but at least we're safe. The equipment is stable, and there's nothing dangerous to us here."

Dana hadn't even considered the equipment; how easily a running machine could have fallen on her while she was out cold.

Wade positioned himself beside her, his back against the wall.

"What are you doing?"

"Getting more comfortable," he said, stretching out his legs and leaning his head against the wall, his eyes closed.

"Why aren't you figuring another way out of here?"

"Like I said, there's no way out."

How could he be so calm? He sat there, seemingly without a worry about how they'd get out. It was infuriating.

Dana leaned forward until she was on all fours before getting her feet under her. Her knees wobbled, but she stood on her own. She looked back to flash Wade a smile filled with pride, but his eyes were still closed tight. Dana poked out a finger toward his face to catch him peeking, but he didn't flinch. She snatched up the flashlight and took a tour of the room.

It was as Wade had told her. The heavy equipment was undisturbed. The vents were too high. Even if there was double the equipment to pile on top of each other, she still wouldn't be able to reach them. Dana checked behind panels and shifted a rack of towels to one side to look for more ventilation shafts, but found nothing.

She circled the room until she stood in front of the main doors again, the charred remains of the console reminding her of what had happened. Thankfully it hadn't been a full console terminal, or she might not have survived the electrical surge. Dana beat the edge of her left fist against the doors and shouted for help. Then she leaned against the door, pressing her ear to it, and listened for anything coming from the other side.

Nothing.

Defeated, Dana returned to where she'd been sitting and slid down to sit next to Wade to wait, placing the flashlight face up again between them.

His smirk was back. "Told you."

"I needed to see for myself."

"Feel that?"

Dana put her palms against the mat and nodded. "We're not moving."

"I think whatever it was took out the engines. We're not going anywhere."

"I should go stand by the door in case someone passes by."

Dana moved to stand, but Wade's hand snaked out and grabbed her shoulder, avoiding her burned arm. He turned his head and opened one eye.

"Not so fast. You need to relax."

"I'm the captain of this ship. I believe you take your orders from me, not the other way around."

The look she gave his hand, still on her shoulder, would have melted any other officer. Wade, however, held her gaze. His hand remained firm, keeping her in place.

"You're injured, and the dizziness could return," he

reasoned. "It would be great if you didn't make things worse for me."

"For you?"

"Yes. As you said, you're the captain. If you become incapacitated because of your stubbornness, I'll be in command of the ship, and then I'll be forced to work."

The laugh escaped before she could slap her good hand over her mouth. Dana quickly regained her composure and shrugged off his hand. He let go, and she settled in next to him, careful not to touch him. She still gave him a side glare, though, wanting to wipe that know-it-all smirk off his face.

"They'll come for us," he said. "Just wait."

"Fine."

They sat in companionable silence. Dana had lost track of just how long they waited before something knocked against the gymnasium doors. Before Wade managed to pull her to her feet, something else hit the door with a loud metal-on-metal *thwack*. She and Wade were standing side-by-side when a male ARI with short blond hair forced the doors apart.

From behind it, Maggie came rushing in, the flashlight in her hand shining blindingly into their eyes.

"Hey, do you mind?" Dana asked, throwing up a hand.

"Oops."

The light in Maggie's hand lowered, and Dana could make out their features again. The ARI remained at the door, but the corridor behind it was still black. It seemed the power was off throughout the ship. She was about to ask about it when Maggie stopped in her tracks, looking Wade up and down. Then her eyes went to Dana's burned arm.

Maggie lifted her left hand to her hip and shook her

head. "Well. Looks like you figured out how to get him out of his clothes again, Captain."

Dana's mouth fell open, but before she could respond, Wade was moving forward and wrapping his arms around Maggie.

"Come on, Mags, it's nothing. I sacrificed my shirt to save my captain's injured arm."

To her horror, Dana looked over and realized that the blue strips wrapped around her hand and arm had come from the shirt he'd been wearing during his workout. He'd been sitting there bare-chested the entire time, and she hadn't even noticed in the dark.

Maggie's pink lower lip protruded in a pout. She glanced around the room, as if expecting to see someone else. No doubt she was wondering what they were doing in the gym alone together.

Wade shrugged it off. "You know me. I'm quick to provide help to a damsel in distress." He gave her a playful pinch at her waist and a peck on the cheek. He guided Maggie toward the door, then turned to smirk at Dana behind her back.

Dana set her teeth and balled her left hand into a fist.

To make matters worse, Wade paused to tell the ARI, "The captain needs medical attention. Make sure she gets to the med-bay."

Dana wanted to scream at him, but she had a pounding headache, and burns that needed attention. Besides, it wouldn't do her any good to be seen wearing strips of her first officer's shirt.

"See what's going on in the engine room, Commander, then report to the bridge," Dana said to his back.

"Yes, Captain."

Maggie giggled at something he said in her ear as he leaned on her for support. They didn't appear to be a couple having problems, like Wade had hinted at. Maggie had come straight away to help him, knowing where he was even if she didn't know with whom. Wade might have been exaggerating.

"I am perfectly capable of carrying you to the medical bay, Captain." The ARI held out its arms. Both were covered by sleeves, but the left hand lacked the realistic skin of the right, exposing the internal wiring and metal.

Dana gave his arms a measured look before she turned her attention to its face. The ARI was almost twice her size, but she still managed to look down her nose at him.

"Try it, and I'll have you disassembled and used for scrap."

CHAPTER 4

EARTHA

The room spun as Eartha tried to make sense of her surroundings in the dark. After she'd been dropped to the floor from the bed where she'd been journaling, everything went dark. Something had landed on her, which after a careful, sightless search, she figured must have been the bedside lamp. The pieces of its base lay broken underneath her hand, and she had to feel around in the dark to avoid them as she made her way back to the bed.

Eartha had been hiding in the Rogan's quarters since the death of her planet. It was better than the ventilation shaft she'd spent most of the journey in so far, but she had a hard time enjoying it, knowing she'd never see her mother and father again. Hadn't she longed for a bedtime, proper meals, baths? Now she found herself under someone's charge again, and the restraint of it choked her after so many days spent looking after herself.

The Rogans were a sweet couple, and had always seemed to her to be in a kind of sync she'd never seen before. Eartha's parents often argued because of their contrary personalities, but they made up passionately. At thirteen, she knew full well that what her parents had told her at five was "night wrestling" was, in fact, making love. It had embarrassed her to imagine her parents kissing the way she wanted to be kissed herself, but now she'd have done anything just to hear their voices again.

The Rogans responded to things in the same way, often at the same time. It was as if even their thought patterns were always in harmony. However, in the week she'd been with them, Eartha had watched them fall out of sync with each other. She wondered if it was just something that happened when people had children, or if it had something to do with her. It seemed every time they discussed her presence, they launched into another standoff, neither side giving way until a truce was called, the discussion tabled, but never resolved.

Eartha caught the pained looks on both of their faces when they thought she wasn't looking, but she didn't know how to help. She'd tried to make herself invisible, fading into the background like a piece of the furniture. Mr. Rogan wasn't happy with that at all. He'd insist she play a game with him until they were both rolling on the floor with laughter. Then she'd catch Mrs. Rogan's eye, who seemed to grow more displeased the more boisterous they became.

Mrs. Rogan said she was worried about Eartha being discovered, but Eartha saw a wariness in her eyes when she spoke, as if there was something about her she didn't trust. It had been there that first day she'd stepped into their quarters, and that tightness had never quite left her furrowed brow or down-turned mouth. In all the time that she'd known them, she'd never seen the couple at odds, and Eartha felt responsible for the rift growing between them, though she hadn't exactly had a choice in the matter.

She'd made the unfortunate mistake of telling the Rogans about the feelings she got about things. About how they warned her about things. When they'd scoffed at her, she'd told them about the plants strangling her in the night, and that she'd begged Ari not to go near them, fearing for his life. Mrs. Rogan had pulled away from her, not wanting to believe it. Mr. Rogan's eyes had gone sad, but he'd pulled Eartha tight against him in a big hug, as if he could replace the strangling vines. She'd told them about her teacher, and the car accident that matched the one in her nightmare, and how Eartha had flown through the air before hitting the ground.

They hadn't believed her, and the discussion had turned into another argument that they'd had behind their paper-thin bedroom door. Their voices grew louder, debating whether they were capable enough to care for a girl who might be insane. Of course, they hadn't used that word specifically, but she knew what psychiatrists were for, and the idea of meeting with one made her stomach churn.

That morning, Mrs. Rogan had stayed behind to make her breakfast. They'd sat at the table and eaten together in silence. She didn't tell Mrs. Rogan about her feelings anymore. The woman seemed to only ask about them as if she were testing Eartha for mental stability. Mr. Rogan would listen as if they were the most important thoughts in the world. He was a lot like her father in that way.

Just thinking about it made her tear up over her breakfast.

"What's wrong?" Mrs. Rogan had asked in a stern voice, as if Eartha's tears were a personal affront.

"Nothing," Eartha mumbled.

"There's obviously something wrong, or you wouldn't be crying."

Eartha didn't want to talk about her dead parents. Talking about them broke her heart in a million pieces. She was getting tired of losing pieces each time she tried to put them back together again. Being with Mr. Rogan made her not miss them so much. Being alone with Mrs. Rogan made her wish she'd stayed in the crawl space behind the ventilation grate in engineering.

If only it was just her and Mr. Rogan... they'd both be happier.

"I understand if you're still grieving. We all are. Sometimes it helps to talk about it. It's like diagnosing a problem with the engines. You can hear the irregular patterns in the way it runs or feels in the ship's stuttered movements. It won't tell you what's wrong, so you have to work the problem backward. Figure out what's the diagnosis by the symptoms. For example, when it makes a *tinking* or a *thunking* sound." She seemed to catch herself rambling and stopped. Mrs. Rogan pushed herself away from the little dining table, standing stiffly. "Maybe when Eric gets home, you'll want to talk to him."

Mrs. Rogan cleared away their plates. They clattered against each other angrily, as if she couldn't hold them steady. She didn't press Eartha to speak again. Mrs. Rogan grumbled her goodbye and dashed out of the cabin. It wasn't long after

Eartha had climbed into their bed to write a new poem that the whole ship lurched and then went dark.

Without the Rogans and Ari, she didn't know what to do. When someone came knocking on the door to see if anyone was inside, Eartha buried herself under the blankets and waited for them to leave. There was only one rule in the Rogan's cabin she couldn't and wouldn't break.

She would never, ever, answer the door for anyone—no matter what.

CHAPTER 5

Even with the help of the ARI, it took ten minutes for Dana to get through the growing crowd in the med-bay and treat the burns on her right hand and arm. She flagged down a nurse in transit and made quick business of getting in for her second-skin patch and out again. She zipped past the slow trickle of injured stumbling into the med-bay to get to her quarters. With the power still off on the ship, it took longer than it should have to force her way into her quarters. The ARI had long since been released to attend to other important duties.

The patch on her hand was easing most of the pain, but with only the one she couldn't budge the door. She flagged down two crewmen passing her way to help her inside. Dana changed into her uniform in record time. She decided to hide her one treasure. It was unlikely anyone would venture into her quarters or tamper with anything, but she wasn't going to make it easy for them if she was wrong.

Satisfied she'd hidden her things well enough that it would take a team of sniffer dogs to find them, Dana strolled out of her room and up to the bridge. She marched through the open doors onto the unlit deck.

"Captain on the bridge!" Wade called out, using his flashlight to put a spotlight on her.

There were only two other officers on the bridge. One of Barnes' security team, Lieutenant Adrien Valente, a tall, bald, black man with a severe expression, stood at the tactical station. Wade, as her first officer, had found a uniform and was fully dressed again. She did her best to suppress the arresting image in her mind of him shirtless.

"Commander Chance," she addressed him with an incline of her head. "Report."

"Communications systems are still down, and we don't have locations on all crew members yet. Most have managed to get to their posts, though they can't be reached until we get our systems up and running."

Dana shook her head in frustration. "With only one ARI, there's no telling how long it will take to get everyone needing assistance to their stations, but I sent it on its way about thirty minutes ago. What about our key systems?"

Ensign Cliff Harden strolled onto the bridge a moment later, looking haggard, but in uniform. His normally well shaped afro was lopsided, and disappointment etched his mouth.

"Just in time, Ensign," Wade said. "I thought you were on the bridge before the outage?"

"I was. After the lights went out, I went to see if anyone needed help getting out of their quarters." The way Cliff's voice dropped, Dana had a good idea whom he'd gone in search of, and from the look on his face, he hadn't found her.

"Lieutenant Westlake?" Wade asked.

He shook his head. "No sign of her. I went to her quarters, but there was no answer. She must have been out."

"What's it going to take to get us back up and running?" Dana asked, changing the subject.

Cliff stared down at the console in front of him. "All our electrical systems were compromised. The backup system is what's keeping life support functioning and allowing us minimal computer access. If we don't get everything up and running in full, we'll be out of air in less than three hours. The main COMP interface is offline, so that's an estimate. Whatever took out the systems did a good job of it, because I can't even tell you what else might be wrong with the ship."

"Where are my chief engineers? Esme or Eric should be here."

"No one's come up from the engine room," Cliff reported. "Though I suspect it will take some time for them to gather a report and walk it up here. Last I checked, Eric was in engineering. Everything was down, including our engine core. It will take a few hours to get it warmed-up again before we'll be able to move."

"Life support is our number one priority," Dana stressed. "I don't care if we have to create a chain of fifty people to pass information between here and the engine room. I need to know what's going on, and what they need to get it done."

"Yes, Captain. I'll see what I can do," Wade said, exiting the bridge.

She turned back to look at Lieutenant Valente. "Where's Barnes?"

"He's not reported to the bridge. I was assigned the late shift, and I've not left my post." He gave a significant look to Harden, which the latter ignored.

"We need those comms up and working. I want to find our people. Can you fix it?"

"Not until we have power to the system," Valente said. "Although it looks like another backup system is up and running."

Cliff bit his lower lip as he looked down at the monitor. The emergency lighting came on, and they turned off the flashlights.

"Where are we on life support?" Dana asked.

"Sixty-five percent and holding," Cliff said. "Another blast, though, and we'll be gasping."

Her shoulders set in a hard line. After everything they'd been through, she couldn't let everything fall apart now. "I want to know who's responsible for this. Lieutenant, take a flashlight and go and get Barnes. Coordinate a search and rescue effort with the ARI, if nothing else."

Valente nodded and left the bridge.

"We all know it was the Coalition, ma'am," Cliff said, an edge to his voice.

"First off, Ensign, I already warned you about calling me ma'am. Second, we can't be sure until there's been a full investigation." Dana thought for a moment, adding, "But, that said, you're probably right. I'll speak to Shu as soon as our primary systems are back up and running."

He squared his shoulders at the reprimand and seemed to refocus.

"Yes, Captain."

Dana sat in her chair, tapping her fingertips on the armrest. She was forced to wait as her people walked to the bridge to deliver their reports orally. Passengers were gathering in the Commons, waiting for news. Most had been locked out of their quarters or needed rations. Two people stuck in the lifts when the power was disabled, were rescued and pulled to safety. The reports trickled in slow and methodical. Dana worried they were exerting too much energy, using too much air as they ran from place to place, but it couldn't be helped.

For a moment, the engines sputtered to life. Dana leaped to her feet and held her breath. Maybe Wade and the engineers had figured out how to get everything running again.

It lasted less than a minute before the engines died again. Life support dropped to a meager forty-five percent, and their emergency lighting took another hit. She pulled out the palm flashlight so she and Harden weren't sitting in the dark.

"Captain, I got a brief message from Commander Chance," Cliff said.

"What did he say?"

"I didn't reach the end of the message, only that the Chief's wife was taken to the med-bay. She was knocked unconscious, and Rogan went with her."

Dana's heart sank. "By the Merciful! Does that mean there's no one in the engine room other than Wa— Commander Chance?"

Cliff shrugged. "From what I could see, yes."

Nancy came through the open doors just as Dana was ready to lose it.

"Lieutenant Westlake, nice of you to join us," Dana said as Nancy dashed over to take her seat at the helm. There was no bite in her voice only a hint of sarcasm.

"My apologies, Captain. I couldn't get out of the room. It took forever for someone to pry open the doors."

"I stopped by your quarters," Cliff said with a frown. "You

didn't answer. I'm sorry, if I'd known you were inside, I would've—"

Westlake cleared her throat. "I wasn't in my quarters." Dana watched the flush of embarrassment crawl up her neck and into her cheeks as she avoided Cliff's stare.

"Oh. Sorry, I didn't mean—It's just—" Cliff couldn't seem to stop sputtering. "I mean... it's none of my business if—"

Dana had heard all she wanted to hear. She had enough trouble onboard without worrying about interpersonal relationships. The ship was dead unless they could get the engines back up and running.

"Right," she interrupted. "Lieutenant, you've got the bridge. I'll be in the med-bay, retrieving our remaining Chief engineer."

Chancellor Jeremiah Evans marched onto the bridge through the open doors. He puffed out his chest and lifted his chin, as if preparing to chastise a child. "Captain, a word please, in your office."

"Not now!" Dana hissed as she brushed past him. He stammered something about protocol and decorum that she ignored as she bolted out of the room. Without the lifts, she was forced to climb through the maintenance shafts, and had to pause while she encountered other members of the crew as they did the same.

When she caught several passengers milling about in the corridors, she redirected them to their cabins.

"There's no power there either," one complained.

"Yes, but we need to keep the corridors and shafts clear for the crew while we work to get the ship running again," Dana explained tersely.

"Who did this, Captain?"

A young man in an expensive suit asked the question. His matchstick-thin wife, her mousy brown bob tragically disarrayed, clung to his arm, looking ready to faint if anyone dared speak to her.

"We'll notify you of our current situation as soon as we have vital systems up and running again. We are on backup life support, which means you roaming the ship is only going to burn through our reserves faster. Please return to your quarters."

The crowd of people who'd gathered around her as she spoke dispersed, seeming more amenable to going back to their rooms. Had it only been a week since these same passengers had been banging on her cabin door, demanding answers?

Dana clamped down on the anger and frustration welling up inside her, forcing her jaw to relax to keep from grinding her teeth. She needed to be calm when she spoke to Chief Rogan. No matter what, she wasn't leaving the med-bay without him.

CHAPTER 6

"United against tyranny we stand."
- CAH Creed

Long before she reached the doors of the med-bay, Dana knew there was a problem. Injured passengers and crew were taking up residence on either side of the main doors along the corridor. That wasn't a good sign. They'd run out of beds, so the nurses were doing triage outside of the bay. One nurse flitted among them with a tablet in her hand, taking notes as she assessed their needs, hurrying from person to person, asking questions and inputting notes. Her stringy blonde hair had come loose and stuck to her tired face. Dana addressed her first.

"Ms. Stewart?"

"Yes, Captain. Jennie."

"Right, Jennie," Dana repeated, filing away the name for later. "I'm going to get you some help down here. I want these people moved to the cargo hold. We'll send you beds, and whatever supplies you need—just make a list. I'll coordinate someone to handle it before I leave. We need to keep the corridors clear."

"Someone with medical training would be great." She rolled her eyes and then, as if remembering who she was speaking to, straightened to attention.

Under the circumstances, Dana didn't hold the slip against her. "Do what you can with who you have for now."

"Yes, Captain."

Inside the med-bay, Dana found Dr. Jabar elbow deep in surgery. Two of his staff were holding flashlights above him while he worked. The other two seemed to be physically monitoring the patient's vitals. That explained why no one had come to the bridge. It looked like every available staff member was here, saving lives.

Instead of disturbing them, Dana spoke to the nearest able-bodied person in motion.

"Ensign Jones?"

The young woman, sporting a short black pixie cut, stopped mid-stride, keeping her palm light focused on Dana's chest and out of her eyes. "Yes, Captain?"

"How are you feeling?"

"Good as new," Jones said, flexing her leg in front of her under the flashlight as if surprised to find it intact.

"Excellent. I need you to track down any crew members not actively working on the engines or electrical systems. Whether they have any medical training or not, get them down here to help move the non-surgical patients out of the corridor and down to cargo bay three. Until you're done, you and your people will be taking orders from Nurse Jennie Fillmore. She'll have a list of equipment she'll need gathered there. I want you to take care of it. Understood?"

"Aye, Captain."

The first issue dealt with, Dana turned in a slow circle until her eyes landed on her Chief Engineer, Eric Rogan. Esme lay on one of the few suspended beds. Eric's head lay on its edge, at his unconscious wife's side. His hands were clasped together around one of hers. Because there were no lights on in the med-bay, all the other patients lay in the dark. For the moment, they all either seemed to be sleeping, or unconscious.

From what Dana could gather with the palm light she carried, Esme was breathing on her own. The man in the next bed had a battery-powered oxygen mask that pushed air at him as he slept. Dana knew little about medicine outside of fieldwork, but for now, it seemed Esme was stable.

Eric didn't move as she approached him from behind. She kept the flashlight on the floor as she called out to him. After the second time, he lifted his head and acknowledged her.

"Captain?"

"How is she doing?" Dana asked. She wasn't sure why she was whispering. Despite the quiet corner, the rest of the med-bay was in constant motion; the remaining staff ran around, treating the severely injured. It seemed the surgery was complete, and the team scattered to help those who'd been lying quietly in the dark. They spoke at a normal level, conferring with each other on diagnoses and prognoses of her people, seemingly unhindered by the lack of light.

Eric's silence made her want to keep talking.

Dana kept her voice low. "She's strong. I know she'll pull through," she said, putting a hand on Eric's shoulder. "Dr.

Jabar is busy with other patients, but I'm sure he'll have an update soon."

There was another long pause before Eric spoke, his eyes looking past her at something in the distance.

"We were arguing. It was stupid, really. We never argued before we found—" He seemed to catch himself before he looked up at her, his eyes pleading for understanding. "We don't argue. Ever."

"Were you arguing before the systems shut down?"

Eric nodded.

Dana understood loss. There wasn't a person on the ship who didn't. But she imagined for Eric this wasn't at all the same. He lived and worked with his life-partner. Esme had even taken his last name, as was the ancient custom. That said it all.

"The ship isn't moving," Dana explained, trying to be tactful while expressing the direness of their situation. "We need your help to get it running again."

He didn't respond.

"Eric, did you hear me?"

"The power conduits are blown. Idiots set off an EMP." He swore to himself, then rubbed a hand over his face. "Excuse me, Captain. It was the Coalition. They left their usual mark on everything. I should have been sweeping the engine room daily. It didn't even occur to me after the messages arrived that anyone would still work for those terrorists, trying to destroy our last chance at life."

Dana nodded. She was less surprised and more disappointed that they'd made another attempt on the ship, this time taking advantage of their collective grief. She made a mental note to go down to the brig next. Shu would be the first to feel the wrath of her anger.

One problem at a time, she told herself.

"I need you to get to work on those power conduits."

Eric shook his head. "I'm sorry, I can't."

"Do you understand what I'm saying?" Dana heard the sharp tone of impatience but couldn't hold it back.

"Someone else can handle it. Get the Commander, he's got an engineering background." He continued to clutch Esme's left hand with his right, as if it would tether them together. "I'm not leaving my wife."

Eric's voice had risen until others in the room turned to stare at them.

"What's going on here?" Dr. Jabar asked, joining them. His face was half-covered with a surgical mask.

Dana scowled back at him. "I'm just discussing an important matter with my chief engineer."

He glared at her from behind the mask. "Captain, if you haven't noticed, we're a little busy here." He turned away from her, still speaking as he checked on the man in the next bed. "We've got people flooding the corridors with minor injuries, as all the major ones have already taken all our beds."

She didn't have time to explain how far out of line he'd tread. Instead, Dana kept her voice level and her face neutral, even as her jaw tightened.

"I won't be long," she told him, then turned back to Eric. "Chief, I need you in the engine room. No one else has the skill or ability to fix this problem. We won't be able to get to where we're going if you don't figure out why the ship is floating like a dead stick."

"Didn't you hear me?" His voice struck out in anger, but his lower lip trembled as he fought back more tears. He looked down at Esme, fear and worry etched into the lines of his face. "I'm not leaving here until my wife wakes up."

Dana leaned in, keeping her voice whisper-quiet as she spoke in his ear, not wanting to alert anyone else to the gravity of their situation. "If the ship doesn't move, we'll run out of life support. So will your wife. If you want to see her get well, we need supplies—supplies we can't find on this ship. We need to get moving, and fast."

After a long moment, Eric nodded, but didn't move. The blond-haired male ARI she'd sent to help in the rescue effort returned to the med-bay. It approached Eric without acknowledging Dana, as she'd been expecting.

"Chief Rogan, you are needed in your quarters to attend to an urgent matter."

Annoyed by its lack of protocol, Dana spoke directly to the ARI. "Chief Rogan and I are in the middle of a discussion, ARI... I'm sorry, what number are you?"

"I am ARI number three. I apologize for my rudeness, Captain," it said, as if realizing for the first time that she was there. Perhaps in the low lighting, it hadn't recognized her. "The Chief left something very important in his quarters, and he asked me to remind him when it was time to take care of it."

Eric's head snapped up. For a brief moment, she saw his eyes and his mind clear. Then he looked back down at his wife. He lifted the hand he held to his lips and kissed it gently before standing up and letting go.

What did the ARI mean he had something to take care of

in his quarters? Dana was about to ask him about it when Eric spoke.

"I'll see to the engines right away, Captain." He wiped a hand over his eyes, then nodded to Dana before he rushed out of the med-bay.

ARI number three excused itself and followed Eric out of the room without a second glance in her direction. It was strange behavior for an ARI to not ask if she, or anyone else in the room, needed help. Their primary function was to attend to everyone's needs. Perhaps it was malfunctioning. She made a mental note to speak with Dr. Walker, the ARI specialist.

After the med-bay doors slid closed behind them, Dr. Jabar came over to read Esme's vitals. Dana noted that from his high cheekbones and lean stature, he looked to be from the western hemisphere. The people there clung to their origins. After almost being exterminated from Blue Earth, when given the chance, they had been the first willing to settle on other planets.

"How long has Chief Rogan been here?" she asked him.

He held Esme's wrist in his fingers, checking her heart rate. Once he had his number, he continued his examination, speaking as he did. "He arrived with her and hasn't left until now."

"And ARI number three, how many times has it been by?"

"I didn't notice." He lifted an eyebrow in challenge. "I can barely keep up with the warm bodies."

"Of course, Doctor." Dana waved a hand in dismissal, then turned her attention back to Esme. "Will she ever wake up?"

"I'm not sure. It's up to her now. Comas can last for days,

weeks, months—or longer. No two cases are the same. Though she took a nasty hit to the head, all her other vitals are stable." Dr. Jabar turned from Esme and met Dana's eyes above the illumination of the palm-light. "Is it true what you said about our life support?"

She nodded gravely. "If we don't get on our way, we'll either suffocate, or starve. Neither is on my agenda for this week." Dana needed to leave, but not before learning all she could from the doctor. "Your report?"

"Oh, yes. I was going to send it up to the bridge by way of one of the nurses, but since you're here... We've had over fifty passengers and crew members in and out of the bay. They range from minor burns to coma. One crewman was killed when his antique sword impaled him in his quarters. He bled out before anyone could pry open the doors. There are somewhere between seventy-five and eighty-five minor injuries being tended to at the moment both here and in the cargo bay." He gathered himself and added a brusque, "By the way, thank you for that."

Dana sighed. She hadn't been fishing for gratitude. "Don't hurt yourself trying to thank me for doing my duty," she said, rolling her eyes to the ceiling.

"If that's all," he said curtly, already moving on to the next patient.

"Yes, thank you, Doctor."

They'd had enough loss, and this would just be another crippling blow to their already low spirits. Dana already felt the weight of it settling on her shoulders, wondering if perhaps she should have continued their investigation into the Coalition members onboard more publicly.

She ran a hand over her burning eyes. She had to get to

the brig before she was dead on her feet. With the lift off-line, it was going to be a long crawl, but it was a necessary one. There was only one person she knew on the ship who might have answers, and it was Shu. The sooner she got those answers from him, the safer for everyone it would be.

Dana walked out of the med-bay just as the lights went to full. Then she felt the rumble of the engines as they rolled to life beneath her feet. Dana thanked the Merciful. They wouldn't die before they got to the next planet. It also meant she wouldn't have to climb through the shafts to the brig.

When she reached the detention level, she moved to the door of the brig. The palm reader recognized her authority and slid open. She let out a curse as she stepped inside.

The guard lay on his back, his vacant eyes staring up at the ceiling.

Brian Shu lay sprawled face-down on the floor of his cell, dead.

She wouldn't be getting any answers today.

CHAPTER 7

"May the Majestic keep you safe from harm;
From troubles deep and all around;
May the Majestic keep you safe from harm;
Prayers and entreaties that you may be found;
May the Majestic keep you safe from harm;
For friends and family of any lost soul;
May the Majestic keep you safe from harm.
Alive with body and mind made whole."
-Prayer for the Lost First Verse
Ancient Holy Writings Scroll 21B

Dana stared at the two corpses lying on the brig floor. From the lack of any distinct rotting smell in the room, they hadn't been dead long. Why hadn't security been alerted if there had been a problem down here?

Dana reached for the communication panel and signaled for Doctor Jabar.

"I thought from our earlier conversation you understood. I'm up to my elbows here, Captain," came the exasperated reply. "If they're already dead, then there's not much else I can do for them."

"I need the time of death and cause. This is an official murder investigation."

Jabar let out a huff. "Fine... I'll send someone. If you find anyone else, unless they're still alive, don't bother calling me again."

Dana didn't like the doctor's attitude. He was becoming more of a jerk as the day went on. She understood they were all stressed, and he had a lot on his plate, but it didn't excuse his behavior toward her. She would have to have a conversation with him once all of their emergency needs had been dealt with.

Next, she called Wade down to the brig. When he arrived, he looked down at the two bodies and swore under his breath.

"What do you think happened down here?" he asked.

"I'm not sure, but I'm beginning to think whatever happened to our ship was a cover-up for what was going on down here."

Wade looked doubtful. "You think someone cut the power to the entire ship to kill Shu?"

Dana shook her head as she took in the room. "No... I'm wondering if they hadn't already done the deed before the power was cut."

Behind her, the brig's door opened, and another figure appeared. She almost thought it was Doctor Jabar, but it couldn't have been unless he'd created and successfully used a miracle hair growth hormone in the last few hours. Other than that and the friendly smile, he and this new man were identical.

"Doctor?" Wade asked, as if the man's appearance had also thrown him off.

"Not exactly. You probably already know my brother, Randall. I'm Rido Jabar, and Captain, I have to tell you, you're more stunning up close than I thought."

He took her hand and brought it to his lips. Dana's mouth fell open as she tried to search for the words to tell him to back off, but they wouldn't come.

Wade cleared his throat—loudly—and Dana turned to him, breaking the spell. She snatched her hand out of Rido's. "Yes, well, these are the bodies I need you to take a closer look at."

Rido lifted a shoulder and let it fall, then turned to the security guard on the floor, kneeling next to him and studying him for a few moments. "See the bruising on his knuckles? It looks like he tried to beat his way out of the room." He lifted one of the man's eyelids and checked his neck. "The blood vessels in his eyes are ruptured. I suspect they both suffocated in here."

Dana nodded. She'd also noted the bruising on Shu's hands. "How long have they been down here?"

Rido shook his head. "I don't know. Forensics isn't..." He paused, as if searching for the right word. "It isn't what I do. If I had to guess, I'd put it sometime around when the power went out."

"What kind of doctor are you?" Wade asked, his arms crossed over his chest, looking at Rido with suspicion.

"I'm not a medical doctor. I'm a Healer. Also the ship's mental health specialist."

Dana looked at Wade. He raised an eyebrow at her as if to say, 'should we even trust this guy with our dead?'

"Medicine has been in my family for generations," Rido continued. "However, only my father, sister, and brother chose the traditional medical paths. I chose the path of my grandfather and my uncle. They were also Healers." He lifted his chin and stared between them as if waiting for a reaction. When none came he continued.

"I learned most of what I know from them. The mental health specialty was something of a side interest of mine. Randall has been able to open my mind to some of his treatments, and has had his mind opened to some of mine." Rido lifted his shoulders and let them drop. "My brother said he needed help, so I came to assist."

"We'd like a full report from Doctor Jabar as soon as he's able," Wade said, still frowning at the man. "There's probably a murderer on board, and we need to catch them before they choose another victim."

"Of course, Commander." Rido bowed low to Dana, and she felt a flutter kick in her chest when his dark eyes met hers. A smile spread across his full lips, lifting his high cheekbones even higher.

Two crewmen who'd been prescribed to help arrived with a pair of hoverbeds to carry the bodies away.

"I'll have a full report on the official cause of death within a few hours," Rido assured them. The door closed behind him and the crewmen shortly after, and Dana let out the breath she'd apparently been holding.

"I don't like him," Wade said, returning with her to the security station.

She couldn't disagree more. In contrast to his cold twin,

Rido was charming and warm. She'd never seen two men more distinctly different, such polar opposites.

Wade's dislike was something else altogether, and Dana wondered how he'd react if she dated someone on board. She couldn't deny the thought had occurred to her the moment she understood the truth of the *Hope*'s mission. They were the last of humanity. Eventually, they'd all have to pair up to raise their children. She hadn't imagined doing so herself.

Dana waved a hand in front of her face, dismissing the thought. "Never mind him. What can you tell me about the moments before their deaths?"

Wade turned back to the console and read off the details. "According to the security log, the last authorized visit was last night's evening meal. Four hours after that was shift change. It seems no one entered or exited the room until your hand opened the door thirty-two minutes ago."

"The guard on duty, he was scheduled to be relieved at what time?"

"This morning at oh-six-hundred."

"Right around the time the lights went out."

Wade nodded.

"Who was scheduled to come in?"

"I don't have the duty roster here, but I can have that information for you within the hour."

"Make it happen. I need to get back to the bridge. Get me audio and vid from the brig camera. I want to see it for myself."

Wade nodded again, then asked offhandedly, "How's Esme?"

Dana hadn't forgotten the hollow look on her unconscious face, or the desperate, crushing pain in Eric's eyes as he refused to return to engineering.

"She's asleep. Comas are unpredictable. According to Jabar, she may wake up anytime, or not at all."

"Eric's back in the engine room. I think he's going to work himself beyond exhaustion. He and Esme are an indivisible pair in every way."

Dana had seen it, too. She'd never met a couple more in sync. Finishing each other's sentences aside, they were also incredible when they were solving problems together.

"Speaking of couples," Dana added, "we'll need to notify Mrs. Tan of her husband's death."

"I can take care of it," Wade told her. "Getting the video footage shouldn't take more than a few minutes."

Dana's shoulders sagged forward in selfish relief. She'd been dreading the thought of visiting Jun Tan the moment she'd found the bodies. In the meantime, she had no witnesses and no Coalition member in custody to question.

Wade finished up at the console, and they walked out of the room together. She waited until a group of civilians passed before asking the question on her mind.

"Are we making any progress on the messages?"

Wade shook his head. "Without the ARIs, it's slow going. We have the one doing several searches at once. I'm going through them with Barnes one at a time, but it's a chore. Barnes is still swamped with the rest of his security duties. I've got other departments to oversee. We don't have enough eyes, to be honest."

"I know. If you need more people, get Harden and West-lake to help you. Harden is our relative language expert. He might catch something that the rest of us won't. Westlake has the time, as our ship isn't going anywhere very fast." Dana rolled her eyes in frustration. "Outside of the bridge crew, I'm not inclined to trust anyone else. It's too sensitive. Someone got a message on to this ship from the CAH, and they're keeping the group's original mission active. I believe they also silenced our only lead. We need to be able to protect our people."

Wade nodded but his eyes were far off.

"What?"

"It occurred to me I might not be the most impartial person on the job, myself," Wade admitted his voice dropping to a whisper. "Especially after admitting how I felt about not knowing what was on Maggie's vid."

Dana paused mid-step and pulled him to one side of the corridor so she could look him in the eye.

"I gave you the assignment because my security chief is otherwise occupied and you're my First Officer, not so you could go digging around in your girlfriend's private business." Dana clipped her scolding tone before she continued, her voice softer this time.

"Every relationship needs trust to survive. If you watch her message without her permission, you'll lose her respect, and, most of all, her faith in you. I wouldn't presume to know much about relationships, but if you watch it, using this as your excuse, you need to be prepared for her to end things. Lack of trust is usually a deal-breaker."

She continued walking, leaving Wade to catch up.

Wade rubbed the back of his neck. "I'll keep that in mind."

Dana noticed the same exhaustion she felt gripping him as well. He'd been working for as long as she had, and besides that, he'd been running all over the ship while the communications system was down.

"Speaking of messages, did you ever find the girl whose message was never delivered?" he asked.

The girl had slipped her mind with everything going on. She hadn't had time to give it another thought.

"No. Whoever she is, she wasn't scheduled to be on the ship. I went as far as making sure she wasn't a lottery winner." Dana shrugged. "I can't find her anywhere, and no one's come forward to claim the missing message, so I have to assume it was some tragic, unfortunate mistake. With everything else going on, I'm not all that worried about her. May the Merciful keep her in His care," Dana said, quoting the ancient psalm.

"May the Merciful keep her," Wade echoed.

CHAPTER 8

On the bridge, Dana found the rest of the crew had finally arrived at their stations.

"Captain on the bridge!" Barnes bellowed.

Dana stared at him. He was her chief of security and should have been on the bridge long before she'd arrived. She hadn't seen him all morning. "Where have you been, Barnes?"

"I was helping coordinate rescue teams on the passenger levels. I didn't think to send a messenger until Lieutenant Valente arrived. I apologize." Barnes inclined his head to her, but there was a challenge in his eyes she didn't like.

She opened her mouth to reply when Ensign Cliff Harden spoke up. "The Chancellor is waiting for you in your office, Captain."

She suppressed the frustrated sigh that wanted to escape her. "How long?"

He shrugged. "I'm not sure. Close to an hour, maybe."

Dana let out a huff and went to her office. She found Chancellor Jeremiah Evans inside, pacing from wall to wall.

He didn't leave her waiting long to find out how he was faring, rounding on her, eyes blazing.

"Do you know how long I've been waiting to speak with you?"

"No."

He muttered a stammer at her clipped response. She moved past him, preferring her desk between them as she sat down and started reviewing the files and reports she'd requested.

"I won't be ignored, Captain Pinet. You and I both know things are escalating out of control."

"True." Again, she kept her eyes on her work, ignoring his demand for attention until he slammed an open palm onto her desk.

"How dare you just continue to brush me off!"

Dana dragged her eyes from her monitor to his face. Up close she noted his olive skin was beginning to show his age. The deep lines of his eyes and mouth more pronounced than ever. She felt she'd given him plenty of warning, but he was pushing her too far.

"What do you plan to do about these—" he waved a hand as he searched for a sufficient word to describe things, deciding on "—these chaotic events? My wife can barely sleep in our bed for fear of what's next."

"Are you saying that your wife is refusing to sleep in your bed? That sounds like a personal matter. May I suggest you visit the psychologist."

Chancellor Evans's pale face turned bright red, and his eyes bulged in their sockets. "You purposefully misunderstood," he gritted out. "My wife is afraid for her life."

"I suggest that you practice maintaining a sense of calm, as your own dramatics may worsen the situation."

"I would hardly consider fear of another Coalition attack dramatic. I'm tired of being forced to sit idly by while you muck up this entire operation." He squared his shoulders. "I demand a meeting. The senior officers, the president, and I, should discuss how things will be handled from this point forward."

The chancellor continued to outline his plans for a classic witch-hunt. Dana remembered it from her Blue Earth history studies. Back then, people had been superstitious and backward. Women with a mind of their own were labeled witches so the Puritan men could rid themselves of such contagious thinking. However, they were no longer in those times, and she was the captain of this starship. If her father were here, he'd never have tolerated such disrespect. She wouldn't breed distrust and panic by searching the quarters of every passenger and crew member for corroboration of Coalition involvement, and the chancellor had no say in the matter either way. He could not be allowed to dictate matters to her here.

"That's unnecessary and unwise," she started coolly, keeping a tight rein on her temper. "We don't want to send Coalition collaborators into hiding. I've already met with my officers and debriefed them on the situation. We are in the middle of a large-scale investigation. That's all you need to know at this time." She met his glare with one of her own. "You have no involvement in running this ship, and what you say has no bearing on what we plan to do. I won't remind you of this again. Now, I'm very busy handling the current crisis. Please see to your wife. Good day."

The Chancellor was left blustering as he stormed out of her office. Dana pressed her palms to her eyes. The day wasn't over, and she was already exhausted.

Returning to scanning through the files, she found the one she wanted—the video of the brig. She scanned the footage, looking for anything that might lead her to who might have been responsible, as the men in the brig gasped for air. She watched the security guard beating against the doors until he fell. When they had both gone still on the floor, the lights went out.

"Captain, there's a call coming in from the Commander," Cliff said over the comms.

"Put it through," Dana said without taking her eyes off of the vid. "Commander?"

"Captain, we have a problem."

WADE WAS ALREADY WAITING IN THE SECTION OF THE MED-BAY designated as the morgue when Dana arrived. Mrs. Jun Tan was standing with her arms crossed over her chest, and Rido and Randall Jabar were off to one side, arguing about something so loudly she thought they might start swinging at each other.

She stepped in. "Gentlemen, what seems to be the problem here?"

The twins were face to face, clenched fists at their sides, breathing hard through their nostrils. At the sight of her, Rido broke out in a smile.

"Captain," Randall growled, "tell these people I need to

do an autopsy to determine the time and cause of death. Without it, a murderer might go free."

Mrs. Tan folded her arms over her chest. "He's my husband, and I insist he be kept whole."

"She has the right to her beliefs," Rido said, coming to the woman's defense.

"I don't understand the problem," Dana said. "You can have your memorial service, and then the body can be delivered to Dr. Jabar for the autopsy."

"Part of the service involves the burning of the body—whole," Wade whispered to her.

Dana let out a heavy sigh.

"So, you see, Captain, either we get a good look at the body now, or never," Randall said, then lifted a finger, pointing at his brother. "This is your fault. You should never have gotten involved."

"What was I supposed to do?" Rido protested. "It's up to the family to decide what to do with the remains. She is allowed to have her faith. Just because you choose to believe in the almighty god of science, doesn't mean others can't make a different choice."

"Take your ancient scrolls and backward notions with you when you leave!"

Their voices rose again, and they were so close to pummeling each other Dana didn't feel safe getting between them. Thankfully, Wade stepped forward before a hand could be raised.

"Dr. Jabar, let the captain handle this," he said, his voice restrained. "Rido, thank you for your assistance, but this is between the Captain and Mrs. Tan."

"I'm only here as a support to Jun. If she would like me to

leave, I will heed her bidding." Rido gave her a look that said he wouldn't leave unless she expressly said so. Mrs. Tan nodded her assent for him to depart. He inclined his head toward her before leaving them alone.

"Commander, you are free to go," Dana said. "There's some business I believe you still need to attend to."

"Yes, Captain," Wade replied, heeding her order and following after Rido.

Dana stood with her arms at her sides, waiting for Jun to mirror the movement. She released her arms with reluctant agreement.

"Believe it or not, I understand your reluctance to release the body," Dana told her. "My grandmother used to say, 'When all else fails, let it wash away with the next rain.'" Dana caught Jun's wide eyes and nodded. "Yes, she was also a Believer. To be honest, I'm not entirely sure what they did with my grandfather's body. He died before I was old enough to understand. But those words have always stuck with me. Out here, in space, we don't get a lot of rain, but I never interpreted the phrase in a literal way. You see, there are lots of ways to understand the will of the Majestic."

Jun's eyes filled, and her bottom lip quivered as she stroked her belly. No doubt she was thinking of her impending child. The tears she'd been holding back fell down her round cheeks. "He wouldn't even care, you know." She shrugged and sucked in a breath. "I talked about the Majestic, but he never seemed to buy into the idea that there was anything greater. He said, 'If you're waiting to be saved, you'll be waiting a long time.'" She nodded, then her posture stiffened. "We fought about that for a month before he finally gave in and apologized for making light of my belief."

"Can I make a suggestion?"

Jun stared at her, but didn't answer, so Dana continued.

"Have your memorial service, everything short of the cremation, and then let our doctors check the body. It may be able to tell us something about who killed him. Then, when we're done, the body will be released to you for the final step in your ceremony."

Mrs. Tan bit her bottom lip to keep it from trembling, then she nodded without saying another word.

Dana had turned to go when she called out to her from behind.

"Captain, will you attend his memorial service?"

How could she answer that? She didn't want Jun to change her mind, but she also had enough integrity to know that lying to the pregnant widow was wrong.

Dana turned to face her. "No."

It was simple, and didn't require any explanation. She bowed to Mrs. Tan in ultimate respect, and the young woman inclined her head. Then Dana left the med-bay.

To her dismay, Rido was waiting just outside. "How did it go?"

She didn't slow down, forcing him to follow her. "Fine, no thanks to you."

"I apologize for interfering, but I knew she wouldn't go for it, and she had to be informed. I trust everything is settled now?" His lip curled into a smile, as if he already knew the outcome.

Dana stopped and turned. If she could level him with a look he'd be a pile of ash.

"As a matter of fact, it is. Not that it's any of your business. She's agreed to allow the autopsy after the first half of the ceremony, and then she'll be allowed to cremate her husband once the doctors have what they need."

Rido nodded in understanding. "Excellent. I'll help Jun prepare for her husband's ceremony. If I can be of any more assistance, I trust you'll let me know?"

"I think I've had enough of your help," Dana said, walking away from him. After several steps, she had the distinct feeling she was being watched, and turned to find him staring after her. Flustered, she turned away again, wondering what in the stars she was going to do about him.

CHAPTER 9

ERIC

Chief Eric Rogan dragged his aching body back to his quarters with as much enthusiasm as a prisoner on death row. He'd gone back to the cabin with Ari that morning to tell Eartha what had happened. She'd been so upset that she'd cried for almost an hour. He'd had to reassure her Esme's coma wasn't her fault. Then he'd left her to deal with the engine room, where he turned a disaster into a reasonable mess.

It hadn't taken long to figure out the EMP had permanently fried over half the ship's control systems and with the backups down it had taken most of the day to get through the repairs. Even with everything he had to do he hadn't been able to take his mind off of Esme for a moment.

Even now, Eric fought through the perceptible limp. He'd

been daydreaming when he rammed his leg into the base of a console in front of Lieutenant Dix.

Dix had been mortified, and his stream of apologies had only made it worse, drawing the attention of everyone in engineering. Eric knew how they were looking at him now— a man whose wife had been in a coma for three days and might never wake up. It brought him deference and side-eyed glances filled with pity, none of which helped in the least and only managed to piss him off. Outside the doors to his quarters, he stopped to stretch and twist his aching back one more time, but nothing relieved the dull, constant pain. Eric wanted to fall face first onto the nearest soft spot in the room. It would have been the sofa, but the moment he came through the door and found Ari Three in the kitchen, he paused. Eric's stomach let out an angry growl, reminding him he hadn't remembered to eat during his entire shift. He vaguely remembered someone handing him an energy bar, but he didn't think he'd even bothered to eat it.

Ari prepared dinner with expert movements. He turned to add a dash of seasoning to a pan with his one good hand still covered with the synthetic skin. He used the mechanical one to gingerly pull two plates from the cabinet and place them on the table. It seemed Dr. Walker had yet to find what he'd needed to add the synthetic skin to the limbs Ari had lost to the prehensile vegetation on planet 2396.

He'd wanted to help, but with everything going on he'd hardly had time to sleep anymore. Though he looked forward to the meals Ari prepared for them as did Eartha. She usually waited for him, but maybe she'd gotten tired of waiting for him to come home after his shift.

"What are you making? It smells delicious," Eric said, managing a small smile as Ari looked over at him. Sometimes he looked almost human, with those gray eyes and bleach blond hair that always looked effortlessly styled.

"I am preparing tacos. Eartha has not eaten, so I started dinner for you. There will be enough left over here for the two of you to have a second meal." He seemed genuine in his concern.

Eric waved a hand at him. "It's great, really. Thank you for all your help. I can't keep an eye on her and do my job at the same time. Without Esme—" Eric's words stuck in his throat. The moment he thought of her, he lost his appetite. The idea of sitting down at their table to eat without her made him feel ill.

Every day he tried and failed to imagine a life without Esme. Without the ARI, he'd have curled up into a ball next to his wife and never left. However, the ARI wasn't his personal property. They'd assigned five of them to the ship to help all of its crew and passengers. When the others had been destroyed, it meant ARI Three was the only one left to assist the entirety of the *Hope*. Eric was plagued with guilt for taking up so much of its time.

"Am I keeping you from something else?" he asked.

"No," Ari replied simply. "However, you should know Eartha is not handling the loss of Esme any better than you are."

Eric swore. Of course. He'd been mired in his own loss, not realizing Esme's situation might have affected the girl as well. She'd be thinking of the worst outcome. Eartha had just lost her parents, and you couldn't get any closer to home than another situation like this.

"Where's Eartha now?"

"She is in your room," Ari replied. "To settle her, she is watching her message from home."

Eric frowned. "Where did you get the message?"

"I downloaded the original file as soon as they arrived and stored it within my memory. I thought if she saw hers, it might help calm her." Ari cocked his head to the side, an oddly human gesture. "Was that appropriate?"

"It's a great idea. But how did you know she had a message? She wasn't even supposed to be on the ship."

"That is true." Ari tilted his head again, as if processing the question, before he straightened. "I deduced whoever placed her on board would have knowledge of the messages, thus concluding there would be one for her."

It was a reasonable assumption, and Eric nodded in agreement. It was a good move, but he wondered what state Eartha would be in now after watching the message from home. He and Esme had cried for a full day after getting the messages from their families.

Eric had no idea what he could even say to her. He didn't have the words or energy to comfort himself. How was he supposed to raise the girl on his own? When he'd taken Eartha in, he'd imagined he and Esme doing everything together.

"Chief Rogan?" Ari's voice cut through his thoughts.

He must have been standing in the middle of the room staring at the wall for a full minute. He sighed and nodded as he made his way to the bedroom. The door slid open, and he found Eartha curled up on the bed, her back to the door. He could hear the vid playing on Esme's communication device. He kept his distance, monitoring the video from behind her.

A large black man with no hair was staring into the screen and speaking. He had to be her father. Tears were streaming down his face.

"I miss you so much, darling. Don't worry about your mother, she'll be fine. I brought someone who I think you'll miss as much as us."

The large man wiped at his eyes, then stood up and moved aside, allowing a young girl to sit down. She was about Eartha's age, with a turned-up nose and red-rimmed green eyes, and she spoke fast and with intensity. The conversation began some place in the middle, as if they'd been talking for hours. She stared at the camera as if she could see her friend on the other side. She reached out and touched the lens, then her voice dropped to a whisper, and Eric had to step forward to hear her.

"I know I made it sound like I'd kissed him, but I hadn't. But don't worry. Before the world ends, I'm going to walk right up to him and say, 'Jeremy Cross, I'm going to kiss you until your brains melt.'"

Eartha let out a giggle along with her friend, and then slapped a hand over her mouth. Eric jumped at the sound, as so far, to his knowledge, Eartha didn't laugh. He wondered how many times she'd watched the message.

"Anyway, don't forget your pinky-swear promise." She held up her pinky and crooked it at the camera. "We're best friends forever. No sea, mountain, river, or person can divide us. Us for one." The girl said the words without looking away.

"One for us," Eartha whispered back to her. She linked her pinky fingers together instead of holding it towards the camera.

"Sorry to interrupt you."

Eartha jumped to turn off the device. She didn't have a room of her own, and at her age, she needed one. It was becoming more difficult to maintain any privacy. He and Esme had been arguing about that the morning the EMP went off, and now all he wanted to do was go back in time and tell his wife that they were going to the Captain together to tell her about Eartha. Captain Pinet would probably have given them bigger quarters on the spot. Maybe then Esme wouldn't have been in the cargo bay, looking for a spare cot and bedding. Then that crate would have never fallen on her.

"I need to shower, and then I'll join you at the dinner table," Eric told her, pushing the thoughts away. "The smell of Ari's dinner is making my mouth water. I think you'll love it."

Eartha crawled out of the blankets without a word. Still clutching the communicator to her chest, she made her way out of the bedroom.

Eric showered quickly, sliding into a pair of gray sweats and a blue T-shirt with BUGALOO written in bold white letters across the chest. He and Esme had gone to the concert when they'd been dating, and though she hadn't loved the band, she'd loved the soft souvenir shirts he'd gotten for them.

He joined Eartha at the small, square dining table. She pushed the food around on her plate, but it didn't look like she'd taken a bite. Ari stood watching awkwardly from the kitchen.

"Ari, are you going to sit with us?" Eric asked him.

Ari's head tilted to one side as if calculating before responding. "I do not require sustenance."

"Yes, I'm aware of your limitations, but we could use the

conversation." Eric pointed to the empty chair that didn't belong to Esme.

Ari sat down in the seat he'd indicated with his arms hanging at his sides. "Are the tacos not to your liking?"

Eric realized he hadn't touched his plate either. "No, they're great." He took a bite to prove it. They were good. He chewed and swallowed, but the food hit the bottom of his gut like a ball of lead. He couldn't eat anymore, and gave up trying.

"Are you going to see Esme tonight?" Eartha asked.

She didn't know how much it hurt to hear her name, so he cleared his throat and answered. "Yes. I'll see her and report back. I'm sorry you haven't been able to visit her."

Eartha lifted one shoulder in a half shrug.

"I'm sorry I haven't been home much, either. The ship needs a lot of my attention right now." He forced positivity he didn't feel into his voice. "But it won't be long before Esme wakes up. She'll be back here reminding us to pick up our things in no time."

Silence.

Eric looked at the ARI, pleading with his eyes.

"It is time for me to see to my other duties," Ari said, rising from the chair, missing the cue entirely.

"Thanks a lot," Eric grumbled.

"Thank you for allowing me to sit with you during your dinner. I look forward to doing it again," the Ari said, his tone polite. "Eartha, please remember to tell Chief Rogan about the disturbance earlier today."

Eric's attention sharpened, looking between the two of them. "What disturbance?"

The ARI didn't stop to explain, continuing out the door as

if he hadn't spoken. Eric looked down at Eartha, but her head was turned away, staring at her plate.

"Eartha, did something happen today?" he asked.

Her voice was barely a whisper. "I felt someone watching me."

Eric looked around their quarters as if he'd spot a peephole in the bulkhead. "What makes you think someone was watching you?"

"It's like before. I can feel someone in here with me," Eartha explained without looking up. "It creeps me out. Ari said he couldn't find anything."

"Are you sure it's not a waking dream?"

Eartha rolled her eyes. "I know you don't believe me, but it's true."

"Are they here now?"

Eartha let out a sigh of frustration as she threw her napkin onto the table. "No, they only watch me when you're not here." Her head dropped into her hands as she continued to stare down at the food still on her plate.

Eric looked at the top of her curls and wished desperately, for the hundredth time, that he wasn't alone, that Esme was there to help him. She'd been right about there being something different about the girl. It disturbed him how certain events seemed to support her notions.

Regardless of her strange ideas, though, nothing could change how he felt about her. He wanted Eartha to stay. His heart ached at the thought of turning her over to the captain. Isn't that what he'd been trying to explain to Esme? She hadn't been able to see his side of things before, but she'd wake up, and then she'd come around.

"I believe you," he said, and watched her lift her head at

last, her eyes searching his face. "Just do me a favor. If you think they're going to hurt you, use the comms system to call me like I showed you."

Eartha nodded, and he watched a small smile spread across her mouth. He'd said the right thing. He couldn't wait to tell Esme.

With one hand, he pushed his plate to the side, still not ready to eat. Maybe after his visit to the med-bay.

"Is there anything you want me to tell Esme tonight?" he asked.

Eartha considered it for a moment. Then, with her eyes focused on his, she said, "Yes. Tell her when she wakes up, everything will be better. There's a surprise waiting for her."

"Oh? That sounds good. What are you planning to give her?"

"Nothing." Eartha looked down at her plate again. "It's not from me."

Eric reached over and lifted her chin so she could face him. "So there isn't a surprise?"

"There is, but it's not a surprise from me."

Eric frowned. "Who is it from, then?"

"I don't want to tell you. It's not my surprise. But trust me, you'll both be happy." She pulled away and dug a fork into her meat, breaking apart the taco before taking a bite. "This isn't bad. Not as good as Esme's, but it's okay. She'll be home soon, and we won't have to eat Ari's cooking much longer."

Eric frowned. She sounded so sure. But something made him ask her the next question with all seriousness. "Really? How soon?"

Eartha looked up, as if thinking, then shrugged. "I don't know. But not until the aliens show up."

The hairs on Eric's arm stood on end. "What aliens?" he asked, a chill of fear sliding down his spine.

"The aliens watching us."

CHAPTER 10

Who was Eartha Singh?

That was the question Dana kept coming back to as she watched the 3D vid of Michael Singh breaking down on camera again. He reassured Eartha that her mother had done the right thing.

Dana wondered just what she had done.

Why did Michael Singh believe his daughter was onboard the Hope, even though her name was nowhere to be found on the manifest?

It wasn't much of a leap to assume a worker on the ground crew had smuggled their daughter onto the ship to save her. However, despite its importance, no one had come looking for the lost letter. No one had claimed the strange name, either—Eartha, no doubt a namesake variation of their planet of origin, Earth. Their history was a grim one, the name a unique choice for a young girl whose grandparents had probably never even set foot on the planet where their ancestors had fought—and lost—the Great Purge.

The first humans were assigned the role of planet-caretakers by aliens only known as the 'Benefactors.' When they'd returned to find the planet dying from the barrage of damage that had been done, and the people near to annihilating themselves, they'd taken action to cleanse the planet at the highest level.

Dana leaned forward toward the vid when the girl's best friend appeared. Her shiny brown hair and freckles would have made her a striking beauty, had she lived. She talked about boys, the way young girls were inclined to do. She admitted to Eartha that she'd never kissed a boy, but that she was planning to rectify the situation as soon as an available specimen presented himself.

Dana had giggled at the girl's bubbly personality the first time. Even through her tears, her positivity shone through. She reminded her so much of Bonnie Porter, her friend from the academy, that it was difficult not to cry the second time she watched the vid. Dana sat stone-faced the third time as the girl's laughter turned to tears, looking for any clue as to where Eartha might be found.

The young girl was long dead now. Their planet, Zelenia, destroyed a month ago by an asteroid they'd named Harvey. This young Becky had no family onboard the *Hope*; Dana had already checked the manifest. There was no one left behind who knew her to mourn her. Her lost friend, Eartha, would sadly never receive her message. The only comfort was that the asteroid's trajectory and impact had made their deaths instantaneous. None of them had suffered.

The father, eyes still red, but dry, returned to the camera with promises that Eartha's life was more important than she knew. He said he tried to track down her and her mother, but it was too late. It was his next words, though, that didn't make any sense.

Michael Singh glanced over his shoulder, as if someone might be watching him, and said, "Raising you was the greatest privilege any father could dream of. You're my child in every way that matters. When your birth family comes for you, please remember that much. Embrace your differences. They're what make you so special."

Who were her birth parents? Why wasn't there any record of her adoption into the Singh family?

"COMP, pull up Zelenia citizen record for Singh—first name Michael."

Dana stared at the man in the vid, wondering who he might be. His daughter was nowhere to be found on the ship. No one had seen the girl. For all Dana knew, she may have been injured in the original Coalition bombings.

The computer interrupted her thoughts, listing off the information she'd requested. *"Singh, Michael. Born 4293.6.30 to Roger and Beatrice Singh. Husband to Susan MacLaren. Father to Eartha Singh MacLaren."*

"COMP, pause read-out. Display Michael Singh's family photos."

Eartha's bright smile filled the screen between her two loving parents. The girl had a large mane of curly black hair, and her eyes slanted ever so slightly upward, like a cat. The full mouth and high cheekbones looked to be her father's, but her eyes were her mother's. Eartha's were brown and her mother's green, but they were the same shape.

Then she saw it.

"Computer, enlarge and enhance image—upper right quadrant."

The image enlarged, and Dana gaped as she looked at the woman who'd given her the tour of the *Hope* when it had still been docked. Eartha's mother had been the well-dressed woman who'd designed the ship, who knew every inch of her.

She'd been amazed at how the woman had known so much about the ship. Dana had caught a strange sadness on Susan's face at times and had wondered about it. She thought it was because the engineer had been mourning the loss of her project. But apparently Susan MacLaren had known the truth. She'd planned to put her daughter onboard, perhaps even hide her, as she knew the ship inside and out. Perhaps it was the assurance that her daughter would survive without her that had been the reason behind the melancholy expressions.

But they'd found no evidence of the girl on the ship.

Had someone discovered what she'd planned to do? Dana wondered. Had they stopped her before Susan had the chance to hide her?

Dana looked closer now at both parents, still shaking her head. Eartha looked like a perfect mix of the two.

How can this girl be adopted?

Dana searched for close relatives for potential connections, but every child born to either side of the family had been accounted for. Then she cross checked the manifest for any family onboard that might be hiding the child. Her search came up empty again.

Dana reviewed the girl's limited school and hospital records. There had been nothing of note in either, nothing in her records to indicate she wasn't the biological child of Singh or MacLaren. She was an average student with an above average interest in the sciences. It seemed she'd taken after her mother in that regard, focusing most of her studies on engineering and design.

The door chimed and the computer announced President Muñoz.

Dana closed the 3D rendering of the message and turned her attention to the door. "Enter."

"Captain," he greeted as he entered. "I realize you're a very busy woman, but I wanted to stop by and see if I could be of some help to you."

She held out a hand, gesturing to the chair in front of her desk. "I appreciate you stopping by. And thank you, but you've done plenty in the last month."

Dana had come out of mourning in a haze to find he'd put together an amazing memorial for those lost on their home planet. It had been a tasteful and inclusive event to mark the occasion.

"The ceremony was lovely," he agreed, taking the offered seat. "I wish I could take credit for it, but as you know, my wife is a genius when it comes to party planning, and with Abigail Evans involved, the competition alone was enough to make it a success." He smiled, then sobered, no doubt picking up on Dana's current mood.

Dana tried to muster up a smile, but it probably looked as forced as it felt on her face. "People can be unpredictable when grieving. The two of you standing with me helped a lot of the passengers and crew."

"I couldn't help but notice when you answered the door you seemed a little spooked. Is there anything I can do?"

On Zelenia, President Hector Muñoz had made a name for himself for being not only reasonable, but wise in matters of global scope. Unlike Chancellor Jeremiah Evans, he rarely forced his views on anyone. Instead, he spoke to others with respect, taking a genuine interest in people. His concern evident on his round face and in his warm, coffee-colored eyes. Dana wondered what he'd think of their little mystery.

"Do you remember Sarah MacLaren?" she asked.

Muñoz sat back in his seat and stroked his hairless chin. He shook his head. "I can't say that I do."

"She was one of the principal engineers who designed this very ship. It appears she was planning to smuggle her daughter onboard."

Muñoz leaned forward in his chair. "I'm intrigued."

Dana turned on the 3D imagery from Eartha's video message. Muñoz watched with apt attention, and let out a soft 'oh' when the message ended. The image of Singh's face, his eyes filled with tears as he pleaded for her safety, sat suspended above Dana's desk until she tapped the off icon.

"So you see," Dana continued, "we believe this girl was supposed to be hidden onboard the *Hope* by her mother."

"Is there any evidence that she succeeded?"

"None." Dana watched Muñoz trying to work it out for himself. "I can at least confirm that she's not here, but it doesn't sit well with me that there's no record of her being with her parents at the time of the end."

"Might she and her mother have been discovered before our launch?" Muñoz reasoned.

"That's my guess, but with no one left behind, there's no way to get confirmation. With everything happening on board, we've crawled the entire ship, looking for explosives planted by the Coalition. If there'd been any sign of her, we'd have seen it by now."

"Did anyone ever claim that missing shoe?"

Maggie had done a fantastic job of including a brief shot of the shoe and a message on her evening broadcasts. Almost everyone watched her, so it was likely that most of the ship had seen the shoe at least once. The president was the only one to ask her about it. Dana turned and pulled the small, pink running shoe from the bottom desk drawer where she'd kept it, expecting someone to claim it at any time. She placed it on the desk between them.

Muñoz raised his thick black eyebrows at her. "Could be a young girl of thirteen, considering the size and style."

Dana nodded. She hadn't put the two facts together until now. It would also explain the raids on the Commons if the girl was onboard, scavenging for food.

Her stomach dropped when she remembered all the injuries that had been sustained during the last attack on the ship to cover up the murder of Shu and the guard.

"There's been so much activity, if she is onboard, she might be hurt," Dana said, giving voice to her worst nightmare. The last thing she wanted was to find the girl dead in a conduit somewhere.

"Easy to lose track of someone in all that's been happening, but it might explain some of the events that have so far been a mystery," he concluded.

Then she remembered the night she'd heard someone in the vents above her. At the time, she'd thought it was someone working for the Coalition, or maybe even a crew member. Now, she wondered if it hadn't been the young girl.

"It's starting to add up... a few unexplained incidents, the shoe, and now this message... She may very well be onboard, but hiding in plain sight. Or she's hurt and needs help." She nodded slowly to herself. "We need to search the ventilation shafts. I think that might be where she's hiding." Dana stood and gave a slight bow to the Muñoz. "You've been a tremendous help, Mr. President."

He stood as well. "I did nothing. I only helped you put together a couple of clues. You did the rest. However, if I may share another idea?"

"By all means," Dana said, coming around the desk to walk him out.

He started for the door. "There may be a way to get the passengers to help us with this."

"How?"

"Put out a bulletin for everyone to be on the lookout for the girl. Put her image on every monitor and display unit until people recognize her on sight. If she's onboard, someone may spot her."

Dana nodded. "I like it. I'll alert the crew to begin a grid search of secured areas and maintenance shafts of the ship."

"With your permission, I'll enlist my wife, as well as Chancellor Evans and his wife. We can ask around at some gatherings we attend where there are children. She may have made a friend or two who, for her own good, may give her up."

It was an excellent idea Dana hadn't even considered, and she said so. "Thank you, Mr. President," she said as the doors to her office slid open.

She'd set things in motion to track down the girl immediately. She knew deep down the girl had to be onboard, or it would be the most tragic of endings, and Dana was nothing if not a sucker for a happily ever after.

The sight of Commander Wade Chance heading her way reminded her how much she wanted her own happy ending.

CHAPTER 11

Wade followed Dana into her office. "What do you have for me?" she asked as they both sat down.

Wade cleared his throat. "Well... I wish we had more. The original files were corrupted."

She frowned. "Corrupted how?"

"I have no idea. We could only get a partial download to the ARI. When I went to check the original file, I found the data was corrupted."

"I don't think that's a coincidence."

"Nor do I." Wade leaned back in his chair. "The question is, who had access to corrupt the original data file that was sent to you through a secured channel?"

Wade sat there, the question hanging between them as she stared back at him.

Then understanding dawned, and Dana touched a hand to her chest.

"Are you saying you think I did it?"

Wade leaned forward in his chair with a frown and shook

his head. "No! Did you think I was—? No. What I mean is, it might have arrived corrupted."

Dana nodded her understanding. "You mean from the ground..." She hadn't thought about someone from the Coalition getting access to the information from their side. It was entirely possible. "Is there any way to find out when the file was corrupted?"

Wade shrugged. "I can try. Right now, we're using all our resources to go through the messages we've got, and we've come up with nothing."

"Someone with access to those files, access to the brig, and access to the areas where the bombs were placed... I don't like it. There's a connection, Commander, and I want to find it."

"Even with the corrupted files, there's a lot to work with. The ARI Three can run the search passively, looking for anything suspicious, while we go through our list of people with first access and work our way down. The ARI narrowed the first search parameters to just over fifty people. We'll need to go through those ourselves." He sighed. "It will take several hours to complete. Although, we haven't yet ruled out the Coalition using nuanced language or a coded overlay to ensure that only the intended watcher gets the message."

"Aren't they resourceful," Dana said, her voice dripping with sarcasm then she bit her lip in thought. "Have you added anyone to the team?"

"I'm going small on this one. The less crew, the better. For the moment, it's just Barnes, Eric Rogan, Westlake, Harden, and I."

"Good thinking. If you'd like to give me a few vids, I can go through them in my quarters."

Wade stood up from his chair, but he didn't turn to leave.

Dana furrowed her brow, looking up at him. "Is there something more, Commander?"

"No, not really." He puffed out his chest and flashed her a half-smile. "I wanted to inform you; Maggie's video was one of the first few flagged by the ARI. I handed it off to Barnes for review."

Dana smiled at him. He seemed so proud of himself.

"So, she's all clear?"

Wade scoffed. "If she weren't, Barnes would have her in a cell by now."

Too bad. Dana's idea that Maggie might be hiding ties to the Coalition disintegrated. It didn't mean she wasn't hiding something else from him. There had to be some reason, other than Wade, that the woman grated on her nerves. No, Barnes and Wade were friends. If there were anything on her message for him to worry about, Barnes would have told him.

Wade gave her a curt nod, making for the door, but before he reached it, he turned back. "Are you all right?"

She must not have been doing a very good job of hiding her feelings.

"Yes, I'm fine."

"I missed you again this morning. You must get up at oh three hundred to run these days. That's true dedication."

He laughed, but Dana averted her eyes, looking for a distraction.

"I haven't had my work out yet."

"Oh," he said.

Wade seemed to swallow his disappointment in a hard gulp. Before she could make up an excuse about getting back to work, Cliff broke in over the comms.

"Captain to the bridge."

Their conversation officially tabled, Dana gave Wade a nod and moved through the side doors of her office to the bridge, Wade following behind her.

"What have we got?" she asked as she entered.

Nancy's hands flew over the helm, her face screwed up in confusion. "There's something on the port side of the ship, Captain."

"What is it?" Wade asked.

"I'm not sure. I thought it was another sensor echo, but..." Nancy's words got lost in the focus on her search.

"But what, Lieutenant?" he prompted.

"It keeps coming back. There it is again. I think... I think it's following us."

"How long has it been there?" Dana asked, but Nancy didn't answer.

"Want me to light them up, Captain?" Barnes asked.

Dana shook her head. Firing on them could prove disastrous. They didn't have unlimited weapons or power. Without knowing what the other ship carried, they could find themselves outgunned.

"No. Continue scanning and see if you can figure out what their ship is carrying. There's no need to start a fight we can't finish."

"Should we try hailing them?" Wade asked.

"I can't get a clear read on them, but there's something out there scanning us," Barnes said.

"Defense shielding up and signal red alert," Dana ordered. "Everyone to their stations."

Wade put in the command. The emergency lights went to full, and the sustained siren alerted everyone onboard they were to operate in emergency mode.

"This could be our first contact with a new species," Wade said, rubbing his hands together. The excitement on the bridge was palpable.

"Harden, hail the other ship with our standard greeting," Dana said.

"No response," Cliff said. "Of course, I'm not entirely sure they're receiving us." There was more uncertainty in his tone than usual.

Dana faced the main monitor. To the naked eye, there were only stars, but if there was something out there, it might be hiding. The only way to know for sure was to make it visible by some other means.

"Amplify the scanner ahead of us," Dana said. "Let's find something to make them visible even for a second. Do we have anything we can bounce off their hull without appearing hostile?"

"We don't have a lot of anything that wouldn't be considered an attack... Any suggestions?" Wade asked the other officers.

The bridge remained quiet while they all thought.

Barnes chimed in, "We could try a particle spread."

Wade nodded. "It's not really like firing on someone directly, and we'll be able to make them visible for a moment."

"Let's try it," Dana said.

The particle spread burst out in front of them and continued beyond the range of the sensors.

"No bounce," Nancy reported from the helm.

"Let's check the port side," Wade said.

Again, nothing.

"Let's not be so predictable," Dana said. "Hit them from our back end."

They all watched as the particles spread into a pattern before bouncing right back at them.

"Gotcha!" she crowed. "Put it on the monitor. I think we'd all like to see it." Dana waited with crossed arms. The direct hit revealed an alien ship visible on their bow. "See if you can get a scan of them now, Barnes."

The ship disabled its reflective shielding and moved to take a position off the bow of the *Hope*. It had an almost oval, beetle-like shape, with the engines positioned on either side, strong but maneuverable. There was no shine on the vessel, as if it had endured many years of space travel.

"They're trying to scan us again, Captain," Cliff said.

"Let them," Dana replied. "We're not the ones hiding."

"We're picking up multiple armaments at the ready," Barnes reported. "I think they have enough to take us down."

"Understood. Hold." She gave the command with one raised hand.

It was as if they all held their breath, waiting to see what the ship would do next.

"Ensign, open a hailing channel," she said.

"Channel open," Cliff replied.

"Unknown vessel, this is Captain Dana Pinet of the *Starship Hope*. We are from a recently destroyed planet within this system, and we're in search of a new home. Who are you, and what are your intentions?"

"That should get their attention," Wade said, keeping his voice low.

"We've stated our business, now let's see if they'll do us the courtesy of imitating our example," Dana agreed.

She paced between her seat and the helm. She had so much nervous energy she wasn't sure what to do with it. Friendly relations with a new species was monumental. Would they be able to communicate? Would they look like them? Work with them to find a new planet?

Dana tried to keep her expectations low. They didn't seem interested in them as a people. They might not even reveal themselves. If they moved on, her ship wouldn't be able to follow them.

"They're answering our hail," Cliff announced. He stared down at the console, a confused expression on his face. "Wait..."

"Put them on the main viewer."

Dana meandered to her chair and crossed her arms again as she waited. Then she crossed her legs and stared at her nails as if they were the most interesting thing in the world.

Then the screen lit, and Dana's nails were immediately forgotten.

The aliens on the other ship were nothing like Dana expected. The first thing she noted was the amount of hair that seemed to engulf them. It grew from their heads, limbs, and most of their face, leaving only a small bare section around their eyes and cheekbones. Other than that, they seemed to be anatomically similar, and even wore clothing, including metallic breastplates that looked heavy and bulky. They reminded Dana of something she'd seen in a book of Earth's history. The breastplate had been used to protect oneself against enemy fire before the invention of polyabsorbant cloth. They had only two eyes that she could see, a nose, a mouth, two arms... perhaps they also recognized the similarities.

Nothing happened for a full minute as the two bridge crews took in each other. Dana noted that the one who appeared to be the leader wore a brighter metallic chest plate than the others. He also had an oversized head with long blond hair, and something about his proportions seemed off, but other than that, he looked similar to the Zelenians.

"You are a strange species," the leader said at last, his voice more high-pitched than she'd expected. "May we speak?"

It was strange to hear her language coming from his lips. The other crew members also seemed surprised by the address. His two dark eyes shifted from left to right as he waited for her to answer.

"How is it you speak to us in our language?" Dana asked as she uncrossed her legs, waiting for an explanation.

"We have technology. We speak with aliens easy. How do you get so far without?"

Dana bristled at the note of condescension in his voice. "We are equally surprised by your rude behavior," she shot back. "Is it acceptable among your species to make yourselves invisible while scanning another ship?"

The alien laughed, and she saw inside his mouth; a pink tongue and short, dull teeth.

"You are correct. So rude we are. Many sorries may we meet you. I am Ashwin Zeppel of the Des freighter. We are Fashin Teku. A great many stars from here is our planet—Wakuba."

Dana nodded. Without star charts, she had no idea how far off Wakuba was, but the Fashin Teku didn't need to know that. She put on her best smile, but still refused to leave her chair. "What do you want?"

"We offer our deepest sorries." Ashwin inclined his head. "We understand what it is you have suffered, as our people once lived on twin planets."

Dana leaned forward in her chair, intrigued by the statement. "What is your purpose in this part of space? Why are you following us?"

"We have scanned your ship, and we see that you are in some trouble. May we help you?"

Dana looked to Wade, who shrugged, then turned back to the main viewscreen. "What do you have in mind?"

"It is the custom of our people to speak nose to nose when there is something important to be discussed. Is this likely?"

"Ensign, mute audio." Dana looked to Wade. "Should we allow them onto our ship?"

He crossed his arms over his chest. "I want to say no. However, then you'd just insist on going over there to meet with them. I don't trust them with you, so they'll have to come here. We'll keep a security team with them at all times."

Dana nodded. Better for them to be cautious then foolish in cases like these. Her people's history with alien species wasn't great, and, in this case, she didn't want to put her people in danger.

"Ensign, resume audio," she said, turning to face the monitor again. "We welcome you, Ashwin Zeppel, to be our guest."

"May I bring two?"

"Of course. If you have a small shuttle, it should fit in our—"

Dana's next words were cut off as the viewer went black, leaving them staring at the outside of the ship.

"Were we cut off?" Dana stood up and Wade joined her. "What did I say?"

"I'm not sure what happened," Cliff said as he stared baffled at the console. "The transmission just ended."

Then, without warning, the three Fashin Teku materialized in front of her on the bridge. Barnes, with lightning reflexes, had his weapon out and trained on the three aliens immediately. Wade stepped in front of her, his arms raised out before him to shield her.

Ashwin raised his short arms up and out in the same manner as Wade.

"We come with peace in mind?"

CHAPTER 12

"Thy enemy is any person with hands that carry a disagreeable taste."

- Fashin Teku Proverb

Dana needed to get control of the situation. Her crew had their weapons pointed at the short captain's hairy head. The entire bridge was at attention, wondering how the aliens came to be standing in front of them.

"At ease," Dana called out. "I believe this is another one of their technologies."

Ashwin and the two others with him held up their hands, looking to Dana in confusion. She gave Wade and Barnes a nod, and they lowered their weapons.

The Fashin Teku were a trifecta of color and representation. The three of them were so short that Dana was still a head taller than the tallest of them. That one was the darkest of the three, with long blond locks that flowed down his back. The two males had long beards that trailed down their breastplate-covered chests to their bellies. Each of them wore small metal decorations in their hair that kept it out of their faces. They reminded her of the ancient Earth fairytales about gnomes. Their eyes were large to match their mouths, making their heads appear even bigger than they were. Other than that, they seemed to have five fingers on each hand, no extra limbs she could detect, and carried no weapons.

"Many sorries, did we frighten you?" Ashwin asked. "We mean no hostility."

Dana had to push down her own rush of adrenaline to step forward with a smile. "Welcome to the *Hope*. We're pleased to meet you in person. You're correct, your mode of transportation is unfamiliar to us. Please forgive our reaction and tell us more about it."

Ashwin nodded, his long beard quivering.

"This is our bridge, where only officers are permitted," Dana continued explaining.

"Oh, I understand. This is a forbidden area."

"Yes."

Captain Ashwin Zeppel was astute in his assessment of the situation, and maintained a safe distance from her and the others while keeping a smile on his foreign features. "We meant no disrespect," he said, then he stepped forward, careful to keep his movements slow and deliberate when she reached out a hand to shake his.

However, instead of shaking it, he grasped her right hand and gave it a sloppy lick. He seemed to test the taste on his tongue before nodding to the others.

"You honor us."

When he released her hand, it was all she could do not to wipe it off on the leg of her blue and white uniform.

Ashwin gestured behind him. "This is my second-in-command, Tovar Vaziri."

It was the female who stepped forward, her bright red hair falling in waves almost to her feet, intricately braided and decorated with metallic bands that shifted with each movement, catching the light. Her pale skin and figure were in direct contrast to the other two, though she also had a beard of sorts that lay flat against her chin and draped down her neck.

She seemed agitated, but when she smiled at Barnes, showing off black and gray teeth, she showed no fear. She held out her hand, and when Barnes reached down to shake it, she turned it over and gave it a lavish lick, as her captain had done.

"That is Lieutenant Commander Peter Barnes," Dana said, nodding in his direction, proud that he'd maintained his composure. "He is our chief of security." Then she gestured with one hand to Wade. "This is my First Officer and second-in-command, Commander Wade Chance."

"Ah, wonderful," Ashwin said with a clap of his hands. "This is my third in command in charge of security, Oli Serei."

When Oli reached out to Wade, they shook hands once, but before Oli could lick Wade's hand, he pulled it back and shook his head.

"No thanks, I'm good."

It took a moment for them to recover from the shock. Dana was quick to jump in to continue diplomatic relations.

"I apologize, Ashwin, not all of our people are as refined

as yours." She shot a glare at Wade for his lack of diplomacy. "Please come with me. The bridge, as I mentioned, is for designated crew only. We have a more comfortable area for welcoming guests."

Without another word, the three followed Dana out of the room. She signaled with a tilt of her head that Wade and Barnes should follow. Dana was optimistic she could convince them they weren't from some backward planet, but bringing security was standard protocol. The same seemed true for the alien race.

She gave them a brief tour of her office, and then moved on to the adjoining senior officer's conference room.

"Please, sit down," Dana said as she gestured to the chairs. However, she realized her mistake when it took each of them two tries to climb up onto them. Due to their stature, they kept their chairs pulled back from the table to avoid hitting their heads. She watched them pull their long head hair to one side so they weren't seated on it.

Dana sat across from them, Wade taking the chair on her right and Barnes on her left.

"Your ship's insides are lovely," Ashwin said once everyone had settled. "Not what we are expecting."

"Do you encounter many aliens in your travels?" Dana asked.

"Yes, of course. Don't you?"

"We admit we're new to this part of space. Our people haven't explored this far out before."

Ashwin frowned. "That's not true. We've met your species before."

She wouldn't have been more surprised if he'd said they were hiding a third eye under all that hair. Wade and Barnes both sat forward in their seats, intrigued, but Dana shook her head. She didn't want to lead this discussion with their wants and needs. She didn't know much about these aliens, but she didn't imagine they had a reason to lie about something like this, and given time, might voluntarily tell them much more.

"When did you have occasion to meet our people?"

Ashwin waved a hand in the air. "My father was commander. Over four decades in the past. I was a boy. Your people were unpleasant, skittish, without hospitality."

Wade and Barnes looked at her with an expression of disbelief and wonder. She shook her head. She had no idea whom they had met, but it hadn't been Zelenians. They were too far from home, and her father would have most certainly known about any alien contact, had there been any.

"Pardon our surprise, but I find your story hard to believe. We are the only known Zelenians to explore space since our arrival to our planet from Blue Earth centuries ago." Dana pulled up the 3D imagery of their planet as it had been. "This is Zelenia, our former home. As I mentioned, we are the last. We are unaware of any others. Where did you encounter these people?"

Ashwin stroked his beard. "Many moons and stars ago... I think on a different star chart. I was no more than a muffit." He shrugged. "They maybe killed themselves."

Dana frowned trying to make sense of their words. She ran through the possibilities in her head. Could there have been others from her world? There were no records of such travel. Had a faction of their people splintered off during the relocation to Zelenia?

Their history on Earth didn't have the kind of ending that could be forgotten, a scar on their people they had endured for centuries. It had kept them from pursuing contact with alien species in general—to their detriment, it seemed.

Dana's mind raced with the possibilities. The search for more humans was only second to them finding a new planet to call home. Distrust this early in their relationship might scare them off, destroying any chance at getting any more information out of them. "It's our privilege to meet you, and begin renewed relations with you, if you'll permit it."

Ashwin seemed pleased by this news. He smiled before launching himself across the table to grasp her hand again. Both Barnes and Wade shot to their feet, ready to defend her, but after Ashwin licked the back of her hand again, he climbed back down and, with the help of his companions, managed to get back into the chair. She wondered how they would feel if they were taught the Zelenian way of greeting. She'd do anything to avoid more of the unpleasant licking.

"Can we provide help to you on your journey?" Ashwin asked again, his eyes wide.

"We are in search of a planet that will be compatible with our species," Dana explained. "Have you come across anything that might suit us?"

Ashwin sat back to give it some thought. He chittered to his two companions. Only the female, Tovar, answered. The other, Oli, remained quiet. He shook his head, never quite taking his eyes off of Wade and Barnes, who'd settled back into their seats.

"Many sorries. I wish we could give help to you. The other planets we've been are no good." Ashwin put a hand on his hairy chin and stroked his beard. "Maybe we can do a thing. Let me have the conversations with my people, and we will help you on your way."

Dana smiled at Wade and Barnes. "Excellent. We are also unfamiliar with your technology. Is that something we can discuss later?"

Ashwin shifted. This time she caught the subtle tap of a fingertip behind his ear. They all seemed to have a small device there. Dana listened to their chittering conversation for a moment, but couldn't understand a word. The devices must be used to speak and understand other languages.

They debated the subject among themselves. The Fashin Teku language had clicks and grunts that appeared to be a part of its grammar. At one point the female sneered at her, and Dana wondered what Ashwin said to get her to calm down. For the moment, they had no regard for anyone else at the table.

"I suspect they can't understand us either," Wade whispered, keeping his voice below the level of the aliens. "Would you like me to dig deeper into their technology on my own?"

Ashwin gave him a strange look before he continued to debate with his people. The conversation was dying down, so Dana had to be quick.

"Yes. I'd like to know their capabilities, even if we can't replicate them at the moment," Dana whispered back.

The three aliens tapped the back of their ears again in unison. Ashwin's words were once again understandable.

"Again, many sorries for the long time. My people and I think we have misled you. We do not have the law of free exchange of technology with aliens. If we share too much, we might have to battle our own technology." Ashwin held out his hands, palms up. "You understand?"

"Of course I do," Dana replied. "We will appreciate anything you can do to help us."

"Your propulsion mechanisms are not well functioning. Oli is an expert. We are very happy to help you repair so you may be able to travel again. We also have maps that go further than a small distance." Ashwin tilted his head. "Will that be of help to you?"

Dana's smile was genuine. "That is very generous."

She had less than a moment to congratulate herself on her success when the computer interrupted her by announcing Chancellor Evans and President Muñoz at the doors of the room.

She nodded to Barnes to see to the door. The Fashin Teku watched with interest as Barnes made the attempt, but failed to keep them out.

"I will not be refused entrance, young man!" the Chancellor snapped, barging in past him. "You'll have to arrest me."

He swept into the room, arms wide as he smiled at their guests. A more subdued President Muñoz trailed in after him.

"I apologize for our tardiness. We weren't expecting guests." Chancellor Evans gave Dana a reproachful glare. "Captain Pinet, it is disappointing to see you are in diplomatic talks with new aliens without us. We assumed you would call upon your dignitaries when such need arrived."

Evans extended his hand to the aliens in greeting. Ashwin and the others took in their distinct clothing and smiles. President Muñoz was wearing a formal uniform, complete with medals. The Chancellor had opted for a bright blue uniform with gold accents.

Ashwin and the others looked to Dana for confirmation of the chancellor's words. She had established herself as their leader, and they wouldn't move until she cleared them.

"It is true," she said, nodding at the two men. "This is Chancellor Jeremiah Evans, and President Hector Muñoz. In our world, they are the ambassadors of our people."

The three leaped to their feet and grabbed the nearest hand, giving them each a sloppy kiss. The two men looked uncomfortable but said nothing before bowing low to them. It seemed to thrill the aliens to learn a new greeting. They each bowed back in turn. Both men's ability to keep a straight face impressed Dana. They were correct—they had a lot more experience in diplomacy than her.

Dana stood and gestured to two empty chairs at the table. "I apologize gentlemen. Our guests' arrival was a shock to us. They have a technology that allows them to dematerialize and materialize at will. There was no time to signal for you to join us, as we've just sat down. Please forgive me and join us."

She'd meant to get their attention, and she had. Both the Chancellor and the President stood staring at her with raised eyebrows, then looked to their guests.

"How are they able to speak our language?" Muñoz asked, settling into one chair.

"They have a technology that allows them to communicate with alien races," Dana explained, sitting down. She smiled, trying not to give too much of her excitement away. She planned to further discuss their stand on sharing technology with things like communication devices once they were more comfortable with each other.

As the Chancellor was adjusting to his seat, the computer announced Maggie Brooker's presence. Dana took one hard look at Wade. He threw up his hands and shrugged, a sly grin never leaving his face. "I didn't say a word. I've been here with you the entire time."

Dana rolled her eyes. She knew better than to try to keep Maggie out. "Permission granted, I guess," Dana said to the computer. "Can I help you, Ms. Brooker?" she asked as the woman sashayed inside. "This is a closed meeting."

Dressed in a powder-blue skirt and blazer, in direct contrast to their dark blue crew uniforms, she drew every eye in the room. "Yes, Captain, but I'm the official historical recorder. New alien relations fall under a monumental historical event, so it's only appropriate I am in attendance. Besides, the passengers and non-bridge crew will want to see our visitors. We don't want people to be startled by our guests' unique appearance, now, do we?"

She didn't wait for a response as she approached the Fashin Teku, extending a hand to the nearest one—the female. Dana was still debating about whether to throw Maggie out, but thought it would serve her right to embarrass herself. She had no idea what customs these aliens revered, and their greeting alone might be enough to get rid of her. Dana gave the Fashin Teku another nod, and they climbed out of their seats again to greet her.

Tovar took her outstretched hand, giving it a wet lick. Maggie returned the gesture with an open mouth kiss on the alien female's hand. Her response must have been accurate, because the aliens were so enamored with her, they each shoved their hands in her direction. She took her time leaving a wet kiss on each of them. They encircled her, all chattering at once. Even the silent one, Oli, who before now hadn't said a word in their language, was introducing himself.

Dana leaned in and whispered low to Wade, "Now what?"

"I'm not sure, but whatever it is, I think Mags just made us look good. Let's go with it, and later we can claim it was all our idea." Wade smiled, and Dana had to stifle a laugh.

The Chancellor clapped his hands together to get everyone's attention back on him. "I've just been speaking with President Muñoz, and we've decided. In honor of our new guests, I'd like to host an evening of entertainment."

"Chancellor," Dana said, rising from her chair in protest. So far, the aliens had offered little help. In fact, in her mind, they were still in the early negotiation phase of discussions. Besides that, they didn't have the rations to support a party for an unknown number of aliens. Before she could interject further, Ashwin moved to stand in front of the seated chancellor.

"What defines an evening of entertainment?" Ashwin asked.

President Muñoz answered with a warm smile. "It's where we have a small party where the guests share their unique skills and talents for our enjoyment."

"Don't worry, you'll love it," Chancellor Evans chimed in. "We'll have demonstrations of our music and the arts while partaking in light drinks and snacks. We may not fill your bellies, but we'll fill your hearts."

Ashwin and the others switched off their communicators again to confer excitedly in their language, this time with wild gestures. When they finished, the three of them bowed in front of the chancellor, to his undisguised pleasure.

"We accept your entertainment. May we bring food and drinks to exchange?" Ashwin glanced at Dana. "Is that an equal gift?"

Chancellor Evans leaped to his feet, a smile spreading

from ear to ear. "I believe it is. In the meantime, I'd love to give you a tour of our ship."

"Chancellor, that wouldn't be appropriate," Dana said before he could take two steps toward the door. It had never been her intention to offer a tour of their entire ship. "There are security concerns that need to be addressed in advance. Besides, the Fashin Teku have agreed to help with some of our repairs. I believe those concerns take precedent."

She'd spoken through tight lips, her hands stiff at her sides. The chancellor had taken over the delegation. Dana made a mental note to remind him of his overstep at a later date, as she didn't want to embarrass him or herself in front of their guests. She still wanted to get access to some of their technology; it might reflect poorly on her if she lost her temper now.

"Come now, Captain." He waved a hand in the air as if to erase her protests. "I'll take Ashwin with me, and the others can see to the work with you."

"I am security for my captain. Where he goes, I must go," Tovar interjected with a glare at Dana.

She nodded. "Of course, you are welcome to go with them."

Chancellor Evans called President Muñoz over to join him. Maggie turned and followed them out, asking questions of Tovar even before the door closed between them.

"Lieutenant Commander," Dana said through gritted teeth, "will you also accompany the Chancellor on his *tour* and be sure that he avoids any restricted areas?"

Barnes nodded, rushing out to obey her order.

Dana crossed her arms and sighed. "Commander, please see Oli to the engine room. I'll let Chief Rogan know to expect you. Perhaps you can get our engines and other systems back up to a hundred percent before our little party this evening."

Wade and Oli departed, and Dana returned to the bridge on her own.

Cliff was leaning over the console, and Nancy was turned away from the viewscreen so she could watch Dana come in. No doubt they were excited to hear what had happened during their first sit-down with an alien race. Dana relayed the highlights, omitting her agenda. It would be best if few people knew what she was planning.

"Do you think we should trust them?" Nancy asked.

Dana had been wondering the same, but her needs outweighed caution for the moment. "What's that old saying? 'Beware of strangers with smiles and arms wide, bearing the perfect gift'?"

"Yeah, that was my feeling, too," Cliff said as he rubbed the back of his neck.

"Ensign Harden, go over the scans of their ship," Dana said. "I want to know what they're carrying as far as weapons. They may be small, but their technology is grand. I want to figure out a way to get my hands on those translators." She settled her attention on Nancy next. "Lieutenant Commander, keep an eye on the sky. They may not be traveling alone. I don't want any surprises."

"Aye, Captain."

"Are we invited to the night of entertainment?" Cliff asked.

Dana smiled. "Yes, Ensign. Formal attire. It will be bridge crew and invitation only."

Nancy chuckled, then covered it with a cough.

"That means you, too, Westlake," Dana added.

"Does that mean you're wearing your red dress this evening?" Nancy asked.

"No."

She giggled. "Too bad. I know Ensign Harden was looking forward to it."

Cliff's dark skin covered his blush, but his wide eyes and open mouth gave him away. "I never—Captain, I swear—" he stammered.

Dana stifled her laugh with one hand. "Relax, Ensign. The Lieutenant is just teasing you. But be on your best behavior this evening, and someday you might just see that red dress."

CHAPTER 13

Dana tapped her monitor twice to bring up the image of Dr. Jabar in his office. It was a rare occurrence, since most days he was running around treating patients. He appeared rested, and she wondered if he'd slept. He'd gone prickly when she'd confronted him on it, and decided it wasn't a battle she wanted to fight today.

"Thank you for speaking with me," he greeted her. "Have you reviewed the autopsy reports I sent yesterday?"

"I did, but I found it hard to believe."

"I ran them twice, which is why it took twice as long to get them to you."

"Are you sure about this?"

"Quite sure," he said, frowning. "As I said, I ran the tests twice. They died at roughly the same time. All of the oxygen was removed from the room, suffocating them. There was no air in the room until you entered, breaking the seal and they'd only been dead for a few hours. That's why the smell of the bodies wasn't overbearing."

"There wasn't any sign of poison or something else?" Dana asked.

He shook his head. "If someone did this on purpose, they didn't touch either of the bodies. They'd recently eaten a meal, so there would have been some evidence of poison had it been present in the food—severe cramping, vomiting—but there was nothing in the bodies or their immediate environment to indicate such. From my findings, there were no signs of ingested or inhaled toxins. The damage to their hands was self-inflicted."

"So they died, slow and painful, trying to get out."

"They knew what was happening to them." Dr. Jabar's face was grim. "You don't think this was a mechanical malfunction?"

"Killing the only identified member of the CAH, and being the only room on the entire ship with a reported oxygen loss?" Dana shook her head. "This was no accident. Though, I believe they tried hard to make it look like one."

Dana ran a hand over her face. She was missing something. She needed to figure it out before it was too late. Then she remembered the other casualties from that day.

"How is Esme? I spoke with Chief Rogan earlier, but I didn't have the guts to ask him. He wasn't exactly in a good place."

Dr. Jabar shook his head with a weak smile, he seemed to recognize her genuine concern. "The good news is that she's stable, but her condition is unchanged. She's not conscious and I don't know when or if she'll ever wake up. We just don't have the necessary facilities here to help her. If we were back on Zelenia..." His voice faded in the way it did for all them when lamenting personal loss rather than an occupational one.

If they were back on Zelenia she wouldn't be responsible for handling a murder investigation, a missing persons hunt, or managing the survival of their race. She nodded in agreement. "Yes, I know. Thank you, Doctor. Keep me informed."

He nodded back before he disconnected, and the display turned to black.

Dana sighed to herself as she accessed the footage of the brig again, bringing it up on her monitor. She paid close attention to the security guard as he pounded and scratched at the door. Seconds later, Shu also dropped to the floor, gasping. She grimaced, but didn't look away. It was a horrible way to die.

She noted the time and realized something strange. The man on duty that evening was not the man who should have been there. She checked the data again. Why hadn't Barnes mentioned it when they'd gone over the room?

"Computer, Lieutenant Commander Barnes to my office," Dana ordered.

A moment later, he entered from the bridge. His eyes shifted to her monitor and then back to her face. She scanned his facial reactions for any recognition, but he wasn't giving anything away. She pointed to the still image of the brig surveillance vid. "Lieutenant Commander, what am I looking at here?"

Barnes leaned in, pretending he hadn't already seen it. "Looks like footage from the time of the localized EMP."

"Yes. However, the EMP didn't cause this."

His bright red eyebrows drew together. "How do you know?"

"Someone triggered these systems to go off before the EMP took effect. You can tell by the end of the vid and the loss of power."

Barnes raised one bushy eyebrow. "You think someone did this intentionally?"

Dana watched his face for any clues he might be hiding something, but saw only the sincerity in his expression.

"Yes. Look here." She advanced the video forward until they were watching the two men die. "According to the autopsy reports, both men suffocated. This means someone had removed the air from the brig at this point. They also had access to the security codes to lock down the doors so neither of them could get out."

"Do you want me to launch another investigation?"

"I feel like you already have your hands full. Who could do something like this?" Dana asked, though she already knew the answer.

Barnes rocked back on his heels, crossing his arms. "Life support systems are primary clearance only. Everyone on my team has the means. No lower-level crew member would have access. If we're looking at murder, then I'd have to begin the investigation with my people, though I don't know anyone who could do this. Lieutenant Adam Wesley was one of us."

Dana nodded. That had also been her original conclusion.

"You were assigned to the duty roster for the time in question," Dana continued, watching as his cheeks flushed. She didn't know if it was from guilt or the subtle accusation.

"True, I was originally assigned to take brig security, but I was already in the middle of another investigation. I needed more time to work on it, so I assigned Lieutenant Wesley."

"Why didn't you mention this before?"

Barnes' face faltered a second before he stood erect, his shoulders pulled back at attention. "I didn't know *I* was under suspicion for the murder in question." Then his eyes went to the wall behind her.

Good. He understood how this was going to go. She was going to question him until she was satisfied he had nothing to do with it. Dana began firing off questions.

"Who changed the roster?"

"I make all changes to the security roster myself."

"Why did you make this particular change?"

"Commander Chance has me assigned to review footage of the vid messages from our family and friends. It's a lot to cover, even with the help of the ARI. When I'm not at my station, I'm watching them for any clues that might lead us to Coalition ties. I changed the roster over a week ago to accommodate the new workload."

Dana watched him as he gave his report. Clean. No holes but one.

"Can anyone say where you were during the EMP burst?"

"No. I was alone in my quarters," he said, then cleared his throat. "A *real* coalition member would probably have some kind of alibi. I don't."

He had the nerve to give her a side-long glance. Dana understood and respected it. She didn't want her officers buckling under every interrogation. Besides, she'd had the same idea about the alibi. If he was a coalition member, he'd have done better than that.

"There's a shortlist of people capable of changing the life

support protocols in the brig," she continued. "Besides you, who else is unaccounted for during that time?"

Barnes frowned. "I don't know. I'll have to check them out one by one, and they won't like being accused any more than me."

"No one's accused you. I was eliminating you from the suspect list. You'll need to do the same for your team." Dana leaned back in her chair. "The Coalition runs deep, and is alive and well on my ship. Now the person who had the answers we need is dead. That's not a coincidence."

Barnes remained thoughtful for a moment before he spoke again. "If someone manually entered the security codes... they might have watched from a monitor."

Dana snapped her fingers. "That's it. I want to know where your team was when these men were killed and find out if someone was tapping into this feed."

"You don't think it's someone with a grudge against the CAH?"

She shrugged. "It could be. At this time, I'm not ruling anyone out. Shu was never working alone. He understood what would happen to him if he talked. I think someone got tired of waiting to see if he'd break. I'd like to clear security before we move on to the next phase of the investigation."

Barnes nodded. "We're still looking into a few passengers with some redacted histories."

Dana stood and came around her desk to see him out. "Keep this quiet, but get me some answers. With everything that's going on, I don't want any trouble while we're hosting the Fashin Teku."

"Yes, Captain."

"By the way, how was their tour with the chancellor? Is there anything we need to worry about?"

"I don't believe so. They hardly got a word in. The chancellor did all the talking. Ms. Brooker could probably tell you a bit more, as she was invited to join them on their ship."

Dana's arms dropped to her sides as she stammered. "What?"

"She didn't clear it with you?" Barnes shook his head when Dana continued to stare at him. "Figures. When they'd finished the tour, she was invited to go back to their ship with them," Barnes explained. "They left with her in the same way they'd come. I would have stopped her if I'd known."

Dana placed her hands on her hips and bit back the words that threatened to tumble out at Maggie's idiotic behavior. The woman was going to give her a heart attack before she turned thirty. "I want her position monitored, and she is to see me as soon as she returns."

"Yes, Captain." Barnes snapped his shoulders back.

"I appreciate all the work you're doing. Keep me abreast of any progress. You're dismissed."

CHAPTER 14

ERIC

C hief Engineer Eric Rogan took the lift to The Commons. Lieutenant Commander Barnes had asked him to take the lead on questioning a Mr. Franklin Jennison about some missing information in his file. It was unlikely that he was CAH, so Eric had been tasked to do some light questioning of the man and report back. He'd put it off as long as he could while dealing with other matters on board that had taken precedence, but now the ship's engines were back online and, for the moment, Esme was stable.

He rarely ventured to the Commons now that he had Eartha to care for in the evenings. The space was designed to be a large communal dining room with a glass-domed ceiling and a large wall of windows that offered sweeping views of the stars. The space was, by far, his favorite outside of engineering. By now, the morning crowd had thinned, and he spotted Franklin Jennison right away.

The old man with the weathered brown skin and tight white curls was seated at a table with the genius kid who'd won the academic ticket for his entire family to be on board. The two of them were often seen together sitting with a large 3D game between them. Four virtual platforms hovered in front of them as each tried to outwit the other in strategy. The boy, his unkempt hair dangling in long strands across his face, wore a scowl of concentration. If Eric understood the game correctly, the older man was winning.

It seemed Jennison also talked nonstop, despite the rule of silence during gameplay. The boy bit at his fingernails, working out his next move, while Jennison talked, keeping only half an eye on the game. Eric pulled up a chair and watched the last few minutes of their game play out, catching the end of the man's story.

"In a shocking twist, the detectives discovered transport passes proving Kate Jeffries and John, Jr. were alive. John Jeffries was released as it was clear then he hadn't killed them. All charges in the case were dropped. The authorities continued the search for his missing wife and child for several years. They never did find them. Some think that John found them first." When he finished his story, Jennison turned to Eric. His kind brown eyes, sunken within folds of wrinkled skin, looked Eric over once before turning back to the game. "Can I help you with something, Chief?"

"If you have a moment, Mr. Jennison, I wanted to ask you some questions," Eric said with a nod to the boy. "It would be best if we had some privacy."

"It's fine, we were done anyway. A genius doesn't like to be beaten more than twice in one day." He looked to the sullen teen, grinning as if they shared the joke. "Do they?"

The kid grumbled as he reset the board, intent on playing another round.

Jennison continued to stare at the boy, who made no reply. "Are my quarters suitable? It's about time I had my afternoon nap." Jennison pushed back from the table and stood up.

Eric nodded. "That'll work."

The boy crossed his arms over his chest and huffed as he slumped in front of the reset board.

IN FRANKLIN JENNISON'S CABIN, ERIC COULDN'T SEEM TO FIND a place to rest his eyes. The garish colors and sea of knick-knacks crowding both the surfaces and the walls didn't seem to fit his initial impression of the unassuming old man. His outfit—a neutral tan, along with simple brown sandals on his large brown feet—stood in stark contrast to the brass orna-ments and brightly painted fabrics hanging from the walls.

Eric ran a finger along a set of carved creatures so small they could fit in the palm of his hand. One bore large ears and a snout that reached down to the bottom of its feet between two white horns. He'd never seen anything like it before. Some of its paint had faded with time and handling.

"What is this?" Eric pointed to a large gray animal with wrinkled skin and a snout that hung to the ground.

"It's called Loxodonta Cyclotis." Jennison grinned with pride. "Majestic creatures that once roamed the African forests of Blue Earth. They were killed off long before the invasion of Earth. It's an original—hand-crafted. Arrived on one of the original ships to Zelenia. I got it from my great grandfather."

"Really?" Eric set the figurine back down where he'd found it. "What about this?" He pointed to a carved bone with strange writing, placed on a metal stand.

"Oracle bone script. It's not an original, since it predates space travel." He waved a dismissive hand. "Most of these items are replicas. The originals are far too expensive."

Eric was so caught up in the room he'd nearly forgotten his reason for being there. He cleared his throat, then started in on his questions.

"First, I want to preface this by saying you're not in any kind of trouble, Mr. Jennison. We're performing a routine investigation following the bombings, which have been credited to the Coalition."

"Yes, there are members on board. I've heard the rumors. Call me Franklin."

"We're looking into the background of the crew and passengers. During that process, you were flagged."

Franklin nodded and moved to sit down on his gray couch, adorned with bright pillows. He motioned for Eric to do the same.

Eric sat and leaned forward, placing his elbows on his knees. "Do you know that a lot of your personal records are blacked out?"

"I can imagine they would be."

"Excellent. Then I need you to tell me what records are missing, and why."

Franklin shook his head. "I'm sorry, but I'm not at liberty to share the details of those missions."

"Missions?" Eric echoed, frowning.

"Yes, the records of which were redacted due to the nature of the assignments. There were innocents involved—and not-so-innocents—and the government wished to keep their identities a secret." Franklin waved his hand, then stood up and reached for an empty glass, staring into as he spoke. "The Chancellor and the President will corroborate my story."

"I see. It must have been tough," Eric said, watching Franklin carefully. He'd started his research into the man with a very different opinion of him. He had been able to give his reasons for the missing information but now he stood in front of Eric looking lost.

"It was a difficult time in my life. You know... I have three adult children, and more grandkids than I can fit on my lap." He placed the glass back down as if changing his mind about his thirst. Then he returned to his seat on the couch. Though he smiled, his eyes were sad. "They say the boys are most like me, but my daughter, she's like her mother. Even looks like her. We built treehouses, went camping when I wasn't on duty, and drove across the country in the family car. Years of memories that should erase the fact that we lost a child."

"You had a fourth child?"

"We did. April. She was our first, born in the winter. She... she died two winters later. That was the year I took the most dangerous assignment of my life. I just couldn't bear to be home." There was a vacant look in his eyes as if reliving the year. "By the time I got the second assignment, I was over it. I retired early."

A silence crept into the room while Eric waited for Franklin to speak. He didn't. Franklin had shared something so personal it seemed only right Eric share something of his own.

"Esme and I have been trying for years to have a child," he said quietly.

Franklin seemed to look at him as if seeing him for the first time. "Oh? I'm sorry."

Eric shrugged. "It's gotten to the point where I don't even mention it anymore."

"Kids?"

"Sex."

"Ouch." Franklin stood up and moved to pick up the glass again, then grabbed a bottle he kept hidden under the chair and poured an amber liquid into it. He passed it over.

Eric took a sniff and shook his head. "I'm on duty. I shouldn't."

"Personal conversations should be shared over something harder than water. I won't tell if you won't."

Eric sipped at the drink and after the warm liquid travelled down his throat he grinned. "Pure?"

"The purest alcohol you'll find on a starship." Franklin crossed his arms, clearly proud of himself. "I haven't had a sip myself in over fifty years."

Eric's brow furrowed as he regarded the glass. "So why do you hang onto this stuff?"

"For times like this. When I meet someone who I think might enjoy it," Franklin said somberly. "It almost destroyed my marriage once—the drink. My life, more accurately. I like to think having it around reminds me what I traded it for."

Eric took another sip and sighed.

"I usually keep it hidden in the closet. There's a light blue box in the back on the shelf."

"Why are you telling me that?"

"If something should happen to me, I'd... like someone to know where I keep it." He gestured at Eric. "Someone who'd appreciate it."

Eric waved him off.

"I know my chances of making it are slim." Franklin smiled. "All the same, I'm going into my cryotank with optimism."

Eric didn't return the smile, his heart sinking a little in his chest. This wasn't the time to break the news that the damaged cryopods were irreparable. He and Esme had been all over them, along with the other engineers. It had been the captain's decision to keep people in the dark until they knew for sure there was no way to make them viable.

"I've seen that look before. The cryopods took a good hit. I know. But I'm old, and if I get to the point I think I might not make it, I'm going to request one anyway." Franklin nodded quietly to himself. "That said, a man doesn't get to be as old as me by worrying about tomorrow. We'll figure something out, because I plan to be there when we reach new ground––I promised my grandkids."

"Good point." Eric finished his drink in one last swallow and set down his glass. "Thanks for the drink."

"Anytime." Franklin stood to see him to the door.

"Oh, don't get up. I'll see myself out. Thank you for being upfront. I'll let the captain know about your circumstances. If we need anything further, we'll let you know."

"You do that," Franklin said.

Eric was at the door when Franklin cleared his throat.

"About that other thing," he said in a low voice. "In my experience, women prefer action over talk, no matter what they say they want. Take hold of her and *show* her how you feel. That'll go a lot further than words and bring you a lot closer to having a baby than what you're doing now."

Better advice than any of the fertility doctors, Eric mused as he saw himself out.

CHAPTER 15

It feels good to be lost in the right direction.

B y evening, the entire ship was buzzing with anticipation for the exclusive event with the Fashin Teku. The Commons dining room had been converted into a performance hall, complete with an elevated platform and seating for the event's fifty guests. By the time Dana arrived, her people were already mingling with Ashwin and his friends.

The Fashin Teku were true to their word. Though they'd arrived a half-hour late, when they returned to the *Hope,* they'd brought with them a large variety of food. No one was happier than Dana herself to see the colorful array complimenting the beverages they were able to serve. With the way their cook could preserve and prepare meals, the food, if pleasing, would last them several days.

Dr. Jabar made a thorough examination of all the gifted

refreshments and found it to be mostly plant-based. There seemed to be nothing that would harm them. The meat was a trickier matter. Most of the crew hadn't had anything that looked so fresh in a long time, and once it was cleared, people were making a point to try each variety they could get their hands on.

Dana picked up something that looked like a cracker with a jam-like spread and popped it into her mouth. The flavors were what she suspected, a salty-sweet combination. It was all she managed to get down before the third trio of Fashin Teku came over to greet her. She noted that, in general, they traveled in threes, regardless of their rank. Ashwin told her it was their custom for each of them to acknowledge the person in the room with the most control.

The thirty or so Fashin Teku in attendance dressed in what looked to be their version of formal attire—long tunics in creams, tans, and greens. They'd replaced their metal chest plates with fabric panels in metallic tones, still representing the plate's insignias on the softer material.

All of them wore varying themes on the blend of metallic and neutral tones, but Dana noticed that Ashwin was the only one wearing a metallic royal blue with gold-colored accents, perhaps because he was their captain. He wore his hair braided in an intricate style for the occasion, and his charming manner made him the center of attention everywhere he went. The others had pulled back their long, wavy hair at the nape of the neck, their faces framed by loose plaits or with two single braids. The women decorated their hair and neck beards with more elaborate bands and metallic clips, but otherwise their clothing was the same.

The guest list included the senior officers of both crews.

Dana watched with pride as they seemed to get along with each other. Most of her crew had dressed in their military finest or formal clothing, if they'd brought any. Probably like her, they hadn't planned on pulling them out until they'd awakened from their cryopods and reached a new world. Perhaps they'd find another occasion to celebrate.

Dana discovered her gown while digging in a trunk of things she'd saved from her mother. She never thought she'd use any of it, however, a formal cream gown that she'd kept seemed to fit the evening. There were no sleeves, but it came up to her neck, and showed off her bare arms and shoulders while clinging to her curves before dropping straight to her knees. When she'd seen the attire of the Fashin Teku, she was glad she'd gone with it instead of something too bold, like red.

In the back of her mind, Dana was working out how to convince Ashwin to help the *Hope* acquire some of their technological advancements. They were still low on food goods and supplies. The last planet they'd encountered had been unsuitable; the air, being completely toxic, had prevented them from even setting foot on its surface. They wouldn't have enough resources to continue their journey if they didn't find a suitable planet soon. With the Fashin Teku's technology, they'd be able to materialize food and materials from a planet without setting foot on it, and even one of their communication devices could save them from disaster with another alien encounter. Dana had confidence the Fashin Teku would also see it that way. Ashwin had promised her star charts and maps of their system that might help them on their way, but without the translation devices, they wouldn't be able to stop and ask for directions.

Wade was standing with Cliff and Nancy when she pulled him aside.

"How did it go?" she asked Wade with a nod toward the Fashin Teku.

He gave her a once-over before taking a sip of the wine in his hand. "According to Lieutenant Westlake, with engines at full, we'll be in range of another planet in less than twenty-four hours."

"What about the other thing?"

Wade paused and smiled as a triad of Fashin Teku passed by them with drinks and food in hand before returning to their discussion.

"They have more than a few technologies we could use, including the molecular relocation device. They were very skilled at fixing our systems, as if it were child's play. Oli kept trying to figure out why the engines wouldn't go any faster than our maximum, so I think they're accustomed to moving at much higher speeds."

Dana nodded. "Let's see if we can stretch out this encounter one more day. I'd like to see if there's anything we've got onboard that interests them. We might arrange some kind of trade."

"I'm already on it. The entertainment is the most antici-pated event for them. Mags is recording the entire evening to create clips of the night for the passengers. We could make it available to them as a gift, should they desire it."

"Good thinking," Dana said into her drink. The bubbles of the clear liquid tickled her nose and left a sweet taste in her mouth. "She was on their ship earlier today," Dana added, smiling when Mrs. Muñoz met her eye from across the room.

Wade nodded tightly. "I know. Maggie convinced them she wanted to do an exclusive interview on their ship. It was the only way to get the inside story about the Des." He shrugged. "We might learn something from the footage."

Dana looked at him askance. "You knew she was going over there and didn't consult me?"

Wade rolled his eyes. "Of course not. She didn't tell me anything about it until she was back. Though, I'm not sure we could have stopped the Fashin Teku's molecular relocation technology."

"I don't like her making a decision like that without clearance from me," Dana said between her teeth.

Wade's frown matched how she felt. "Agreed. Permission to speak freely?"

Dana turned to face him, wondering what he was going to tell her about Maggie she didn't already know. "Of course."

There was a playful twinkle in his eyes as he trailed them over her again. "That dress is stunning on you."

She got over the shock of the compliment quickly and gave him a dismissive glance. "Make sure I see that footage before anyone else does."

He bowed to her still grinning like a fool. She watched him stroll away, then looked up and caught President Muñoz and his wife, Maria, waving her over a second time. They were wearing matching smiles and shades of purple as they greeted each guest.

Dana leaned in as she approached and caught the delicate scent of Maria's perfume as their cheeks touched.

"Our new friends have made quite the impression on us with their delicacies." Maria said as she popped something round and crunchy into her mouth. "Nothing looks familiar, but it all tastes great."

"I'm glad Dr. Jabar was able to run a quick scan of everything to see if any compounds would be dangerous to us," Dana replied. "He assures me the food and drink are safe for consumption, though he's not familiar with their flavors. You've been warned."

"Good thinking," President Muñoz said.

"Eat and drink at your own risk?" Maria smiled and gave her a conspiratorial wink. "I like a little risk with my meals."

Dana picked out a gooey, gummy thing from one of the nearby trays and ate it. The salty-sweet mixture which seemed to embody everything was in this item too, and she liked the interesting texture, even though it stuck in her teeth. She was still discreetly trying to dig it out of her molars when Dana heard a bell ringing. She looked up to see that Chancellor Evans had brought an actual bell. He stood on the elevated platform, waving everyone into the seats he'd arranged in a semi-circle for the evening's event. Like the others, she rushed to fill up a small plate to enjoy from her seat while she took in the entertainment.

The semi-circle of staggered seats gave everyone a clear view. Abigail Evans sat in the front row to offer her husband encouragement in the form of loud hooting and clapping. Dana rolled her eyes and caught Wade, seated to her right, looking at her and doing the same. Their shared laugh was cut short when Maggie tugged on Wade's arm.

She couldn't see Maggie's face on the other side of him, which was probably for the best. Dana was still angry about her blatant disrespect for ship protocol. She'd already requested the woman to come to her office—an invitation

Maggie ignored. Dana vowed to rectify the situation at her convenience, even if it put the other woman out. She was the captain, and this wasn't something she could ignore.

Once everyone was in their seats, Chancellor Evans spoke, his voice booming over the excited whispers of the crowd.

"Ladies and gentlemen, I'd like to welcome you to this evening's festivities. We have an unbelievable show for you. Among our passengers and crew, we have a plethora of entertainers, and tonight you're in for a special surprise. When you see all the talent we have in store for you, I guarantee you'll leave here wanting more."

He clapped his hands together, encouraging the applause for himself before continuing.

"Let's start with our first act. One has the voice of a songbird, and the other plays the guitar. In their *Hope* debut, let's welcome Felix Gregory and Richard Taylor to the stage."

As the chancellor exited the platform, the lights dimmed, and a spotlight illuminated the performers. The musical duet was mesmerizing. She had no idea Ensign Gregory was so skilled with the guitar.

To her surprise, Dana found herself lost in the variety of talents from those on board. One of them was Luke Geyer, a handsome young man with heavy dark brows and shoulder-length chestnut hair. Dana remembered him because he was the only student who'd gotten a hundred percent on his scholastic abilities' exam. At sixteen, he'd saved his family by procuring a large suite onboard the *Hope*. She had no idea he was also a skilled artist.

Luke had agreed to do portrait sketches of the Fashin Teku during the reception, and now presented his work from the stage. The beautiful images he'd made with pencil and paper must have thrilled them. Their excited speech patterns and joyous clapping filled the room. Things were going well for him until he requested some kind of compensation in exchange for the images he'd created.

Chancellor Evans eased the young man off of the stage. "We're providing our entertainment free of charge this time, Mr. Geyer, since our guests have been generous and provided all the food for this evening. Please forgo your usual sale, and give our guests a gift they can bring home and treasure, as there is no one with a skill like yours."

The chancellor's diplomatic approach was smooth, practiced, and impressive. Luke nodded in agreement and moved off the small stage, handing out the sketches to their models. Dana admired the boy's skill, but his request for further compensation could be misunderstood.

Their guests seemed confused at first by the request, then Ashwin laughed it off. The others laughed with him, and didn't seem at all upset by the boy's rudeness. Dana released the breath she'd been holding. Thanks to the chancellor, the event moved along, and they soon forgot the incident in the shadow of more admirable talent by the next performers.

The evening progressed, and after an hour and a half, Dana was cursing her shoes and wondering how many more acts the chancellor had scheduled. Regardless of her fatigue, she was happy to see their guests applaud with enthusiasm after every performance.

Then it seemed the end had come. The chancellor stood in front of the audience again, recapping the evening's performances from the center of the platform.

"I hope you have all enjoyed our lovely banquet of talent

this evening." He waited for the applause to subside before continuing. "How many of you are listening and thinking, is that all? Well, it's not. We have many more with the skills and talents to entertain you."

Dana stifled a groan.

"But not tonight."

The chancellor laughed at his own joke, along with the rest of the audience. Dana was among them. She wanted nothing more than to escape their guests, throw her shoes across the room, and climb into bed.

"To close out our festivities, we're going to do something a little different. Our next guest has no idea that they'll be performing tonight."

The audience murmured in anticipation, wondering who it would be. Dana glanced around along with the others, hoping it wouldn't be a long performance.

"This person needs no introduction. She's multi-talented and comes recommended by some of the highest of our respected leaders, who rest in peace on Zelenia. She's been playing the piano since she was a child. Although we couldn't get a piano onboard, we managed to find something that comes close to the same sound."

Dana's stomach dropped, and a buzzing began in her ears.

He wouldn't dare.

She remained transfixed as one of the crew moved behind the chancellor. The woman set up a chair and a small stand with a piano length sheet of keys rolled out on top. The chancellor couldn't be thinking of her.

"Let's welcome up our beloved Captain Pinet!"

The sound of his voice warbled in her ears as he called

her name. Every person turned at once, cheering for her and encouraging her with smiles and pats on the shoulder to take the stage. She wasn't sure when it started, but she caught the chanting of her name somewhere in the haze. Dana couldn't imagine anything worse. She hadn't played in years, and she hadn't told a soul she could.

Wade turned to look at her, his eyebrows drawn together in question. He mouthed something, but it was a blur among the other looks and cheers.

"Don't make me beg you to come up here," Chancellor Evans said when she still hadn't moved. He shook his head. "All right, fine. She needs some encouragement, everyone. Let's give our captain a warm welcome to the stage!" Chancellor Evans lifted his arms up and down to get the crowd more excited.

Dana shook her head, but someone pulled her to her feet, and the momentum of pats on her back and cheers pushed her up to the platform. Once she stood behind the seat at the piano, it didn't take long for the chanting to die down. It got so quiet, when someone in the back of the room coughed, the echo forced someone else to hush them into silence again.

Dana looked out into the crowd, scrambling for an excuse —anything that would get her off the stage and back into her quarters without causing an intergalactic incident—when Captain Ashwin Zeppel stood up.

"Please, Captain." He whispered the words from the front row next to his wife, encouraging, but not demanding.

Dana sat down at the piano and placed her hands over the keys. Her fingers felt so stiff. She stretched each one, rolling her hands into fists, then extended them outward. At first, nothing came to mind. Seconds that felt like minutes passed as she sat there, the entire room waiting for her to begin.

Her father used to love to listen to her play. She imagined herself in front of him now, playing in their home while her mother made them one of his favorite meals. Her mother talked non-stop about whatever had vexed her that day, and her father would roll his eyes and nod to the piano. She heard him as if he were right there in his favorite reclining chair.

"Play something, baby girl."

CHAPTER 16

Dana's fingers found the notes as if her hands and this strange table of keys belonged to one another. She played her father's favorite song. The room melted away as the notes made their slow build to the chorus. She was humming along at first, and then she was singing in full voice. The room's acoustics were perfect echoes, bouncing back to her in time. She sang through the ache in her heart, belting out the words as if she could reach her father with them one last time. It was a song of lost love, lost family, a lost world.

When the last note rang out, she felt as if she'd spilled her soul on the stage for everyone to see. Afraid to look up, she waited until she heard the first boisterous claps from the audience. It was Wade, and he was standing up, a bewildered expression on his face. He'd never heard her play. He was probably just as surprised as everyone else. Why hadn't she shared that part of herself with him? She wondered if it had to do with her father's death.

The chancellor ran up to the stage, encouraging the

crowd to applaud even more. Dana stood up from the portable piano and gave a slight bow to the audience before she excused herself from the room. On her way out, she caught several women in the audience, including Maggie Brooker, wiping away tears. Ashwin and his people stood at the door and congratulated her on her performance. She couldn't catch the words through the haze. He placed something in her hand and she gripped it, not trusting herself to look at it right then.

Her throat was raw with unshed tears, and she desperately needed to be alone. She dashed out the doors and didn't breathe again until she'd reached the corridor. It wasn't until she arrived at her quarters that she finally looked down, remembering her sore feet and the item in her hand.

She opened her fist. In it was one of the behind-the-ear translator devices. Dana placed the device in the top drawer of her chest of drawers and took several deep breaths. She kicked off the cream heels, throwing them across the room and vowing to toss them into the nearest incinerator in the morning.

After a languid bath and some time to herself, Dana thought she'd be ready to sleep, but the evening kept replaying in her mind. Wade had stood up and been the first to start clapping. Dana hadn't even met his eyes for fear of what she might see. The loss she was sure she'd find in them compounded by the loss she fought inside would have overwhelmed her.

The thought of sharing that part of herself with him made her skin flush, and she was thankful there was no one around to see. She couldn't remember why she'd kept so much from him. She'd been so filled with grief for so long...

Instead of climbing into bed, she opened the third drawer of her dresser and pulled out her memory box. She ran her fingers along the hand-carved etchings, as she often did to calm herself. This time she lifted the lid and pulled out a small memory drive. She already knew what it contained, but she connected it to her thin tablet anyway. The words came up on the screen, and when she pressed the audio, it was her father's voice she heard.

FROM: CAPTAIN STEPHEN PINET
    To: Cadet Dana Pinet
    Date: 4323.2.11
    Hey Baby Girl,

    Sorry I missed your Space Fleet Academy ceremony, but I knew you'd make it all on your own. You've never let anything stand in your way. Too much like your old man, if you get my drift. They used to say, 'don't put all your eggs in one basket'. You don't want to end up like me. You and your mother rarely see me, and it's not because I don't want to be around, but because my duty comes first.

    I hope someday that you're able to understand. If given the choice, be happy.

    I know you told me not to step in, but they reached out to me after you took your entrance exams and let me know the board was going to accept you. I didn't get you in or anything, so put the hairs on the back of your neck down. One of your professors is a good friend of mine and I spoke with him only after you were placed for the results, nothing else. You have my solemn promise, Peanut.

    Things here are heating up. It looks like we're designing a few more ships. It's the biggest project that's come through in years. I *couldn't pass up the opportunity. I wish you and your mother were with me. Try to do something nice for her this week. You're going to be as busy as I am, but one of us has to make the effort when we're around, and you're the closest. She depends on you when I'm not there. It's my fault, but I trust you'll take care of her, anyway. Use my credits and take her to one of those spa days she likes to give herself. You should enjoy one too, Cadet. You won't get any pampering where you're going.*

The video is one we snapped of the crew here, just wishing you all the best. We're a family, too, and they feel like they've helped raise you. In a way, some of these old goats did.

Have fun on your new adventure, baby girl, and don't forget to remember your dad. I'll hold my hugs inside until we see each other again.

Your time will come,
Dad

A TEAR FELL FROM HER EYE AS SHE RE-READ THE DIGITAL correspondence. The date stamp was the day she'd arrived at the academy. She remembered hating him at the time, scrolling past the message, refusing to read it. He'd missed what had been, up until that point, the most important day of her life. Now she cherished the words and the image of him sitting around a large table with his crew, many of whom she recognized, and who had stayed close to her family now that he was gone.

Her father had been dead now for almost five years, but Dana couldn't remember a time when she didn't want to cry at the thought of him. Maybe it was the guilt. At times, she and her mother had been too hard on him. He'd been a good father and husband, though he'd barely lived long enough to prove it.

Either way, that song held too many memories. She'd lost herself in the moment. The ache had come rushing over her from the first note she'd played and haunted her beyond the last.

CHAPTER 17

Dana sat up in bed, listening for what had woken her. Her eyes were still grainy from crying herself to sleep, making it difficult to make out shapes in the dark.

"COMP, lights to dim."

As her eyes adjusted to the light, she tapped a finger on her tablet's clear display to check the time. It was close to oh-five hundred ship time. She strained to listen for any changes or alarms, then she felt it, and her body went rigid.

The room was absolutely still, the silence so unnatural her body went to high alert as she leaped out of bed.

The engines weren't running.

"COMP, lights to full," she called to the computer. It complied. There were a dozen possibilities why the ship wasn't moving, but if it had been something like an explosion, they would have contacted her before now. Thankfully, the party would have died down hours ago, and the Fashin Teku would be back on their own ship. "COMP, what's wrong with the engines?"

"The engines are not currently in operation."

"Tell me something I don't already know," Dana grumbled as she pulled on her uniform.

"Please clarify."

"Forget it. Initiate yellow alert. Senior officers to the bridge."

Dana rushed out of her quarters. The alert signal would be silent except for those who ventured outside of their rooms. The crew at their stations would check critical systems while awaiting further instructions.

By the time she reached the bridge, she'd passed several other crew members as they headed to their posts. As soon as the doors opened, she called out, "Report."

Barnes, Westlake, and Harden were already at their stations. Wade hadn't yet arrived.

"Systems are down, and the med-bay is reporting multiple thefts, Captain," Cliff replied. "They suspect the Fashin Teku. Dr. Jabar is requesting your presence as soon as you can manage it."

"Theft?" she echoed, the words he was saying not making any sense. She shook her head to be sure she was awake. "Are the Fashin Teku still on board?"

Before Cliff could answer, Wade stumbled onto the bridge. There was a trickle of blood from a wound on the back of his head, drying on the neck of his uniform. Cliff let out an unintelligible gasp of surprise.

Wade answered the question, "No, I suspect they're long gone."

"You're bleeding, sir," Nancy said, pointing to Wade's head.

Wade shrugged off her concern and turned his attention back to Dana.

"The Fashin Teku?" Dana asked, dread tightening her stomach.

"Yes," Wade said. He grimaced with pain. "After the performance, I watched them relocate themselves off the ship. Later, I was in the corridor near the med-bay when I caught one tampering with one of our panels. I asked what he was doing, and he was stuttering a response when something hit me." Wade rubbed the back of his head. "They shoved me into a ventilation shaft on deck four. When I came to, I saw the alert and came straight here."

"Elevate that alert to red," Dana said. The lights turned red, one long alarm signaling the crew and passengers of the change. "Where are they now?"

Cliff stared at the console in front of him, shaking his head. "They're not within range of our sensors."

"You should report to the med-bay," Barnes told Wade quietly.

"Later."

"What's the status of our engines?" Dana asked. "Is there anyone down there?"

"There's no answer down in engineering," Cliff replied. "The comm panels must be down."

"Keep trying. I'm on my way to the med-bay. If they contact you, let engineering know I'll be there as soon as I can."

"Yes, Captain."

Wade took a hesitant step toward her. "Captain, I should go with you."

"Absolutely," Dana said, starting for the door. "I'll walk you there, and they can get you cleaned up."

"I meant as protection in case there are still aliens on board," he said, following after her.

"The only one who needs protection is you from falling on the floor," Dana said with an exaggerated eye roll. "Barnes, gather your team and run a full security sweep of the ship. Report back any suspicious activity. Begin questioning the guests from last night. Let's make sure everyone is accounted for, and no one else is stuck in a ventilation shaft. Westlake, you have the bridge."

Dana followed Wade into the lift, riding it to the fifth level and the med-bay. Wade leaned against the back wall, his eyes closed.

"Don't get comfortable. You probably have a concussion."

"Last night... your performance was beautiful." He kept his eyes closed as he spoke. Maybe he knew she'd squirm under his gaze.

Dana kept her eyes on his mouth, looking for any hint he might be mocking her. The night before, she was so sure he'd enjoyed it. Now, facing him, she wondered if she'd imagined it all.

"I don't think I've ever seen you so honest and open," he said, then hastened to correct himself. "Not since our time on the *Atlantis*, I mean. You were different back then. I thought I'd never see the real you again."

Dana cleared her throat as the doors of the lift opened. She stepped out, needing to be in front of him to catch her shortened breath. She turned back as he swayed toward her, and she reached out, catching him as he teetered.

"Whoa... we need to get you looked at. Hang on to me."

"If only I had," he murmured, putting some of his weight on her, draping an arm around her shoulders.

She shuffled them forward. "How did you get to the bridge in this condition?"

"I think the initial adrenaline is wearing off. I didn't feel so sleepy before."

When they reached the med-bay, Dr. Jabar and his assistant were there, alone. His assistant worked at cleaning up in the lab, where some of their supplies must have been taken.

"He probably has a concussion," Dana said without preamble.

To the doctor's credit, he rushed over to help Wade to one of the empty beds. Dana glanced over and saw Esme, still peacefully sleeping. Thankfully, they hadn't disturbed the comatose woman.

"She's hooked up to the secondary life support system," Dr. Jabar said when he caught her looking over at Esme, as if reading her thoughts. "If they'd tried to move her or remove her, it would have set off alarms. I'm sure that's why they didn't bother her."

"It looks like the Fashin Teku charmed their way onto the ship and used their molecular relocation system to come back and take what they wanted," Dana said as she watched him work.

He patched up Wade's injury using a thin medicated wipe that cleared away the drip of dried blood and provided an antiseptic. Then he administered something using a palm-sized injector that made the Commander wince.

"Yes." The doctor's voice was dry, but she could see the vein pulsing in his forehead that belied his calm demeanor.

She'd seen it once before, when he'd been arguing with his twin over the body of Brian Shu. "They took our embryos, their stasis containers, and several other medicines we had locked away for critical care."

Dana walked over to the med-lab where the embryos had been stored and stared at the blank wall. The small boxes had been lined up from floor to ceiling and wall to wall. Every single one was gone. She wanted to scream in anger and frustration. Instead, she clamped her lips tight over her feelings and took a deep breath.

"Why?" Wade said. He slid off the medi-bed, swaying a little on his feet.

"Why they took them is anyone's guess," he looked at Dana, "but I don't have to tell you what that means."

Dr. Jabar let the gravity of the situation hang between them.

Wade shook his head, looking from Dana, who was now pacing, back to the doctor, confusion etched on his face. "Is anyone going to tell me what this means?"

Dana ignored his question, clenching her hands into fists. She wasn't sure what to do next. "How much of the medicine did they get?"

"They've taken everything that was locked away," Jabar said. "All we have left is what we have in our medical cases. One per medical staff—that's a total of five, before you ask."

"This seems to be the focus of their attack on our ship. They must have learned about the embryos during Chancellor Evans' tour," Dana reasoned. "Then they made plans to come here after the evening of entertainment."

"I understand the embryos represent our race as a people, but I thought they were insurance, not necessity."

Dr. Jabar ran a hand over his face. "What are we going to do?"

His unspoken question hung in the air. If they got them back, would they even be viable?

Dana leaned over and put her hands on her knees, trying to breathe. She suddenly thought she might faint.

Doctor Jabar put his hand on her back and rubbed gently. "Can I get you something?"

She shook her head. "We don't have enough for scrapes and bruises, let alone for a weak captain."

"You're not a weak captain," Wade said, reaching out to take her arm.

Dana snatched it away from him, stepping away from them both. "Yes, I am. A weak captain who let those pirates on board with open arms. I let them steal the future of our race right out from under me, because I thought they might give us some of their technology."

Wade took a step back. "Wait, what?"

Dana let out another audible groan.

"The embryos are the means of our survival as a species," Dr. Jabar explained slowly, as if speaking to a child, keeping his voice low. "Even with the number of women on board, there isn't enough genetic variety for us to rebuild our society."

Wade covered his mouth with one hand as the information sunk in.

"Captain? Are you all right?" Dr. Jabar asked again.

She was far from all right, but she pulled herself up and rolled her shoulders back.

"I need to get to the engine room," Dana said, walking out without another word.

"Wait," Wade called out behind her. His footfalls raced to catch up. "This isn't your fault."

Dana ignored his attempt to placate her. Who else was to blame for what happened on her ship? She was the captain. The blame couldn't go any higher.

"We were all fooled by them. You couldn't have known they would betray us," he said, as he caught up to her.

Of course, she knew. All one had to do was pick up a history book. When had humans ever had peaceful relations with aliens? Ones that didn't end in betrayal? Dana could kick herself for being so gullible.

"When I find those Fashin Teku, they'll wish they'd never crossed us," she said, as they reached the engine room. "Chief, what have they done?"

Eric ran a hand over his grizzled face. He hadn't shaved, and his hair was standing up—no doubt because he hadn't bothered to wash it. He'd been notably absent at the Fashin Teku party. Dana had planned to ask him about that, but thought she already knew the answer. Esme was still lying in the med-bay, unconscious, and he looked like he hadn't slept in days. He was likely depressed.

"They knew exactly what to do to leave us floating out here like a log on a lake," he said.

"What about the systems they helped fix?" Wade asked.

"Interestingly enough, those remained intact, as if they took pride in their work. It's the part they got to that's got me confounded." He threw his hands up and let them slap against his thighs. "They cut thruster lines aft and stern. We've got no juice to even limp, but they kept the system running well enough to keep the primary support systems working so they wouldn't trip any alarms."

"How soon before we can get moving?" Dana asked.

Eric shook his head, his shoulders drooping. "Longer than you'd like."

"I need those engines back up and running as soon as you can. Even if we're not going fast, we need to keep moving."

"I understand," he said, turning away from her. The ring on his left hand, a small silver band, reminded her that she'd wanted to give him an update of her own.

"They also hit the med-bay and labs," she said softly.

Eric's eyes widened, and she saw the fear etched out on his face as if he'd spoken it aloud. She watched his body lean away from her as if to run.

"Esme was left undisturbed," she added quickly. "Dr. Jabar says he's got her on an auxiliary system, but had anyone attempted to touch her, they would have tripped an alarm. She's fine."

Eric nearly sagged in relief. "Guess that means none of us better get sick then."

"Agreed. We're running on less than nothing in there, and they made off with more than I'm willing to let go. Get me those engines, Chief."

Eric nodded. He started giving orders, and the entire engine room picked up speed.

Dana turned on her heel, heading for the corridor while Wade followed. Things were worse than she'd imagined. She didn't like how defenseless they'd been left.

"Did we ever get those shielding specs?" she asked as they rode together back up to the bridge.

"No," Wade said, shaking his head. He gave her a curious look. "You think we're going to need the shielding more than the engines, don't you?"

"I don't want to consider it, but what kind of Captain would I be if I didn't?"

"The kind that's doing the best she can with what she's got."

Dana didn't want to dwell on how they'd gotten there, only on how to get back what had been taken.

Back on the bridge, Barnes hadn't yet returned. Cliff, as their center point of contact, would have the most accurate information now.

"Report," Wade called out.

"Reports are still coming up, but so far it seems they took something from almost every critical system. They even stripped us of more rations."

"By the Merciful, what didn't they take?" Dana hissed. She ran a hand over her face. Another major blow to the kneecaps like that and she'd collapse.

"It was a sloppy job. Most of the things they took we can replace with supplies from the storage hanger," Cliff said. "Chief Rogan sent up his report, and says several power coils are missing, and the thruster lines were cut. Once the power coils are replaced, they can reconnect those lines, but he estimates it'll take several hours to get the job done."

"Do we have the frequency they used to communicate with us?"

"Yes," Harden said, checking the console.

"See if we can use that signal to help us track them down."

"Track them down?" Nancy echoed as she swiveled to look at Dana from the helm.

"Yes, Lieutenant, and see if you can track them using their

shield frequency the way you did before. Their last known trajectory, breadcrumbs—just do it."

There was a curt nod and a determined line where Nancy's smile used to be. "Yes, Captain. I'll see what I can do."

Dana turned her attention to Barnes as he entered the bridge. "Do you have a report for me?"

"I do, but I'll highlight the relevant bits. None of them remained on board. They didn't take anything from anyone personally, and no one suspected the Fashin Teku were capable of anything like this. The ship is secure."

"Wait, Captain," Cliff said, frowning down at the console. "It appears the aliens left behind a recorded video message."

"What, how?" Wade asked.

Dana waved a hand through the air, dismissing his question. "It doesn't matter how at the moment. Put it on our main viewer."

They all turned to look at the screen as the image of Ashwin appeared. Dana had to fight the urge to hurl something at his grinning face.

"My dearest, Captain Dana. Many sorries. It is rude for me to speak to you so familiar after what we have done. However, we want to extend to you many thank yous for the joyful entertainment you gave to us last night. We brought you food, and you have shown us something we will keep in the memories and pass down to our children."

His eyes shifted, as if he were being prompted to continue.

"We are often low on the things we need. We take what we can, not because we enjoy the hurting to anyone. We need to survive if we are to reach our people back on the home worlds. We did not mean to make you desperate, but we must take care of our people, as do you."

Ashwin sighed, as if he didn't want to say what was next.

"I am pleading you, please do not attempt to follow us or to retrieve your things. It will only bring more pain and loss to you, and I do not feel the strong desire to destroy your ship. You possess no means of attack, so do not try. But in case you do want to partake in the foolish idea, I will tell you. We took something from the med-bay labs you'll miss. I assure you we will care for them as if they were our own, but if you give to us many troubles, your cargo will be thrown into the space before we defeat you."

"That's the end of the message," Cliff said.

The entire bridge sat silent for a full minute. Dana could only hear her heartbeat racing in her ears as the rage settled into a ball in her stomach.

"You have your orders," Dana said woodenly.

"But you heard them," Barnes protested. "We'll be putting the rest of the passengers and crew in danger. As your security officer, I advise you to reconsider."

Dana turned around to glare at him, then spoke loud enough for the entire bridge to hear her.

"I want this ship in pursuit of those pirates as soon as it's ready."

Wade took a step forward. "Captain, may I have a word with you in private?"

"In my office. The rest of you have plenty of work to do, so get to it."

Once they were inside and away from the others, Dana saw the doubt clouding Wade's face, and knew she was in for a fight. She steeled herself against it.

"Captain, permission to speak freely?"

Dana crossed her arms over her chest. "Let's have it, Wade."

"I think you're making a mistake."

"In what way?"

"We need to consider all the angles," he started, gesturing with his hands as he spoke. "The aliens that stole from us have an invisible shield, armaments, and technology that is beyond compare. Chasing after them could not only delay us finding a home of our own, it could end us."

"So, you're saying we should count our losses and move on?"

Wade considered her words for a moment before shrugging in agreement. "We could find ourselves worse off if we don't take care of ourselves and our people first."

She wanted to tell him the real reason she was so scared to lose the embryos. The words were on her tongue and she swallowed them along with the disappointment she felt when knowing she'd never be a mother.

"Don't you see?" Dana threw up her hands in frustration. "They stole our future. We might not last more than a couple generations now. If we don't pursue them, what will become of our embryos? We need to know. Best case scenario, they're alien grub. Worst case, our children might be genetically modified or forced into slavery." She shook her head resolutely. "We may not have what it takes to defeat them. But we may find something they want more than our embryos, and we'll be able to offer them a trade. Either way, we can't just walk away. We need to track where they've gone and initiate pursuit."

Wade ran a hand through his dark hair before he nodded.

"Okay... Okay, so we've got to track them down. We've also got to increase our ability to face them head-on. Maggie took a tour of their ship. If I know Mags, she took video they don't even know about."

"Make sure to include Chief Rogan, Ensign Harden, and the ARI in the review," Dana told him. "They might catch something you'll miss. Let Harden know I've got one of their translation devices and if he's game, it's his to use."

Wade nodded, then gave her a sidelong glance.

"What is it?"

"Are we still not going to talk about your performance last night? Or maybe you were thinking we'd pretend it didn't happen, like everything else in our past?"

Dana wanted to wither him with a look, but her glares had never worked on him. She shrugged, looking away from the intensity behind his stare. "This is not the time."

He frowned, then straightened. "You have a good eye for detail. If you review the footage, you might find something that no one else will see."

Dana shook her head and stretched out her fingers to keep them from clenching at her sides. She still had several things to do that couldn't wait. "Not yet. I'm not feeling objective enough to even look at them. For now, you have your orders, I need to get this ship moving and after those thieves to get back what's ours. Have President Muñoz and Chancellor Evans report to my office immediately."

CHAPTER 18

"If you don't care about it enough to hide it, then let the one who finds it alone."
- Fashin Teku Proverb

President Muñoz and Chancellor Evans stood watching Dana uneasily, while she paced in front of her desk, lifting and dropping her hands. Their heads ping-ponged back and forth, neither willing to open the conversation. Every two or three paces, she'd stop and start to say something, then change her mind. She didn't know where to start on all the things they'd done wrong, and how she blamed herself more than she could ever blame them.

The chancellor gave up waiting for her and spoke up first. He blubbered through his first attempt. "Captain, let me be the first to say, this was all a—"

"No," she interrupted, stopping mid-stride. She lifted a finger and pointed at both of them. Though they were both taller, she intimidated them into silence. "Chancellor Evans, I want you to listen very carefully to what I say next. I've tolerated your insubordination and disrespect for the last time. You've done nothing but condescend my position and rank. You were presumptuous in inviting our guests onto our ship before I even had a chance to establish a security protocol with them."

"It wasn't entirely our fault, Captain," said President Muñoz. He was kind to take on some of the blame, knowing it mostly belonged to the chancellor.

"And I'm not entirely blaming you. I let you overrule my better judgment, but it is the last time I will do so." She clenched her hands around the top of her desk's chair, leaning forward. "From now on, when I make a decision, you will abide by it, and without contest. I'm in command of this ship and its safety, and you will respect that, or I'll see you spend the rest of this voyage in the brig."

Both men nodded, their faces somber and contrite.

She nodded once, sharply. "Good. Now that we're clear, I need your help. Please sit down."

If she wasn't so upset, she'd have laughed at the identical expressions of confusion on their faces. Neither seemed sure what to do. They took the two chairs facing her desk. Dana sat in hers, and folded her hands in front of her.

"The Fashin Teku have stolen our embryos."

Muñoz leaned forward his mouth agape. "What?"

"They've threatened our lives and the lives of the embryos if we attempt to pursue them. My instincts say that we should go after them. Our future as a people depends on those embryos."

"What if they've already sold them or something else by the time we reach them?" Evans asked. He'd been quick to go there, as she'd done herself.

Dana didn't want to concede. She'd considered the possibility that they'd been lied to, that the embryos were already on someone's plate. However, from what she understood about the Fashin Teku, they dealt in quick trades, drop-offs, and piracy. They wouldn't hold on to the cargo any longer than necessary if they didn't need it.

"It's a valid concern, but not one we can afford to worry about at the moment. Our priority is to the ship and its complement. I need you to be the people's voice and my ambassadors." She met their eyes. "Meet with the passengers. Listen to their concerns. Keep them calm with limited, but accurate information."

"Wouldn't that be better coming from you?" Chancellor Evans asked, glancing to his left and right as if someone would jump out and scare him.

"It would. However, I'll be too busy attending to ship's business. At the moment, we're working on getting our engines back online, and we'll soon be in pursuit of the aliens. Which means it's time for you to step up and perform your diplomatic roles on board. In future alien relations, I'll call on you as needed, but only once I've fully vetted anyone who sets foot on this ship." She looked hard at them both. "Is that understood?"

"Yes, Captain," they said in unison.

"Fantastic. Good day gentlemen. You've got plenty of work

to do." Dana looked down at her monitor as they stood and shuffled out in silence, not waiting for them to leave before placing her next call.

She sucked in a breath. This one was going to be another handful.

CHAPTER 19

Dana sent Maggie a message to come and see her in her office at her convenience. She had some questions that it seemed only Maggie could answer.

Maggie arrived shortly after the call, dressed in a muted blue jumper and flats. Her auburn hair was pulled back with an elastic binder and draped over one shoulder. It was the second time Dana had ever seen her looking less than camera ready, not that it mattered. She was still annoyingly stunning.

Dana laid into her about leaving the ship and protocol for a solid ten minutes before she sat back down and visibly calmed herself. In a surprise twist, Maggie hadn't said a word, which was wise considering the circumstances. Now that she'd gotten her feelings on the matter out of her system, she needed to ask Maggie some questions about the Fashin Teku ship tour's vid. Again, without any resistance she handed over the video she'd taken while interviewing the aliens. Dana put it into her COMP. The two watched together as the 3D vid played between them on the desk.

"They told me it was storage," Maggie said with a shrug when Dana paused the vid.

"What kind of storage?"

"The none-of-my-business kind," she shot back, then shrugged. "Well, they didn't use those words exactly. It was something more like, 'Ms. Brooker, you wouldn't be interested in a boring storage shed. Come, we'll show you more of the command center.'"

Dana raised her eyebrows. "And you let that go?"

Maggie waved a hand in the air. "Of course not. What kind of reporter would I be if I let every Tomack, Dali, and Harry try to throw me off the real story?"

Dana grinned, unable to keep from leaning forward. "You got something?"

Maggie sat back in her chair and crossed the opposite leg over the other while she draped one arm casually over the back of her seat. Her bright red lips curved into a seductive smile. "I didn't say that."

Maggie's default setting seemed to be how to get information or favors from male counterparts. The performance had no effect on Dana, and she sat back and put on her most bored expression, waiting for Maggie to continue.

When her tactic didn't work, she uncrossed her legs and scooted her chair so far forward, she could rest her elbows on Dana's desk. She continued the story as if she'd been holding back the best part. No doubt she had, but Dana listened as if they were discussing the weather. She wasn't going to be baited by the reporter and she had the feeling Maggie was leading up to something.

"They were certainly acting odd, but at the time, I didn't know what they were planning." She leaned in conspiratorially. "Most people don't know this, but I usually carry two cameras besides my audio recorder. One camera is visible and collects visual data only, and the audio device I hold in my hand, also in clear view."

Dana kept her tone bored, but her mouth went dry in anticipation. "The second camera does both, I'm assuming?"

"It does. That way, I always get the real story, even when my subject believes they are off the record."

"The way you did on the planet's surface?" Dana asked.

"I always keep it right here." Maggie pointed to the top button of her dress. "It fits behind the crease or button, depending on the outfit."

"Tell me you have a second recording of the Fashin Teku ship."

It was Maggie's turn to smile. Her green eyes lit up like a cat's in front of a bowl of warm milk.

AFTER MAGGIE LEFT HER OFFICE, DANA PULLED UP THE footage of the Fashin Teku ship again. If it hadn't been for her leaping onto their ship without permission, they'd have nothing. She'd have to remember that in the future.

Maggie had talked her through everything the first time they'd watched the vid, but she wanted to watch it again and see if anything stood out. The audio recording of her questions and their answers was on a separate device. Maggie played it through once, but Dana found it more distracting than helpful in this case. The vid, however, had picked up a clear view of the room where they'd denied her access.

It appeared to be a type of storage bay. There were

unmarked and marked storage containers inside. Dana slowed the vid down and reversed it several seconds to make a mark of the labels, none of the symbols matching each other. They seemed to be various configurations and colors. Could they be more stolen cargo from other species? It was highly probable the Fashin Teku had mastered their technique of piracy and duped many others besides themselves.

Several times, Maggie stopped and asked questions of the Fashin Teku that they refused to answer or ignored as they redirected her attention to some other part of the ship. In front of one guarded door stood a particularly obstinate male who had blond hair like the captain but wore a no-nonsense expression. He had argued with Maggie about going in for a quick peek. The closed door never opened, despite the light touch she gave his shoulder and the stroke of his beard that made his cheeks tinge red. Maggie was *good*. Dana had never seen a more subtle yet insistent form of prodding. Whatever was behind that door, it must have been important. The guard wouldn't budge, despite whatever she was offering him.

Dana went over the footage again and again. She was scanning for angles, anything that revealed what the Fashin Teku agenda might be, or how their technology worked.

After her eyes had gone dry and irritated, she gave the viewing a rest. She hadn't found anything particularly helpful, but she had a feeling she'd be needing that vid again. She wasn't done with the Fashin Teku whatever they thought. She wouldn't be intimidated by them either. Whether they left them behind or they were thrown out into space, the embryos' fate was the same. Dana imagined she knew what her father would do in this situation and she was prepared to do the same.

"*No prisoners, Baby girl.*"

CHAPTER 20

EARTHA

Eartha sat straight up from the couch that had become her bed. Ever since the Fashin Teku had come and gone, she'd finally been able to sleep through the night. Something had woken her, though. According to her tablet, it was still early morning. She should have slept until breakfast.

Though Mr. Rogan still hadn't believed her, she knew they'd been following the ship for days. When she said he shouldn't go to the party with them, he'd listened to her. At the time, she'd thought she was making progress with him. In the end, he hadn't wanted to go to the party anyway. He was planning to stay home all along. He didn't want to go out and pretend to have fun while Esme was still in a coma.

Instead, they'd stayed in their cabin and watched old vids he watched when he was a kid. Eartha laughed at them. Her mother and father hadn't watched a lot of vids as kids, so most of what she'd gotten were new shows but hearing Mr. Rogan laugh had put a smile on her face. He'd stayed up with her until she fell asleep in the middle of one, and then he'd put her to bed.

She'd had a dream about Esme. An important one—a good one. She'd have enjoyed it until morning if something hadn't woken her up. She listened a moment for the sound of alarms and heard Eric moving around in the bedroom. When he came out, he stopped short of the door, shocked to see her awake.

"The ship's not moving. I need to go see what's going on. Stay here, and don't come out for anything. You're probably going to see emergency lights and hear the alarms, but you'll be fine here. I'll send Ari by as soon as he's free."

"Mr. Rogan, wait, I had a dream about—"

"Not now, sweetheart. This is an emergency. We'll talk about it later, I promise. Can you do as I ask?"

He had his sandy brown eyebrows up to his hairline, his eyes questioning. Not leaving the cabin through the ventilation shaft was implied in the question.

Eartha nodded, and he rushed out the door, leaving her alone in the empty room.

That had been hours ago. Mr. Rogan hadn't returned once since then, not even for a quick meal. He must be very busy if the ship was still quiet, and he'd been at work in the engine room the whole day.

Ari never came to check on her, and she wondered if he was busy helping people, too. Eartha looked up at the familiar ventilation shaft. She could make her way through them and find out what was going on, but it was risky. Mr.

Rogan had told her to stay put, to not climb through the ventilation tubes anymore.

What if there was someone else hiding in them now? The aliens were about her height. What if they were still somewhere onboard?

She didn't want to see them up close. The images from Maggie Brooker's report had been enough, strange beasts with dark teeth and hair down to their ankles. She couldn't understand why no one else seemed to see the malice behind their eyes. They smiled not from pleasure, but because they were planning to hurt them.

Eartha had wanted to warn the captain about them the very first day, but Mr. Rogan didn't think it was a good idea, saying the captain had enough to deal with at the moment. Mr. Rogan had insisted the aliens had helped in the engine room, increasing their speed and adding several adjustments to components that the ship already had in stock. He'd said the ship had never run more smoothly.

Now the ship wasn't moving at all, so Eartha knew she'd been right again.

Sometimes she hated being right.

Why didn't adults ever believe her? Even after all the proof she'd offered Mr. Rogan, even he hadn't believed her in the end. She knew it from the sad way he'd looked at her, as if she needed to talk to a mind-shark. She wasn't insane. At least she didn't think so, though crazy people probably thought the same thing. This was different, though, and when she acted on what she saw, she helped people. Ari was almost living proof. Though he wasn't alive in the regular sense, she'd saved him from being destroyed. He'd even said so when he'd thanked her.

Eartha dressed, and then waited a while longer. After she got bored with watching vids, she cleaned the small cabin. She changed the sheets and made the bed, just like she'd been taught. Then she made sure all the dishes were clean and put away. She didn't want anything to be out of place when Mrs. Rogan arrived. She would be awake soon, and Eartha didn't want her to be alone while everyone was off taking care of the broken ship.

When she ran out of things to keep her busy, Eartha sucked in a breath, and moved to the door. This couldn't wait. It slid open, and she found herself standing in the corridor, watching people rushing from one end to the other. The lights on the wall were the yellow of warning lights. Things were still in chaos, but people seemed to be too busy going about their business to be concerned with a kid roaming the halls.

It was only after she'd made it to the lift that she realized she'd never actually gone anywhere using it. What if it didn't work?

The doors slid open, and she stepped inside. She entered and spoke to the COMP system.

"Med-bay?"

The lift chirped in response before it started moving upward. It stopped without a word, and the doors opened to an identical looking corridor. Eartha had to follow a crew member dressed in the uniform of a nurse to find the right set of doors, or she might have missed it. The nurse hurried along, never looking back.

Everyone inside the med-bay seemed to be cleaning up something in the lab and didn't even notice her come in. Eartha tiptoed over to where Esme Rogan was lying peacefully with her eyes closed. It looked like she hadn't moved at all that day.

Eartha stared at her, willing her to open her eyes. At first, nothing happened. She reached out and held her hand. It was cold, limp, lifeless. Eartha willed her own heat into the woman, but she remained still.

Then, as she was letting go, her hand twitched. At first, Eartha thought it had been her imagination, but then Mrs. Rogan groaned, her eyes struggling to open.

"It's okay," Eartha whispered. "You're not alone. You can open your eyes now."

A man with a ponytail on the other side of the room heard her speaking and turned to stare at her. His face was curious, but he didn't interfere or ask what she was doing there so she kept her attention on Mrs. Rogan. Instead, he watched her for a moment, then called out behind him.

"Get the doctor. Esme's waking up. And get her husband up here."

Eartha knew she shouldn't be there. Everything in her being cried out that she should go, but she didn't want Mrs. Rogan to be alone when she opened her eyes, so she stayed, even when the doctor came and checked her pulse and breathing.

"Esme? Esme?" he said, leaning on her other side and stroking her arm. "Can you hear me?"

Esme's eyes fluttered open, and she slowly took in the room and the faces around her. Eartha squeezed her hand and their eyes met. She thought Mrs. Rogan would be mad, maybe snatch her hand away, but she didn't. Instead, she let out a thin sob and pulled Eartha close. She'd done the right thing coming to be with her, even though it meant that everyone now knew she was on board.

Mr. Rogan barged through the doorway less than two minutes later. He was breathing heavily, like he'd run the whole way.

"Chief, she's awake," the man with the ponytail said, waving him over.

Ari trailed him, and while Mr. Rogan took the place of the doctor, Ari came around the table and stood beside Eartha. The Rogans were whispering over each other and kissing each other's faces and hands.

"When?" Mr. Rogan asked a few minutes later.

"Just now," the doctor told him. "We called you as soon as we saw her conditioned had changed."

"Is she recovered? Can she come home?" he asked, not looking at either his wife or Eartha.

"I'll just need to run some tests, and then she can recover in her quarters." The doctor then gestured to Eartha. "This little girl was here when we arrived. Do you recognize her?"

Mr. Rogan seemed to notice her for the first time. "Um... yes."

"What's your name, little girl?" the man with the ponytail asked, but Ari eased Eartha behind him before answering.

"Wait, I can explain–" Mr. Rogan began, but Ari beat him to the rest.

"Her name is Eartha Singh MacLaren, and she's a stowaway."

"Oh no," Mr. Rogan muttered, running a hand over his face.

"What?" the two men said at the same time. Eartha noticed for the first time how similar the doctor and the man with the ponytail looked in their expressions. Though they dressed very differently, they each had the same mouth and eyes, like brothers.

Esme Rogan coughed, and all the eyes in the room darted to her. The doctor handed her a tube of water with a straw she could sip from. Then she spoke, her voice barely above a whisper.

"Eartha is our daughter."

CHAPTER 21

Just as the doctor said, Esme was awake. Dana walked into the med-bay with Wade at her side and couldn't help smiling when she saw Esme sitting up on one of the hover beds, a wan smile on her lips and her husband at her side. It was more than Dana could have imagined for the two of them.

However, there seemed to be too many people in the room. In her head, she placed each person, trying to figure out why there were so many.

Dana's eyes went to Rido Jabar, and he gave her another one of his mischievous grins. Then she saw ARI Three and a little girl that seemed to be hiding behind him. Not too little. She was probably twelve, and she had a familiar face, as if Dana should recognize her. The almond eyes, the poof of black curls at the nape of her neck.

Then she realized who the girl must be.

Dana's eyebrows flew up. This was Sarah MacLaren's daughter. The woman with the same almond eyes who had given her the final tour of the ship, and, as its designer, knew more about it than Dana herself. Her father, Michael Singh, was the large black man in the unclaimed vid who'd broken down over her departure, the one whose best friend had both giggled and cried before asteroid Harvey had destroyed their world.

The answer to the mystery that had consumed her before the Fashin Teku now came rushing back.

"Captain, Commander, I hope you're not making a fuss for me," Esme said as she sat up straighter in her bed. There was light in her playful eyes, though she looked pale enough to see through.

Eric held her left hand in both of his and straightened, pulling his shoulders back as Dana joined them. His eyes darted to Eartha, and then back to her.

"At ease, Chief," Dana said. "We came by to see how you were doing, among other things." Dana's eyes fell on the child half-hiding behind ARI Three.

Either Esme didn't see her look, or didn't care as she continued on, not letting anyone else get a word in.

"I slept for a week, so I'm still groggy. I might need to sleep for another, as apparently being in a coma is exhausting. Fill me in on everything, what did I miss?"

The girl behind the ARI stepped forward as if on cue, her eyes never leaving Esme's face.

"There were these really ugly aliens. They followed us for days, and then they pretended to be our friends so they could sneak onboard and steal from us."

Esme was putting on a brave face, but she was tired, and the conversation Dana wanted to have with Eric was one she couldn't have in the med-bay.

"That about sums it up," Dana said with a nod to the girl.

"Thank you, Eartha. Chief, in my conference room, and bring the girl with you. I have a few questions."

"Captain, I'd like to be a part of anything that concerns my family," Esme said, her eyes darting to the girl.

"I must insist," Dana said. "You need rest if you're going to return to your cabin, and I'm sure your husband will be able to answer my simple questions." She inclined her head. "Nothing, however, will be decided without you. You have my word on that."

Esme nodded. Eric lifted her hand to his lips and kissed her knuckles. Eartha stood on her toes and leaned into hug Esme. The woman gave the girl a gentle kiss on her forehead, then whispered something only the three of them could hear.

"I would also like to be present, Captain," said ARI Three.

"You?" Dana asked doubtfully.

"He's the one who found her," Eric said.

She cut her eyes at him. "And you didn't inform me?"

"It's a long story," Eric said with a tired shrug. "But I think you should allow Ari to join us."

Dana wasn't sure exactly what that meant, but it seemed important to the family, so she conceded. She leaned in and spoke to Wade. "See that Dr. Walker also joins us."

"Right away," Wade said, dashing off to make the call.

CHAPTER 22

The last time Dana had been seated at this table, the Fashin Teku had been on the other side of it, making a fool out of her. This time, she sat on one side with Wade, while on the other side sat Eartha MacLaren Singh and Eric Rogan. The girl sat with her feet tucked under her, gnawing on her fingernails.

The ARI sat on the other side of Eartha, and on his left was Dr. Noah Walker, the ARI engineering specialist.

Dana didn't speak right away, letting the weight of the moment settle. She looked over the girl's olive skin and big, curly hair. She could see such a strong resemblance. The fluffy curls and light brown skin were like a perfect mix of her mother and father. The eyes were just like Sarah MacLaren's. Again, Dana wondered how this girl could be adopted. She wore a child-sized uniform, her hair pulled back from her face in a pink bow low on her nape. She wore a different pair of shoes, but she was sure if she pulled out the pink running shoe from her desk, it would match her size. Dana mentally checked off that mystery as solved.

Dana leaned forward on the table, lacing her hands together. "Let's start with you, Eartha. Please tell me how you got on this ship."

The girl cleared her throat. "My mother."

Dana nodded to Wade, who got her a glass of water. Eartha took a sip and continued.

"She snuck me on a couple nights before the launch."

"Your mother is Susan MacLaren?" Dana asked.

"Yes."

"How long were you living in the vents before the Rogans found you?"

"My mom told me to stay hidden for fourteen days. She told me to count them. When I came out, I saw what was happening to Zelenia..."

Her voice faded as her eyes filled with tears. Eric reached over to pat the girl's arm. Eartha turned to look up at the ARI, who reached out and took her right hand with its mechanical left.

Dana wasn't sure which of them was more fascinated by their connection—herself, or Dr. Walker, who seemed to be leaning so far over in his chair he might lose his balance and tumble to the floor any moment.

"Did your mother tell you what would happen?" Wade asked. His tone was prodding, but gentle.

She shook her head. "I didn't even get to say goodbye to Becky or anyone." Eartha's lip quivered. Her feelings were so close to the surface. These questions were becoming too difficult for her to answer.

Dana turned her attention to the present. "How did you meet the ARI?"

Eartha cleared her throat. "I used the tubes to get around

at night. I went out when most people were asleep. In the Commons, people talk a lot about what's going on around the ship. So, I went there a lot. When the Commons closed down for the night, I'd climb up and get food from the kitchen."

"Ah, the kitchen thief," Wade said with a snap of his fingers, as if solving the case.

Dana ignored his outburst, turning back to Eartha.

"I met Ari there," she continued, "and he promised to keep my secret."

"What?" Dr. Walker stood, towering over them. "Why would you do such a thing?"

Eartha's expression fell, and she looked more worried than angry. "He didn't do anything wrong!"

Dana held up a hand and gave Dr. Walker a look that made it clear she didn't want any more outbursts. He sat again and leaning forward his eyes intent as he focused on Eartha.

"That's what you call it? Ari?" He asked, encouraging her to continue.

She looked at him in confusion. "That's his name."

Before the doctor could interrupt again, Dana continued her questioning.

"That's where I believe you came in," she said, turning her attention to the ARI.

"Yes, Captain. I met Miss Eartha in the Commons during one of my shifts."

"When you discovered the girl in the Commons, why didn't you report her existence at once?" Dr. Walker asked the ARI.

If an android could squirm, its hesitation would have sufficed as proof. Its expressionless face tilted to one side as it considered the question. Then its eyes went from Dana to Eartha and back again, ignoring Dr. Walker altogether.

"Eartha was very... compelling in her reasonings. She convinced me that her existence should remain a secret until her life was no longer in danger. Once the Rogans knew of the situation, I left it to them."

"But—"

Dana cut off Walker's outburst with a hand. She wanted the whole story before he interrupted again.

"Have you lied, falsified, or omitted any other relevant information pertaining to the safety of this ship, passengers, or crew?" she asked the ARI.

"No, Captain. In all other respects, I have performed my duties to the best of my abilities."

Dana nodded, satisfied for the moment that it was telling her the truth.

"The Rogans have been taking care of you?" Dana asked Eartha. She'd mentally omitted the word 'hiding', substituting it instead.

Eartha nodded.

"Do you like staying with them?"

Eartha looked up at Eric and nodded again. "Yes. They're the parents my mom wanted me to have."

"How do you know that?"

"She told me to find the Rogans as soon as I came out of the vents."

"I see," Dana said, sitting back in her chair. There had been something in the way Sarah MacLaren spoke about the couple that Dana remembered as strange. Now it made sense, since the woman was preparing to leave her only child in their care.

Dana stood up. "That's all. Thank you all for your honesty. Dr. Walker, you're dismissed, and you can take the ARI with you. Wade, please bring Eartha back to the med-bay. She'll need a full medical workup. She'll be near to Esme, which should make them both happy."

"Aye, Captain."

Eartha looked from the ARI to Wade and shook her head. Her legs had curled up as she pressed herself into Eric's side, looking terrified.

"You don't need to be afraid of the doctor," Wade said, a broad smile on his face. "He won't hurt you. He only needs to create a medical record for you in case of an emergency."

The girl refused to budge.

"We can bring her, Captain," the ARI said, and Dr. Walker stared at it in surprise, as did the others in the conference room.

"Excuse me?" Dana asked, unsure if she'd heard it correctly.

"Dr. Walker and I can escort her to the med-bay. It is on our way, and I think she will be more comfortable with me."

Dana glanced at the girl, who unfolded her legs and ran to the ARI. He was protective of her, and was oddly sensitive to her needs for a machine. Dana nodded, still trying to work out their strange relationship, then remembered something.

"Fine, take her with you. And please relay my instructions to Dr. Jabar."

The ARI nodded, taking Eartha's hand in its right, the flesh-looking one. But before they took a step to leave, Eartha turned back.

"Are you in trouble?" Eartha asked, looking at Eric with concern.

His face softened. "I'll be fine, sweetie. Go with Ari, and I'll come down and see you in the med-bay when I'm finished."

Eartha's dark brown eyes were full of worry, but she nodded, and turned back to the ARI, who was waiting for Dr. Walker, looking as baffled as she'd ever seen him.

"Dr. Walker, I expect to be informed immediately if and when you find the cause of this." Dana waved a hand in the direction of the ARI. "I want to know how it could disobey a programmed directive."

Dr. Walker's shoulders hunched. "Yes, Captain."

Eartha walked behind them, but, at the door, turned back once again.

"His name is Ari Three. When you say 'the ARI', it makes him sound just like any old machine, but he's not," she said. "He's my friend."

Dana's brows lifted. "Oh?"

"Yes. He was there for me when I needed him, and he stayed away from the trees like I told him." Eartha shrugged. "That's why he survived."

Eartha ran out the door to catch up with Dr. Walker, who hadn't bothered to wait. When the door slid closed, Dana turned to Wade, then back to Eric, who was trying his best to keep his eyes fixed on the wall behind her. It didn't stop her from firing questions at him one after the other.

"While you and the ARI—" She caught herself, then tried again. "While you and Ari have been hiding her, has anyone else learned that Eartha was onboard?"

"No."

"You haven't confided in anyone?"

"No."

"She's been in your quarters and has never left since you found her?"

His eyes flicked her way, then went back to the wall. "Yes, and not until today."

"How did she know about the prehensile vegetation on Planet 2396?"

It was Eric's turn to shift uncomfortably. "I don't know Captain. Just like I don't know how she knew the Fashin Teku were trouble before we did."

There was something different about the girl, but perhaps even the Rogans didn't know what it was.

"Right... and she left your quarters for the first time to see Esme, who had been in a coma until this very day?"

"She's just a child. She's lost everything, Captain. All Esme and I wanted was to give her something stable." He shrugged. "We don't know much about raising kids, but we know she needs a family."

"You knowingly and willingly hid a stowaway onboard without my knowledge. That fact, Chief Rogan, is why you and your wife will have a formal reprimand written into your records. It might not mean much right now, but it's the most I can do." Dana's shoulders fell forward as she sighed. "I need you in the engine room, getting us moving, and Eartha needs a place to live."

Eric's eyes lit up and Dana knew she'd done the right thing. "She can stay with us?"

Dana nodded. "The Commander will work on getting you larger quarters as soon as possible."

"Th-thank you, Captain," Eric said, standing up and saluting.

"You're welcome. I suppose I don't have to tell you the engines are your priority at the moment?"

"No, Captain. I'll just tell my girls the good news and get right back to work."

"You're dismissed," Dana said, laughing as he dashed out.

"Those two are going to have their hands full," Wade said, "but I'm happy they're together. It could have gone another way."

"Agreed. Try to get them moved before Esme's out of the med-bay. It will give Eric and his new daughter a chance to surprise her."

Wade nudged her with one shoulder and winked. "You're such a romantic."

"Yeah... I'm learning."

CHAPTER 23

Captain's Log: 4327.9.25

T hings are bad.

We made first contact with the Fashin Teku. They robbed us. I've declared war on them, the way an ant is at war with a foot. We're tactically outmatched, but we haven't given up.

Once we locate a fuel source and food, we're going after our embryos. They'll still be viable, and we'll find them before it's too late, because we must. I must.

They never meant us to be awake for this trip. Food stores and medical supplies are low. Our fuel expenditure is also higher than it should be because of our contact with the aliens and planet 2396, where we lost two of our scientists.

But it hasn't been all bad.

We discovered a stowaway on board, and she appears to be different from the rest of us in a way we don't fully comprehend.

Our numbers are still biologically growing, and with every newborn face, there's another Zelenian looking to me to get them home.

I'll lead my people home. It's more than my job or my responsibility—it's my purpose.

I don't know what tomorrow will bring, but whatever comes, we'll face it together. At the moment, we're still flying, and I haven't given up. There's a planet beyond our charted stars waiting for us, and our people will find it.

CHAPTER 24

"Before the Great Purge, men rode on the backs of loud mechanical beasts through city streets and proclaimed themselves gods. All the while, disapproving eyes observed their folly from the heavens."
- The Book of Ages

In the ancient days on Blue Earth, there was something called a "mutiny" on large boats made of wood that sailed the planet's seas. When the ship's crew disagreed strongly enough, they would force its captain out—usually into shark-infested waters. Dana had never seen a shark, but being thrown out an airlock into open space had to be worse than being eaten by a large fish. In space, there was no chance of survival.

She wondered how many more mistakes she could make before her own crew threw her out. It was on her mind as she stood in front of her senior officers, bridge crew, and the ship's two ambassadors. They sat around the long oval conference table, staring up at her in anticipation.

Since their journey had begun, nothing had gone according to plan. The Coalition attacks and the piracy by the Fashin Teku had left them with limited resources. The last planet they'd visited had taken their terraforming science specialists, and nearly all the ship's small army of ARIs.

Now with limited supplies, a crippled ship, and no embryos, Dana had pursued the Fashin Teku. Instead of searching for a new planet where their species would slowly die off due to the lack of genetic variety, they would go after the alien pirates. The possibility of losing their own lives in the pursuit was highly likely.

The question remained whether her crew would continue to follow her on this almost positively suicidal mission, or overthrow her authority, thinking her insane, but they needed their embryos. Not every woman on board could have children the old-fashioned way.

She wasn't about to tell the room she was one of them.

She sat down at the head of the table and played the hand she'd been dealt.

"Chief Rogan, what is the state of the engines and fuel?"

"We've got the engines back, including the upgrades that the Fashin Teku put into place," Eric said. "Thankfully, they didn't drain the fuel lines. We're moving faster than any Zelenian ship made before this one."

"What about food and water?"

Wade sat forward. "According to Chef, we've got the rations we had from before. The Teku took all the food back that they brought, the fresh food he was keeping in stock, and most of the specialty drinks. Water we've got, thanks to the recycler system."

"Are there any planets nearby?"

"No captain," Cliff answered. "There are no known planets in this sector. We went well beyond the border of our charted space over a week ago. We could be a few days, or a few years from the next habitable planet."

"And with the loss of the ARIs, we'll be at a tactical disadvantage," Dana mused. "To be honest, we depended on their strength and durability to deal with hostiles. The designers of the *Hope* didn't plan on engaging with any hostiles while we were in cryostasis, which means we must ramp up our defenses in the meantime. I want our invisibility shielding back up." She turned to Barnes. "Lieutenant Commander, where are we on the CAH investigation?"

"We're still trudging through the vids when we're not dealing with our regular duties but, to be honest, we're not making a lot of progress."

She nodded her understanding. "We've got other security priorities that you need to cover. We may need to consider increasing your force. Let's table it for now, and focus on the immediate dangers."

"We haven't had any CAH activity since Shu's death," Barnes went on. "It might be the end of their agenda."

"Perhaps, but I'm not going to be sitting around wondering if someone's going to try to blow the ship out from under me. Keep at it."

Barnes nodded. "Yes, Captain."

"We're dealing with at least one new mouth to feed, not to mention the ones that will come. Dr. Jabar, how many births are already on the books?"

He ran a hand over his face. "Without giving out any names, we currently have five pregnant civilians and two crew members, making seven births over the next year that we're aware of."

Dana's eyes grew wide. So many in so short a time. She'd only known about two, not including Eartha. She wondered who the other pregnant women might be.

"With the current situation being what it is, there will be an increase in our population," said Chancellor Evans, breaking into her thoughts. "It's in these situations that people come together. They're staring mortality in the face. It's a natural reaction."

Dana turned to Nancy. "Lieutenant Westlake, what's the update on the Fashin Teku?"

"Clif–Ensign Harden and I have been able to extrapolate their trajectory based on their shielding signal," she replied, a tinge of red rising to her cheeks.

"Do you have a plan, Captain?" President Muñoz asked in a mild, undemanding tone.

Dana made eye contact with everyone before she spoke her next words.

"I don't have to tell you what a serious position we're in. However, this is what we signed up for. There were never any guarantees that our mission would be a successful one, but that's not how they promoted this thing. I want the rest of the crew and the passengers to remain positive." She focused her attention. "Chancellor and Mr. President, I'll need you to continue to keep the passengers and crew spirit's up with shipboard activities."

"Never saw myself as much of a cruise director," Chancellor Evans muttered with a huff of disbelieving laughter. President Muñoz chuckled along with him.

They both stopped laughing when Dana's expression didn't change.

"You're serious?" President Munoz asked.

"After your successful party the other night, you've proven yourselves capable of distracting the passengers while we figure out our next move. I appreciate your flexibility in this matter."

Chancellor Evans refused to be so easily dismissed. "Does that mean you don't know what you're going to do next? Captain, I beg you to reconsider our experience in diplomacy—"

Dana held up a hand to stop his plea. She needed their help, even if she didn't want it. They'd give it, even if they didn't like it.

"I value your assistance, gentlemen. However, I need a moment alone with the crew. You will be notified again if I require your expertise. In all other matters, you'll receive updates along with the rest of the passengers."

The two dignitaries stood up and shuffled out of the room. Dana waited a full minute after the doors slid closed before she spoke again.

"What I'm asking of you is no small task. I need to know you're with me one hundred percent."

"You're still planning on going after the Fashin Teku," Wade said, finishing her thought.

Dana nodded. There were several surprised gasps. Her two senior officers, however, didn't look surprised at all.

"Thoughts?" she asked.

"Let's go get them," Nancy said.

Cliff and Wade verbally agreed.

"This is ludicrous," Barnes protested, frowning in disbelief at them all. "I can't imagine a worse idea. It's bad enough that this entire mission has been one big conspiracy gone wrong. Now you want us to lay down our lives for embryos? I say we take the lives we have and live out our days in peace."

Dana listened to him stone-faced, keeping her true feelings as hidden as possible.

"Although I don't share his reasoning, I have to agree with Commander Barnes," Eric said, surprised at himself. "Maybe it's because I have a family now and the others don't. I have more to lose than just some hypothetical children. I have a wife and child here. The last thing I want for them is a life with an expiration date." Eric leaned forward on the table with his hands splayed in front of him as if pleading. "Until we have the resources to keep ourselves well fed and defended; I think we should leave the Fashin Teku to themselves. We don't know what our future holds. We could find allies in other aliens with the technical resources to go after the Fashin Teku."

Dr. Jabar lifted his hand from the table to speak. "Although we never considered the possibility before, it should be noted that we could be physically compatible with other alien species we encounter. Any slight variation could be enough to keep our future generations alive. Of course, that would require extensive research into their genetics, but I believe we have a scientist on board who could determine the possibility."

Dr. Jabar and Eric's reasonings were sound. They were all things Dana had thought of herself, but she couldn't shake the one thing that persistently nagged at her. She sat back in her chair and fiddled with her fingernails before folding her hands in her lap.

"When I was a kid, there was a boy in my virtual studies that used to bully me from the age of ten until I was almost fifteen years old. He'd create fake profiles for me and pictures of me in embarrassing situations he'd share with the other students enrolled in the classroom platform. My mother, teacher, even the principal told me to ignore him. Said he'd go away faster if I didn't engage him." Her hands tightened around each other. "I tolerated his taunts and insults for five years. When my father returned from a space flight mission and found out what was going on, he sat me down and told me something I'd never forget. Bullies prey on the weak and scared because they are a reflection of themselves. To stop one, you have to let them know you're neither weak nor scared."

Dana looked around the table again, meeting their eyes as she spoke.

"The Fashin Teku are swindlers. They believe we are weak and scared. If we allow them to steal from us without recompense, they'll think they can do it again. Or worse, they'll tell other aliens we're easy targets."

She let that idea sink in and saw from her crew's wide eyes that several of them hadn't considered that scenario until now.

"I believe there's more to lose by giving up than we do by pursuing these pirates," she went on. "Another factor to consider is that without more expansive maps, we're flying blind. The only thing we have is a fading emissions marker pointing us in the direction of the Fashin Teku. If we follow them, we might not only find them, but we may encounter more habitable planets."

"Or we could end up prey to some other aliens," Barnes muttered. "We don't even know where they went."

But the others were already considering her plan.

"True, but we have their trajectory," Dana said resting her palms on the table. "It's not much. I'm your Captain, and I'm willing to fight for all of you, but I won't order you to pursue the Fashin Teku. I'm asking you to let me find these pirates and get back what belongs to us."

"How long will you pursue them?" Eric asked. "What if we run out of resources in the meantime?"

It was a valid question, and one she'd already considered.

"All I want is to keep after the Fashin Teku until we either get our embryos back, or find a new home—whichever comes first." Dana watched them contemplate the possibilities. "Do I have your full cooperation?"

Everyone seemed to agree, except for Barnes.

"Barnes?"

"As your security officer, I want to emphasize for the record that this is a bad idea." He frowned down at the table. "However, you have my full cooperation, Captain."

That was good enough for her.

She nodded to them all. "You've got your assignments. For now, dismissed."

Everyone left the preparation room except for Wade.

"Commander?" Dana asked once the door had closed, leaving them alone.

He inclined his head. "Captain, you're holding something back. I'm just wondering if it's this briefing, or something else."

Dana sighed and put her chin on her clasped hands. Wade moved closer, reaching out to take one of her hands in his.

"It's Mitchell."

"Dr. Mitchell?" he echoed. He thought for a moment then remembered. "The scientist who was killed by the plants on Planet 2369."

"Yes. You probably didn't know, but he served with me on my last assignment." She kept her eyes on their hands. "His wife is one of the seven women pregnant onboard. That's two children without fathers."

Wade didn't speak, only kept his hand over hers.

"Is it showing?" Dana asked.

"Is what showing?"

"The defeat. Is it showing on me?"

"No, it isn't." His hand tightened slightly on hers. "I think it's because you don't believe you're beaten yet. Besides, you've always been able to keep your feelings in check. That's what makes you a great Captain." He grinned at her when she looked up. "And I promise I'll inform you of the first signs of weakness."

She huffed out a soft laugh, turning her hand over until she held his. It was nice to hold Wade's hand in hers again as friends. Dana was confident no matter what happened, he'd be there, and she was grateful.

"You're so warm. It's so cold out here and you're always warm."

"I'm built that way." He took her by the chin and turned her face up toward him. "It's okay to be excited."

Dana pulled back, running a hand over her hair. "What do you mean?"

"You don't need to put on a show for me. I'm your first officer, but I've been your friend since—" He stopped short, then seemed to make up his mind to continue, "—for a long time. I can tell when you're holding back your excitement. You're eager to be doing something. I feel the same way."

"I am excited," she admitted. "Excited, hopeful, terrified. But I can't bear to lose any more of them." Dana stood up to pace. The energy always seemed to build up in her, and she needed a release. She was overdue for a run. With everything happening, she hadn't made the time. "This could be my biggest mistake yet."

"I know," Wade said, standing up. He started to say something more, but she cut him off.

"No, you don't. How could you? When I close my eyes at night, their faces haunt me. They're always with me."

Wade looked at her closer. "You're not talking about Zelenia, are you?"

Dana shook her head. The incident at the Breezy Blue might as well had been yesterday. She took a deep breath to clear the scent of burning that permeated her memory.

"It was almost a year ago Dana, when are you going to forgive yourself?"

He moved to stand beside her, and when she continued to pace, refusing to make eye contact with him, he put his arms out and placed his hands firmly on her shoulders to hold her still.

"You can't change the past." He tilted her chin up toward him. "Look at what's around you. Despite everything, we've got a real chance here."

Dana had to fight the growing heat rising in her chest when he gazed into her eyes with that kind of intensity. She turned away, letting his hands fall. He'd caught her up against the wall, and she had to move past him to put more physical distance between them.

"How's Maggie holding up these days?" she asked.

Wade sighed. The moment his girlfriend's name was mentioned, the air in the room cooled. There was a wall of safety dividing them again with Maggie's name on it. "She's good. She's been going over the alien footage." He rubbed the back of his neck. "I think she's trying to stay busy because she feels like she overlooked something."

"It's not her fault. None of us saw it coming." Dana moved to the preparation room table and leaned one hip against it as she crossed her arms. "I've been over the footage myself, and she got more than I expected. Perhaps we can turn it into an advantage. She's excellent at what she does."

"True, but for some reason, the women in my life don't believe me when I say it." Wade's mouth lifted in a smirk.

Dana ignored it. "Tell her I've got a little assignment for her."

"Sure. What were you planning to have her do?"

"A little public relations piece."

CHAPTER 25

Maggie sent the footage for the next day's broadcast as promised. She'd agree to do the update as soon as possible and put it into the next broadcast of *Maggie's Minutes*. Dana sat back on the couch in her quarters in her white fuzzy slippers and fluffy white robe to watch it. Her last days visiting the spa, her mother had insisted she buy them. As she sipped her tea, Maggie was on the screen speaking directly to the camera.

She explained about the Fashin Teku and the current state of things. She'd done her research. Maggie had included what sounded like official numbers for survival from Dr. Jabar. Her voice played over clips of video she'd taken on board the Fashin Teku ship. Even after she'd already seen the entire video, the sight of them put her teeth on edge. Their false smiles and waves as they were planning to come back that very night and steal from them.

"Before we sign off, I've got another exclusive story that you'll only get here. After the dramatic events of yesterday, you'd think nothing else could be worth talking about, but you don't want to miss this."

Maggie had a twinkle in her eye, as if she couldn't wait to spill all of her secrets. Dana knew the tactic well and still leaned forward in her seat.

"I'm joined today by our Chief Engineers, and power couple, Eric and Esme Rogan, and the newest member of their family young Eartha MacLaren Singh." The screen seemed to move back as it took in Maggie sitting in a chair with the Rogans and Eartha on a light blue couch.

"First of all, let me say hello and officially welcome you on board, Eartha."

Eartha's eyes were wide with nerves, but she answered in a clear voice.

"Hello."

She kept her eyes glued on Maggie's face.

"Now, I understand that you recently turned thirteen. Is that right?"

"Yes."

"Congratulations." Maggie was still leaning forward as if trying to get more out of her, but Eartha's responses remained clipped.

"Thank you," Eartha said.

Dana thought the girl's answers were too stiff and practiced.

"You're here with the Rogans because your mother hid you onboard the ship in a conduit close to engineering. Is that right?"

"Yes," Eartha said.

There was a cut in the footage before the camera returned to a closeup of Maggie's profile.

"Do you know why your mother risked everything, the lives of your family, and your life to place you in that conduit?"

Then the camera cut to a closeup of Eartha's round face.

Eartha shook her head to the negative. Her lips clamped shut. Maggie didn't let up this time. She followed it with another question.

"Can you describe to us what it was like that night your mother brought you here two days before launch?"

Eartha took in an audible breath, then spoke. "It was still dark, and I was sleepy because I was supposed to go to school in a few hours. She didn't tell me anything at first. Not until she put me in a crate to hide me to get into Nova Base."

Eartha relaxed into her story, and her voice increased in volume. The camera never left her face, but Maggie's question could be heard off screen.

"Were you scared?"

Eartha nodded, her bottom lip quivering. "I didn't know she was going to leave me there. I didn't know I wasn't going to see them again." Tears welled in her eyes and fell down her face.

Dana found her own eyes welling with tears.

Maggie continued when the girl stopped. "You mean your parents?"

"My dad didn't even know. He didn't get to say goodbye. My mom—I was angry at her at first. I thought there was going to be another ship. There was supposed to be another ship."

The anger in her voice echoed the one inside of Dana. She'd felt that same frustration—the same anger when she'd learned the truth.

Eartha leaned into Esme's side and the woman wrapped

her arm around her, clutching her close. She leaned down and whispered something that the microphone didn't catch. Eartha nodded and lifted her face for Esme to wipe away the tears. Maggie's camera highlighted them perfectly so the moment, though private, could be felt by the viewing audience.

Nice touch. Dana smiled as she took another sip of her tea. It was already getting cold, but the interview was heating up.

"Eric and Esme let's go to you, first let me say I'm happy to see that you're both well after the harrowing last few days. Esme, you sustained a concussion and were in a coma for a week. Can I say, you look amazing?"

"Thank you, Maggie," Esme blushed and the color in her cheeks only added to the glow of her face.

"When do you return to duty?"

"I feel great and I suspect I'll be back on duty in a couple of days."

"Glad to hear it. I'm sure your husband is too." Maggie turned her attention to Eric. "While Esme was in a coma, Eric, you were juggling your duties on board, with the loss of your wife, and a grieving orphaned child. How did you do it?"

"I'll be honest, it wasn't easy," Eric swallowed the emotion that kept him from saying anything more. It was clear from the widening of his eyes he hadn't expected it, but the camera zoomed in on his face as if ready for it. "Esme is my entire world, I wasn't so sure I could go on without her." He choked back the emotion again and Maggie reached down and handed him the glass of water. After a sip, he continued. "Eartha needed me, she'd just lost her family, just like the rest of us, and she thought she might lose another parent even before she got to know her."

Maggie jumped in, giving him a chance to take another sip of the water.

"It takes a special kind of person to take in an orphan. As I understand it, the reason Sarah MacLaren placed Eartha so close to engineering was because you knew her mother and worked alongside her as she built and designed the ship."

Eric glanced at his wife. At her nod, she continued.

"Sarah knew this ship better than anyone. Eartha is her only child, and we were honored her mother entrusted her in our care." Esme gave Eartha another squeeze as she settled into her husband who clutched her right hand in his.

"How did she know what no one else seemed to, that the world was ending?"

"We don't know," Esme answered.

"Did you know?" Maggie asked.

Eric shook his head. "No, we had no idea like everyone else we were shocked to learn we were the only survivors."

Esme squared her shoulders and spoke up, "We don't know how she found out the truth. All we know is she did what anyone in her position would have, she tried to save her child."

Maggie leaned back as if letting that information settle over them before continuing.

"Neither of you have ever been parents before, and adoption is such a rare thing in our world. How long did it take for you to adjust?"

The Rogans shared a smile as they looked from each other, then down to Eartha.

"We're still adjusting," Esme said.

Eric turned back to Maggie and continued. "Eartha is

helping us, and she's patient with us when we don't get it right the first time."

Maggie let out a quick laugh as she crossed one leg over the other settling in to listen to their story. The next question was quick and unrehearsed. Dana saw it in the looks on their faces—surprise and then resignation.

"Despite what you've all been through and perhaps because of it, I'm wondering why you didn't report finding Eartha right away?"

Eric was about to say something, but Esme put a hand on his thigh and nodded. He seemed to take a moment to calm himself. His cheeks were red as he defended their choice.

"We discovered Eartha at the same time as we learned that we'd lost an entire planet of friends, family, and memories."

Esme jumped in then, "Eric and I were in mourning along with everyone else. We didn't feel it was the best time to tell everyone. With the sabotage and my coma, we thought it was more important to focus on keeping the passengers and crew safe," Esme said.

Dana noted that she'd used the word 'we' when talking about the decisions Eric made while she was in a coma. They seemed united now in front of the cameras, Dana couldn't help but wonder if it had been so unanimous in the beginning.

Maggie continued with the harder questioning. "When you discovered Eartha's existence, were you afraid the Captain would take her away from you?"

Eric looked to his wife and then back to Maggie. He swallowed hard before he answered. "We made a huge mistake not telling the Captain immediately."

"We both regret it, even though our reasons at the time seemed sufficient," Esme said. Her shoulders hunching forward.

Eric continued gesturing with the free hand that wasn't clinging to his wife's. "In all honesty, of course, we were concerned she might be taken away from us and given to more experienced parents. Regardless, that wasn't the reason we didn't immediately tell the Captain. People make mistakes when they're grieving, and we've accepted the punishment that was given as fair and just considering the circumstances."

Maggie nodded as Eric finished speaking, and then she turned to Eartha.

"Eartha, you've got some very generous and hardworking people taking care of you. What do you think of them?"

Eartha looked up at the Rogans, then back at Maggie.

"I love them," Eartha said.

After her declaration, every adult in the room teared up. Eric was the first to regain his voice.

"We love you too." Eric reached around his wife to embrace them both in a fierce hug.

Maggie wiped a tear from her own eye as the camera settled back into view of the entire group.

"Thank you both for sharing your story with us and welcome aboard, Eartha. In a time of loss and confusion, it's nice to know there is still plenty of love and kindness on this ship."

There was a cut in the angle, and she was speaking directly into the camera again.

"Well, everyone, you heard it here first. Pirate aliens, and a stowaway. Just another week on the *Hope*. This is Maggie Brooker signing off."

Dana sat back with a sigh. It was an excellent interview. Had they been back on Zelenia, Maggie would be looking at a journalism award. The piece would go a long way to smoothing over relations between the Rogans and the rest of the crew and Eartha with the rest of the passengers. Dana was impressed, which meant she owed Maggie one.

AFTER THE BROADCAST WAS SENT OUT, MAGGIE SHOWED UP IN her office. Maggie sat across from Dana, her hands clasped in her lap and her leg bouncing as if she were ready to bolt for the washroom. She wore the same brown dress with the large white dotted pattern she'd worn for the broadcast. Dana saw from the red rimming her eyes that she'd been crying. The make-up hid most of her distress well enough, but she'd seen Maggie up close too many times to miss the telltale signs of it.

Dana pushed the newest batch of reports aside and turned to face her.

"You reviewed my broadcast," Maggie said abruptly.

It wasn't a question, and Dana thought she heard the hint of annoyance in her voice. Maggie would, of course, be ruffled by the idea of having anyone seeing the broadcast ahead of time, but in this case it was necessary. Dana did, in general, like most of Maggie's broadcasts, but she wasn't about to admit to it now.

"I did, and I appreciated your spin on both stories. You kept to the relevant facts about what happened with the Fashin Teku. You've made my job a little bit easier in the sense that I don't have to explain why we're going after them. Eartha's introduction to the rest of the passengers and crew was also tastefully done."

Maggie lifted a shoulder. "I do have some diplomatic experience."

Dana thought it was an interesting word choice. It took some level of diplomacy to ease tensions between people, and there would certainly be tension on board now that Eartha was out in the open and they were hunting down pirates.

"I remember." She leaned back in her chair. "You got far more footage of the Fashin Teku's ship than I imagined."

"Anything to further our mission to find a new home." Maggie bit her lower lip, as if in that moment trying to determine if there was something more she could have done. "I had thought to get something more valuable, like details on how to incorporate their technology, but—"

"You got enough. So, tell me why you're really here. It's not to talk about your broadcast." Dana purposefully left out mentioning her red-rimmed eyes.

Maggie shifted in her chair again. "I'm here to discuss my future on the *Hope*."

Dana raised an eyebrow at her. "Oh?"

"Yes. I would like to discuss future planetary missions, and also a seat on the bridge."

Dana made a soft sound of surprise. "Whatever makes you think you belong on the bridge?"

"Other than my accurate reporting, I believe my diplomatic skills may be an asset."

"We already have diplomats on board," Dana countered, even though the thought of the chancellor made her purse her lips in annoyance. The last thing she needed was someone else on the bridge who didn't know protocol or procedure. The thought of it set her teeth on edge.

Maggie straightened up, pulling her shoulders back and lifting her chin. "Not the kind that can carry a hidden camera and adapt to whatever customs or language they use."

Dana noted her confidence but didn't share it. Maggie was referring to her skill with and acceptance by the Fashin Teku. They'd only taken to her so quickly because she understood their simple but important greeting. It hadn't stopped them from robbing them of everything they'd given and more. It also didn't address her near-to-complete break down after her visit to planet 2396. She'd been a mess after that, and Dana wasn't eager to have someone on the front lines who wasn't mentally and physically prepared to withstand such blows.

Dana shook her head. She already had the best of the best serving on the bridge, and she wouldn't diminish any of them to squeeze Maggie into a role she hadn't earned.

"I can't have you on the bridge. It isn't just an issue of safety, you have no training or knowledge of bridge protocol. Do you expect me to allow a passenger on the bridge when there are still capable officers who've actually attended the academy?"

"I'm willing to learn," Maggie insisted. "I've got the time, and I'm prepared to put in the work."

"Yes, but who has the time to teach you? The Commander is out of the question. I need him on the bridge."

Maggie seemed to ruffle at that idea. "It never crossed my mind to ask for him. I assumed I'd be learning from the best, and that would be you."

She was good. Dana remembered a phrase of her father's —this one knows how to butter you up while picking your pockets, looking for loose change. It was something from old Blue Earth, but it still rang true in her mind. Maggie was ambitious, but her flattery wouldn't work this time.

"My busy schedule doesn't allow me to teach you, either. You know exactly what we're up against, and at the moment, your services are neither needed nor desired."

Dana sat back in her chair. She'd been harsher than she'd intended and didn't want to lose the very fragile peace between them over something like this.

"Look, Maggie, what you do is stellar. I'm not just saying that. Everyone loves your broadcasts. What you're asking for is out of reach at the moment, but that doesn't mean it always will be. We're going to be on this ship for some time, and, eventually, you might get your wish. For now, I need you to keep doing what you're doing and reign in the ambition. You've got no one left to impress. Is that clear?"

Dana looked down in dismissal.

"No."

Dana's eyes slowly rose from her reports to stare up at the other woman. Maggie's leg was no longer bouncing up and down on its own. Her green eyes were clear, and her hands lay still in her lap.

"Wade is my boyfriend," she continued. "He's not my father, or my keeper. If he doesn't want me on the bridge, that shouldn't factor into your decision."

Dana's eyebrows drew together. She was sure she must be hearing things, because what Maggie was saying didn't make sense.

"I've always liked that you didn't back off of a story once

you got hold of it," Dana said, "but in this case, you've got your teeth in the wrong bone. As the Captain of this ship, it is my right to make decisions about my bridge crew. It has nothing to do with my first officer. His relationship with you is irrelevant, I thought I made that clear. However, in this case, I think you're confused. Commander Chance and I have not discussed you working on the bridge in any capacity."

"Fine. I just thought—" Maggie's arms came up around herself, and she looked away, as if offended. "He told me you'd say no. I thought maybe he was blocking me."

Her eyes were dangerously close to swimming in tears, and Dana wanted to back away from her desk, but there was only a wall behind her. "We haven't spoken yet today, but whatever issues you're having with him, they're yours, and don't serve any hidden agenda on my part. Are we done here?"

Maggie nodded, but it seemed like it was more to herself. "Yes. Of course. Thank you for seeing me."

Dana nodded back, not sure how else to respond. Something was going on between her and Wade. She'd have to talk to Wade if she wanted to keep their private business off the bridge. That meant she'd have to talk to him about it. Nothing made her more uncomfortable than conversations with him about Maggie, but in this case, it seemed unavoidable.

After Maggie left, Dana braced herself, then called Wade to her office. He stood at attention in front of her desk, and she waved him into a chair.

"At ease, Commander. Your girlfriend came in to see me."

He tensed. "I already know what she asked you. What I don't know is what you decided."

"I told her the truth. At this time, we have no need for passengers on the bridge in any capacity."

Wade let out the breath he'd been holding. "Thank the Merciful," he murmured.

"I'm asking this not as your Captain, but as your friend," she prefaced, meeting his eyes. "What's going on with you two?"

Wade sighed. "I wish I knew. I went by her quarters, and she's going on about sitting on the bridge so she can take notes and report on events and raving about being on the front lines regardless of the danger." Wade shrugged, then leaned forward, his elbows on her desk and his head in his hands. "I told her how I felt about her putting her life at risk. The next thing I know, she's throwing me out."

Dana sat back, her eyes searching his for any hint that he wasn't being completely honest. "She's an adult. You knew her job was to be the ship's official recorder of events. What did you think that she'd sit in her cabin letting you take the camera for her?"

He sat up, looking at the wall, avoiding her gaze.

"No," she breathed.

"Yes." He grimaced. "I mean... I said it, but I didn't mean it the way it sounds."

"What the sou were you thinking?"

Wade shook his head. Then he reached into a small pocket hidden in his uniform and pulled something shiny out of it, holding it in his palm.

A yellow-gold ring with three square-cut colorless gems in a low setting.

Dana's breath caught at the sight of it. She'd thought things were serious between them, but she'd assumed their engagement would be a verbal understanding. It was the more modern thing to do these days. The ring said it was much, much more.

She stood up and walked around the desk to see the ring up close. Set within the aged, worn metal, the brilliant prisms caught and reflected the light. "I haven't seen a real one of those in ages. Where did you find it?"

"I had it made, like in the old days," he said, holding the ring between his finger and thumb. "I wanted a physical symbol of our love, one diamond for every year we've been together."

Wade slumped in the chair, staring at the ring in his fingers for a moment longer before he slid it back into the invisible pocket near his chest.

"I'm afraid of losing my fiancé. Not to someone else, but to her job. She could die out there. It's my duty to lead the scouting missions, and if she's there, I'll be honest, I won't be thinking about protecting the ship. Instead, I'll be preoccupied with protecting her."

"Have you told her this?" Dana asked.

"I have. She's as stubborn as you ever were."

She huffed out a laugh and returned to her side of the desk. "Yeah, well, that's different. You weren't carrying a ring around with my name on it."

When she sat down and looked up again, he was staring at her in the oddest way.

"What is it?" she asked.

His concern had melted away. In its place was a disappointment she recognized, the betrayal and hurt still there in his penetrating gaze. She'd seen that look when they'd returned from the *Atlantis* and she'd pushed him away. Now she struggled to break eye contact. Nothing worked, not even when he spoke her name in the softest whisper.

"Dana," he said with another sad shake of his head, "what makes you think I didn't carry a ring for you?"

Horrified at the thought, her mouth opened and closed as she searched for something to say—anything to erase the last five minutes of their conversation, to go back to when things were uncomplicated. *What had she done?*

She thought back to the conversation they'd had when she'd told him she didn't want to see him anymore—couldn't see him anymore. Had he hinted at it back then? Was there something more in his face, in his voice, that spoke of the commitment he'd been ready to make that she'd been unable to see?

"But you didn't, did you?" she asked, hating the eagerness she heard in her own voice, more so because she didn't know the answer she wanted to hear—yes or no. Either one would break her in two. She treasured the friendship they'd managed to build again, and she didn't want that to change, not for anything.

But the thought that she'd shot him down before he'd even had the opportunity to ask...

Wade opened his mouth to answer, but Dana's communications link beeped, and he clamped it closed.

Something told her she'd never hear the answer now.

"Yes?"

The computer's masculine voice spoke the message:

"Incoming message to Captain Dana Pinet from Dr. Randall Jabar."

She nodded at Wade in dismissal. He stood up without a word and left her sitting there. She stared after him, even after the door had closed on his back, and knew she'd be replaying this conversation over in her mind again and again, wondering what he'd been going to say.

Dana shook her head to clear it, then hit receive on the message flashing on her monitor. It wasn't Dr. Jabar's face, but several screens filled with medical jargon before she reached the conclusion. She stared at it, not sure what it meant.

EARTHA SINGH MACLAREN - TEST RESULTS:
INCONCLUSIVE

CHAPTER 26

Dana went to see Dr. Jabar straight away to discuss Eartha's test results. After an hour-long conversation, she'd been left with more questions than she'd had going in.

Eartha had passed her physical and cognitive exams. She hadn't been worse for wear after spending her first two weeks onboard living in the ventilation system. However, there were some DNA markers that the doctor couldn't identify, ones that left them wondering more about her biological heritage.

As she listened, Dana thought of the mysterious message Michael had left his daughter. He'd mentioned something about her real family. Despite looking like the perfect blend of Michael Singh and Sarah MacLaren, it appeared they'd adopted her. If so, then who were her real parents, and where had they come from? Why did she look so much like them, but wasn't their child?

Dana stood outside the door to the Rogan's new cabin. It took less than a minute for Eric to answer her call.

"Captain," Eric said as he signaled the door to open, speaking loud enough for his voice to carry behind him.

Esme popped out of one of the private rooms and caught her eye. Dana watched her quickly enter the room and gather up two pieces of misplaced laundry, hiding them out of sight. Though they'd just moved, everything seemed to have found a place in the new cabin. Dana had done the right thing in getting them new rooms as quickly as possible. Eric and Eartha, no doubt, had arrived early enough to arrange things for Esme while she was still recovering in the med-bay.

"Captain, what a surprise," Esme said, coming to stand behind her husband.

"I'm not in uniform. It's Dana." She looked down to be sure, so tired that for a moment she had to make certain that changing her clothes hadn't only been in her mind. She saw the white running shoes and pea-green tracksuit she often used for workouts. "I wanted to come by to check on my newest passenger."

"Sure, come in, Cap—" Eric caught himself, but still seemed unable to relax enough to call her by her first name.

"Can I get you something to drink?" Esme asked.

"I'm fine. I was hoping to have a moment with Eartha."

Dana looked around the cabin. It was much larger than their old one—two bedrooms instead of one, divided by the sitting area, and a larger kitchenette and dining space. The sitting area had a large vidscreen on the wall between two port-facing windows. The dark blue sofa had two matching sofa chairs on either side, clustered around a low wooden coffee table.

Esme led Dana to the chairs, and they sat together while Eric went to get Eartha from her new bedroom.

She noticed small decorative touches throughout the area which incorporated their love of geometric art and free-standing clay sculptures. There were a few personal items scattered about that she assumed were Eartha's—an antique children's book on the side table alongside a framed digital image. It held a still of Eartha with her parents, sitting around a table, laughing at something off-camera with a pizza between them. There was a slight repeated movement, catching them settling in for the photo. It was heartwarming to see the Rogans had made such an effort to make Eartha feel at home.

Dana swallowed hard at the sight, thinking of her own family photos. Her mother had kept a similar one of their family on the mantel. She didn't like thinking about that mantel being obliterated to dust.

"Has she done something wrong?" Esme asked in a low whisper, brown eyes filled with worry. Though her skin had a glow that reached her cheeks, she looked much healthier. It was hard to believe she'd been in a coma for over a week. "We're doing our best to keep tabs on her, but she's curious about the ship, and it's hard to keep her cooped up in here after so much time in the vents."

"Not at all, I promise," Dana said, placing her right hand over her heart. They were protective of her already. It was good, but unnecessary at the moment, since Dana's intentions were benign.

Esme sat fidgeting over the state of their cabin. Her eyes kept going to the table filled with their dirty dishes from their evening meal. She was going to make an excellent mother.

"I trust she hasn't gotten into any trouble already," Eric said, returning from the bedroom alone.

"No, nothing like that. She's our newest passenger, and there's little to nothing of her on file. I'd like to talk to her if I could, make sure she's adjusting to life out here. Learn a little bit about her and where she came from, if she's up to it."

"I thought she was in her room, but it looks like she's gone out. You'll catch up to her in the Commons. She likes to hang out there with Mr. Jennison and Luke after she completes her homework."

She nodded. "I assume you've heard from Dr. Jabar about Eartha's test results."

Dana watched a worry line form on Eric's forehead. He glanced at his wife, then back to her. "Yes. However, inconclusive doesn't mean much to me."

"We're engineers," Esme added. "We don't care much about where she's from as much as where she's going."

Dana smiled lightly at that. "You've noted that she's a bit different."

"Yes," Eric said, finally taking a seat on the couch beside Esme. "She has these feelings about things. At first, we ignored them, but we've recently learned the importance of taking them seriously."

"See that you do. I don't know where her intuition comes from, only that it can be helpful to us if we run into any more trouble. It's probably best to keep that information about her to ourselves. It doesn't do any good to frighten her with what we don't know. Let's just be as supportive as we can until we find out what makes her so different."

Esme nodded, wringing her hands in her lap.

"Is there something wrong?" Dana asked.

"No, only..." Esme looked like she was going to be sick with nerves. "We're pregnant."

"What?" Dana stood up to hug her, and Esme almost broke out into tears. "Seriously?"

"We don't want to tell anyone just yet," Eric said, holding on to his wife with one hand and shaking Dana's with the other.

"I understand. You've had some trouble in the past, correct?"

"I've never reached full term, but we're thinking that maybe this time..." Esme's voice trailed off as she looked at Eartha's door.

"Don't worry," Dana assured her. "No matter what, we're here for you. I have faith that Dr. Jabar will do everything he can to help you through it."

"Thank you, Captain," Eric said, forgetting she was still out of uniform.

"I'd better go and see if I can catch up to Eartha. Just so you're aware, I'll be digging into her past a bit. Nothing formal. If you'd rather accompany me, I don't mind."

Eric looked at his wife and shook his head. "No, please talk to her. And if she says anything about us, will you tell us what we can do to improve?"

Dana saw the sincerity in their eyes. They so badly wanted to do right by Eartha. They would give her a warm and loving home, and that was more than any orphan could ask for.

She nodded and stood up to leave. "How are you both adjusting to being new parents?"

Esme's face flushed, and she looked down. Eric looked over at her. "It's a steep learning curve," he said rubbing Esme's back.

"Since I'm not a parent, I can't even imagine. You might

talk to someone about it. Mr. Jennison is an excellent choice. I believe he's a grandfather, and it seems he already knows Eartha." She shrugged. "But I'm sure there are plenty of parents around with advice on raising kids."

"We'll keep it in mind. Thank you, Captain," Esme said as her eyes went to the hand she held over her flat belly.

"I'd better go see if I can find your daughter," Dana said, and had the pleasure of watching both of their mouths grow into huge smiles.

Dana found Eartha where the Rogans said she'd be. Mr. Jennison and Luke Geyer sat across from each other, playing a complicated game of strategy, while Eartha sat beside them, looking on. Mr. Jennison sat with his brown arms crossed over his chest, waiting for Luke's next move, his eyes never leaving the boy or the boards, though his white eyebrows wiggled up and down whenever he was about to make a move. Luke's mousy brown hair almost reached his shoulders, even when tucked behind both ears. He stared with his nose near to touching the middle board as he squinted at the pieces, like they would tell him what to do next.

Luke's sketchbook sat on the table beside him. It seemed to Dana he was never without it. He'd been the young man at the Fashin Teku event who'd drawn detailed sketches of people after only moments of meeting them. Of course, afterward, he'd demanded payment for his work, which had been, at the time, a rude gesture. In hindsight, she wished he'd gotten his way.

Dana watched Mr. Jennison and Luke make several moves before she interrupted them. "Excuse me, gentlemen."

"Captain," Mr. Jennison said, addressing her, his face crinkling with a welcoming smile. He refused to use her first name, despite her telling him he could in their off-hours. He reminded her so much of Charlie that she had to suppress the sudden wave of loss, remembering the old security guard who'd been left to his fate back on Zelenia.

"Mr. Jennison," she said, respectfully using his last name. "I see you're teaching these two something about strategic battle."

"I'm doing my best, but the two of them are as thick as a pair of bricks."

Luke looked up at him with exasperation, and Eartha covered her mouth and giggled. It seemed he had a way with both adults and children.

"I thought I might borrow one of your charges and invite her for a bowl of ice cream."

Both Mr. Jennison and Luke looked from Eartha to Dana and back again.

"Me?" Eartha said, pointing to herself.

Dana smiled. "If you would do me the honor."

Eartha didn't hesitate before leaping up. "Sure. But I'm not supposed to eat anything after supper."

"Don't worry, I cleared it with your parents," she said, testing out the word and waiting to see if there was any reaction from her. There wasn't. It was good. Since they were a family now, they should get comfortable with using and hearing the titles as soon as possible. Dana then leaned in and whispered to the older man, "Mr. Jennison, if you get a chance, the Rogans might need some help with the fundamentals of child developmental psychology."

He nodded, his eyes twinkling with mischief. Dana winked at him and put a finger to her lips. She didn't want them to think she'd interfered. However, she'd learned she could count on Mr. Jennison for his discretion.

Dana chose a table near to the bar and away from the wall where Mr. Jennison and Luke had been sitting. She used her ration credits to buy one dish of double chocolate for herself, and a mix of both chocolate and vanilla for Eartha, per her request.

"So, how's it going being the new kid?" Dana asked.

Eartha lifted one shoulder, then let it drop, scooping up a large spoonful of ice cream. "It's okay."

Dana made a pleased sound in the back of her throat as she finished licking her spoon. "Things on the ship have been a little crazy lately."

Eartha nodded.

"I wanted to talk with you a bit about your parents, if you're up to it."

Eartha shrugged one shoulder again and Dana accepted it as a 'yes.' She didn't understand kids much, but she remembered being one. It was a similar tone to the one she'd used when her mother asked her if she liked something she couldn't get out of doing.

"Is Luke your boyfriend?"

Eartha's cheeks turned pink, and she dropped her spoon in her bowl, staring wide-eyed at Dana.

"I only ask because he keeps looking over here at you. It's a sure sign he likes you."

Eartha turned her head to look across the room and caught Luke's eye. They were both quick to look away.

Dana grinned at their exchange. "It's okay. He can't hear us, and I won't tell anyone."

Eartha stared at her with what looked like a mix of frustration and apprehension. "I thought you wanted to ask me about my parents," she said, a little bite in her tone.

"True. I was wondering how old you were when you were adopted."

"I just turned thirteen."

"No, I mean the first time you were adopted," Dana said, keeping her tone neutral.

Eartha's eyebrows drew together in anger. "I wasn't adopted."

"Your father's message seems to indicate otherwise."

Eartha's eyes widened, and she abandoned her bowl of ice cream. "You saw my message?"

"Many times. It was before we knew you were onboard. As Captain, I need to be familiar with everyone on the ship. When we received your message, we didn't know who it belonged to, and I'd been trying to figure it out until I met you in the med-bay. I wasn't sure how or why we'd received it."

Again, Eartha looked down at her abandoned ice cream and shrugged. This was going about as well as treading through mud in high heels.

"Any idea why he would mention your 'real' parents?" Dana pressed.

After another moment of silence, Eartha spoke.

"I don't understand why he said all that. It doesn't make any sense."

"Isn't it possible? It's not like you'd remember it."

"No, but I've seen the video of my mother in the hospital holding me after I was born. I saw the stills of her when she was pregnant with me. How could I be adopted if I was born in the hospital?"

Her question was a valid one, and yet the way she spoke made Dana feel as if she were saying it to convince herself, too.

"That is a mystery."

It seemed she wouldn't get any answers tonight, and Eartha had started to withdrawal into her thoughts. Dana switched tracks again.

"Since I know a secret about you, I'll tell you a secret about me—to make it fair."

Eartha dragged her eyes up from her bowl of ice cream, focusing intently on Dana's face. Dana figured she would have to make this good to be convincing. She glanced over at Luke and saw his eyes had found their way back to their table. There was one secret that might do the trick.

"No one else knows this, so you'll have to promise to keep it a secret."

Eartha nodded, but it wasn't enough. Dana wanted to be sure the girl understood she was a friend and an ally. She reached out her pinky, as the girl in the message had done, and watched Eartha's eyes light up in understanding. She reached out and took Dana's pinky with her own, her mouth gaping open in surprise.

"Okay, there's this guy I used to like," Dana said lowly. "He's on the ship, and we're not together anymore. He loves someone else, and that's okay, because now we're just friends. But to be honest, sometimes I miss him."

Dana brought a spoonful of ice cream close to her mouth and wondered if that was a little too adult of her to share.

"You mean Commander Chance," Eartha said, and took a bite of her ice cream.

She shifted her eyes to Dana's face. The ice cream hit her

throat in that instant and Dana choked. Eartha had made that connection a little too fast. She must have looked surprised, because Eartha continued.

"It's okay. Everyone knows about you and Commander Chance."

"Really?" *Here's to having no real secrets on this ship.*

"Not about you missing him, but about you both being together once."

The blood rushed to her face, and Dana was grateful for her sienna skin. "How did you come by that information?"

"People like to talk when they think no one's listening."

"I see," Dana said, and meant it. The *Hope* wasn't a big ship, and gossip was inevitable when people were prone to boredom.

"You still like him, but you're not sure if he likes you," Eartha said.

"No, it's not like that. We're just friends. Besides," Dana leaned forward in her seat to whisper over the table, "between you and me, he's getting married to someone else."

"Ms. Brooker?" Eartha made a face, and then she looked out into the stars, as if thinking. Then she shook her head. "No, I don't think he's going to marry her."

"What?"

"They're probably not going to get married."

The hairs on Dana's arms rose, and she put her ice cream bowl down on the table. At first, she wondered if the girl was just trying to be sympathetic, but she seemed certain. There was no hint of humor on her face as she continued to eat her ice cream. Dana crossed her arms to warm them against the sudden chill that had seeped into her. *What had the doctor said about Eartha?* She showed some unusual markers. The DNA tests were 'inconclusive,' whatever that meant.

"Why would you say that?" Dana asked.

Eartha glanced up at Dana and smiled giving her a one shoulder shrug. "Sometimes I get feelings."

"Feelings?"

"It's like..." Eartha struggled for a moment. "...like an antenna. When something's wrong or off, it tells me."

Dana didn't understand at first. She asked her next question anyway. "What does it feel like?"

"It's not always the same. Sometimes, if it's something or someone close, it hurts in my stomach. Sometimes it's a sound in my ears, like an alarm. It doesn't happen all the time."

"Like when we went to the surface of that planet, you had a bad feeling about it before we touched down?"

Eartha shook her head. "That was different." Eartha shivered as if too cold. "I told Ari about it, but he said he still had to go because he was under your orders."

Eartha's anger was obvious in the glare she leveled at her. She would have blamed Dana if the ARI hadn't returned. *Thankfully, it had.*

"Right, Ari," Dana said. "You have the same feeling about the Commander and Ms. Brooker."

Eartha scrunched up her face. "No, I just don't think they'll get married," Eartha said with a shrug, looking uncomfortable with the subject. If Dana was being honest, she wasn't so comfortable with it herself.

She picked up her ice cream and took her final two bites. "Well, I'm out of ice cream. How about you?"

Eartha picked up her final scoop and with a grin and finished hers, too.

"Let's get you back to your game." Dana stood up. "I'm glad we talked. Now that we've shared some secrets, we're friends. If you have any trouble onboard, I want you to come and talk to me."

"Thanks," Eartha said as she stood. Then she lowered her voice to a whisper. "He still likes you."

Dana didn't have to wonder if she was speaking about Wade. "What makes you say that?"

"You said if a guy keeps looking over at you, it's a sure sign he likes you." Eartha leaned closer to the captain and whispered, "He's looking at you right now."

The hairs on Dana's arms stayed erect as she lifted her eyes and caught Wade's. He was sitting at the bar alone. The minute she made eye contact, he acknowledged her with a nod, but unlike Luke, he didn't hurry to look away. Wade brought his drink to his lips, keeping his eyes on her. *How long had he been sitting there, watching her?*

Dana turned back to Eartha and pasted on a smile. "Anyway, it was nice catching up with you. Can we do it again sometime?"

"Sure."

Eartha walked off, returning to her game before Dana could ask her anything more. She stared after her, wondering what she'd meant. By the time she turned back to Wade, he was gone.

CHAPTER 27

Dana took a brisk walk around the upper deck to work off some of the chocolate ice cream she'd had before she returned to her quarters. She planned to spend the rest of her off-hours soaking in a hot bath. Dana plopped down on the edge of her bed to slip off her shoes. She saw the message-waiting light on her tablet and began scrolling through the messages. There wasn't anything that required a response before tomorrow. She put the messages on audio-only mode and cranked it loud enough to hear while she started the bathwater.

The first message was from Esme; her soft voice filled the room. "Captain, thank you so much for taking time out with Eartha. We appreciate you taking an interest in her. Let us know how it went this evening and if there's anything we should be looking out for."

A second message marked 'urgent' came in while she was still reading. She groaned at the sound of it.

"Barely off duty, and there's already something. What could it be this time?"

Dana listened to the first part of the message before she turned off the water and raced back into the bedroom. She picked up the tablet and turned off the audio, so she could read the message with her own eyes.

TO: *Captain Dana Pinet; Commander Wade Chance*
   FROM: *ARI THREE*
   MESSAGE: *While running a continuous scan through the vid messages sent from Zelenia to passengers and crew of the Starship Hope, I was able to find and flag five messages as extremely suspicious with highly probable Coalition coding, references, or correlations. The questionable messages containing coded messages from the CAH were sent to the following:*
   Ensign Brian Shu
   Doug Applebaum
   Kate Wallace
   Luke Geyer
   Commander Peter Barnes
   Recommended course of action: immediate arrest and confinement for the safety of the crew, passengers, and ship.

Dana double-checked the timestamp. *Less than thirty minutes ago.* Why hadn't the ARI just told her about what it had found while she was in the commons? Then she remembered Wade had been in the Commons speaking with the ARI. He may have

"Computer, put me through to the bridge."

She'd have to deal with the night-shift as everyone else would be off duty.

"Yes, Captain."

"Have a security team meet me outside of Lieutenant Commander Barnes' quarters immediately," Dana ordered.

"Uh, yes, Captain. Right away," Ensign Gregory stammered.

She didn't bother with her uniform, jumping back into her runners, retrieving her sidearm, and dashing out the door, heading for Barnes' quarters. According to the report, the ARI had delivered the information to Wade. She'd also have to ask him why when he'd received the report, he hadn't come to her directly. *What was he thinking?*

Lieutenant Valente and three other security guards were there standing at the ready when she arrived. There was a light sheen of sweat on his bald head, the only indication he might be nervous about what they'd find inside.

"Captain?" he asked.

"We have a list of four suspected CAH operatives," she prefaced. "Barnes made the list. I know what he means to you as your superior officer, but I'm asking you to set it aside until we can confirm or disprove his involvement with the group. That goes for the other four members on the list as well."

She waited for each of the three members of his team to nod in agreement.

"Valente, release the security locks." She took a step aside away from the panel, so he could open the door.

"Computer, security override, Valente: Echo Bravo four-nine-two Green."

The COMP system chirped an alert before the male voice responded, *"Security code not accepted."*

Valente frowned in confusion. "I'm sorry... I'm not quite sure why it's not giving me access."

"Barnes must have restricted your access, but he can't

keep me out. Step aside, Lieutenant." Dana took his place. "Command code authorization: Pinet Alpha six-seven-four-two-eight." The doors released, and she entered, weapon raised.

Inside, she saw Peter Barnes and Wade in a stand-off, each of them pointing their own weapon at the other. She moved to take her place beside Wade.

"That's quite enough, Barnes," Dana warned. "You'll have to answer for your involvement with the Coalition, but for now lower your weapon, or I promise you I will have no trouble putting you down."

Dana wanted him to test her. She had every reason to hate him right now, and she was sure that Wade would have done it himself if she hadn't barged in.

What was worse, giving him a trial, or throwing him out the airlock? At that moment, she couldn't decide, and that meant she had to take him into custody. He'd wait out the results of their investigation in the brig, along with the others on the list.

She lowered her weapon, but she saw Wade stiffen, his arm remaining outstretched as if he couldn't control himself.

"Commander Chance, stand down!"

When he didn't budge, she moved in closer.

"He's not worth the weapon's fire."

Wade spoke through his clenched teeth in anger. "He almost killed us all."

Dana lifted her hand, slowly putting it in Wade's sightline before tapping his breast pocket, the one where he'd placed the ring. "You have more than most have on board. We'll take care of him."

Dana signaled the security officers in with a nod. Two

members of the security team held Peter while a third put durometal wrist restraints on him—unbreakable by human hands.

She reached up and put a hand on Wade's shoulder. His body was stiff with rage, and his hand clutched the weapon like a lifeline. In one smooth motion, she relieved him of the Shock-Glock. She put it aside on the side table and checked the readout. It was at the highest setting. At close range, he could have crippled Barnes if not worse.

Peter snickered, glaring at Wade. "You have no idea who she is. I've seen her vid. She's not telling you the truth because she doesn't think you're man enough to handle it."

Whatever he meant by that, she didn't know but the show had gone on long enough.

"Take him to the brig," Dana called out over her shoulder. "Detain everyone on the list I gave you. I'll deal with them in the morning."

Valente and his men rushed out with Barnes between them. Wade stood like a statue, staring at the place where Peter had been. He looked down where his weapon sat on the side table. "I was ready to do it... If you hadn't arrived..."

"You're a good person," she told him. "You would have been meting out justice, but I want to make sure there's nothing more we can get from any of them before we go to that extreme. He may have been working with the Fashin Teku as well."

"Yeah, I thought that, too," he said as he let her guide him out of the room.

"Tell me exactly what happened."

Wade rolled his shoulders as he sucked in a breath. His eyes were still on the wall as he spoke.

"After the messages were corrupted, I didn't think there was any way we'd be able to find the incriminating messages. The ARI had downloaded an uncorrupted file for Eartha when she was still in hiding. It flagged four messages other than Shu's. He approached me in the Commons and showed me the list of names. At first, I couldn't believe it. I mean– Barnes was my friend."

"I know, but why didn't you tell me the moment you found out? We were both in the Commons. We could have come here together."

Dana glanced around the cabin. There was nothing to indicate Barnes did anything more than sleep there. He had no personal effects on any surfaces and the walls were bare. She ignored the closed bedroom door. She imagined the walls decorated with the faces of her crew as it had been in Kristoff's home after he'd blown himself up with the Breezy Blue. It wasn't something she could face. She'd leave it for Valente to handle.

"I needed to see for myself. I wanted him to look me in the eye and at least try to deny it. He didn't."

"So, you left it to the ARI to send me a message that I wouldn't get for thirty minutes." She let the doubt into her voice. It didn't make sense. He was her second in command. He should have followed protocol and the ARI should have informed her immediately.

"No, I instructed the ARI to deliver the message to your tablet instead of interrupting you."

"Why?"

Wade turned looking her in the eye at last. Then his eyes shifted to the left before landing back on hers. She braced herself for a lie.

"I didn't want you here when I confronted him." Wade squared his shoulders. "I knew what I was doing, and I had every intention of seeing it through."

Not a full lie, but only half the truth. Dana could understand the need to lash out in revenge, but Wade hadn't been personally affected by Barnes' actions. Maybe there was something she didn't know. Before she could ask, he spoke up.

"He was our chief of security. Every command, every structure in place designed to keep out the terrorists he thwarted. He had the position and the clearance to actively sabotage our entire defense against them, and I was his commander."

"And I'm yours. How do you think I feel?" Dana reached out a hand and this time he relaxed into her touch. "When the time comes, justice will be brought. But for now, I want you to get some rest."

Wade nodded distractedly. "You're right, thanks." They reached the door to his quarters a few minutes later. When Dana tried to let him go, he held on, forcing her to look up at him.

"Thank you. You were right. I have someone else to take care of now. I'll propose to Maggie as soon as she forgives me for being an idiot."

There was a hard *thunk* in her chest, but Dana kept her face expressionless.

"Congratulations." The word came out woodenly, for fear she'd give away her disappointment.

"I don't care what Barnes said. I'm not suspicious of her anymore."

"I'm truly happy for you." Again, the words came out perfunctorily.

Wade nodded as his cheeks grew red with embarrassment. "You know, at first, I was hoping you wouldn't be."

"Why wouldn't you want me to be happy for you?" Dana asked, wondering what he meant by it.

"I don't know. I figured if you had stronger feelings for me back then, you'd be a little upset by it. Maybe I was still holding a little bit of a flame for you." His eyes fell to the floor. "I'm glad I didn't make a fool of myself."

Dana took in a deep breath to steady herself so she could continue to keep her feelings in check as the next words tumbled out. "You're assuming I didn't have strong feelings for you back then."

She hadn't meant to say that much, and she was grateful that he kept his eyes on the floor for once.

Wade gave her a light shrug.

"If things were reversed, and I was getting engaged, would it upset you?" Dana asked. She didn't know what she wanted his answer to be until he spoke.

"I don't think so. We've both moved on. I still want the best for you, but I don't think it's me anymore."

Dana choked on the words but forced them out. "We're friends again, and that means a lot to me. Besides, Maggie's a strong woman who knows her own mind. I think she's right for you." Dana lifted a hand to pat his arm before letting it drop back down to her side, too heavy for the effort.

"Thank you," Wade said. "That means a lot to me, too. Despite what we've been through, I have no regrets."

Dana clamped her mouth closed rather than lie.

"Goodnight," he told her, turning away with a smile on his face.

She was glad he'd turned away before he could see the tears fall down her cheeks. She wiped them away with the back of her tracksuit sleeve and hurried to her quarters.

CHAPTER 28

ESME

Esme thought things at home had improved. It seemed being in a coma had helped. Eric had taken on more of her duties and kept their family fed despite living on rations. He must have been working hard to earn so many extra credits. She'd promised to bake him something special for their anniversary. It was coming up, and they'd earned some time alone. Mr. Jennison had volunteered to look after Eartha while they had an evening in the virtual suite. He'd become a staple at their place, and with the captain's blessing, had helped them into their new home. She loved the space—not so much the cleaning, but the privacy it afforded them.

Since her return, Eartha hadn't spoken of being watched or had any nightmares, either. Her behavior in all things had been impeccable. For example, when they'd finished dinner, Esme asked her to clear away the dishes they'd used.

"Yes, ma'am," Eartha said. She'd jumped up to see to the task while Esme eyed her with suspicion. The girl was up to something, but she wasn't sure what it was.

When she'd finished with their dishes, the three of them curled up on the couch to watch a classic vid. By the end of the movie, Eartha had grabbed her grandmother's quilt and slid down to the floor in front of them for a better view. Esme lay against Eric's chest with a blanket wrapped loosely around them.

A wave of contentment swept over her like never before. She reached down and touched her flat belly. Eric's hand found hers under the blanket and he rested it on top. When the movie was over, Eartha stood up. She stood taller than when she'd first come to stay with them.

"I'm going to bed. Esme can tuck me in if she wants to," Eartha said. She shrugged as if she didn't really care, but Esme had learned to read her subtle hints. The girl seemed to crave being a part of both their lives and their daily routines.

Esme gave Eric a look when Eartha was out of hearing.

"What's she after tonight?"

"I have no idea, I swear," Eric said, holding up a hand.

"She's been like this for days—doing all her chores, cleaning up after herself."

"You'll have to tell me after she speaks to you," Eric said, giving her a gentle nudge off the couch.

"It might be about a boy," she said, goading him.

Eric sat up, suddenly wide awake. "A boy? *What* boy?"

"I don't know, but I intend to find out." Esme leaned down and planted a teasing kiss over her husband's furrowed brow.

As she walked over to Eartha's room on the opposite end from theirs, she tried to imagine what she might want to discuss. Eartha was developing into a young woman, maturing, and she needed a woman's guidance. Esme only hoped she might be that woman for her.

That was probably it. She wanted to have some 'girl talk.' Eartha must be worried about her friend, Luke Geyer. The cute older boy who shadowed Mr. Jennison all the time turned out to be a member of the Coalition. He'd been arrested along with three others including, Barnes.

Esme plopped down on the edge of Eartha's bed. "How are you feeling since they arrested your friend?"

Esme glanced up at the sketches that Luke had made of her and Mr. Jennison still hanging on the walls above her bed. Beside them were two of her school project schematics. Luke's portrait of Eartha was exceptional. It had made Esme suspicious of the boy. Eartha was only thirteen. Now that he was likely to be convicted of colluding with the CAH she wasn't too worried. He and Eartha were separated indefinitely, and it was probably for the best.

"It's fine. I know he didn't do anything."

Eartha didn't meet her eye, and Esme wondered if there was something more there. The last thing she wanted to do was make the boy more appealing by declaring him off-limits. Instead she chose a safer path.

"Is everything else all right?"

"Yeah." Eartha sat quietly for a long moment, then took a breath. "I want to ask you something."

Esme lay back against the bed's headboard, one hand in Eartha's hair. She loved playing with the tight curls, and had been speaking to the ship's hairdresser about different braiding styles she could try. "Whatever it is, you can tell me. What's bothering you?"

Eartha turned toward her and reached out, splaying her fingers across her belly.

"When the baby comes, is it all right for me to call you and Eric mother and father?"

Esme raised a hand to her belly, covering Eartha's hand with her own. It seemed warmer than before. She fought the urge to pull away. Esme's throat was dry, and she was sure it still hung open, though, for the life of her, she couldn't remember how to close it. When she didn't answer, Eartha continued.

"It'll be less confusing for the baby."

Esme found her tongue at last, but her brain was still slow to respond. "Who told you I'm pregnant?"

Eartha shook her head. "Nobody. Will it bother you if I call you mother?"

Esme gulped down the emotion in her throat and smiled.

"It doesn't bother me at all. I'm sure Eric will be fine with it, too."

Eartha's hand finally let go, and Esme felt like she could breathe again.

"He's going to be amazing," Eartha said. "I can't wait to meet him and be friends."

The girl threw her head back into the pillow and looked up at her. Esme was trembling. There was no way the girl could know the sex of their child before the doctors.

Or could she? Hadn't the Captain believed them when she'd learned about Eartha's gut feelings? The doctor had confirmed her genetic markers differed from any other human on board.

What was she, that she could see so much so soon?

Esme slid out of the bed and leaned over, placing a light kiss on Eartha's forehead. She reached over and turned out the light. She made it to the door before Eartha spoke from the dark.

"Good night, Mother."

In the softest whisper, Esme answered, "Good night, Daughter."

Esme returned to her room, still wondering about the exchange with Eartha. Eric lay sprawled across the bed, as usual, and she had to climb under his heavy arm and leg to get under the covers on her side. Eric mumbled in his sleep as he snuggled closer.

"Honey?" Esme asked. She repeated herself twice before he answered.

"Yeah?" he yawned, snuggling up behind her with his mouth close to her ear.

"Didn't we promise each other we wouldn't tell anyone about the baby? I have my own expectations to worry about, I don't want to have to deal with everyone else's."

"Yep."

"Did you tell Eartha?"

"No."

"What?" She half-turned toward him to see his face. She couldn't make out his features, a mere silhouette in the dark.

He yawned again. "I didn't tell her."

Esme reached for the light and, with a tap, it was on at half full. Eric groaned, turning away from the light, snuggling his pillow instead of her.

"Then who told her?"

"What?" he muttered groggily.

"She knows about the baby."

"How could she know about the baby?"

"That's what I'm trying to figure out," Esme pressed insistently.

"Well, it wasn't me."

"I can't imagine Dr. Jabar or the captain breaking a confidence on purpose." Esme worried her lip in thought. "One of them might have said something about it in front of Eartha by accident. She might have heard something while she was there."

"Esme."

"I don't have a clue where she heard it, but you should ask her about it tomorrow. No, maybe I should talk to her about it." Esme rambled on. "She might be guessing. But she's thirteen, how could she guess at something like that?"

"Esme." His voice was insistent this time, snapping her out of her monologue.

"Yeah?"

"Turn off the light and go to sleep."

CHAPTER 29

Dana used the auto-dispenser to prepare a cup of her favorite sweetened hot tea in one of her four white mugs and turned on the ship's evening broadcast. She settled in with the plaid throw from her old couch over her knees and the latest vid report from Maggie Brooker.

"Well, have we got news or what? Welcome to *Maggie's Minutes*. I'm Maggie Brooker, bringing you the latest onboard news from around the ship."

The vid was a close-up of Maggie, her red hair falling in waves around the shoulders of a crimson dress. She wore a bright red lip tint to match the ruffles that filled the bottom of the frame.

"First off, the time has come for the Coalition trials to begin. Our hearts and minds are on the seven members of the Committee of Justice. Tomorrow begins the first round of closed testimony from the accused. I sat down with the family of the youngest apprehended, a minor by the name of Luke Geyer. He is the eldest son of Oliver and Kate Geyer, and I spoke with them about how they felt about their son's imprisonment."

The screen faded into a cozy scene from inside Maggie's quarters. She sat on a single soft gray armchair while the Geyers sat beside her on a blue couch. Two glasses of water sat untouched on the table in front of them.

Maggie wore a muted brown dress with ruffled edges that came to the top of her crossed knees. It was one of Maggie's more serious outfits. She even had her hair pulled tightly back in a schoolteacher's bun. Somehow, she switched between two cameras, one over her shoulder, the other one a wide shot. The one over her shoulder zoomed in on both parents.

"He's just a child. He's a good boy who got in with bad friends. Who hasn't?" Kate asked, her voice rising to shrill. "He shouldn't be in jail with the rest of the criminals. This is overkill."

Oliver cut her off from saying more. "He's a genius. It's not his fault he saw holes in the government's cover-up. Let's not forget this was a cover-up from the start. His reasons for joining the Coalition are not surprising considering his level of intelligence and his search for truth."

Maggie sat forward. "The Coalition was intent on ending the very mission that saved his life. Shouldn't he pay the ultimate price for that?"

Kate's hand flew to her mouth as she let out an anguished sob.

Sou she's good! Dana thought.

Oliver put an arm around his wife, pulling her into him before he spoke. "He's a genius. The only student to get a perfect score on the Academics exam. That's what got him and his family off of Zelenia. Luke hasn't lifted a finger against his people since our departure."

"So you believe he can be reformed?" Maggie asked.

"Luke's been a productive member of our new society here. We believe he'll continue to be the kind and caring big brother he's always been. He saved his family here, as well as those to come."

Oliver placed a protective hand over his wife's belly. Her hands covered his, and they both looked up at Maggie.

Dana spit out her tea and slammed the cup down on the table.

"She's pregnant?" Dana asked out loud, despite herself.

"You're pregnant?" Maggie asked, her voice the perfect echo of Dana's.

They both nodded, unable to speak beyond the emotion. Maggie let the moment drag out in silence.

Oliver eventually cleared his throat. "We want nothing more than for Luke to meet our new child. Make no mistake, this mission to find a new home is dangerous. There isn't a day that goes by we don't think we might lose one of them along the way, but not like this."

"Not like this," his wife echoed softly. Then she put a knuckle between her teeth to keep herself from sobbing.

Maggie cut the scene at that point and the next shot was of her alone. Dana sat back in her seat; glad she'd insisted that the seven new Justice Committee members cease watching Maggie's broadcasts. They could always count on her biased reporting to sway public opinion. Look at what she'd done for Eartha, who was now just another kid on the ship. People hadn't spoken about her being a stowaway in the last two weeks.

"What will become of them and the other families of the accused Coalition members? It's in the hands of our Justice Committee, may the Merciful be with them."

Maggie shrugged and gave a long-suffering sigh. She turned toward the wide-angle camera as it zoomed in on her face.

"That's breaking news folks. We've got another passenger on the way. That makes seven in all. If you haven't congratulated the new moms-to-be, don't worry, you'll get your chance. There will be a welcome aboard party for all of our new arrivals. That's not the only party in our future."

The vid zoomed out from her face getting the red ruffles of the dress at her knees. Maggie was a polished professional, eyes never wavering as she looked into the camera lens with her hands out in front of her.

"We'll be live with the verdicts, and other ship's news as it happens so be sure to watch. Don't forget to join me for the new morning special edition, as we take a stroll through history in our *Blast From The Past* segment with one of our favorite storytellers, dear Mr. Franklin Jennison. I'm Maggie Brooker, and this has been *Maggie's Minutes*. See you next time."

CAPTAIN'S PERSONAL LOG: *4327.9.26*

I'm addicted to Maggie's gossip show, and my diplomatic skills need work. Wade and I have a great relationship, though I won't be caught dead in the gymnasium alone with him again. However, after Eartha's comment about them not getting married, I have to say I've been more interested in their relationship than I probably should be.

"Computer, delete the last sentence, then continue recording."

As a judge on the panel, I've already analyzed my own bias in the case. I expect the Committee and the other two judges to make up for my lack of impartiality. None of the judges will be issuing verdicts, which will shield them from most of our partialities. The three of us will have to confer and agree on sentencing in the end, and I couldn't think of two men more different to offer a balance. We will begin hearing testimony over the next few days. I'm optimistic that with investigations into the Coalition members complete, we can come to a satisfying resolution for all, and I won't have to deal with this ever again.

There's nothing worse than staring at a fifteen-year-old kid who thinks he's getting a death sentence.

CHAPTER 30

Doubt kills more dreams than failure ever will.

Dana's evening routine on a good day or a bad one didn't change much. After the evening broadcast, she changed into her workout clothes and hit the gym. Since the unfortunate incident with Wade, she'd been careful to avoid getting stuck alone in the gym with him during early morning workouts. He hadn't been upfront with Maggie about sparring with her, and though she missed it, she didn't want to be the cause of any strife between them.

Dana had switched to evenings shortly after, and though she found the floor and gym more active, no one bothered her here. Dana waved to Cliff and Nancy, who were on the climbing wall, and made her way to the virtual runner, putting on the visor before starting the machine. The platform allowed her to walk or run in place while simulating the virtual terrain she saw through the visor. Halfway through running a desert landscape, she came to an oasis, and she slowed down to begin her cool down.

Another avatar appeared on the scene, and though she didn't recognize the face, the voice was unmistakable.

"Good evening, Captain. May I join you?"

Maggie had chosen a female avatar with bright-green feline-like eyes, but that was where the similarities ended. The image wore a sharp, black bob that bounced and twirled when she moved, so different from the long, wavy red hair that was a part of Maggie's signature look. If she hadn't spoken, Dana might not have recognized her. The fitted sports bra and short shorts in hot pink, however, looked like something straight out of her wardrobe.

Dana didn't stop to answer the question. She didn't need to, as Maggie continued speaking as if she had.

"I'm so glad I ran into you. I couldn't wait to talk to you about something."

Dana's heart rate increased despite her cool down.

"Whatever made you come to this location?" Maggie said, her avatar looking around them. "The desert is so dry and hot. I know we're not really here, but I'm sweating to death already."

Dana smiled to herself. It was precisely why she favored the beaches and deserts. Space was cold. The warmth of the program helped.

But now Maggie was working up to something she was sure she wouldn't like. When had the woman ever sought her out and not complicated her life?

"Wade and I are neck-deep in wedding plans, and we need to address some finer details. He's expressed interest in having a more traditional wedding."

Dana listened, making a non-committal sound in her throat as she bent over her toes. So, he'd done it. He'd asked Maggie to marry him after all. That must mean Maggie had forgiven him for not taking her advancement plans onboard seriously.

Strange he hadn't told her himself. Dana lifted her visor to glance over at Maggie, and noticed she wasn't wearing the ring. That was curious. She might have put it aside for her work out, but it was unlikely she'd continue to do that for the rest of her life. Rings were an old tradition, but one that both partners usually decided on early. Dana knew about the ring, but she couldn't exactly ask about it without revealing the fact that Wade had shown it to her first.

Maggie rambled on about choosing wedding colors while Dana eyed the exit. It looked like Cliff and Nancy were finishing up their climb and might be leaving soon. She could make up an excuse and follow them out if she hurried. Dana reached for her towel, intending to leave Maggie there, when the woman ripped off her visor and stopped the program.

Maggie put down the visor and climbed down from the machine with no more than a sheen of sweat on her skin and started stretching as if she'd run a marathon. She was limber, and didn't mind showing off her flexibility.

Dana cleared her throat and turned to leave when Maggie spoke up.

"You do this every day?" Maggie asked.

Dana watched Cliff and Nancy wave as they left, along with her excuse.

"Yeah."

Dana reached for her water and took a long drink. She

needed to work on limbering up. Her muscles were strong, but always too tight, always a little too cold. She noted that most of the gym had cleared out and there were only two other passengers left huddled in the corner, looking steeped in gossip, each hanging on to the other's words.

"Now I know how you keep up your amazing figure," Maggie said.

Dana rolled her eyes. Maggie refused to end the already dead conversation. She was after something and Dana didn't have all day to figure out what it was.

"What do you want?" Dana asked, eyeing her with suspicion.

Maggie tipped her head. "Can't a couple of girls just talk?"

"Sure they can, so spill it. What are we talking about?"

"Give me a minute, I just need to..."

Maggie pulled her feet together toward her body and leaned over them with a groan. Her flexibility was ridiculous. Dana looked on with envy as she completed a full split stretch.

"I have a formal request to make of you."

Dana had a sudden desire to inch away from her, but Maggie's intense gaze held her fixed. If Maggie wanted on the bridge, she'd have to go through some extensive training, and she was putting her foot down about that, no matter what she'd come to say.

"Wade and I are not Believers, as you know, so there are only a few options for marriage ceremonies. As our captain, you're the only one who can give us the traditional military marriage we were hoping for. We'd be honored if you would perform the ceremony."

Something in between Dana's ears popped.

What did she just say?

When she didn't say anything, Maggie fidgeted in place, then rushed to fill the silence.

"You can say 'no'. I mean, I don't expect you to say 'yes'. The Chancellor or the President can officiate the wedding, but... we want you. Would you be willing to do it?"

"Are you serious?"

Dana hadn't meant to blurt out the words, but there they were. Like a comedy sketch, Maggie nodded, a grin spreading across her face.

"Wade said he wanted *me* to officiate his wedding?"

"Yes." Maggie shrugged. "He said I could have whoever I wanted."

Dana's insides groaned, and she wished she'd left the gym the moment Maggie had shown up. How was she supposed to attend the event, let alone officiate it? She wasn't even sure she should.

What had Eartha said? 'No, he won't marry her.'

Dana wasn't sure why, but she thought Eartha might be right. However, that didn't help her immediate problem of getting out of officiating their wedding.

"I don't know," Dana hedged. She didn't like the idea of agreeing without Wade being there.

"I know the two of you have a history, but we're all friends now, right? It's the kind of thing that friends do for each other. I know you would stand up for him, anyway, so why not just marry us?"

Dana stared back at Maggie in wonder. There was a vast difference between standing up for someone and marrying them, and she knew it.

"I'll... I need some time to think about it."

Maggie's head tilted to one side, and then she nodded.

"Good, because it will look so much better for all of us if you perform the ceremony."

There was a finality to her words that Dana didn't quite understand. "What do you mean?"

Maggie lifted one shoulder again, as if she hadn't just implied something. "I just meant that seeing the three of us standing up for each other will put an end to any rumors about the two of you getting back together."

Dana's surprise must have been on her face, because Maggie laughed.

"You can't be serious?" she asked, green eyes flashing. "You haven't heard the talk on the ship that the two of you are having an illicit affair behind my back?"

"What?" Dana hadn't heard any such rumors, but the idea that they were out there made her feel like she was still running in the desert. "We are not having an—we are not." Dana couldn't even say the word.

Maggie waved it away with one manicured hand and grinned at her. "Of course you aren't. That's not the point. The fact that people on board think so is the problem. I've done all I can to make it clear that we're happy, but I don't like idle gossip."

Dana raised an eyebrow. She knew half the reporters out there were the biggest gossips she'd ever met.

"I report real news, not gossip," Maggie said when she caught Dana's skeptical look. "There's an enormous difference. It's important to us that we have not only your support, but your seal of approval."

Dana swallowed the lump in her throat. She didn't know what to say, so she did her best to stall. She'd have to talk to

Wade. Regardless of what Maggie thought, she wasn't convinced that he'd approve.

"We're saving the ring for the ceremony and everything," Maggie said with a pout as she looked down at her naked finger.

Time. That's what she needed. More time.

"I've never done it before, and I want some time to consider what's involved," Dana said firmly. "A lot is going on, as I'm sure you know."

"Of course. Take some time." Maggie smiled as she picked up her towel and water, following her out.

Guilt crept up, tightening Dana's chest. She should have just said no. It wasn't like she'd ever performed such a ceremony before. She replayed the conversation, looking for all the places she could have politely refused, then chastised herself for not doing it in the first place.

"Wade was right about you," Maggie called over her shoulder as they parted. "You're a good friend."

Dana's heart sank. A lump of regret formed in her throat. She and Wade had come a long way, but she wasn't sure they'd come that far.

CHAPTER 31

The Justice Committee gathered three days later to the anticipation of everyone on board. Dana's stomach was in knots. She hadn't slept well since learning the names of the four accused members of the CAH. Followed up with her conversation with Maggie a few nights ago, it had only gotten worse. She hadn't been back to the gym for fear of running into either of them. She didn't even know how to breach the subject with Wade, who hadn't mentioned it to her or even seem to be aware of the request.

Dana made her way to the conference room and checked to see if her hands were steady for the third time. *All good.* Before she'd left her quarters, she'd eyed the wooden box in the drawer where she kept her tin of nanodots. She'd decided once again she didn't need them—though it had been close, as she wasn't sure she could pass as someone with calm nerves after the nights she'd been having. She tried to channel the nervous buzzing into putting a gleam on her formal dress coat and buffing her black boots. By the time she made it out the door, she'd felt better.

Of course, half-way there, she'd almost turned back. Several crewmen passed her in the corridor saluting and giving her nods of encouragement. Everyone on the ship knew what she was about that morning and her chest tightened around her heart at the thought. She reached her empty office and, once inside, took a deep breath, quieting the dead voices of the past.

The conference room had been transformed to accommodate the hearings per her specifications. The large table that normally dominated the room had been removed. Three seats were given to the judges: herself, President Hector Muñoz, and Chancellor Jeremiah Evans. All dressed in their formals, they sat in a semi-circle around the curved side of a wooden table.

The remaining seven chairs were placed to the left of the judges in a row against the viewport side, facing the center of the room. The committee that would fill them was responsible for listening to the testimonies and deliberating in order to come to a consensus on the verdict for each individual. Once the vote was received from the committee of seven, it was up to the judges to pass the sentence.

Four women and three men made up the committee. Four were passengers, and three were crew members. They had done their best to choose a diversified group from the ship who could render a fair verdict.

The accused would be brought in one at a time, seated in front of the three judges during their questioning. They were each allowed a defender, though most represented themselves, and didn't require anyone to speak on their behalf while they answered questions from the judges. The proceedings were closed to all, including immediate family members.

Luke, the youngest in custody, would be permitted the presence of his father. At the end of the day, the seven Justice Committee members would be dismissed, and would return to hear any remaining testimony until all were heard. Only then would the Committee be allowed to deliberate. The day's proceedings would be recorded and the vids available for review by the Justice Committee and the judges during their private deliberations only.

Maggie Brooker had been more annoyed than the rest to be shut out, but it had been a unanimous decision that the testimonies were not made public. Dana had to think of the safety of her passengers and crew. Should any of them be given leniency or have their charges dropped, nothing they said during the hearings could be used against them.

The first person to testify on behalf of himself was Barnes. Dana and the other judges thought getting him out of the way early would move things along. He didn't request any representation. As the head of security, there was no one willing to stand up for him, not even Wade, who'd once claimed him as a friend early in their voyage.

His testimony was brief and to the point, and he answered all of the questions posed to him.

"Are you a member of the Coalition Against *Hope*?"

"Yes."

"Were you responsible for any of the bombings on board the ship?"

"No."

"Are you responsible for the death of Brian Shu and his security officer Lieutenant Adam Wesley?"

"Yes."

"You admit to planting an EMP on board and knocking

out several of the ship's necessary systems in order to cover up their deaths?"

"Yes."

Dana sat stone-faced, boiling on the inside. *How could they have been so fooled?* A man on her security team, vetted by the world government, had been working for the Coalition, right under her nose, for months. It took all she had to stomach his open court confession.

After his testimony had been concluded, she'd rushed to the adjacent bathroom and threw cold water on her face. She couldn't stop seeing Kristoff. He'd been there at the Breezy Blue the night he, along with the CAH, had blown up her friends. Had Barnes been among them, planning and plotting to keep her grounded? That had been their agenda, so why were they still active? Even knowing their ship carried the last survivors of Zelenia, and potentially the last humans in the universe, why would they continue to act under the orders of a group that was long dead?

She didn't want to believe the answers, but they'd been asked, and he'd answered.

"What is the Coalition's agenda now that Zelenia is destroyed?"

"I don't know."

"Are there any more members that haven't already been identified?"

"I don't know."

"Did you have anything to do with the Fashin Teku, or did you assist them in any way?"

"No."

After Dana had gathered herself, she'd joined the president and the chancellor back in the main room to adjourn the proceedings for the day. Muñoz had given her a sidelong look, but she'd ignored him. She probably looked shaken, but the last thing she wanted to do was talk about what the Coalition had already cost her. She couldn't let it influence her judgment. These people, despite their involvement with the CAH, probably had nothing to do with what had happened to Samantha and her other friends that night at the Breezy Blue. She and the other two judges would have to come to a consensus on fair sentences for each individual on her ship.

The youngest and last member to sit in front of them, the following day was Luke Geyer, the genius/artist who spent most of his time with Mr. Jennison and Eartha. Mr. Jennison had chosen to represent the boy and spoke like someone experienced in presenting cases to a court. Dana couldn't recall anything in his record stating a history in law, but he'd dressed in a nice suit and carried himself like someone who'd studied. The older man was full of surprises.

"Ladies and gentlemen of the Justice Committee, your honors, Luke Geyer had absolutely nothing to do with the tampering of this ship before or after take-off. I ask that you dismiss his case, and let him get back to school, where he belongs."

"Hardly! The boy is a known terrorist, and he can't be allowed to roam free," Chancellor Evans bellowed.

"Chancellor," Dana said, holding up a hand to quell further inevitable outbursts. How many times today was she going to have to pull on his reins? "Please, Mr. Jennison. Make your case."

Luke's father sat beside him, wearing a solemn expression and clutching the arm of his son's chair. Luke leaned away from him and the table in front of them, his eyes on the floor as if he wanted to curl in on himself and disappear. She wondered if he'd inherited the artistry or genius from his father, looking over the man's short hair and brooding features. Dana found the father as handsome as his son would be, though Luke wore the features in a wild, untamed way. Watching their body language though, it was clear the boy drew no comfort from his father, and she wondered what kind of conversations they'd had before he'd been brought in for his hearing.

What had brought him to the Coalition in the first place? Luke was too young to have taken part in what happened to her people. Dana watched him listening as he chewed his fingernails but kept his head down. When questioned, he'd been as direct as the others. Other than Barnes, none of them had admitted to sabotaging the ship directly. Unlike Shu, they'd seemed relieved to come clean about their marginal involvement with the group, and none of them had ever seen their leader—a man that was now a speck of dust floating in orbit around the space where Zelenia used to be.

Mr. Jennison continued listing off the boy's educational achievements, saving his entire family by passing the *Hope* Academic Achievement placement exams with the highest marks ever recorded. He spoke of his own relationship with the boy, peppering in stories of his own misspent youth. Dana regarded the Justice Committee, looking for any reactions in favor or against the boy. Their expressions were tired and, for the most part, neutral.

Mr. Jennison continued his argument, moving in to appeal to their sensibilities. "Luke has been an upstanding member of our society for some time, and he has a right to survive beyond a childhood club. Once again, I implore you to consider dropping the case against him. We shouldn't allow his intellect to be squandered. He can still be a valuable member of our new world if given the chance."

"Childhood *club*? I don't think so. Would you have us turn a blind eye to his activities just because of his age, Mr. Jennison?" President Muñoz was leaning forward. "On the one hand, you speak of his astounding intelligence, yet out of the same mouth claim he shouldn't be responsible for his actions. Which is it?"

Dana turned to Muñoz as he spoke. He kept his cool, his hands flat on the table in front of him. His question was one the committee was no doubt asking themselves, and it was smart for Muñoz to have brought it up.

Leave nothing unsaid so they have the full story with which to make a judgment, she thought.

Chancellor Evans gave Luke's father a significant grimace. "It shows a certain deficiency in the family unit. He seemed to have ample time to take part in this kind of truant behavior. Despite his academic record, he was often missing from class and insubordinate toward his instructors. Is this the same young man we're talking about?"

Luke's father stiffened as he glared back at Evans, his mouth in a hard, thin line. Family members were forbidden to speak unless called for testimony, or risk being kicked out of the proceedings altogether. He reached for his son, but Luke pulled away.

"Your Honors, this boy will pay for his past crimes, but he did nothing deserving of death."

After Mr. Jennison's final plea, the judges directed a few prepared questions at Luke.

"Luke Geyer, this court will tolerate nothing less than the absolute truth from you. Is that understood?" Dana asked.

Luke nodded.

"We'll need a spoken confirmation for the record."

Luke cleared his throat. "Yes, I understand."

Dana sat back and let Chancellor Evans speak. They'd selected him to ask the first set of questions. Luke answered in a clear and concise voice. Then Chancellor Evans went off-script.

"For the record, can you tell us when you joined the Coalition Against *Hope*?"

"Two years ago."

"How did you find them? Or rather, how did they find you?"

"A Coalition member came up to me at my school after I said some things to my teacher about the government lying to us about the meteor."

"What lead you to that conclusion?"

"I used the telescope my father bought me to track the meteor. I did the math. What they were saying about its trajectory was impossible. I knew the rock would collide with our world and the government was keeping the truth from people."

"Why didn't you tell an adult instead of joining the Coalition?"

"I tried. I told my teachers, my counselors—no one would listen..." Luke sighed as he gave his father a sidelong look. "Not even my parents."

"So you joined the Coalition and bombed facilities instead."

"No," he insisted, sitting up straighter in his chair. "I didn't even know about that at first. I didn't do anything, really. They just asked me a bunch of times how I had done the math. I wrote everything out so a monkey could understand it, and they used it to fuel their movement." He deflated a little. "I was just trying to get the word out."

"Is it true you were involved in the destruction of the first *Hope* construction facility?"

Luke's eyes went wide in surprise. Dana and President Muñoz also stared at Chancellor Evans. The sabotage of the first facility wasn't public knowledge. It was even more shocking that Chancellor Evans thought Luke had something to do with it.

"No... no, I didn't do that."

"Strange," Evans pressed on, "because if the information you gave us earlier is correct, then you were already a member when that facility was bombed. It put us months behind, which put the entire project at risk."

"I wasn't even there," Luke insisted desperately.

"No, but it's your math that fueled the movement, without which we might have been able to build two ships instead of one."

Luke shook his head, looking with concern to Mr. Jennison and then back to Chancellor Evans.

"I'd like to call a brief recess," Mr. Jennison said.

"Yes, that's a good idea," Dana quickly agreed. "Let's take a fifteen-minute recess."

The Committee and the judges retired to their respective rooms to confer on what they'd heard. Dana followed the other judges into her adjoining office. On her way out, she saw Luke rise from his seat on shaky legs. Mr. Jennison put a reassuring arm around his shoulders before whispering something in his ear that made him nod in agreement.

Once they were alone, she turned on Chancellor Evans.

"What was the meaning of that? You have a set of questions to ask for a reason."

"Yes, Chancellor, that's not good form," President Muñoz agreed.

"I'm using tactics that work in the judicial system," Evans replied smoothly. "Neither of which either of you have any experience in."

"I beg your pardon, you're not the only one with court experience," President Muñoz argued, his fists on his hips in challenge.

"Not as a judge." Evans waved a dismissive hand. "Your jury experience hardly counts here."

President Muñoz shook his head and angrily muttered to himself about the chancellor's pompous attitude.

"Gentlemen, please," Dana said, "keep your tempers and your personal agendas out of the proceedings." She looked to Evans. "Do you have any other surprise questions for the defendant?"

"No, I just wanted to rattle him. We've questioned them all, and we're still about where we started—no new leads, no real agenda. They're still a danger to everyone on this ship. We need one of them to break."

"Fine, I appreciate your..." Dana paused to avoid saying what she wanted to and instead filled in, "enthusiasm for the truth. However, next time you plan to go off script, Chancellor, don't. He's just a kid. You had your chance with the other three and found nothing. There's no need to fabricate something that isn't there. The leaders of the Coalition kept their identities a secret, which means we don't know who they are, and their agenda was probably only told to those in the inner circle. It's a smart play that saves their people from revealing anything they don't know. So let's move on, shall we?"

The two men nodded, and followed her back out into the conference room, filing into their respective seats. Dana's shoulders felt heavy with what was to come and didn't envy the responsibility of the Justice Committee.

Luke and his father were both composed once more, sitting side by side. Before they could begin questioning Luke again, Mr. Jennison spoke up.

"My client would like to speak to the three judges in private."

There was a gasp from the Justice Committee, none of them expecting it, least of all the judges. Dana's heart was pounding as she looked at the young man as he rose to stand in front of them, his shoulders back and his chin lifted.

Mr. Jennison nodded to Luke to continue.

"I want to invoke my right to be heard off the record."

"Why?" President Muñoz asked.

Dana found herself leaning forward in her seat, waiting for his answer.

Mr. Jennison nodded again to the boy to continue when he looked to him. Luke turned his face back to them.

"I have information that is not publicly known, and probably shouldn't be told to everyone all at once for fear it will damage the morale and functioning of the ship."

Dana sat back and looked to each of the men beside her. The chancellor was frowning at Luke while Muñoz met her gaze and shrugged. The murmuring of the Justice Committee behind her said they were also thrown by this new development. None of the other accused had made such a request. However, he seemed certain, and whatever he knew, Mr. Jennison agreed. He'd obviously given him the words to speak for himself.

Dana gestured for Luke to follow them back into her office, adjacent to the conference room. Once they were in the room with the door closed, Dana took her seat behind her desk. The President and Chancellor took the last two available seats, moving them to either side of her, as they'd been in during the hearing, leaving Luke and Mr. Jennison to stand in front of them.

"All right," Dana began, "we're listening."

"First of all, I have seen the face of the CAH leader," Luke told her. "At least, I know who he was when Zelenia was destroyed. Eddy Wong was a friend of mine from school. We were in most of the same classes." Luke shrugged, as if embarrassed to be put in the same category. "That's where they reached out to me. His older brother was the leader back then, and they were looking for people like me—young and smart—to join them."

Chancellor Evans let out a guffaw. "Wait, are you saying a sixteen-year-old kid is the leader of the CAH?"

"Sir, please let him finish," Mr. Jennison said, raising a hand.

Luke frowned. "Eddy Wong makes me look like a kindergartner. He and his brother were brilliant together. They knew about things no one else seemed to know or understand, but I didn't really know what they were doing at first. Like everyone else, I was only told what I needed to know about whatever I was working on, and that was all." He looked at his shoes. "When Eddy asked me to do some research about the meteor activity in the area, I did. I liked astronomy, and since my father gave me the telescope, I was sort of into it. I tracked the asteroids in space, their trajectories, and discovered something no one else had said so far."

"What?" Dana asked.

He looked up, still not quite meeting her eye. "All the asteroids seemed to be aimed at Zelenia. They weren't random rocks that happened to be traveling through our orbit, they were directed at the surface by someone, something."

Dana felt the hairs on the back of her neck stand up.

"What do you mean, they were aimed?" Chancellor Evans asked, leaning forward.

"I mean those asteroids were not on a trajectory toward our planet until something pushed them into our orbit. The world government knew they would eventually destroy the planet because the sizes were getting bigger, their path to our planet more consistent."

Evans looked doubtful. "How do you know that? We have scientists with telescopes much more powerful than yours, and probes that report back everything they find."

Luke shrugged. "I don't know. But I told Eddy what I'd found, and I showed him the math to prove it. He took it to his brother. It wasn't long after that there was a bombing on the original *Hope* base."

"This is absurd," President Muñoz said, sitting back, crossing his arms in front of his chest. If the asteroids were targeting our planet, our people would have caught it.

"I doubt it. Not many can do the kind of dimensional statistics that Eddy and I do. And basically, if you're not looking for intelligence behind the activity, you probably wouldn't even notice it. They were subtle, but the shifts were there. Those asteroids, going as far back long before Viola, weren't accidentally passing through. They were shifted from their original trajectories and pointed at our planet."

"Why?" Dana asked in a low whisper. Her father had died because of Viola. She'd watched him save most of his crew and turn his ship into a strong enough projectile to throw Viola off its course.

What if there was intelligent life behind it? Someone wanting to destroy them rather than a series of random events would speak to an even larger problem.

This time, Luke looked her in the eye. "That I don't know, but I think Eddy figured it out. He sent me this really cryptic message on what to look out for. I already erased it, but he told me there was someone on board who didn't belong with us."

Dana and the other judges had seen the message. She didn't correct him, as it didn't make a difference, but after hearing what Luke had just said, it took on a whole different meaning. Dana nodded as he continued, her thoughts still on Eddy Wong's face and the message that was included about someone not being who they claimed to be. She'd thought it the ramblings of a brainwashed Coalition member. Now, knowing he was their leader changed everything.

"Who is this person that doesn't belong?" Dana asked.

Luke shifted his weight from one foot to the other, fidgeting now.

Eddy's words floated in the back of her mind: '*Protect the species.*'

Dana thought of Eartha and her almost strange ability to understand events before they happened. If it was the girl, she knew Luke wouldn't want to throw her to the wolves. Dana looked at the other men, leaning forward in their chairs. If they knew what she knew about Eartha, they might not see her the way she did.

"That detail aside," Dana said, drumming her fingers softly on the table, "you didn't want this conversation to be on the record. Is it because you didn't want the others to know who the CAH leader was? Not to be insensitive, but it hardly matters now. You could have told us all of this in the conference room."

"No... there's more." Luke squared his shoulders and lifted his chin again, as he'd done before they'd entered. "At the time I was doing work for the Coalition, it wasn't only for the trajectory of the asteroid. I was also researching the possibility of there being other ships built and launched. As far as I know, there were three other ships in various levels of production when our ship left Zelenia."

The Chancellor blustered while the President gaped. Dana wasn't sure what to say.

"Luke, please tell the judges how you came to this conclusion," Mr. Jennison said with a satisfied smile.

"I used math. I plotted the known location of the first *Hope* project, then determined that with similar characteristics and financial backing, there were six other locations around the world capable of duplicating the project. I didn't know they were going to attack the facility. We wanted people to know the truth. The world government was keeping everything a secret and limiting the list of people getting on the ships."

Luke waited a beat looking from one disbelieving face to the next before he continued. "Eddy thought he was making a point by grounding the ships. He wanted to force the hierarchy to admit they were lying. I thought it was a stupid idea, and I told Eddy as much. Grounding the ships, even temporarily, with a planet-killer so close was ridiculous. When he wouldn't listen to me, I made plans to get my family on the *Hope*. I took the academic route because I knew I could pass it."

"What?" President Munoz asked. "If there were other projects, wouldn't you think we'd have known about it?"

Dana looked to Chancellor Evans. He didn't seem as surprised by this information as he should be. He sat pensive and quiet, which wasn't his way at all. He liked to fight and flounder, and for someone learning there might be as many as three other ships that had survived, he should have been as confused as the rest of them.

Dana caught President Muñoz's glare at Chancellor Evans, who must be coming to the same conclusion. *What was Evans hiding?*

Mr. Jennison caught the expression, too. "You don't seem surprised by this, Your Honor," he said, addressing Evans. "My charge was seeking to tell people the truth when our government refused to. The Coalition's methods were deplorable. However, Luke Geyer's involvement, you'd have to agree, was, at the most, informative. He didn't lift a hand to kill a child, worker, or crew member on or off of this ship before or after takeoff. He should be assigned to community service, but we beg that the death penalty not be pursued in his case."

"We'll need to confer as a group," Dana said. "For now, let's return to the conference room so the Justice Committee can be released for the day."

The men all agreed, though Muñoz was still staring at Evans like a snake in the grass.

Dana stood, moving back into the conference room and speaking to everyone present. "We're adjourned for the day. Ladies and gentlemen, please return to your cabins. I must repeat—do not share what you've learned today with anyone. Not with each other, not even on record for yourselves in any form. You'll have plenty of time to discuss the testimonies in the morning. Try to eat and get some rest, you've got a long day ahead of you tomorrow." She nodded to dismiss them, then turned to address her other two judges. "I'd like to see you both in my office for a moment."

Once the door to the room closed, Dana whirled on Chancellor Evans.

"What do you know?"

Chancellor Evans moved to the drink dispenser near her desk and grabbed one of her cups, filling it with cold water for himself. He took a sip before continuing. "Of course there were other ships."

Dana's knees wanted to give out. She quickly sat down.

President Muñoz paced the room, stomping from one end to the other. "Why wasn't I informed? I'm the President of the Southern colonies. Someone should have told me from the start."

"They kept the identity and the locations of the other ships a secret for two reasons," Evans replied. "One, the Coalition's following had grown into a full-on terrorist group. We didn't want to risk losing the other ships. The other was obvious. The more ships there were, the more excuses there would be for people in positions of power to bribe their way onboard. They told only a handful of our people, and we prevented the news reports from reaching beyond our colonies to other parts of the world."

"It's true?" Her voice warbled in her ears before the room tilted to one side.

Dana tried leaning to keep upright but tipped out of her chair and onto the floor. She must have blacked out for a second because President Muñoz and Chancellor Evans were leaning over her with worried expressions when the room came back.

She blinked, and the sound in the room returned. Her cheek stung; had the President slapped her?

"Captain, are you all right? Should we call the doctor?" Muñoz asked.

"I'm fine," she said. "Just help me up." She'd fallen on her arm, and it would probably be sore, but nothing more. She was more embarrassed than anything. The need for a nanodot was like a hunger. Dana didn't have to look down to see her hands trembling.

The two older men helped her back into the chair. President Muñoz sat across from her at the desk while the chancellor turned to the drink dispenser. He placed a full cup of water in front of her and she downed half. The glass clinking to the desk as her hands shook. When her mind was clear again, she spoke between clenched teeth.

"Are you telling me we're not the last of our people?"

Chancellor Evans grabbed a glass for himself and took a long sip of water and shrugged. "Once they chose me as a passenger for the *Hope* project, they stopped informing me of the progress of the other ships. However, there were three other ships that may have been ready by the deadline. It's possible, but we don't know if they made it." He looked down at the cup in his hand. "When we reached the rendezvous coordinates, we were the only ship to see the planet destroyed. If the others had made it, they would have been there."

"That's only if the captains knew the other ships existed," Dana seethed. "They could have been within communications range, but if we weren't looking for them and they weren't looking for us..." she let them fill in the blank.

"Everyone knew about *Hope*," Evans said. "However, they may not have been prepared to launch."

"Someone may have sabotaged them," President Muñoz murmured.

"Perhaps none of the others survived," Chancellor Evans said, almost to himself.

"Why you?" Muñoz asked.

Evans finally looked up. "The information was only told to those who needed to know. If you'll forgive me, Mr. President, your seat was always secure. The rest of us had to beg, borrow, and steal to get a seat on a ship. Once I learned of the project, I reached out to everyone I knew who might be involved in any part of the continent. I won't give away names now, because it hardly matters, but some of those contacts paid off."

Dana could imagine it. If there had been even one other person like Evans, there had to be more survivors. But all this time, she had been working with only half the information. It had taken a fifteen-year-old kid to tell her the truth.

"How could you keep something like this from us for so long?" she demanded. The frustration seeped out as her fist hit the desk. "What did you think you'd gain? We're already on our own. The existence of another ship could mean the difference between life and death out here."

"People wouldn't know what to do with that information now. They might think we should turn around, go looking for them instead of for a new home. Our mission is unchanged," Evans said, staring down into his glass and taking another sip.

"No, but this information cannot remain a secret," Dana argued. "That's exactly how groups like the Coalition gain legs."

"What difference will it make?" Chancellor Evans asked with a wave of his hand. "We have all the Coalition members in custody."

"That we know of," said Muñoz.

Dana put her heavy head into her hands. "I'm currently racing down the Fashin Teku because of our stolen embryos. If there is even one other ship, it won't matter, and we're doing all this for nothing."

President Muñoz leaned over her desk and reached out a hand. She took it like a lifeline. "The fate of the embryos still matters," he told her, looking sincerely into her eyes. "Keep in mind we have no idea what they intend to do with them. In this state, they could just as easily be born as slaves to another race as eaten."

Dana had given that some thought, and she gave the president a nod. He was right, of course. It wasn't only for their genetic potential. They were humans, and they couldn't be left in the hands of pirates, no matter the circumstance.

"What should we do about Luke's knowledge of the event and the Justice Committee?" she asked then placed her hands on the desk to steady them.

"Nothing for now," the Chancellor said. "Regardless of the outcome of tomorrow's verdict, Luke will be given a pardon. As the youngest member, blah, blah, blah, he'll work off his debt to society rather than face the death penalty. He has the ability to change."

"He could tell someone else," President Muñoz reasoned.

Dana shook her head. "He already has. Mr. Jennison knows the truth."

"We need to insist that the boy keep everything he's told us a secret, at least until we find out if there are any other survivors," Evans said.

"And if we encounter one or more of the other ships?" Dana asked.

Evans shrugged. "By then, no one will care that we kept the truth from them."

The three of them waited in silence for her decision. In her gut, Dana knew this was a bad idea. Government secrets had already spawned a terrorist group whose members had reached her ship. Though the surface logic was sound, she couldn't help but feel that Evans was still holding something back. There would always be some that wouldn't understand.

She kept seeing Wade's face, the look of betrayal when he'd learned the truth about their home planet. Dana never wanted to see that disappointment on his face again but knew she would.

CHAPTER 32

EARTHA

The trouble with being the oldest is that there's no one to tell you that when a baby is coming, you'll be ignored. Worse, you become invisible. When Esme had called her 'Daughter,' Eartha thought things had changed between them. Their excitement about the baby thrilled her, and she thought it would bring them closer together as a family.

Instead, she was more like an outsider than ever. At least that's what Eartha thought when she arrived in their quarters after her day at school.

Eartha knew how much it meant to the Rogans to be having their first baby. Eartha had been one of the first to congratulate them. According to Ari, Esme's record showed several medical visits to a doctor that helped people who couldn't have babies, but to Ari's knowledge, they'd never actually grown a baby this long until now. Everything would be fine if it wasn't she'd have had a feeling about it before now.

She'd burst into their quarters so excited to tell them about how well things were going now that everyone seemed to have forgotten all about her stowing away her first couple of weeks on board. Since Luke's arrest, along with those of the other Coalition members, she had no one to talk to about her problems or accomplishments in school. After classes, Mr. Jennison was busy helping Luke, and she hadn't made any other new friends yet.

Eartha liked her new teacher and most of her class. Mrs. Hill was fun, and she didn't teach like any instructor she'd ever had before. She seemed to understand the way Eartha's mind worked and spoke to her in a way that made perfect sense.

Eartha and Luke had been given a special project to work on before he'd been arrested. They'd come up with an idea on how to make a molecular-reproduction device from existing technology. Mrs. Hill had loved the idea and couldn't wait for them to present their project. Eartha had since gotten an extension, as her lab partner was sitting in the brig. She'd tried to go see him, but she didn't have the proper clearance and had been told more than once by the guard on duty that she shouldn't associate with Coalition members. Though she didn't see him that way. He was her friend.

When Eartha submitted what she'd gathered together for her report, Mrs. Hill insisted that a copy be forwarded to the captain. She said it was to review the project specs in case there was an immediate real-world application. It might even get her access to speak to Luke.

Eartha was so excited to tell the Rogans that when she arrived and found them engrossed in yet another baby discussion, she couldn't hide her disappointment. She missed sharing the important things with the people in her life who mattered. It used to be Eric. Now that he and Esme were on a split schedule, they were both either busy working or sleeping. When they were together, it was all about the baby.

"Well, what about the one I proposed?" Eric asked.

"Your aunt's name? You mean the one with the—" Esme laughed instead of finishing her sentence.

"It's a cool name, and it's already in the family."

"No way. That time we were at the thing, I almost—"

"I admit, that was gross," Eric said as he shook his head.

"I know!"

It was exhausting to listen to them finishing each other's sentences and then laugh at jokes that she didn't understand. She grew tired of waiting for them to speak to her or to stop, since they wouldn't. Coming in the door to their cabin had ceased to work a long time ago. Eartha launched into her story midpoint, dropping her bag in the center of the cabin.

"So, at school today, Mrs. Hill said she really liked our project. There's a possibility that the captain will approve it for production on the ship." Eartha waited for a beat as they glanced in her direction, then returned to the tablet in front of them. No doubt it had the list of names they were debating.

"That's great, honey," Eric said, ignoring the bag in the middle of the floor.

"Dinner's almost ready. Get washed up," Esme said. She glanced in Eartha's general direction without meeting her

eye. Instead, she spoke at her, without actually acknowledging her by name.

Eartha tromped off to the restroom to steam clean her
hands. The light on the sink turned from red to green when
the bacteria had been removed. She waited while the blow-
er's hot air dried her hands, then pulled them out and stared
in the mirror.

For years, Eartha believed that when she turned thirteen,
she'd feel older, be more confident, be more... something.
She pulled her hair back from her face and looked at her
profile. Her round cheeks were about the same, and her hair
had grown about an inch longer than before, but she was
otherwise unchanged. By this time, she and Becky were
supposed to be getting ready for her first kiss with James.

She shook her head, remembering her first day of school,
seeing James sitting there with his older brother Luke. She'd
stared at him, her mouth hanging open until Luke had
snapped his fingers. She hadn't put it together that they were
brothers until she saw him. The two brothers didn't do much
together other than school, but when she arrived, Luke
preferred sitting with her more than with James. He said it
had something to do with their different interests.

The two brothers didn't look that much alike, mostly just
their hair. Luke wore his long and unkempt while James
always kept a shorter, cleaner haircut. They also didn't have
many of the same interests. James was still into various physical activities, while Luke spent most of his time with her and
Mr. Jennison.

Eartha thought back on her last afternoon at Becky's
house, calling James. She remembered that his older brother
had answered. It had been Luke calling James to the phone

that day. It was so weird how things like that happened. Now, she couldn't imagine trying to be James' girlfriend, even though they were the same age. He was just as cute as ever, and when he smiled at her, she still felt a little weak in the knees, but Luke was her friend now. It felt weird to crush on his little brother while hanging out with him.

When she let her hair back down, the ends caught the light and Eartha noticed a slight change. It looked like sun damage, but she'd been in space. She wondered if hair could change color with the lack of light from Zelenia's two suns. Eartha let her hair go, and the thick curls bounced back into place high and wild around her head.

Eartha huffed and shook her head at her reflection. No, she was thirteen now, and she didn't seem different at all. If anything, she felt more alone than ever. *How could she be jealous of an unborn baby? What was her problem?* She wanted to talk to Luke and ask him how it had been when his siblings had come along, since he would soon have four. Did he ever get jealous of them?

She couldn't imagine he would be. Luke seemed to want nothing to do with his family most days, but maybe things hadn't started off that way. Maybe once upon a time, he'd been the center of his parent's attention, and then they'd just moved on to the next kid, the way Eric and Esme had done with her.

It wasn't something she could talk to with anyone else, including James. She just didn't have any other close friends.

Eartha resolved in her heart to be patient. She'd just have to wait for Luke. He'd be out of the brig eventually. If he'd been a bad guy or something she'd have known it by now.

Though her own mixed feelings about him could be the reason she wasn't a hundred percent sure.

Eartha reached up to block the brush of cold air at her neck. A reminder that she never seemed to be alone. Since the baby, she'd made the choice not to mention the cold brushes of air to Esme or Eric. They didn't need another reason to look at her funny or worse; not to keep her in their family.

When she opened the door, she saw they had moved her backpack to the chair. They hadn't even mentioned it. Already eating, they were still in the middle of their conversation when she moved to sit down. Her food had been placed in front of her empty seat, getting cold while she'd been in the bathroom fighting with her out-of-control curls.

"Let's see that Dix gets the coolant modulator fixed. I don't want to have any problems with the engine core overheating because, *stars*, we don't have the fuel to waste on another explosion," Eric said.

"Don't think I won't mention it, but it's getting to be a pain in the neck checking up behind him all the time. I really miss —are you going to slouch like that through the entire meal?" Esme asked, addressing Eartha mid-sentence.

"Oh, now you can see me." Eartha threw down her utensils and stood up.

"Eartha, what's gotten into you?"

"I'm tired of being invisible," she said, storming away from the table.

She went back to the bedroom she'd eventually have to share with the baby. They didn't get quarters with three bedrooms, only two. That meant she'd lose all her privacy.

Leaving the table got her in trouble most of the time, but tonight they didn't even bother coming in to check on her.

When she cooled down enough to come back out, the kitchen had been cleaned up, and the living room was empty. Esme had already gone to work, it seemed, and Eric was in his room with the door closed. He was working long days to make up for Esme's short schedule. She worked nights, when there wasn't as much to do, and slept during the day while Eartha was at school. It worked for them, but they'd seemed to have forgotten they had a daughter at home with no friends.

Maybe it was because they didn't think of her like a *real* daughter. She tried to push down the thought since they had saved her and taken her in, just as her mother had planned. Eartha grabbed her school bag and returned to her room. She finished Mrs. Hill's assignment before getting ready for bed. She lay on the blanket, stewing with anger until she heard Eric's door open. Eartha scrambled into the sheets and threw the blanket over her head, after he tapped on the door. When the door slid open, he rapped softly against the door frame once more, waiting for her to answer before he opened it.

He stood over her a moment and whispered, "Eartha, are you asleep?"

Eartha listened to him sigh when she didn't answer, but kept her head buried under her pillow, refusing to respond.

SHE WOKE UP THE NEXT MORNING TO THE SOUND OF ESME returning from her shift. Eartha pressed her ear to her bedroom door, listening to them talking low in the kitchen. From the tinkering of plates and glasses she figured Esme was making breakfast.

"Is she still asleep?" Eric whispered.

"What's *wrong* with her these days?" Esme said. "It's like living with a grumpy old man."

"I don't know. I mean, this is beyond my knowledge. What can I say?" Eric said. There was some shuffling.

"Leave her alone. She doesn't have class until the afternoon."

"Do you think it's her...?" Eric asked.

"Maybe."

"You should ask her."

"*Me?*"

"Well, *I* can't ask her."

They shuffled off into their bedroom, and Eartha screamed into her pillow. They were ridiculous to live with. When she wanted to talk, they were too busy with their baby plans. Now, they thought she was having her monthly. Eartha rolled her eyes as she listened to them, then imagined sitting through breakfast with them while Esme hinted at why she was in a bad mood.

No. She'd rather do anything else.

She threw off the blankets, dressed, and grabbed her pack. She slipped into her boots and listened again at the door. Their voices were muffled—still in their bedroom. Eartha eased out of her room, and when she saw the living area was empty, she made a mad dash for the door. She made it out into the corridor without a word to either of them, then breathed a sigh of relief.

Until she realized the time. She had no place to go.

They forbade Eartha from hiding out in the hatches and ventilation systems. Eric had explained to her how dangerous it could be if something should happen to the ship. She stood in the middle of the corridor, trying to remember all the places she'd been allowed to visit. She usually sat with Luke and Mr. Jennison in the Commons. Ari would be there, but she didn't feel like talking with anyone. Maybe she could just get a quiet table to herself and review her work for school.

The Commons was quiet in the morning, as most people took their breakfast in their cabins. The people chatting at nearby tables were crew, either coming from or going to their shifts. Eartha grabbed a seat at a table near the viewport and placed herself with her back to the room, spreading out her work in front of her. She ignored the star-filled sky, focusing instead on her next math lesson. She found working ahead helped, though she'd never been that good with numbers. It came so easy to Luke and she wished he was there to help her. He usually made the concepts understandable. Without him, she'd have to trudge through on her own.

Eartha had been there for over twenty minutes before she slid the tablet across from her and groaned in frustration. Ari made his way over just as her forehead came to rest on the table.

"Eartha, you are here very early today," he said with a tilt of his head. "Is everything all right? You seem distressed."

"I'm fine," she grumbled, pulling the tablet back toward her. Maybe she could get some reading done for her language studies instead. The math was making her brain hurt.

"You are refusing eye contact, and your vocal patterns are low and inaudible. You are unsettled."

Ari sat down across from her without a word and waited.

He put the tray down on the table he used for carrying dishes and folded his hands in front of him.

Eartha let out a sigh. "I'm thirteen years old. Becky and my parents are dead. My new parents are having their first baby. I have no one to talk to, and I've never been kissed. Translation: I might as well be dead, too."

She dropped her head back to the table and fought back the tears stinging her eyes.

Ari had been there for her when she was still hiding and sleeping in the ventilation shaft. He seemed to want to help her, even when he wasn't quite sure what to do. He pulled out a cloth and handed it to her to wipe her eyes. Eartha took it and dragged it over her face. Then the words she'd been bottling up came pouring out through her tears in a high-pitched whine.

"Why can't they even look at me or talk like they used to? I'm not a little kid anymore, but I feel like they don't even care about me now that the baby's coming."

"You have feelings of jealousy over the new child?" Ari turned his head and Eartha could practically hear the gears processing the information. "This is not abnormal. You are fine," Ari said and sat back, preparing to stand up.

"What? No, I'm not fine," Eartha said, grabbing his hand and forcing him to sit back down.

"You are experiencing feelings of resentment and anger toward the Rogans for the attention they are giving to the unborn child. It worries you that their affections for you have changed. They have not."

"They have," Eartha blurted out. She put a hand over her mouth when she saw a few of the crew members turn in her direction.

"According to my knowledge base, these feelings are normal and baseless. The parents of a newborn are concerned to the point of obsession over details regarding their baby. The older children must make room for the new sibling." Ari picked up Eartha's hand. "You have never been an older sibling. The feelings you have are normal. Your friend, Luke, is an older child. I believe he would understand."

"I know." Eartha shook her head. "But don't you get it? I'm not allowed to talk to Luke while he's in the brig. Besides, he's got more important things to talk about than this."

"Perhaps you can explain your feelings to the captain. She does not have any siblings on record, but she has the authority to give you access to see Luke. Captain Pinet appears to be understanding and fair."

If an ARI could be optimistic, this was what she imagined it would sound like. Right now, that's not what she wanted. She needed a plan.

"I'm not going to talk to the captain about my stupid feelings. Stop being ridiculous."

"I am being perfectly reasonable. It is beyond the parameters of my programming to be ridiculous."

Ari gave her a concerned tilt of his head and she saw he was scanning her, a little habit he'd picked up since that first night he'd caught her sneaking into the kitchen to scrounge for food when she'd been hiding in the crawl space.

"Stop scanning me. There's nothing *wrong* with me."

"I am merely checking to see if you are fighting a cold. Your temperature is slightly elevated. It can make humanoids irritable and paranoid. It could be the reason you are ill-tempered at the moment."

"I'm not sick!"

"Then what prevents you from attempting to see your friend?"

"They won't let me in. I don't have clearance."

Eartha remembered being stricken with panic when security had come to arrest Luke. They'd been in the Commons laughing about something Mr. Jennison said when two men charged over to take him away. They said they'd found evidence in a personal vid sent from the Coalition with instructions to him. Luke didn't deny the charges, only held out his hands for the magnetic cuffs. She and Mr. Jennison had called out to him, but he hadn't looked back as they'd led him to the brig. That was the last time Eartha had seen Luke, and her chest ached from not being able to talk to her friend.

"I need a better reason than a school project to go see him."

"Perhaps *you* are being unreasonable. It is only natural for you to be embarrassed. Your cognitive development, though somewhat different from other Zelanians', is still underdeveloped."

"Ari, go away," Eartha said in a mild tone before turning her attention to the reading she wanted to finish before school. The last thing she was going to do was argue with an android about feelings.

"As you wish. Good day, Eartha."

This time when he stood up to go, she didn't stop him.

CHAPTER 33

At the end of three grueling days of testimony, Dana could see things coming to an end. Of the four remaining Coalition members, three had done nothing violent in support of the Coalition's cause since boarding the ship. Only one of those had a violent history with the Coalition and had already served time. Upon her release, she'd paid to have her records buried just before joining her family onboard the *Hope*.

Tomorrow, the Justice Committee would deliberate on each of the cases and come to their decisions on the verdicts. It was up to her, along with the Chancellor and the President to dole out their sentences. In preparation, Dana reviewed each of the accused's files. She was currently reading up on Barnes when she walked right into the leg of her couch. She dropped her data file, grabbed her foot, and crumpled to the floor in agony. The throbbing pain in her big toe was still intolerable an hour later. When she couldn't take it anymore, she limped down to the med-bay to get something to ease the pain.

It was strange to see the med-bay so deserted. Even during the quieter times, there always seemed to be a team of people there working. She limped to one of the beds to wait for the doctor. The COMP system would have issued the call the minute she entered.

When several minutes passed, she wondered if perhaps everyone had already gone to bed. Dana wasn't ready to give up. She called out twice for help before someone finally answered.

"I'll be right with you," a voice called before its owner came through the doors. He stopped short when he saw who was waiting. "Captain?"

"Rido." She knew the Healer by the long hair he kept pulled back from his face and his bright smile. He always seemed to have an inner joke he didn't share with anyone else. "Where's Randall?"

"He's off duty for now. He hasn't had a real break in some time, and since we're low on medical supplies, he signed me up to cover the evening shift so his staff could get some rest."

Her mouth formed a silent 'oh.' As he pushed her back onto the hover bed, he ran a scanner over her, looking for trouble.

"So, what brings you here?"

"I stubbed my toe. I need something to ease the pain."

"Something bothering you this evening?"

"What?"

"Most people hit things in their own home with their toes, hips, and shoulders when they're not paying attention. Typically, it's because something else is on their minds. It keeps them from watching where they're going."

"Oh... yeah...I was a little distracted this evening," Dana

said, hoping her explanation was sufficient since she had no intention of giving up any details.

She didn't fill the thick silence he let hang between them. Despite his role on the ship, she couldn't share anything with him about the progress of the hearings.

"Thought so." After examining the toe, he nodded. "You've got a lot going on with the hearings and everything."

"Yes, but—" Dana clamped her mouth shut so fast her teeth clicked. It was as if he'd plucked the thought right out of her head.

Rido looked up at her, his brown eyes probing her face. "I heard you might also be officiating a wedding."

"Wow, false reports travel fast. I haven't actually decided if I will or not."

"I perform a lot of different services. The passengers and crew talk, and I'm a good listener."

"Is that so?" Dana looked at him dubiously. He still held her foot in his warm hands. She looked from her foot to his face and raised an inquisitive eyebrow.

"You'll be fine after an hour."

"Aren't you going to give me something for the pain?"

"No."

Dana thought she'd misheard him. "What?"

"Sorry, Captain. I don't dispense traditional medicine in general. Besides, there's none to spare. If you'd like me to perform a healing, I'd be happy to help you with that, but not in here. It's too sterile for that kind of thing."

"Why didn't you say all that before you laid me down with my foot in your face?"

He handed her back her sock, and she snatched it from him. "Because you looked like someone who needed to talk more than one who needed medicine." He shrugged and picked up her boot and handed that to her, too. "Besides, the medicine won't fix the actual problem, only the symptoms. I would prescribe that you stop running into furniture, if you can help it."

Dana hadn't meant to be so harsh. It wasn't his fault they were low on supplies, it was hers. The sensitivity came from more than her foot. Was she so transparent?

"Have you ever had to work with an ex?" she blurted out.

He raised an eyebrow, then the smirk returned. "Often."

Dana hadn't expected such a fast and honest response. She wondered if it was a recent thing, or something from his past he couldn't forget.

"How do you keep your distance? Or do you remain friends after?"

He smiled a knowing smile, then moved to sit beside her on the bed. "Well, some of us have stayed friends." Then he looked up, considering it a moment. "Some of us haven't."

Dana nodded. She'd heard of people staying friends with their exes. In fact, when her best friend Bonnie had been alive, she'd done it a few times. It didn't seem that strange, but the reality was a lot harder than the concept.

"The ones you stayed friends with, how did it go? Was it easy, or was it difficult seeing them with someone else, or vice versa?"

"For some of them, the sight of me moving on was harder than they thought. For others, it surprised me at how jealous I was when they started dating someone else, but eventually we found a rhythm that worked."

Dana wondered which group she and Wade would fall into.

Rido turned and took her hands in his large, warm ones. He had strong fingers, like a musician. "Can I say something that might be out of line?"

She looked at him and shrugged. "Sure."

"I've seen you and Commander Chance together. The two of you seem like good friends, but..."

"You don't think we're meant to stay friends," she finished for him.

"No offense, it just doesn't work for everyone. For some, the passion, the love, is too strong to be substituted for a quiet friendship."

Dana's mouth fell open. She wasn't sure how she felt about him describing her and Wade as being passionate and in love, though her mouth shut when she found she didn't have the words to deny it. It was harder to hear than she thought it would be.

The sting behind her eyes had her clearing her throat and climbing off the bed.

"You said you do healings," she said, changing the subject. "What does that entail?"

"It's—"

The computer's voice broke into whatever he was going to say next.

"Captain, to the bridge."

"Another time, Doc—Rido."

"I'll call on you tomorrow."

She gave him a wave. Dana wasn't sure what a healing involved, but she had the distinct feeling it wouldn't work on her.

CHAPTER 34

"Captain, we've got a planet in range with life-supporting water, air, and plant life," Nancy, already seated at the helm, reported as Dana entered the bridge.

"On screen, Lieutenant," Dana said. Her heart was already in her throat.

The screen filled with a planet not as green as the last one, spotted with brown patches, the blue lines of rivers, and large bodies of water. The planet wasn't very large—about half the size of Zelenia. There seemed to be several clusters of buildings that might be cities.

"Is it them?"

Nancy's ponytail swished back and forth as she shook her head. "I don't think so."

"There's been no comms or ship traffic in the area other than us," Cliff added.

"Have you sent out a hail?" Dana asked.

"Yes, Captain. There's still no response," he said.

"Are you sure they're receiving us?"

"Yes, they're aiming weapons at us," Wade said with one of his smirks.

"Weapons?"

"Yes," Wade said. "The kind that will blow us out of the sky and leave nothing behind."

"Do they know we don't have anything that powerful?" Dana asked.

"They don't seem to care."

Dana closed her eyes for a beat and took in a deep breath before letting it out slowly.

"Open a channel to the planet and broadcast my voice."

"Ready," Cliff said.

She cleared her throat and then spoke with more confidence than she felt.

"This is Captain Dana Pinet of the *Starship Hope*. We're on a mission to find a new planet in which to settle after the destruction of our home world, Zelenia. We are all that is left of our people. We have no hostile intentions. We have no weapons and cannot harm you. Do you have a representative who speaks for you?"

"Maybe they don't have one of those translators," Wade said, gesturing to his ear.

"Harden?"

Cliff nodded. "I'm currently wearing the translator, but it won't work unless they say something."

They hadn't had time to crack the code on the universal translator so they could replicate them, leaving them with just the one from the Fashin Teku. It would have been helpful, but in this case, Dana was unsure if who- or whatever populated this planet were interested in speaking with them.

Meeting new species required finesse, and she hated that she wasn't even sure they understood her.

She sent another silent curse to the Fashin Teku for ruining what should have been an honest exchange.

They waited several moments more before a satisfying beep identified their returning hail.

"It's the planet. They're transmitting audio only," Cliff said.

"That's fine. Let's hear it."

"Captain, we are the Begarans." The male voice sounded like he was speaking around a mouthful of food, but Dana could still understand him. "We wish you to leave our space. We do not desire any contact with you or any of your kind."

Dana looked around the bridge at the confused faces and wondered what they'd done to receive such an impolite response.

"It's on a repeating loop, Captain," Cliff said, a hint of bleak disappointment in his voice.

"Keep the channel open, Ensign." Dana addressed the aliens: "Apologies. We will be happy to be on our way. Since you cannot help us, perhaps you can tell us if you've had any contact with the Fashin Teku?"

A long, intense silence sat between them while Dana waited for an answer. When none came, she continued.

"We ran into some trouble a few weeks ago. A group of aliens identifying themselves as the Fashin Teku on transport freighter offered us food and help with our repairs before they returned using their molecular relocator to rob us. We'd like to track them, but we're short on medical supplies, food, and energy. We would appreciate any assistance you can give in helping us find them."

More silence.

"Should we tell them we're willing to work for food?" Wade asked in a loud whisper.

Cliff and Nancy both chuckled in response. Dana held up a hand to signal them to be quiet. She noted the newly appointed security officer, Lieutenant Commander Adrien Valente, didn't laugh. It seemed he didn't find it as funny as the others. Valente came with high recommendations and had been promoted almost immediately, but Dana had to admit she'd had little contact with him since he'd helped take down Barnes. She made a mental note to make time for her new chief of security.

"Perhaps you would allow us to land so we can scavenge for food," Dana suggested. She never thought she'd have to beg for her people's supplies, but after their recent experiences, she wasn't too proud to do whatever it took to keep flying. "The Fashin Teku have left us with little to nothing to survive. We would be grateful for anything you can spare."

She gave Wade a nod of approval. Even though he'd thrown it out as a joke, it had been a good idea. Their limited knowledge of alien worlds was a problem. The Begarans might have their own codes of conduct regarding giving handouts.

At last, a high-pitched voice replaced the repeating loop.

"We cannot help you."

The signal ended. Cliff shook his head, letting her know they'd been cut off. They waited several minutes but received no further communication from the planet.

"Well, good day to you, too," Dana muttered. "Commander, please record our encounter with the Begarans and their wish to avoid contact with outsiders."

A quiet filled the bridge, disappointment hanging heavy in the air.

"Well, that wasn't very neighborly of them," Wade said, cutting the tension. "And I was thinking of sending them a packet of our finest meal replacement bars."

A burst of laughter came out of Dana, and she had to pull herself together. No one seemed bothered that she'd lost it for a moment. She didn't blame the Begarans for being overly cautious. She'd been burned once herself for not being more careful. Dana wouldn't be so easily fooled again, but at the same time, she didn't want to become so jaded that she didn't show decency to those in need. The losses to their ship and the manifest kept her up at night, always strategizing her next move.

"It was worth a shot," Dana said. "I guess we'll move on and look for someone else to—"

"Captain," Cliff interrupted, cutting off what she was going to say next, "we're receiving something." He stared at the display with his head tilted and his brow furrowed.

"Receiving?" Dana echoed.

When he continued to stare at the display, his mouth hanging open, Wade raised his voice.

"Don't leave us all in suspense. What did we receive, Ensign? A message, a note, a song?"

Cliff looked up from the display and shrugged. "I don't know what it is. It just appeared in the cargo bay."

Dana ran a hand down her face removing a layer of sweat from her forehead and upper lip. "Commander, take a security team and see what they delivered through our shields without so much as a blip."

"Captain?" Valente asked.

He wore a wounded expression on his face. It should have been him leading the team. It was an oversight that needed to be addressed.

She shook her head. "I'm sorry, Lieutenant Commander, that's your team now. Wade, please go with him, and report back your findings right away."

Valente didn't seem too put out by her neglecting him, but she'd have to be more careful when addressing him in the future. It was going to take time before she was familiar with her new bridge officer. It wasn't his fault that she'd put so much trust in Barnes.

"Captain," Cliff called, "I've got a message coming in from Ms. Brooker requesting permission to enter the bridge."

Dana sighed. Of course she'd want to do some kind of 'first-contact' report. "Tell her she can meet me in my office, and I'll give her everything she needs."

A few minutes later, Dana was at her desk and Maggie rushed in looking like she'd just spent a week in the Western Isles. Her skin looked sun-kissed and oiled under the sky blue, off the shoulder shift she wore. Dana never understood the obsession of sun-darkening pale skin. She'd never wanted any color other than her own warm copper tone. Though, in Blue Earth's history, there had been a time when her skin was not favored. Dana struggled to make sense of the idea that the surface of one's skin mattered.

"This is exactly what I'm talking about," Maggie said as she swept in and sat down across from her. "Getting information second-hand is a waste of time. If I were on the bridge, I could have recorded what I needed myself. I'd have the sound of their voices speaking our language, the nuance of how you command—everything. Besides all that, this wouldn't take time away from your duties or anyone else's."

Dana waited for her to take a breath before she spoke. "Are you finished?"

Maggie seemed ruffled, but got control of herself and sat back in her seat.

Dana pursed her lips. "Now, do you have any questions for me about our first contact with the species known as the Begarans?"

Thirty minutes later, the interview with Maggie was complete.

"Permission to go and see what we got from the aliens?" Maggie asked, her eyes already wide with excitement to be on to the next part of her story.

"You'll have to clear it with the Lieutenant Commander Valente. He's in charge down there. If it's not safe, he has my permission to send you away."

"Yes, Captain," she said with a quick fist to her chest in salute as she jumped up from her seat.

Dana let out an exasperated sigh once Maggie was out of the room. At least she hadn't mentioned the wedding again. She still hadn't given her answer about officiating, and she wouldn't until she was sure they'd worked it out between them first. She mentally kicked herself again for not just saying 'no' when the opportunity presented itself.

"Incoming call from Commander Chance," announced the COMP, breaking into her thoughts

"Go ahead."

Wade's voice carried over the comm system. "They sent supplies, Captain. We've got crates with medical supplies, food, and more we haven't figured out yet."

Dana sat up straighter in her chair. "How much did they send?"

"We have over fifty crates of stuff down here." She could hear the excitement edging his voice. "We'll need a team just to categorize and figure out where to store it all."

"I want Lieutenant Commander Valente to go over every crate as a precaution. After that, you can assign a team to take care of the dispersal of the supplies. Then report back to the bridge."

"Yes, Captain."

"Oh, and one other thing. Maggie's on her way down. I told her she didn't have clearance to barge into the bay. That she'd have to go through Valente, as he's technically in charge."

There was a beat of silence, and then he answered, "Understood."

Dana returned to the bridge, where the energy had already shifted.

"We're saved," Cliff said under his breath. Dana caught his relief and addressed it, lest they all get their expectations too high.

"Not yet, Ensign, but it sounds like we'll be better off. If it wasn't for the ingenuity of our gardeners and people like Mr. Franklin Jennison, who lived through the rough times on Zelenia, we wouldn't have lasted this long. The aeroponics bay will be out of fresh produce in a couple of weeks. Let's cross our fingers they sent something he and the others in produce can use."

Dana moved to sit back down in her chair as the bridge crew waited for her orders.

"Ensign, send the Begarans our humble gratitude and thanks. Let it repeat until we're out of range."

"Aye, Captain. Message sent, and according to our sensors, received. Still no response."

"Well, let's get on our way and leave these Begarans to themselves," Dana said. "Helm, resume course."

"Yes, Captain," Nancy said, putting in the coordinates.

CHAPTER 35

"Justice is honesty on display."
-First Zelenian, President Jessica Pierce

D ana paced her office while President Muñoz and
Chancellor Evans watched her like a tennis ball in
play.

"What's taking them so long?"

"These things take time." The President recrossed his legs
and leaned forward. "Captain, you're going to wear yourself
and the floor out if you don't sit soon."

Chancellor Evans stared at the ends of his fingernails.
"You realize as soon as their part is done, we're going to have
to figure out what to do with them. Are we any closer to an
agreement on that?"

"If you mean am I willing to space them all, the answer is
no," President Muñoz said with a note of disdain.

Dana didn't like the idea of a blanket decision. Each

member of the Coalition needed a specific sentence to fit their crimes. She couldn't exactly weigh Barnes' actions against Luke's or any of the others. Two of them had done virtually nothing other than join the cause and speak out against the world government. She couldn't see spacing them just for agreeing with their philosophy.

They weren't a dictatorship. People had the right to their own thoughts. It was only when they made their philosophy something others had to die for that it became a problem. She knew that; even though it had taken the entire three days to stop imagining them in a room with Kristoff planning his revenge.

Before Dana could ask about the time again a message came through.

"Captain, to the conference room."

The Justice Committee was finally ready to announce their verdicts for each of the Coalition members. Dana sat down in her seat between the President and the Chancellor. The Committee had filed in and taken their seats, looking at them and avoiding the faces of Luke's family and two others who were there in support of an arrested CAH member.

The red alarm sounded before she even had a chance to get comfortable in her seat. Dana reached the bridge in less than five minutes, beating Wade, who was nowhere to be seen.

"What's going on?" Dana called out.

"I'm not sure," Cliff replied. "It looks like the Commander sent out the alert."

"Get him on comms," she said, her heart in her throat as she glanced at Nancy. "Is there anything out there?"

"No, nothing on long-range sensors," she announced.

"Well, what's going on?"

"I've got the commander," Cliff said.

"On the main viewer," Dana ordered.

Wade's face filled the screen. He looked ready to lose it. "Barnes escaped."

"What? How?" she demanded.

"During transport, he got away from the guards escorting him. He used some kind of sleeping agent."

"Neither of the guards were injured?"

"No."

"So, he's still in mag-cuffs?"

"Yes. I don't think he'll get far, but I thought it best to get everyone to their stations to be on the lookout. As you were still in the proceedings, I thought a red-alert was the fastest way to handle things."

"Understood, Commander," she said with a wave of her hand. "I'm not going to reprimand you on protocol at a time like this. Make sure the other Coalition members are locked down. I want a bow to stern search of the ship. I want everyone out looking for him. I'm on my way."

"On it, Captain." Wade's face was replaced by the stars outside of the main viewer.

"Do you think someone might be hiding him?" Nancy asked, her face a mirror of the worry Dana was sure was on her own.

Dana shook her head, but she wasn't sure. She bit her bottom lip as she tried to remember the file she'd read on Barnes the other night. He hadn't any friends on board other than Wade. Though the Fashin Teku female had expressed interest in him, she didn't know anything about his personal preferences.

"Any ideas of people who might have been close enough to consider helping him?" Dana asked.

"There was a young lab technician. She seemed the most interested. He didn't give her the time of day, but that doesn't mean he wouldn't..."

Nancy didn't finish her sentence. She didn't need to. They all knew if Barnes was on the run, there was no place he could go off the ship, and he'd probably do whatever it took to survive. Especially since he'd pleaded guilty to all charges without a fight. Perhaps he'd known all along that he was going to run.

Dana was livid. She should have seen this coming. He was their security chief; he knew the ship inside and out, and despite the change in the codes, would know more than she'd like about how they dealt with emergencies on board. He'd taken advantage of the men with him, no doubt people he'd know how to use.

Dana ran a hand over her face. "Ensign Harden, let the Justice Committee know we're adjourned for the day. Tell the Chancellor and the President to return to their cabins. I'm on my way to the brig."

"Yes, Captain."

Dana rolled her shoulders against the enormous ball of anxiety in the middle of her back. After all the trouble he'd caused her, he'd have to ask the Merciful for a verdict. She checked her Shock-Glock settings and adjusted it to the highest one. If he was still breathing afterward, she'd let the Justice Committee deal with him.

THE BRIG WAS QUIET WHEN DANA ENTERED. THERE WERE TWO guards on the door where Wade had arranged to meet her to discuss the investigation so far.

"The two guards he knocked out are in the med-bay, getting something to clear their heads so they can help with the search. There's nothing in his cell to indicate he was planning an escape."

"The others don't know anything?" Dana asked, looking over his shoulder at the three other filled cells. Luke was in the one that had once been Ensign Shu's. In her head, she could still see his body lying near the glass where he'd tried to claw himself out before he suffocated, along with the guard outside. Barnes had been the one to admit to the crime, and she didn't doubt him. What she didn't understand was *why* he'd run. If he was so resolute in accepting fault, why hadn't he taken his own life rather than be captured and killed?

"Nothing," Wade told her. "They're all shocked and worried this is going to change their judgements."

Dana nodded. "Of course it will. We don't know who helped Barnes escape, but we can't trust that they won't help him now that he's out. Unfortunately, in this case, one rotten tomato could turn the rest. We can't take that chance."

Wade nodded, but his mind seemed to be some place else.

"What's wrong?"

"I'm not sure what Barnes has to gain by this," he said, brow furrowed. "If he's escaped, it's not like he can just hop into an escape pod. None of his codes will work."

"All it takes is one sympathetic ear, and he's in a shuttle and on his way to wreak havoc on the rest of the galaxy, carrying his philosophy with him. We don't know who or what we may find out here, but I can't have the Coalition representing us."

She turned to the other cells in the brig. Each occupant was watching her with expectation. Until they re-captured Barnes, they'd postponed the Justice Committee's verdicts and their subsequent sentencing. Their disappointed expressions said it all. They wouldn't be getting out of the brig anytime soon, and they knew it was because of Barnes.

"Did any of you see something that might help us?"

She looked from one prisoner to the next. They either shook their heads or shrugged.

"If you tell us anything that leads to Barnes' capture, it will weigh heavily in your favor during sentencing."

Again, no one came forward. The youngest, Luke, hadn't even stood up from his cell's bench. She doubted they were withholding information. If they'd had any, they'd have spoken up by now, but Dana couldn't risk letting even one of them go free. With tensions being what they were, they could end up killed by an angry passenger or a crew member with a grudge.

No, they were safer right where they were.

CHAPTER 36

Five hours later, after searching the entire ship, deck by deck, they still hadn't found Barnes. The anxiety built inside of Dana until her chest felt too tight to breathe. The absurdity of it all was more than she could stand. She was out of ideas. If someone on the ship was helping Barnes, she needed to find out who, and fast. There may even be more than one person aiding him.

She couldn't let her thoughts take that turn. Those were the kinds of ideas that instilled distrust among the passengers and crew, and the last thing they needed was to be suspicious of each other.

Dana tugged at the collar of her uniform. She was too hot and couldn't wait to cool off in a mist shower. The search for the Fashin Teku hadn't drained them of all their resources yet, and thanks to them, they had contact, limited though it was, with the Begarans, who had generously provided enough supplies to keep them going at least until they ran into another planet or ship.

The moment she stepped through the doors of her quarters she knew something was off.

"COMP, lights to full," she commanded.

The harsh light infiltrated every dark corner, but nothing but the feel that someone else had been there remained. She scanned her kitchen and living area, but nothing was disturbed. In her room, her heart fell to the soles of her boots. Laid out, unpacked, and exposed was her wooden treasure box. Hand-carved by her father, it was open, and everything that had been inside was strewn on the bed.

Dana checked under the bed, along the frame, and in the closet and bathroom before she returned to her most private of items laying out in the open on her bed. Her tin with her anxiety nanodots was there. She opened it and her hands shook. She did the quick count twice. There were three nanodots missing. Whoever had been going through her things had made it clear that they knew about them. Every item from her past had been fondled. Viktor's dog blue identification tag. Her pink memory chip with images of her and Bonnie when they were at the academy. A yellow chip she'd saved with pictures of her family and another blue one from her time with Wade captured on it. The physical precious letters and cards she'd kept inside were all neatly lined up. Three of the expensive cards were from her father. The other two had been from Wade. She'd learned from her mother at a young age, paper was priceless and wasn't something you threw away. Each one would eventually disintegrate on its own but during its lifetime would be invaluable.

Dana wanted to gather them up, but she stood frozen, staring at the items, wondering who would do such a thing. Then the obvious answer hit her between the eyes. Barnes had somehow gained access to her room. She didn't know how, but it stunk of his Coalition disposition. He was letting her know that he knew about her dependency; on the comfort the dots and cards gave her, and if he had time to review any of the chips her true feelings about Wade. She told herself the cards were only a reminder that Wade had loved her once, along with notes from her father. The chips were another matter. If he'd watched what was on it, he'd see her feelings for him ran deeper than she wanted to admit. Nothing inside the box had gone untouched.

"COMP, who's access codes were used to enter this room in the last twelve hours?"

"The Captain's code, and emergency code profile belonging to Commander Wade Chance."

"Not likely."

Dana continued to grumble as she gathered up the memory chips and cards, not caring for the moment they were out of chronological order and mixed together. She was about to cram them back into the box when she saw something black already lying at the bottom. A small square was resting in the empty box by itself. She didn't remember putting it there, but that didn't mean anything. She put it aside, piling the rest of the things quickly back into the place.

Once she had everything, including the tin of nanodots, inside the box again, she closed the lid and was about to return it to its place when she realized it wasn't safe there anymore. Barnes had used Wade's code to enter her rooms and go through her things. Codes could be altered, changed, or stolen. She would ask Wade directly, to be thorough. If he'd touched her things, she'd be able to know it immediately. She knew Wade's face too well to doubt it. Dana was sure it was her former Chief of Security. The violation reeked of him and considering he'd recently escaped it made sense he'd come after her. He was sending her a message.

"COMP, change the access code to my voice authorization only."

"Change complete."

Dana debated about having security come into her room, but then she'd have to explain what she'd found, and there was no way she was going to let them peruse her personal keepsakes. She wasn't in love with Wade anymore, but her memories were hers to keep. Barnes had no right to go through her things. In her mind, she imagined all the ways she was going to make him pay for his invasion of her privacy.

Dana sat down to review the square file between her finger and her thumb, plugging it into the reader. At first, she didn't understand what she was seeing. It was a personal vid file. Barnes had knowledge of the other Coalition members, even if he didn't make himself known to them, as they all claimed. She reviewed every message again, wondering what Barnes had seen when he looked at it. Why had he made a personal copy for himself?

The final vid on the memory card didn't belong to any of the Coalition members. The video was marked for delivery to Maggie Brooker. *Was she one of them?* Dana was about to call for security to pick her up when the auto playback began.

A man named Bill appeared on the screen. He was husky, with light brown hair and red-rimmed eyes. From what Dana could tell, the video was from a former lover. He described their last night together, which had been only days before the *Hope* launch. Bill claimed to love her and was encouraging her to move on in the wake of his death. It didn't implicate Maggie as a Coalition member, but it called into question her loyalty to Wade.

So, this was the piece of information Barnes had threatened Wade with on the night of his arrest. Wade had come to Dana for advice on how to deal with Maggie's secretive behavior when she hadn't shared her message with him. Dana had thought the message harmless at the time, though had questioned the woman's integrity. Why would she keep secrets from the person she claimed to love and wanted to spend her life with?

The evidence sitting on her computer display was clear. Maggie would never share her vid with Wade because it was from a lost lover she'd been with while they were together. Barnes had seen the vid and knew what Maggie was hiding. She wondered if Barnes had threatened her with it. Had he blackmailed her into helping him escape? Whatever he'd wanted done with the information, he'd either been smart enough, or careless enough, to leave it behind.

Dana scrubbed her face with the palms of her hands. He knew the truth about Maggie. Now she knew, too.

The question was *why*? Why had Barnes left this vid for her to find? It didn't make any sense. Regardless of his motive, there was one thing she knew for sure: she wasn't going to have to officiate the wedding. Her new problem was much worse.

When was a good time to tell your ex that his girlfriend had been cheating on him?

CHAPTER 37

Dana's eyes snapped open as she lay on her bed later that night. Every shadow and every noise made her pull the blanket tighter under her chin. The monster in the dark had Barnes' face, and she couldn't stop imagining him overriding the system and breaking into her quarters again. She forced the lights up to full, then lay staring at the ceiling. She rolled to one side to watch the clock on the nightstand, and then the wall opposite the door as she made a mess of her sheets trying to get comfortable. When her eyes, too heavy to hold open, finally closed of their own will, she had nightmares of being chased by Barnes.

By morning, she was exhausted from mentally running and searching for places on the ship to hide. The lack of sleep had given her a headache that the nanodots would cure, but she refused to use them. Dana debated calling Valente down after all and going through her rooms for any evidence, but she knew Barnes was long gone, and had only left behind what he wanted her to find. She still had no idea what she was going to do with that little gem of information, but for now, she decided to get ready for the day, come what may.

The door chime had her grabbing her robe and tying it tight.

"Identify the visitor."

"Rido Jabar," the COMP replied.

"Just a minute," she said to herself.

Dana ran a hand over her face. She felt like she'd only just laid down to sleep. The rumpled sheets said otherwise. She stepped over the abandoned uniform from yesterday, now in a disheveled heap on the floor. The disquieting dreams retreated to the recesses of her mind as she tried to imagine what Rido could want this early in the morning.

The door slid open. His radiant smile greeted her, then faltered before he spoke.

"Captain, I hope you haven't forgotten our date."

Dana put a hand to her forehead. She had forgotten that the healer had insisted on coming by. *Had they set a time?* She couldn't remember.

"I guess I didn't realize we had an official appointment. I apologize. To be honest, we should reschedule."

Rido ignored her as he walked in and positioned a mat in the middle of the floor. He set a small candle on her table and lit the wick. It gave the room the faint scent of woods and spices. He laid out an assortment of bottles. The soft cream pants and robe he wore allowed him freedom of movement and, at some point, he'd slipped off his shoes. Dana noted them near the door. When she turned back, he was sitting on his heels and directing her to lie down on the mat with a gesture of one hand.

"I heard about Barnes' escape, so I squeezed you in this morning. From the look of you, I made the right choice."

"Ouch!" Dana wondered if she indeed looked as bad as she felt.

She got down on the mat, allowing him to guide her into a lying position.

"No offense," he said a smile parting his lips. "I just know healing, and I know when someone needs one. I can see from the bags under your eyes you didn't sleep. The foggy brain, the dullness of your skin... Besides that, the external factors of Barnes' escape, the trial on hold—if you don't need a healing, who does?"

Dana hated when doctors said things like that, as if it should be obvious. She didn't know what a healing entailed, but she was so tired, she didn't have much fight left in her.

"I need to be on the bridge in an hour," Dana said as she slid to the floor and lay face down on the mat.

"It won't take long, I promise, and you need it. You'll be glad we did this," Rido said, pulling down the top of her robe and looking her over. "Your shoulders are almost to your ears with stress."

"How are people doing knowing that Barnes is on the loose?"

"The ship is buzzing with the news. Some people are genuinely afraid. They have children, or they have some history with the Coalition that might make them a target."

Dana realized she should have been more concerned for herself in that regard.

"Everyone is doing what they can." Rido rubbed his hands together. "I haven't heard much sympathy thrown his way. Though, he probably needs some."

"Sympathy?" Dana asked, almost sitting back up.

"Yes," he said as he pushed her back down and continued to work. "He's a man who stood up for his beliefs. Right or wrong, he shouldn't be punished for believing something different from the rest of us."

"I can't believe what I'm hearing. If he came to you, would you hide him?" Dana asked, sitting up and pulling away from him.

Rido sat back and looked up, as if seriously considering it. "No, I wouldn't shelter him. He made his choice. Not one I agree with on a personal level, however, I would offer him some counsel before I sent him on his way."

He held up his hands in surrender when Dana glared at him.

"Am I *allowed* to have my own thoughts aboard your ship?"

His question was a valid one. She'd been considering it when trying to decide what to do about the non-active members of the CAH.

"Of course you are. Just keep them to yourself."

Rido nodded. "I don't know if you've ever been told before, but you're kind of gorgeous when you're angry."

Rido gave her a significant look before his eyes trailed down the front of her robe. Dana looked down at herself, wondering if this was a professional look, or a personal one.

"What are you talking about?" she asked, squeezing the robe tighter around herself when she realized he was looking at her like she was the last chocolate chip in the cookie.

"You have this little crease in the middle of your forehead, and your eyebrows form perfect arches above your beautiful eyes. There's so much fire in you. I've known few women with your passion."

As captain of a generation ship with no set destination, she didn't make for much of a romantic prospect. In fact, until now, she hadn't entertained the thought of taking a lover of any kind.

Her face grew hot as the idea came and quickly left. She had far too many responsibilities to attend to anyone else's needs. Her people needed a new planet, and she wouldn't let her heart—or Barnes—distract her from her duty.

Yes, they were encouraged to procreate once they found a new world, but for most of the trip, they were supposed to be in cryostasis. When she considered her options, she realized once they were settled, she would probably consider Rido—if he were still available. For now, though, it was out of the question.

"Any other gossip floating around the ship?" she asked, changing the subject.

"Nothing I'm permitted to share. Come," Rido said, holding out a hand to her, "I don't bite." He smiled before adding, "Hard."

Dana rolled her eyes before taking his hand. He positioned her on her stomach. With practiced hands, he loosened her robe until it lay on her back like a blanket. He peeled it down her shoulders, exposing the skin underneath. A shiver ran through her as she waited for his warm hands to make contact.

Whatever she'd been expecting, this wasn't it. He opened a bottle near her, and the smell of herbs and flowers permeated her senses. Dana imagined herself lying in a meadow on Zelenia and wondered if that was the point of the oil.

The sensation of his warm, oiled hands against her cooled skin was amazing. She closed her eyes and relaxed into the floor.

"You're extremely tight... and with everything going on... do you want to talk about it?" he asked as his hands dipped lower on her back.

Dana groaned as he worked on the lower lumbar muscles. A memory flooded forward, and just like that; she was sniffling.

"I've said something wrong."

"No, it's not that." Dana let the tears fall to the floor while Rido worked out the tension in her back. "One of the last days with my mom, she was getting something called her bachi realigned, or some such nonsense. She'd love to see me getting a healing like this. It was sort of her thing."

"You absolutely need a bachi realignment, but not today. We'll keep it short and sweet." He turned his focus to her arms. "I don't mean to pry, but something is still bothering you. Is it the ex?"

So, it *was* true. Everyone on the ship already knew about her and Wade's history. It was inevitable on such a small ship. Soon everyone would know everyone else's business. But even Eartha, the young stowaway, had mentioned it. That night she'd caught him staring at her as if he could see something inside... she shivered with the memory.

Still, Dana liked the way he said 'ex' instead of using Wade's name. It made her smile.

"Well, yes... There is something I'm going to have to deal with."

"Ah, officiating the wedding. Have you decided?"

She'd forgotten that he spoke of it when she'd stubbed her toe. She bit her lip considering how much to say.

"The problem is, if things go sideways with them, what am I supposed to do?"

His hands stopped moving. "You expect trouble?"

"In a manner of speaking."

Rido switched to her opposite arm, and she rolled her head so she could watch him work.

"Is it because you want to take her place?" he asked.

If she hadn't been looking at him, she'd have thought his tone serious. In all honesty, no, she didn't want to be Wade's second choice and said so. The words made Rido smile. Did people still believe that could be her motivation?

Rido's tone was still serious. "People are talking, but no one believes you'd actually do anything to sabotage their relationship."

Dana thought about the vid Barnes had left her. Was he trying to tell her something about Maggie, or was he trying to get her to show it to Wade? They'd been friends; was this his way of seeking redemption? It didn't make much sense to her. However, if she were the one to break the news to Wade, isn't that exactly what she'd be doing? Sabotaging their relationship?

"My concern is purely professional," she said. "I don't have time to worry about two people forced to work together who can't stand each other."

"Yes, but the problem hasn't happened yet, so why are you attempting to deal with it now?"

Dana bit her tongue. She couldn't tell anyone what she knew about Maggie. She no intentions of telling Wade until she'd made sure that Maggie wasn't helping Barnes stay hidden. She owed him that much. But the truth was burning a hole in her gut.

"I like to get ahead of things."

"Maybe you can see what's coming before it happens," Rido theorized. "That's probably what makes you such a good Captain and a brilliant pianist." He was quiet for a moment before adding, "Your piece the other night was astounding. Was it an original?"

"Yes," Dana said, then groaned as he reached her calf.

"Don't stiffen up on me now," Rido said lifting her leg and jiggling it in his hand.

She was losing track of time, and she closed her eyes for a moment. At some point, he rolled her over, and she was face up with her robe still laying on top of her. He cleaned off the oil and turned to massage her face and head.

"What do you do when you need healing?"

He let out a small laugh. "You're so practical, Captain. You're all about learning the origins of things and how they work."

"I think you can call me Dana now that I'm on the floor with you massaging my face and feet."

"Dana. I like saying it." He sighed. "To answer your question, I understand how to perform certain techniques on myself. However, when needed, I prefer to visit another healer."

He put his hands on either side of her and gently lifted his hands in the air, closing them with light clap inches above her legs. He lifted his hands to the sky as if pushing something up and out of the room.

"Any better?"

Her mouth went dry and as she tried to croak out an

answer. He retrieved a glass of cold water and handed it to her. She drank half and cleared her throat. "I feel great. I believe you're onto something, with this healing business."

"I'm at your disposal. See you next week? Or sooner, if you'd like."

He smiled again, and Dana noticed how his sharp bone structure softened with the movement. He turned to go, his broad shoulders and strong arms more visible under the fitted shirt he wore. She'd been naked under his capable hands only moments ago. Her voice came out raspier than she'd intended.

"Next week will be fine."

"As you wish." Rido gathered his things. When he passed the threshold, he turned back to flash her another smile. "Until we meet again."

With dimples like his, it was no wonder he had so many exes who wanted to stay friends. Dana dragged her eyes away, letting the door close between them. Again, she wondered why she hadn't noticed the same features in his twin.

Dana rolled her shoulders and sighed. On top of everything, he'd been right. Her mind was clear. She wouldn't worry about anything she couldn't control. Her sense of purpose and duty was now clearer than it had been before. It was a good thing, too. It was time to get dressed and find Barnes before he did any serious damage to the ship or anyone onboard.

When her door chimed, she smiled, wondering if Rido had left the burning candle on the table so he could come back. She picked it up and blew it out.

"Forget something?" she asked as the door opened.

To her surprise, Wade stood staring down at her, his eyes

wide as he took in her robe. Then his eyes dropped to the candle and came back up again.

"Am I interrupting something?"

His voice seemed harsher than usual. He frowned at her, as if demanding an answer. It was all she could do not to blurt out what she'd seen on Maggie's vid. He was going to be so hurt when he learned the truth. Dana couldn't think of any way around it. But he'd come to her for a reason and she'd have to see to Maggie herself, so she had some time to figure it out.

"No, Commander," Dana put the candle down on the nearest surface and turned back to him. "What can I do for you?"

"We have a problem. It's the crates we received from the Begarans."

She frowned. "What's wrong with them?"

"Nothing. But we discovered several of them contained things stolen from us by the Fashin Teku."

Dana felt the tension already trickling back in. Wade nodded as she came to the same conclusion he had.

"All stop. Meet me in the cargo bay."

"Yes, Captain."

CHAPTER 38

"A lie is only a lie until the truth is known."
- Begaran Proverb

As Valente and his security team were needed in the search for Barnes, Eric and Esme had meticulously organized the cargo bay. All the new crates had been pushed to one side, prepped for distribution. The stack of crates piled in the middle of the room were waiting for Dana to address. The open crates were filled with Zelenian supplies, the labels marking their food, drink, and some medical items.

"Report," she said.

"All stop, Captain," Wade replied. "These are the crates we discovered with our labels on them."

"Any sign of the embryos?"

Wade frowned as he shook his head.

"Where are the other crates from?"

Eric stepped forward. "Captain, at first we didn't notice them as being much different."

"They were all crated with their labels until we started opening them," Esme continued. "There are three distinct labeling systems, including ours."

"So, some of the other items might also be stolen goods?" Dana guessed.

"That was our assumption," Wade said, pointing at the crates in question.

Dana walked up and down the organized aisle. There was a group of crates with a large tree symbol. Another with a geometric type shape. The third pile of crates had what Dana understood to be the Begaran label on it, a combination of circles that resembled the structures on the surface of their planet.

"How long until we're in communications range?" Dana asked.

"Not long," Esme said. "If we push the engines a bit, we could be there in several hours."

Both she and Wade looked to the Rogans. They both nodded.

"Yes, she can take it," Eric confirmed. "I'll head there now to keep an eye on things."

"Inform the bridge." Dana's eyes followed Wade as he walked over to the panel before she turned back to Esme. "Leave the supplies where they are for now. I don't want to distribute these other items until we're sure they weren't stolen from someone else."

"But—"

Dana waved a hand. "The crates that belong to us can be returned. Leave the rest." She knew it was a gamble not to keep it all. There might be items inside they could use, but she also knew what it was like to have her things stolen. She didn't want to risk it until she was sure the items belonged to the Begarans and no one else.

Her gut said the third symbol was probably some other unsuspecting sap who'd been duped by the Fashin Teku. However, considering they'd taken the time to repackage their things and send them back, the Begarans might be involved in some shady business of their own. Dana withheld her official judgment on the matter for after they asked the Begarans some more questions.

Esme went back to work, directing her people to remove their cargo from the bay and return it to where it originated.

Dana joined Wade near the comms panel, where he waited for further instruction.

"Commander, a moment please," Dana said. She indicated he should follow her as she made her way to the bridge.

Despite everything going on, the small memory file sitting on the corner of her nightstand was still on her mind. Even though her dreams would insist otherwise, she was relatively sure that no one else could get into her rooms now. Having it still made her anxious. The problem was what to do about what she knew. How could she tell Wade he was planning to marry a woman who'd been cheating on him without telling him? It didn't sit well on her heart or her tongue.

"What else can I do?" Wade prompted.

"At the moment, nothing. Where are we with tracking Barnes? Any sign of him yet?"

Wade's steps faltered, and he shook his head. "I still can't believe he ran. We've searched the entire ship, and he's nowhere."

"Keep looking. We can't leave anything unchecked. While we were scanning the ship looking for explosives, we had a twelve-year-old girl hiding in the ventilation system. If it was easy for her to stay out of sight, I'm not surprised we haven't seen Barnes."

Wade swallowed hard. "Someone could be hiding him."

Again, Dana thought of Maggie and wondered if she was somehow helping him.

"Agreed. Every man and woman who's spent any time with him has had their quarters searched, but there may be more." *There was at least one more.* Dana ran a hand over her face as they entered the lift to the bridge. "We're running out of options here. We haven't seen any signs of life within areas of the ship he might hide in, but I know he's still here. It's keeping me up at night."

Wade nodded. "I wondered, but I didn't feel it my place to ask." He glanced over at her. "We'll catch him. Wherever he is, he can't do much harm without access to the weapons lockers or critical systems."

Dana wondered if he'd had time to break into one of their weapons lockers like he had her quarters. Just thinking about it made her anxious again, and she lamented the three nanodots missing from her stash of seven. She clenched her hands at her sides, trying to think of something else. She blurted out the first thing that came to mind.

"How are things going with the wedding planning?"

Wade waved a hand. "I've pretty much got it under control. Why do you ask?"

It was an innocent enough question, but she wondered why he hadn't mentioned Maggie's request it had been days. The doors of the lift opened to the bridge, and it occurred to her again that Maggie's request might not have been as unanimous as she'd made it sound.

"I haven't given Maggie my answer about officiating yet, but I promise I will, and soon."

Wade stopped short. "Your answer about *what*?"

Dana was suddenly aware of all the eyes in the room on them. "Helm," she called out, "estimated time of arrival?"

"Six hours and twenty minutes," Nancy answered.

"Good. I'll be in my office. Commander?" Dana called out after her. This conversation wasn't going to happen on the bridge.

"She what?" Wade asked the second the doors closed behind them, his voice too loud in the small space.

Dana sat down behind her desk and watched him pace. "So, I take it you had no idea about that?"

Wade ran a hand through his hair. "Of all the stubborn... She's the most thick-headed..." His voice trailed off.

"She assured me she'd asked you, and that you were in full agreement about me performing the wedding."

"I said you would never agree to it. I shouldn't have assumed she'd let the matter drop." Wade shook his head. "I'm sorry. I never would've asked you to do such a thing."

Dana shrugged, unsure, in the moment, why his statement bothered her so much. She didn't want to do it, wasn't planning to do it, and based on what she knew, the wedding would be over before it began.

So why had his quick dismissal of her rankled?

"I guess I should just be happy to be invited and leave the ceremony to someone else."

Wade paused a moment, looking down at her face as if

trying to read her features. Dana knew how to keep her inner thoughts and feelings to herself.

"No, I... I assumed you wouldn't even want to come." His tone was one of surprise. "Somehow officiating was so laughable, I hadn't considered she'd actually come to you with it." His expression was one of confusion. "Did you want to come to the wedding?"

"I thought it was laughable, too, but I told her I would think about it, to get her out of my hair," Dana said, agreeing with his first statement and ignoring the question.

He shook his head again. "I'll take care of it. I'm sorry she came to you about it. You've got enough on your plate."

"Yes, well, it's hardly the time to be planning a wedding. I suggest you push the date back until things settle down."

"I'm way ahead of you, but thanks." He frowned, the confusion still there. "Wait, are you coming?"

"Wade, we're friends. You know I want to support you in whatever you choose to do with your life. Send me an invitation."

Dana wondered if he'd noticed that she hadn't answered the question, relieved she didn't have to mention the memory file. Perhaps the information on the drive could be leaked some other way. If it had been anyone other than Maggie herself, it would have been an easy thing for her to slip the file somewhere. This time, however, it was the reporter's secret that needed to be revealed.

She'd just started to like and trust Maggie. This was something she wasn't prepared to deal with on any level, and she didn't want to be caught in the middle. Her best course of action was to confront Maggie about any involvement she

had with Barnes. Then, *by the stars*, their premature ceremony and doomed marriage could fall apart on its own.

MAGGIE ANSWERED THE DOOR ON THE THIRD CHIME.

"Coming!"

Dana straightened her shoulders. The two security
guards standing out on either side of her had no idea why
they were there and didn't ask questions.

The door slid open and Maggie lifted her long red waves
back over her shoulder as her eyes swept over Dana and the
two guards.

"If you're looking for Wade, he's in his own cabin at the
moment."

"No, I'm here to see you."

"What's with security? Are you charging me with
something?"

"May I come in?" Dana asked as she walked in without
waiting for Maggie to invite her.

"Hey! You can't just barge in here."

Dana ignored her outburst as she took in the room.
Maggie's things were strewn about all over the furniture, and
she had to step over more than one pair of heels as she
circled the room.

"Do you have a tablet nearby?" Dana held up the black
chip and watched Maggie's eyes go wide and round before
she recovered.

Was that recognition or fear? Maggie pulled out her tablet
slipping out a blue memory chip for the black one. The video
started to play, and she gasped.

"Where did you get this? This is my personal and private message," Maggie said baring her teeth.

"It was left in my quarters on my bed," Dana said leaving out the details of her own items before adding, "by Barnes."

"He promised," Maggie said turning off the vid and putting the tablet down on the already cluttered table filled with used glasses and dishes.

Dana moved to the tablet and pulled out the black memory chip.

"Are you hiding him?"

Maggie's blue eyes turned cold.

"I wouldn't hide that snake if he begged me."

"He was holding this over you." Dana held up the chip. "It's possible he persuaded you to hide him in exchange for keeping it quiet."

"I didn't. He never came to me, though he knows I'd never agree to help him run."

"But he did get you to do *something*."

Dana waited a moment while Maggie shifted her weight from one barefoot to the other.

"Yes, I got him something from the med-bay. He said he was having trouble sleeping and if I got him what he needed he'd give me an exclusive in addition to keeping quiet about what he knew."

"When did you slip him the sleeping agent?"

"After his testimony in front of the Justice Committee. I got what I wanted out of him and slipped the agent into his hands." She waved a hand in the air. "It was a simple bump pass. The guards didn't see a thing. I didn't know he was going to use it to escape."

"Fine, so why did he leave the chip in my cabin to find?"

"I don't know." Maggie crossed her arms over her chest and rolled her eyes. "He broke his end of the deal and he pleaded guilty to everything so, some exclusive."

Dana couldn't see anything in the cabin that would convince her that Barnes was there, but she checked inside of the rooms and closets anyway. When she returned to the main living area Maggie was still standing there glaring.

"Satisfied?"

"If he does seek you out for shelter, food, anything, I want to know about it."

"I can do better than that, if he comes to me. I'll find out where he's been hiding and give him up, but what's in it for me?"

"What do you mean?"

"You know what I mean. Wade doesn't know about the vid and he can never know, or everything will be ruined."

"You've already ruined it. Lying to Wade is only going to make things worse. He knows you're keeping something from him and it's only a matter of time before Barnes finds him and tells him."

Maggie shook her head. "No, he'd have done it already, Wade would never believe him."

"It doesn't matter," Dana insisted taking a step toward her. "Look, you two are a great couple, but you won't survive this if you don't come clean on your own. If he learns about it from someone else, he'll never forgive you."

"Is that a threat?" Maggie lifted her chin.

Dana's shoulders slumped and she shook her head.

"No, it's not my intention to break you up. Your relationship with him is your business. However, I could arrest you for aiding Barnes in his escape." She'd probably regret it, but she had a way out of two problems at once. "I'll make you a new deal. If you give up Barnes when or if he comes to you and find yourself someone else to officiate your wedding, I can promise you I won't be the one to show Wade the vid. Though he deserves better."

Maggie stiffened as tears welled up in her eyes. Dana reached the door and turned back as it slid open. She wanted to tell Maggie she could make Wade happy by just being honest with him. They had an opportunity that few others on the ship had. She was a fool to squander it on a secret like this one, but the words stuck in her throat and she left without saying anything more.

CHAPTER 39

After several hours at high speeds, they were back in Begaran space. Lieutenant Commander Valente had given his report only an hour ago, stating that Barnes was still missing despite their continued effort to search non-living areas for him. He was in someone's quarters, Dana was sure of it, but there was no one on his list of friends or enemies who hadn't been searched. He could be coercing someone like he'd done Maggie, but he kept most of his business to himself. She wondered how long Barnes had been planning his escape from the brig. Maggie might not have been the first one he approached.

Barnes was only one of their problems. Dana still had the Begarans to deal with. Why had they lied about contact with the Fashin Teku? Whose cargo had they sent? She planned to get answers.

"The Begarans are within range, Captain," Cliff said.

Dana stood up from her chair and placed her hands on her hips in front of the main viewer. They could see her, even if she couldn't see them.

"Are their weapons trained on us again?"

"Not this time," Cliff answered.

"Inform me the moment that changes. Open comms," Dana said.

At Cliff's nod, she spoke.

"Begarans, this is Captain Dana Pinet of the *Starship Hope*. We discovered something interesting in the cargo you sent us."

Dana's introduction was met with silence. She stood for a full minute, waiting for an answer.

"Are they receiving us?" Dana asked, turning to Cliff.

"Loud and clear, they're just not answering."

"Keep the channel open." Dana continued, "We'd like more information about the alien species that arrived before us. They were carrying stolen goods. Goods you received and passed off as your own to us when we were here a little over a day ago."

It was the strangest thing to be talking to herself with no response from the aliens. Dana looked to Wade on her right. He gave her a nod of encouragement. They'd heard her. It was time to get to the point.

"They stole from us, and we'd like it all returned."

"Their weapons are activated and locked on us," Cliff said.

"Thought it might come to that," Dana said under her breath, then went back to addressing the Begarans. "If they've also wronged you, we will gather anything they've stolen and return it to you. We only want to see justice done. Please, tell us in which direction they went."

This time there was half a minute of silence before the Begarans answered. She recognized the same garbled voice of the representative, though the screen remained black.

"Those thieves are no longer of any concern to either of us. Once we understood what they were after, we gave them a reason to never return. You will be happy to learn in just a few days. They will no longer be a problem for you, or anyone else in this sector. Justice is done."

"What does that mean?" Dana asked, tamping down on the rising anxiety. "Where did they go? What did you do to them?"

They might only be a few days away at maximum speed. Dana did a quick calculation of how much of a lead they had on them now.

"They came here as liars, but they left here as speakers of truth. Unable to lie, they will be destroyed by others, if they haven't already destroyed themselves."

"Can you give us their coordinates?"

"No. It is not safe for you to pursue them. If you come into contact with any of them, you may suffer the same fate."

"We don't have a choice," Dana insisted. "They've stolen our young."

The silence on the other end of the comms made everyone lean forward, waiting for them to speak.

"We will send you the coordinates," the voice said at last. "Be warned, the next time you invade our space, we will fire without question."

"They've blocked our comms, Captain," said Cliff.

"I get it. Helm, have they sent the coordinates?"

"Yes," Nancy confirmed.

"What's our estimated time to that location at top speed?"

"Three days," Nancy said, frowning at her console. "Though, I'm not sure we can sustain ourselves at that speed. We run the risk of running down our fuel reserves."

"I'll talk to engineering. Lay in the heading and go on my mark."

"Yes, Captain," she said, putting in the numbers.

"Mark," Dana said as she sat back down in her seat. "Ensign, inform engineering we'll be pushing the engines a little longer than planned."

"Aye, Captain," Cliff said.

"What do you think we'll find?" Wade asked.

"I'm not sure," Dana said.

"I wish we had their molecular relocation technology," he added. "It would make things so much easier." He looked sideways at her. "From the sound of it, it might be a mistake coming into contact with these aliens again."

"We have no other options. They took our future from us. We can't leave the embryos behind."

Dana wasn't sure they'd ever see the embryos again, but she knew what she was risking if she didn't try. Even if more ships made it off of Zelenia, as young Luke Geyer suspected, the embryos couldn't be allowed to fall into alien hands.

"The Begarans gave us enough to survive on. We may be risking everything going after the Fashin Teku," he reasoned.

Dana tapped her fingers on the arm of the chair. "We've already been over this. They took our embryos. We can't start a new world without them." This was the closest they'd been to the Fashin Teku in weeks and Dana wasn't ready to give up. "If they'd taken half the crew, we'd be doing the same thing. We have to try."

Wade nodded.

"Continue long-range scans of the area. I don't want to miss them." Dana stood up. "I'll be in my office. Inform me of any changes."

Once she was alone, Dana sat down at her desk and stared at her monitor. What did she think she was going to do once they caught up to them? They still had no weapons, no way to take what they needed by force. If they chose to board their ship, they risked being infected with whatever the pirates had been given.

A moment later the door from the bridge signaled.

"Enter," she called.

Wade walked in, letting the door close behind him. "Captain, our estimated time of arrival is still days at our current speed. We can only assume that from those coordinates, they were moving at a more moderate pace, but we won't be sure until we get there. Do you have a plan?"

Dana gestured to a seat in front of her. "I don't. I'm wondering if we've got some large rocks in storage. We can throw them at them as we're making our demands."

Wade was sweet enough to laugh at her joke, and she admired his smile. She would miss it when he learned the truth about Maggie. Ultimately, it couldn't come from her. If she were to maintain her end of the bargain, she had to stay out of it. That was the deal. She'd have to convince Maggie to tell him herself.

"The wedding still stressing you out?" she asked.

"It's unbelievable how a little ceremony like declaring your love for someone in front of friends can become this giant knot at the back of my neck." Wade squeezed his shoulder blades together, wincing in pain.

"I have next to nothing to say on the subject," she started hesitantly, "but I'm told if you love the person, you'll make allowances for differences in preference. Instead of talking to me or anyone else, talk to Maggie. She needs to understand how you're feeling about all this. Encourage her to be open and honest with you as well."

His eyes narrowed as he sat back in his chair. "You say that as if she hasn't been."

"I didn't mean anything by it. It's only that according to you've both been secretive in the past. You don't want to build your future on unknowns."

Wade seemed to think about it as he stared down at his hands. "What would you know about building a future with someone?"

He had kept his tone even, but she felt the bite behind his words.

She took a deep breath and rolled her shoulders back. "I want you to consider it all carefully. Resolve any unspoken mysteries before you get married—"

"If you don't want to attend the ceremony, why don't you just say so?"

"No, you've got this all wrong—"

He was on his feet before she could scramble out of her chair. "So, this is not about how *you* feel about Maggie?"

Dana's mouth clamped closed. She had no idea how to say what she needed to without it appearing like she wanted to break them up.

He took Dana's brief hesitation as his answer. "Well, don't worry about officiating or attending. I know you don't like Maggie, but I had thought you'd be more open to her since she's proven herself to you and everyone else onboard of her worth."

"Wade, this isn't about my feelings about Maggie," Dana said, then hated the words as they reached him.

"Then what is it? Are you so bitter you'd rather see me unhappy than with someone I love?"

"Absolutely not." Dana took a deep breath to steady her next words. "I'm sorry if I ever gave you that impression. Like I said, we're friends. I want to see you happy more than anything. If I didn't, I never would have gone to your house that day."

Wade gathered himself, seeming to consider her words, listening for the truth in them. He knew as well as she that if she hadn't come to his house and begged him to join the *Hope* mission, he might have died on Zelenia along with the rest of the people they'd left behind.

His words came out in a low growl. "I want to believe you," he said.

Dana stood up from her chair. "You can believe me," she said, putting as much feeling into the statement as she could muster. "I still care about you. If you tell me that Maggie has been completely honest with you, and you with her, then I'd be happy to stand up at your wedding along with the rest of the guests."

He frowned back at her. "What do you mean?"

"I mean... you can't build a happy marriage on top of buried secrets."

Wade raised his arms, letting them drop back to his sides. "I know what I said before about the vid messages, but I'm telling you now, we're good. Why can't you just be happy for me?"

Before she could get out another word, he left, jaw clenched as he hurried out into the corridor.

She sighed and sat down with her cheek resting on her fist.

"Captain's Personal Log Supplemental: Dana, you're an idiot."

CHAPTER 40

The conference room adjoining Dana's office was turned into a war room within minutes. The Justice Committee's chairs and tables were gone, making room for the large oval table again. Dana was unsure how well they would accept her plan, but she needed as many minds on the project as she could get.

Wade sat erect and distant on her left, Maggie between them. The President and the Chancellor sat on her right. Lieutenant Commander Valente had also been pulled from the search for Barnes to help them with tactical plans. He sat next to Esme Rogan on the far end of the table. Eric Rogan had remained stationed in the engine room, monitoring their speed in pursuit of the Fashin Teku.

"Gentlemen, Chief Rogan, Maggie, welcome," Dana said as she looked at each member of the table. "I realize we're in the eleventh hour, and this might not have the Majestic's blessing, but we need to consider all our options. I don't care how outlandish or improbable, I want everything we can think up considered and fleshed out."

Valente, who looked like he was getting about as much sleep as she was, spoke first. He opened the discussion with a plan to ride in firing. He wanted to take them by surprise. "They won't see us coming, especially not this fast. We disable their shielding, their power core, and once it's down, we go over in a shuttle and we take back what's ours."

"I like where your head is Valente, but let's assume we can knock out their systems with our little lasers. We still have the major problem of potentially blowing up their ship. If we accidentally hit the core, we'll lose the whole ship—supplies, embryos, and all. We don't know the schematics well enough to be sure we're in the right place when it comes to hitting them from a distance."

"We have the shuttles," Wade said. He didn't meet her eyes, instead he gazed around the table. "Perhaps if we use them, we can overwhelm their ship with our numbers. They don't have much, but the lasers on the shuttles might be annoying enough to take their attention off what we're doing here."

"Tactically sound. However, with my pilots and fighters divided, we run the risk of losing you in a firefight to a ship with superior gun power." Dana, too anxious to sit any longer, began to pace as she considered their options. "We could use the diversion to get close to the alien ship, even dock with them. Didn't I see a docking hatch on that film of yours, Maggie?"

"Yes, I believe so," Maggie said. Her eyes went to the floor. No, she hadn't told him, and she probably wouldn't. "I've got some ideas about where they might be holding the embryos as well."

"Excellent. As soon as we have them, we won't have to worry about destroying their ship if necessary."

President Muñoz raised a tentative hand. At Dana's nod, he cleared his throat. "Am I the only one thinking we might be able to negotiate with them?"

Dana smiled. She'd expected him to speak up earlier, and she wasn't surprised to hear the idea come from him. Of course, she'd considered it. That had been her reasoning behind inviting him and the Chancellor. However, she knew Chancellor Evans well enough to know he liked to believe he was coming up with his own ideas, not being told what to do by her.

"That's why you were invited to this meeting."

"What do you want from us, exactly?" Chancellor Evans asked.

"We'll be out-gunned," Dana explained. "I need diplomatic options on the table just as much as strategic battle plans. How are we going to deal with a species with superior technology to our own?" Dana spread her hands wide in welcome. "We all know diplomacy isn't really my thing, so I'm open to suggestions."

"Negotiation is our best chance," said President Muñoz. "These aliens are a greedy bunch. It's already put them in ill favor with us and the Begarans. Our advantage is that we're now carrying more cargo than before. We may hold something they want."

"Our virtual technology could make it appear as though we carry more cargo than we do," Esme added, speaking up.

"Chief?" Dana asked her.

Esme place a hand on her stomach and leaned back in her seat. She probably didn't even realize she was doing it.

"Well, it would take some doing to fool their sensors, but we could make it look like there's something worth trading in our cargo bay. It's not impossible to re-create the energy signature of some of our more valuable cargo."

Esme waited in silence while Dana thought about it.

"Can you do it?" Dana asked.

"We're only guessing, since we don't know how much their sensors can get from a scan, but yes, I think it's possible. We just need some time."

Dana frowned. "Time is something we don't have. Get ready what you can. It might be the best chance we've got."

"Regardless of what we could offer them, do you believe they'll return our embryos?" Chancellor Evans asked, leaning over the table towards her. "We don't even know why they took them in the first place."

"It's a valid concern," Wade said. "They've got the technology to blow us out of the sky without slowing down. We don't know the range on their sensors. Even at our top speed, they may see us coming. As much as I want the embryos back, I think we need to protect the people still onboard."

Wade met her eye. There was a challenge in his gaze, but something else, too. He glared at her as if she'd stolen something from *him*. Dana had to shake off the chill. She took two steps, then turned around, letting her hands clap against her thighs.

"You think we should give up," she said.

"What if that's the only way to survive, to live to find compatible aliens or find a world where we can start over?" Wade reached out and grabbed Maggie's hand, making a show of kissing the back of their joined hands. Maggie seemed uncomfortable with the attention for the first time and kept her eyes on the floor.

Dana averted her gaze, focusing on the faces around the table. It was frustrating that he didn't even know the truth, and he was already treating her like a jealous ex-girlfriend. She wasn't jealous of what he had with Maggie, she was only looking out for him—whether he liked it or not.

"What if they were implanted into another alien species?" Esme asked. "We might not be compatible with the Fashin Teku, but there are other races, other reasons to trade them."

"We're responsible no matter what happens to them. What if they're sold into slavery?" Chancellor Evans said, slamming a fist on the table.

Dana raised both hands in the air to calm everyone down before things got out of hand. Emotions were high. It was natural, but they had a mission to accomplish, and they'd never fulfill it if they didn't keep cool heads.

"Why are we playing the 'what-if' game? There are many things the Fashin Teku could do with the embryos in their custody. Let's decide here and now if they're worth the risk." Dana looked around the conference table again, making eye contact with each of those gathered. "You already know where I stand."

The table fell into silence while they imagined all the possible uses for their young.

"We still don't know what the Begarans did to the Fashin Teku." Wade shook his head. "We're assuming that whatever it was, it hasn't already changed the embryos."

Dana grit her teeth and squared her shoulders. He was being obstinate on purpose, but with every objection she overcame, she gained more courage to continue.

"That's a big assumption," she said. "I'm not willing to give up without further evidence. The facts are they have the embryos and no matter what's happened to the Fashin Teku they're in danger. It's the only thing we have to go on at the moment."

When there were no further objections, Dana made the call.

"All right then. President Muñoz, Chancellor Evans, be ready to come to the bridge. Once we catch up with the Fashin Teku, if there's any chance of a diplomatic solution, I'll send for you. I'm relying on the two of you to use your experience to get us through any negotiating obstacles that may arise. Keep your comms close."

They answered in unison: "Yes, Captain."

"Esme, I'd like you and your husband to get to work on that virtual sensor trick. We may not need it, but it'd be better to have it in our back pocket just in case. Maggie, if you find anything else on that video footage we haven't considered, bring it to me right away. The rest of you, thank you for bringing your ideas and open minds to the table." Dana gave Wade a significant look that he ignored. "Dismissed. Valente, Chief Rogan, a moment please."

Esme was the closest, and Dana pulled her to one side to speak first.

"How are you feeling?"

Esme gave her a wan smile. "I'll admit this first trimester has been difficult. I'm cautiously excited, of course."

"I understand. Things being what they are, make sure you take care of yourself and get the needed rest. Dr. Jabar cleared you for duty, but you don't need permission to take some time. It's going to be a little bumpy, so stay away from cargo areas and bulkheads."

"I will, thank you."

She was turning to go when Dana touched her arm.

"How's it going with Eartha?"

Esme shook her head and shrugged. "To be honest, I'm not so sure. She's been moody lately, pretty short-tempered, too."

"The baby?" Dana suggested.

"She blows up any time we even mention the baby. She's probably feeling left out, but we're not sure how to include her."

"Give her a little space. She's still adjusting." Dana tilted her head in thought. They needed help, and there was only one person on the ship she knew of who could calm someone down from a murderous rage. "Have you had a chance to speak with Mr. Jennison?"

"Yes, he's been wonderful. He spends lots of time with Eartha, too. However, lately she's been upset every time we invite him over. I think she feels it might be an intrusion on her friendship with him."

"Is there any other support you need? I know we have a certified counselor on board."

"There's a small discussion group for new parents we've attended. It helps."

Dana bit her bottom lip. Adoption wasn't an easy process, and it seemed Eartha had been adopted twice.

"I'll come by and bring her out for a bit of ice cream one of these evenings, once things settle down."

"Thank you, Captain," Esme said with a quick look to Valente, who stood patiently at the door.

Dana watched her go and said a prayer to the Majestic for her and the baby to make it full-term this time. Dr. Jabar had already confirmed Maggie's report they were expecting at six babies to be born within the year—which was amazing itself. However, Dana couldn't ignore that without the embryos, their species was still in peril.

There were too many unknowns when it came to the Fashin Teku and the stolen embryos. Dana did her best to stamp down the fear in the back of her mind that their molecular relocator had damaged the embryos, or worse, that they had been used for food, or something even more sinister.

Valente had been patient and stood at attention until she moved to address him. Up close, she saw the dark smudges under both eyes, and his usually neat hair had grown unruly. *Is he sleeping in his uniform, too?* It looked like he hadn't slept so much as rolled around in it.

"Are you all right?"

"Yes, I'm fine." He lifted a hand and ran it over his bald head. "I haven't been getting enough sleep. I've tried but—" Then, as if he realized he was rambling, he cut himself off and stood erect. No doubt her own face carried the same marks of stress.

"No sign of Barnes?"

"Just the other night," he said with a curt nod.

Dana's heart leaped. Could they be getting close to finding him?

"He raided the kitchen, so we've set up security there to see if we can catch him in the act. We also found his uniform. We believe he'll be in civilian garb from now on."

"Do you believe he's getting help?" she asked.

"Yes. We're still conducting searches of every cabin for

signs of him, but so far my team has come up short. We're stretched thin."

Dana waved a hand. "I understand. Keep doing your best. Do you have a list of potential allies?"

Valente shook his head and shrugged. "He wasn't particularly close to anyone. He worked with everyone in security, but they all swear they had no idea who he was before his arrest and don't know where he was now. We interviewed all the young ladies he'd spent time with since coming aboard, though... there were only two." His jaw tensed. "I won't give up until we catch him."

"I know you won't, but I want you and your people to get a little more rest. Barnes knows his time is short. He hasn't been a threat to anyone else, and I'm taking that as a good sign. If he wanted to, he could have caused more damage to the ship with all his hiding, but he's not."

"Agreed. There's been no evidence of further sabotage to the ship."

"I have other reasons for wanting your team to get some rest. We'll be facing the Fashin Teku in a few days, and I want my security officer on the bridge. I don't want you looking like you just fell out of bed." Dana shook her head as she waved at his attire. "By the way, where did you find Barnes' uniform?"

"He stuffed it in a recycler on deck three. We've searched every cabin on that deck, but we found no other evidence he was hiding there. He might have done it to throw us off. He knows all our procedures—he practically wrote the manual."

Dana agreed. She also figured anyone helping him could have put that uniform there for them to find.

"That's all for now, Commander. Dismissed."

Dana waited until the door closed behind him, then spoke aloud to the empty room.

"Barnes, where are you hiding?"

CHAPTER 41

"The first and foremost in all the laws of our peaceful citizens is that none shall pass as friend or foe, neighbor or distant. Our family lines will endure as long as our blood endures. One family, pure for all time."
-from The Three Laws of the Begarans

When the Fashin Teku's ship showed up on their sensors, it was obvious that something was wrong, even from a distance. The ship was drifting at an odd angle, its bulbous belly tilted to one side.

"Any answer to our hails?" Dana asked.

"No," Cliff replied. "They're not putting out a distress signal, and their channel is still closed."

"Were they hit by an asteroid?" Nancy asked, staring at the main viewer.

It was a valid question, considering their history with

asteroids. Dana saw the debris as well, but there was something strange about its movement.

"I don't think so... Bring us in and magnify the left quadrant of the monitor."

Nancy moved them closer. Wade magnified the image from his seat.

Then Dana saw what looked to be Fashin Teku bodies floating in space around the freighter.

Her hand flew to her mouth, but not before she let out an audible gasp. The last time she'd seen bodies floating in space, one of them had been her best friend Bonnie. She clamped down against the bile that rose in her throat and focused on the task at hand. She had to remember they were there for the embryos and nothing else.

"Any lost cargo?"

"No, Captain," Nancy said. "Their cargo bay is still sealed. All the... debris seems to be Fashin Teku."

Dana counted about ten bodies. She wasn't sure how many were on board, but there had been only thirty who'd come over when the *Hope* had hosted them. The rest of their crew had stayed behind, but Maggie had recorded lots of areas filled with Fashin Teku.

"Well, if they're not answering our calls, running, or firing, we could assume they're too busy to be bothered with us. Maybe we can sneak on board and get what we came for without dealing with them at all."

"We still don't know what's wrong with them. The air could be contaminated, there might not be any Fashin Teku left alive," Wade said, but there was no trepidation in his tone.

"Either way, we need to know, Commander. We're not leaving here without the truth or those embryos."

"I can take a shuttle and dock with their ship," he said. "If they don't fire on us, we might be able to get on board and find them without getting killed."

"We'll do our best to cover you."

Wade gave her a nod. "Valente, you're with me."

"Take two more of your people, Commander," Dana told him. "Bring our babies home."

Wade and Valente left the bridge, and Dana stared at the main viewer. They were walking into the unknown. The whole situation felt beyond what they'd been expecting.

"Anything, Ensign?"

"Still no response to our calls, Captain," Cliff replied.

This wasn't going as planned. Their precious cargo was in danger on an out-of-control ship.

"Continue scanning," Dana said, shifting about uneasily. "I want to be prepared if there's any change on that ship."

"I'll adjust the scanners to read for life signs. Maybe we can pick something up." Cliff squinted at his console and frowned. "Although, I'm not sure I know what I'm looking at... all we're getting is the Fashin Teku biology."

"Get Dr. Jabar in the med-bay to review the information. It's possible he'll notice something.

"Done," Cliff said. "Chief Rogan is on the comms."

"Put him through."

Eric's voice filled the bridge. "Captain, there's another problem. The scans of that ship over there show a build-up in their engines. I don't know exactly what they're using for fuel, but whatever it is, when it goes, that ship, and anyone nearby, is going to be in the blast zone. I suggest we get out of range."

Dana's heart tripped in her chest. "How much time do we have?"

"I don't know. It could be anywhere between several minutes to half an hour. We don't want to be here when it blows. Our shielding is strong, but not that strong. We're talking a full hull breach."

Dana stared at the main viewer as the Fashin Teku ship tilted, spinning in a slow circle, its nose about to face them.

"Wade," she said over the comms, "we need to get our embryos back. You may need to take them by force."

Dana knew what she was asking. There were a million unknowns. Whatever the Begarans had done to the pirates, any actions that put her crew in contact with them might also infect them. She didn't want to put him at risk, but they were running out of options. They didn't have the molecular relocation technology, and thus had no way to avoid stepping foot on their ship.

"On my way, captain," Wade said.

The security team was gathered and quickly left for the other ship. The bridge crew watched as their shuttle docked with the pirate's ship.

"We're getting a call on comms, Captain," Cliff said.

"From the Fashin Teku?"

"Yes."

"Put it through, and make sure that the shuttle is also getting this transmission." Dana stood up. "We might be able to avoid physical contact. Put them on the main viewer."

"Yes, Captain," he said.

When it appeared, Captain Ashwin Zeppel's face was too close to the screen. His hair lay in unkempt clumps, and his blue eyes shifted in rapid succession from left to right, as if he were looking for someone to come up behind him at any moment.

"Captain Pinet," he whispered through brown teeth. "Many sorries for our past dealings. I beg you, please help us."

Dana could see nothing wrong with him other than his slovenly appearance, and she steeled herself against his pleas.

"We have no intention of helping you. We just want what you took from us."

"I'll send over anything you want, but I beg you to take me and the rest of my uninfected crew back to your ship."

Dana couldn't imagine what could account for the failure of their systems and the chaos behind the man.

"What's happening over there? What kind of infection are we talking about?"

"There's no time," he insisted. "We need to evacuate the ship before they blow us all up. We have the technology to put it in your hold. Will you allow that?"

"I have a shuttle docking with your ship now. Give us what we came for."

"No, too much to risk. You will all get the sick. Don't come to our ship. We come to you in a blink." He closed and opened his eyes slowly in demonstration. Zeppel stared at the screen waiting for her answer.

Dana gave Cliff the signal to cut the audio. At his nod, she took a breath.

"Get the Chancellor and the President up here now."

"Yes, Captain."

Dana heard the signal beep of Zeppel's hails.

"It's the Fashin Teku ship," Cliff relayed. "They're hailing us."

Dana shook her head.

The Chancellor and President seemed to have been waiting almost outside the bridge, standing in front of her within three minutes of being called.

"Gentlemen, I need options, now. The ship is infected with whatever the Begarans did to them. I can't get out of their captain what happened to them exactly, but he's agreed to put our cargo back in the hold in exchange for safe passage for him and his unaffected crew."

"We need what they took from us," President Muñoz said, raising his palms up as he shrugged.

"We should leave them to die for their crimes," Chancellor Evans contested. "We don't have the resources to take care of them, especially if they're carrying something contagious."

She didn't love the idea of vindictive justice, but Evans wasn't entirely wrong this time. If they were contagious, her whole ship might be at risk. They might lose everyone for the sake of the embryos. It wasn't a responsibility she was willing to take on lightly. After all they'd done to catch up to the Fashin Teku, only to be forced to leave the embryos behind now, it would be too much.

"Agreed," she said at last, giving a nod to Evans. "We'll let them send over our cargo, but that's it."

With everyone in agreement, she dismissed the President and Chancellor back to their quarters.

"I believe we should stay, Captain," Chancellor Evans said, looking down at her.

"That won't be necessary. If we run into any trouble, I

don't want you on the bridge. Please, get to your cabin. We don't have a lot of time."

As soon as the two men were off the bridge, Dana initiated the comms. She spoke in a firm, decisive tone.

"Captain, we'll try to accommodate you, but we want our cargo first. Then we can negotiate for your safe passage."

"No, you miss the understanding," Zeppel hissed between his teeth. "We don't have the time. We can bring you every technology we can take with our hands. My people can make your ship faster. We can bring you to the nearest space station and you can leave us. We are making the promise. Please, take us with you."

"The cargo first," Dana said between her teeth. "Don't push me. I'm not interested in being conned again. You'll send it, or you'll never get on my ship." She put her hands on her hips. "One of my shuttles is on its way right now. You'll board it and be brought over physically. That way, if you need to be quarantined, we can keep you contained until our physicians can look you over for any contamination."

His eyes darted again to the left and right, then he nodded vigorously, the braids in his hair falling forward.

"Send the coordinates where you want all the cargo and technology to go."

Dana nodded to Cliff. He sent the coordinates.

"You have them. Send us our cargo."

Zeppel didn't bother to sign off before the screen shifted to black.

"Lower the shields and prepare to receive the cargo," Dana called out.

"We are receiving, Captain," Cliff replied a moment later. "They've dumped a whole lot more on top of our cargo in the hold." Cliff paused, staring at his console readout. "There's something else, too..."

"You know how I hate suspense, Ensign. Tell me exactly what we've got."

"The cargo, some foreign technology, and three Fashin Teku."

"What?"

"Captain, incoming fire!" Nancy exclaimed.

The ship jerked to the left, throwing them all to one side. As they were recovering, another shot fired, throwing them backward.

"Initiate evasive maneuvers!" Dana called. "Get our shuttle back here on the double, Ensign. Send security to the cargo bay and tell them to keep those doors sealed until we can get those three into quarantine."

"Yes, Captain!"

The ship dipped and turned as they did their best to avoid the hits. Thankfully, the fire was so focused on the *Hope* that it seemed to be ignoring the small shuttle.

"Our shielding has been compromised," Cliff reported. "It's down twenty—no thirty percent from full."

"Helm, put some distance between us and that ship."

"I'm trying, but they've got weapons on all sides. I can't seem to get free of them." Nancy put in one coordinate after another, trying to outmaneuver them. "They're in pursuit, Captain."

"What? How? A minute ago they were spinning like a top!"

"I don't know," Nancy said, frustration edging her voice. "It's like they just now realized we were here."

"No... they just realized their Captain is here, and no

doubt they want him back." Dana paced in front of the viewer and stumbled when they took another hit. "Where is my shuttle pod?"

"Coming up fast to stern. The Teku have noticed them, and are firing on them, too."

"Get the Commander on comms," Dana said.

"Captain, we're a little busy here," Wade said. "We're taking heavy fire."

"As are we. Do you remember how to do a Cowboy Roy?" Dana asked.

Wade's expression went from confusion to understanding before he smiled. "Got it!"

The screen went black.

"Cowboy Roy?" Cliff asked.

"Helm, on my signal, I want you to adjust course, turn this ship around, and then put us at a ninety-degree tilt," Dana ordered.

"I'm not sure that's even possible," Nancy said as she input the maneuver into her controls. "Better hold on to something!"

"On my mark," Dana said, watching as the Fashin Teku's ship gained on them. She watched Wade's shuttle get into position. "Mark!"

The *Hope* made a quick change of direction and rolled to one side. The next two hits from the pirate ship hit them instead of the shuttle, and the entire ship shuttered.

"We're down to minimum shielding. We can't sustain another hit like that one," Cliff told her.

"Open the shuttle bay doors and get ready," Dana said.

"They're coming in fast!" Nancy called, watching the shuttle come alongside.

"Match their speed."

They felt it the moment they scooped up the shuttle pod.

"Seal those doors," Dana said, pointing at Cliff. She sat down and strapped in. "Helm, correct our altitude and get us out of here. Put as much distance between us and the Teku's ship as you can."

Before Lieutenant Westlake could engage the course change, a bright light flashed behind them. The entire ship rocked to one side as Nancy fought to get them under control. Dana clung to the arms of her seat even as the restraints tightened over her chest, holding her down. The aftershocks from the explosion took out the rest of their shielding, but they managed to keep the hull intact, bolting out of range a moment later.

"On screen!" Dana called out.

Pieces of the Fashin Teku ship spun off into the blackness. The rest had turned to dust behind them.

"The ship, Captain. It's gone," Cliff said.

"They were gaining us before they just exploded," Nancy said.

"Their engines must have overloaded with all that extra activity."

Dana released the restraining belts and collapsed against the back of her chair, breathing a sigh of relief.

They'd done it. She'd gotten the cargo and hadn't been destroyed by the aliens.

But now it appeared they had one more problem to deal with. Ashwin Zeppel had relocated himself over—along with his two friends—with the cargo. She couldn't risk him contaminating the ship. They'd have to stay in the cargo bay until they were sure the intruders could do no further damage.

"Any life signs remaining?" Dana asked.

"None, Captain," Cliff replied.

"All stop, Lieutenant."

"All stop," Nancy confirmed.

"Ensign, send Commander Chance and Valente to the cargo bay along with a medical team. I want those Fashin Teku quarantined. I don't want whatever they have infecting our ship."

"Done," Cliff said.

"Helm, you have the bridge. We'll give the Rogans time to work on our shields. Continue scanning the area for any planets or signs of life. I'm going to the cargo bay to check on our unwanted guests."

CHAPTER 42

Dana found Wade, Valente, the security team, Dr. Jabar, and his team outside of the cargo bay when she arrived. Dr. Jabar and his people were already wearing contamination suits, designed to keep them from catching anything airborne or otherwise from the Fashin Teku.

"No one goes in without a contamination suit," Dana said, addressing those gathered. "We wait for the all-clear from Dr. Jabar. Understood?"

When she had a verbal confirmation from each of them, she nodded to the doctor and sent him and his two assistants inside. She left two guards on the door while the rest of them changed into contamination suits. They were still waiting after they'd returned to the corridor, waiting for Jabar's okay.

"Commander," Dana said, her breath fogging up the duroglass on her helmet, "good recovery. Any injuries?"

"None, Captain," Wade said, his voice made mechanical by the vocal interface amplifying it. "That was a nice move. I hadn't thought about Roy in years. I assume we got our cargo back?"

"We'll need to inventory everything."

Wade nodded. She wondered if he realized he was speaking to her again, the last few days of tension dissipating with one completed mission. Maybe that's how it would always be between them.

"Once the doctor is done with the Teku, put a team together and take care of it," she added.

Dr. Jabar's voice came over the comms a few minutes later. "Captain, are you in your suits?"

"Yes."

"You are free to come inside."

"Understood."

Wade and Valente followed her through the doors. The doctor had set up a make-shift sonic decontamination shower at the doors using a shipping container big enough to hold five people at a time. The door behind them sealed them in, and the inside doors remained locked. As the three of them stood in their suits, the decontamination process began.

A bright blue light bathed them all for a total of three minutes. Then a green light on the inside of the large box turned on, and the far door leading to the cargo bay opened. One of the doctor's assistants opened the door and gestured for them to follow.

Dr. Jabar stood by the Fashin Teku near one wall of the cargo hold. They'd arranged several crates for them to sit on during the examination. They all stood as Dana entered. She passed the charred remains of the cryostasis pods and figured it was about time they discuss redistributing the usable tech.

Dana spotted the new cargo immediately and scanned for the containers that should hold the embryos. None of the boxes seemed to have the correct dimensions, but they could be repacked within the Fashin Teku marked boxes, as the Begarans had done with their cargo. Their new triad of passengers was standing while the doctor and his team of two were preparing their gathered samples into cases for transport.

When Dr. Jabar saw them making their way over, he spoke to his two assistants. "Bring these to the lab. I'll be with you in a moment."

They turned without a word toward the container door, and Dana heard it seal behind them.

The Fashin Teku were all stripped down to the colored gowns they wore under their uniforms. Captain Zeppel stood with his head bent, but his eyes on her, as if willing her to come and talk to him. Dana noted his two companions—Tovar, the female with the bright red hair, and Oli, the one with the jet-black hair—on either side of him. Both sets of eyes rested on her with suspicion.

Dana walked straight over to Dr. Jabar, ignoring Zeppel and his companions for the moment.

"What are we dealing with, Doctor?"

He shook his head. "I'm afraid I don't know much. They let me collect samples and run some tests, but they wouldn't speak with me. I believe they've been waiting for you." Dr. Jabar rubbed a hand over his face.

Dana turned toward Zeppel. Through the contamination suit, she saw his stoic features waver.

"Commander, take a look at what our friends brought us."

"Yes, Captain." Wade moved to open the containers and review the contents of each.

Dana watched the three Fashin Teku with rapt attention. They seemed more interested in the floor than her face.

"Preliminary scans say they're free of any contaminates," Dr. Jabar reported as they waited, "but I can't be sure until I review the samples in the lab."

"I understand, Doctor. Don't let me keep you from your analysis."

Dr. Jabar's face cracked into an eager smile. His eyes were aglow with excitement. She'd seen his twin with a similar expression when looking at her, and at that moment, her face warmed. She hadn't thought about Rido Jabar all that much since her healing, but when she did, she could admit to herself it was with a fondness she hadn't felt for anyone since Wade.

"Where are they?" Wade called out, storming back to the Fashin Teku. They cowered even more under his intensity.

"Is there a problem?" Dana asked, turning to meet him.

"The embryos. They're not here."

Dana felt her stomach drop out and had to lock her knees. "Are you sure?"

"I've looked through everything they sent." His sad gray eyes met hers and when he spoke his voice was thick with emotion. "There are no embryos at all."

It was as she'd feared. The Fashin Teku had fooled them again.

Their embryos had been destroyed on their infected ship.

"Now what?" Wade asked lowly.

She knew what he was asking. Without the embryos, they had a slim chance their species would survive. Wade didn't know about the other Zelenian escape ships, and now wasn't the time to share that bit of information. Despite the knowledge, she knew finding them would be even more difficult than tracking down the embryos had been.

However, there was one sure way to get the information she needed.

"I'll handle this," she said. "Get a team together to inventory what we've got. Have Westlake scan the debris field for remnants of the embryos."

Wade nodded curtly. "Yes, Captain."

Captain Zeppel kept his eyes on the floor in front of him as Dana approached. His long hair fell to his waist, just like the others. His golden hair covered him from head to toe. Only their faces and palms were without the long hair. The three of them looked more disheveled and unkempt than she'd ever seen them. She wondered what they'd endured on their ship once the others were infected.

She fixed a stern expression on her face to match her boiling emotions. None of the Fashin Teku met her eye. All the better, because if they were to say anything other than the truth, she wasn't sure she'd be able to keep from throwing them out the nearest airlock.

"Well, Captain Zeppel, you've gotten yourself into a bit of trouble."

"Not a captain," he said, still avoiding her eye. "I have no ship. I am Ashwin."

"All right then, Ashwin. We have recovered some of our goods from you and some technology. However, we've noticed a few things missing."

"Yes," he said, his eyes still on the floor.

"Our embryos were not in the cargo hold. We want our

young, and if I don't like your answer, you'll be taking a long walk out our hatch with your two friends."

Dana said a quick prayer to the Merciful that they weren't already in the bellies of the small beasts standing before her. She wasn't sure what she'd do if they said they'd eaten them.

Ashwin heaved a sigh, then finally lifted his brown eyes to meet hers.

"How did you find us?"

"The Begarans seem to dislike you as much as we do. However, it seems they showed you exactly what they thought of you before you got too far."

"The Begarans!" Ashwin's eyes narrowed to slits. His hand caught the other in a fist. "They did this to us."

"You have quite the reputation. We only had to ask nicely, and they told us exactly where to find you."

Ashwin looked up at her again, his face relaxing. "They are treacherous creatures."

"And yet, *you're* the ones who stole from us. They weren't as friendly as you pretended to be, but they gave us lots of cargo and supplies."

Ashwin shook his head. "Because they have your babies."

He blurted out the words, and the other two Teku turned to glare at him. They tapped behind their ears and switched into their native tongue so they could berate him. His cheeks turned red as he blustered, no doubt making excuses for himself.

Dana waited, watching the exchange with her fists clenched at her sides. The buzzing in her ears made it hard for her to concentrate as they grumbled back and forth. Tired of their bickering, she held up a hand and spoke, her voice adamant and clear, drowning them out.

"Our embryos? You gave them to the Begarans?"

The three touched the backs of their ears again and waited for her to repeat herself. Though it hurt her to do it, she repeated the question and waited for their answer. Tovar and Oli turned to look at Ashwin.

"No," Ashwin said, hands flailing. "We traded them for the precious equipment here in your large box area. Many sorries, Captain."

Dana's body was so tense, a touch would set her off. "What the sou are they planning to do with them?"

Ashwin seemed to consider her question a moment, then smiled. "The Begarans need young. They will make babies."

That news wasn't as bad as she'd imagined. At least they weren't food. However, just because they were allowing them to become children didn't mean they wouldn't be put into servitude or used for food later.

"For what purpose?" she demanded.

"The Begarans are private. They don't like many others, but when we told them about you, they were happy to trade." Ashwin nodded, almost to himself. "It was a good deal."

"What did they do to your ship?"

He shrugged, his eyes wide. "I know not. One minute, everything is happy. The next, people are angry and fighting. I could not stop them."

"Why did they infect your crew?"

Ashwin bit his lower lip and stared down at his toes, curling against the cold metal of the storage room floor. "We took more than was agreed."

"Valente, inform the helm to put in a course change," Dana called out, her voice sharp. "We'll be heading back to the Begarans' planet, full speed."

"Yes, Captain."

Ashwin gave her a frantic wave. He lowered his voice to a whisper, as if relaying a secret only the two of them would share.

"I would not go after them now, Captain. You saw what they did to us. They won't give you back your young."

Dana wanted to punch something but would have to wait until she had the gym to herself. It was all making sense. The reason the Begarans had thrown goods at them and then sent them off after the Fashin Teku. They'd done everything they could to keep them on the move, away from them.

If they'd been minutes later, they might not have the knowledge that the Fashin Teku held. The destruction of their ship was supposed to end their search, as the Begarans had planned. Her anger fueled her intention to confront the Begarans again, though the blame for her predicament sat squarely on Teku shoulders.

Ashwin held up two hands in front of him, palms out. "You would like to leave us?"

Dana gave a sarcastic laugh. "It's not the worst idea, I've considered so far."

"Captain, let us to help you." Ashwin took a step forward, but Valente was already there, using his body as a shield in front of Dana.

Dana rolled her eyes. "No thanks. We don't want help from you."

"We have the Begarans' security codes. We carry the codes to their defense systems. If you keep us, you will need us."

When he turned to either side of him for support, the other two Fashin Teku nodded along with him.

Dana put one hand over her mouth and exaggerated a yawn. The Begarans were not backward or slow. They would have changed those codes by now. What he offered was no longer of any value.

"We bring you technology," Ashwin insisted. "The blink drive, the food synthesizer—we can teach you to make them. Your shield and defense—"

"What about them?" Dana challenged.

"They are excellent, but we can help you go faster. We know where to find you better weapons."

Dana stared at him with the most disinterested expression she could muster while inside, her heart was ready to pound out of her chest. Though his comment about the technology had piqued her interest, she'd never show it.

Ashwin squirmed as he ran out of ways they could help, shifting from one foot to the other as he waited for her answer.

"I would rather drop you off at a nearby barren planet and watch you suffer from orbit," she started.

Ashwin hung his head.

"But, since there are no nearby planets, you and your friends will help us integrate your technology into our current systems. You can begin working with our engineers as soon as the doctor says you're clear."

He raised his eyes to meet hers, as if trying to read her thoughts behind the words. The three of them stood wide-eyed and surprised. Dana waited for him to acknowledge her request with a slight nod.

Ashwin grabbed her suited hand before she had a chance to stop him.

"You are benevolent and kind. We were wrong to take

from you your babies. My deepest sorries. We are your servants until the debt is repaid."

"Captain," Valente said when he returned to her side.

Dana snatched her hand away from Ashwin before he got any more ideas.

"Problem?"

"According to Westlake, the engines are still recovering from our last dash to get to the Fashin Teku. We're going to need to cool down before we go anywhere."

Dana groaned.

"The Rogans are working on it."

"Good," she replied. "Let the Rogans know these three will be helping them to integrate the new technology with our own. We need to get back to the Begarans, and fast." Dana glanced around the med-bay. "These three will need accommodations. See if you can find them something."

"Yes, Captain." Dana caught the slightest lift at the side of his mouth. "I'll arrange a few cells to be brought in here for them."

She was glad he had a sense of humor. Barnes had often been too severe, too serious. Of course, that was probably because he was sabotaging their entire mission based on a seventeen-year-old boy's orders.

Barnes, like the majority of the other CAH members onboard, had probably never met their mysterious leader. Dana didn't like that kind of blind trust. She'd decided long ago she didn't want to serve with people who didn't want to serve with her. She'd yet to invite Adrian Valente to dine with her and the other senior officers, but when things had settled, she made plans to do so.

Dana focused her attention back on the Fashin Teku and

smiled without humor. They'd have to work a lot harder to earn her trust this time. Whether Valente brought them cots or actual cells, she didn't care. Their comfort wasn't her priority anymore.

"Have someone from the kitchen arrange rations at their convenience. Keep a couple of your people on them at all times. They don't have to get close, but I want them in the room. We don't want our guests to get any ideas."

Dana wondered if the promise of new tech made her a fool for allowing Ashwin and his friends to stay on board, but they'd promised to help them upgrade their engine systems and install a molecular relocator. She finally had the technology she'd wanted in the first place.

However, with the embryos back with the Begarans, it might be too late. Dana knew next to nothing of the Begarans or what use they might have for the embryos. They had to rescue their young, and this time she wouldn't accept silence for an answer.

"One more question," she said, turning to the three Fashin Teku. "What happens to your people when they're contaminated?"

"They behave against their nature and the eye changes. Mostly angry, but very honest."

Dana couldn't imagine honesty in and of itself being a problem onboard her ship but made a note to keep an eye on the crew for any signs of odd behavior. She trusted Dr. Jabar would do a thorough analysis before clearing the Fashin Teku to leave their quarantine.

CHAPTER 43

Captain's Personal log: 4327.10.3

I picked up my tin today. There are only four nanodots left. The anxiety surrounding me creeps up and holds me by the throat so often in the day that I don't know what else to do.

Rido has offered to counsel me, but there's something too raw and violent about these emotions I'm feeling. But as soon as I swallow one of those little white dots, it works its way through my system, making me whole where the anxiety split me in two.

The truth.

What is the truth, except for words on the edge of a knife, plunged into another's chest? I'm not able to tell Wade the truth. To do so would be to go back on my word and split him in half the way I am. There's far too much that needs to be accomplished on this journey. We won't make it with only half a Captain and half a First Officer.

Barnes is still out there, my secret tucked safely under his *tongue. How many other secrets is he keeping? Only the Majestic knows.*

The Fashin Teku destroyed all of themselves but three.

The Begarans have our embryos, and their devious misdirection will cost them more than they think. In two more days, they'll find out what it meant to cross us.

We may be the last of the human race, but we're not going out without a fight.

EPILOGUE

ESME

"I don't like it. Someone else should have to deal with those pirates," Esme said as she bent down to pick up more dirty clothes from the floor. She held it up for closer examination, and when she noted it was Eartha's, she put it in a pile she'd already collected near the hamper. "Why can't that girl clean up after herself? She must be changing her clothes at least three times a day," she mumbled as she worked.

Eric picked up the pile and put it in the basket for cleaning, pulling the remaining items from Esme's hands and gesturing for her to sit down. Esme resisted, but she gave up, knowing she wouldn't win this argument.

Things between them were tense enough, but she felt the need to speak building inside of her like a wall of water against a dam. The Fashin Teku had left the cargo bay and landed in her lap. She was constantly stepping around them and explaining things to them. Sure, they'd helped with the engines once before, that didn't mean they were indispensable. Esme couldn't wait to be rid of them. Any day now, she would burst.

"Don't we have enough to deal with?" she asked him.

"They're not going to be our problem. We'll work with them to get what we want, that's all and–wait. What do you mean by 'enough to deal with'?"

"I mean we have an adolescent and a baby on the way." Esme rubbed her belly, then caught herself. She seemed to do it whenever she thought of the baby.

"Don't get yourself all worked up," he said.

Esme waved him away as if she were erasing his words from the air. "My point is she's different. And I'm not sure we're..." she searched for the right word, "equipped to handle her."

"Lower your voice, she might hear you," he hissed.

Eric rolled his eyes. "We've been over this." He walked away from her and moved to put their dirty dishes from that morning into the sterilizer. "I'm not getting into it with you about her."

"When are we going to discuss the fact, she virtually predicted this pregnancy before the doctor said anything about it? There's no way she should have known."

"Maybe she's got a special skill that allows her to read people," he suggested. "We don't know that much about her life before."

"Ask her. She'll tell you. She's never even been near another pregnant woman. She knew it was a boy before a test would have even shown anything." Esme lowered her voice. "There's something not right about her."

Eric frowned. He was looking at her as if she'd threatened to kill the girl. He was so attached to her.

What would he think of their baby? Would he push his own child aside in favor of this strange girl? They had tried so many times before, they'd virtually given up. This child was a marvel. They hadn't done any of the things the doctors had encouraged them to do before their last night in their bed back home on Zelenia. Even with modern medicine, a healthy delivery wasn't guaranteed at this stage. What if this child didn't get a chance to open its eyes to the world? She tried to prepare herself, but her imagination insisted on creating a safety bubble around it.

Eric lifted his jaw in challenge. "I don't want to go over this again. She's our daughter, and we're going to take care of her. That's final."

"If you say, 'that's final' to me one more time Eric Rogan, I promise you it'll be the last time," Esme snapped. There were cracks in the dam, anger seeping out like water refusing to be held back. She struggled to bite down on her feelings. It was getting worse every day. Was this normal for pregnant women?

He sighed, rubbing a hand over his face. "I only mean I would prefer we drop this."

Eric reached out and put his hands on her shoulders, but Esme jerked away. The surprise and hurt flashed over his features and held him still. He seemed to notice her real anger for the first time.

He dropped his hands to his sides and lowered his

voice. "Can we at least agree that she's a priority and not a problem?" Eric asked, raising his eyebrows in question.

He cleared his throat when Eartha entered the room, moving past them to get herself a plate of food.

Esme bit down on her next words, keeping her mouth clamped shut.

Eartha eyed them both from under furrowed brows as she moved to Eric's side.

"This conversation isn't over," Esme hissed. She stood up and continued picking up the room. She gathered together another one of Eartha's 'projects', some contraption she was designing with the help of her robot or her friend.

"Eartha, I'm going to ask you one last time to pick up after yourself. This isn't a trash compactor." Her voice was too loud even to her own ears, but she couldn't help it. The cracks in her dam were growing wider.

"Yes, ma'am," Eartha said.

Eric leaned in close to Eartha, but Esme still heard him. "What she means is you've been a little distracted, and we think you need to focus when you're given a chore to do. We're grateful to have such nice quarters, but they won't stay nice if we don't keep it clean."

Eartha nodded. "Yes, sir."

"Come here," Eric said. He enveloped her in his arms, then kissed the top of her head.

Something in Esme's heart clenched at the sight and she rubbed her belly again. He loved that little girl, and nothing Esme said would change his mind.

Eartha looked up and made eye contact with her, and she felt a shiver run down her back. It was as if the girl could read her mind. Esme had a scientific mind, and though she'd never considered it a possibility before, after spending so much time with Eartha, she wondered if telepathy was a real thing.

After gobbling down her breakfast, Eartha was quick to pick up her pack and leave for school. The moment she was gone, Esme felt the heaviness in the air lift. What was it about the girl that put her off? Why did Eartha make the hairs on her arms stand up?

The pain in her back flared up, and she rubbed at it. Esme figured it meant another long day in the engine room. If her back muscles were already tightened like a vise, it wouldn't be long before her feet ached, too.

"You need another hour to get ready," he said with a sigh. "Take your time. I'll get the Fashin Teku set up in the engine room and ready to follow your orders."

"No, you just worked the night shift," she protested. "You need your rest, too."

"I'm fine. You're carrying our child. What kind of father would I be if I forced my pregnant wife to push herself when she needs rest?"

Esme pushed away from him, the anger slipping out again.

"You're the one pulling double shifts. I'm perfectly capable of doing my job. Just because I'm pregnant doesn't mean I'm an invalid. I wish you'd stop treating me like a glass doll."

This time his face quickly recovered from the disappointment and hurt that flashed over it.

"I'll be in the engine room. You can come in whenever you're ready."

Eric walked out the door, leaving Esme wondering why

she'd lashed out at him in the first place. He was only being considerate. Pregnancy was making her loopy. Maybe there was something the doctor could give her to balance out her emotions.

Despite her protests, it had taken her another hour to get ready. Picking up after the two of them had her wondering if she could do it for a third.

Esme marched into the engine room and noted two of the pirates, Oli and Tovar, already there, working with Eric. That explained the extra security she'd seen on her way in. Ever since they'd been cleared by medical, the two Teku had spent most of their time in the engine room, attempting to replicate their molecular relocation technology. In theory, they could transport items from one place to another by breaking them down to their micro-biotic level, then building them back up again in a different location.

"Esme, over here," Eric called out, waving her over. He was beaming, which could only mean one thing. Eric could see the possibilities already. That was his way. He liked to dive in feet first, especially when he knew that the result was success.

"Good afternoon everyone," she addressed the room as she made her way over. "Sorry I'm late. Are we making any progress?"

Ashwin, the former Fashin Teku Captain, popped out from behind a console, making her jump. "Yes, hello, Esme." He bowed toward her and eyed her hand, resting on her belly. She hadn't meant to draw attention to it, so instead crossed her arms as she spoke. They might not be familiar with the biology of human pregnancies.

"Chief," she said, correcting him.

Ashwin blinked twice. Confused he looked to the others for help but they remained silent.

"I am also addressed as Chief, or Commander Rogan," Esme said, giving Eric a knowing look. The two of them had often come up against some resistance to both of them carrying the same title and last name.

"My sorries, Chief Rogan."

Ashwin looked from Eric to Esme, then back again, as if not knowing how to continue. Tovar didn't seem to have the same struggle. Was the struggle for equality between men and women a thing in their history as well? She'd have to ask one day, when she didn't have a million other things to do.

"We isolated the materials to build the device," Tovar said, looking at Esme. "Now is the finding a location to build it."

"I didn't realize that the Captain had already approved of the building project," Esme said.

"She hasn't," Eric said, crossing his arms.

She didn't have to wonder what that meant. He'd asked Captain Pinet, and she'd said no.

"But she's aware that it's possible?" Esme asked.

"Yes, but first she wants a schematic of the project in writing. You and I will need to figure out where to put this contraption."

From the 3D image, it looked bulky and complex. They'd need something that could connect it to the rest of their systems, and it would need some kind of protection from tampering and panels to cover all the exposed wires.

"Well, let's get to work. This thing won't build itself," Esme said, pushing up the sleeves on her shirt.

Eric cleared his throat. "The Fashin Teku don't have much of a written language."

She frowned. "I see... Well, if they can build a 3D model, they can draw, and that will work too. Let's get moving or we'll never finish this thing."

Ashwin and Tovar worked hard on their drawings and made them to specifications, leaving Eric and herself to add the details in their written language. After an hour of work, she gave up wondering when Eric would leave. His shift had ended when she arrived. She didn't need him to supervise her. He was running on pure scientific curiosity now. He wanted to know everything and wouldn't sleep until he did.

When Commander Chance came by to check on their collaboration with the aliens, Esme was glad to report they were making progress. He addressed his questions to Eric.

"When do you think you'll have something up and running?"

"Soon," Eric replied. "It'll take us some time to get the schematic completed, but once we're approved, gathering the pieces won't be too difficult."

"Excellent. Thanks, Chief." Wade gave Eric a slap on the arm and turned to go but ran into Esme. He reached out in an automatic gesture, placing a gentle hand on her shoulder. "You're looking radiant today, Esme," he added. He wore a bright smile as he moved off.

She had to clamp down on a word you didn't use with a superior officer. She felt so violated. What gave him the right to come into her engine room, call her husband Chief, and call her by her first name while groping her shoulder? He had some nerve if he thought he could ogle her like a piece of meat, or worse, touch her as if she were a pet in a shop.

"What's wrong?" Eric asked her. "You've got that look on your face like you're ready to strike. Did the Commander say something wrong?"

"I'd like to know where he gets off touching me," she snapped. "Just because I'm carrying doesn't mean he can just reach out and put his hands on me whenever he wants. How would he like it if I just came up and stroked his arms?"

"I wouldn't love it," Eric said with a knowing smile. When she didn't smile back, he shrugged. "I'm sure he didn't mean anything by it," he said, reaching out and putting an arm around her shoulders, but she shrugged him off.

"He called you Chief and me Esme." Esme wanted to choke back angry tears. "I suppose that doesn't mean anything, either."

"It doesn't. The Commander is a nice guy." He frowned back at her. "Give him a break. You're being too sensitive."

"Too sensitive? And I guess being the mother of your child doesn't give me that right? Your child. Don't you get it? You're not going to play father to Eartha forever. She's a teenager. It's time you stood up for your own child."

"Eartha is just thirteen, I think she's got some time left. Why are you going on about her all the time?"

"I don't, but I notice you do."

Esme's voice was one level below a screech, and the entire engine room turned to stare at them. She noticed Ashwin and Oli look at one another, then take a distinct step back. They *should* get back. She wasn't interested in coddling anyone else today.

Esme took a step toward Eric, her nostrils flaring, her hands on her hips. "You'd better get it through your thick skull. Our baby is coming whether you like it or not, and you're going to be a father to him. Don't forget who's been in your life for the past fifteen years before you became an adoptive father to Eartha." She spat the words out and threw her fist against the nearest panel. It sputtered under the hit.

Eric shook his head as he stared back at her, his own voice rising in volume to match hers. "What's gotten into you? You're acting crazy."

"Oh, so now I'm *crazy*?"

Esme stormed off and out the doors. Eric moved to follow her out.

"Are you two feeling all right?" Ashwin asked as he passed, his hands tapping together nervously.

"We're fine," Eric said dismissively, pausing for a moment. "I wish I could say I didn't see this coming, but I did. You two keep up with your drawings, and we'll be back in a moment. I'm sure the rest of you have work to do, so get to it."

Eric gave the gawkers a significant glare of his own, then turned his attention back to Esme. As soon as they were on the other side of the engine room's doors, he spoke between his teeth.

"What's the matter with you? I knew you had some strong feelings, but *this*?" He waved a hand over the front of her, as if her emotions were something tangible. "Something's wrong."

"You just don't get it, do you?" Esme rubbed her hand over her forehead and pressed her fingers against her temple. "I need a minute."

"Take all the time you need. We'll be here." Eric walked until the doors of the engine room opened, then spoke loud enough for everyone to hear. "Get yourself together, because you're losing it. We don't need any more of your hysterics in here. We're all here to work."

He let the doors close between them.

Esme lifted her jaw off the ground. As long as she'd known him, Eric had never spoken to her in that way. He was angry, and he'd been mean, but she couldn't remember the last time he'd been so upset with her.

It was that girl. Eartha. She was already changing him, and Esme had to do something about it.

She stormed down the corridor, ignoring the looks she received and bumping into Mr. Jennison along the way.

"Oops, pardon me," he said, giving her an odd look. "Are you all right, Esme?"

"It's Chief, and yes, I'm fine. Watch where you're going," she snapped, leaving him and his apology behind.

DID YOU LOVE IT?
If you liked this book in whole or in part, I hope you'll let other people know by leaving a review. The fastest way to get another book from any author, including me, is to review and share the last one. Thank you!

ALSO BY T.S. VALMOND

Starship Hope Series:

Ensign (Prequel)

Exodus

Marauders

Viral

Nexus

Arrival

Verity Chronicles Series

Exile

Divided

On the Run

To be notified about the latest releases, promotions, and giveaways, make sure you're a VIP Reader. Learn more at https://TSValmond.com

ACKNOWLEDGMENTS

Many thank yous...to my readers for continuing the journey with me and the *Starship Hope* crew through unchartered space. *Marauders* is my love letter to space pirates. They make everything a little more interesting, in my opinion.

Being a storyteller is the most fun I've ever had. But being a professional writer takes a lot of work–way more than most people believe. But you make it all worthwhile. I'm still amazed when people reach out and tell me how much they like something I've written, but I'm not doing this all on my own.

Thank you to my editor Jack Llartin for attempting to show me the way of the comma. You've made this book sparkle, and I appreciate your professional diligence.

I want to add a special thank you to Christine and Taria, without whom this book would not have been true to me or made any sense. It's been a rough year not seeing your faces in person, but I honestly believe we'll see each other again soon. (Maybe in two weeks?)

Thank you to my loving and supportive husband, Matthew. He not only listens extensively as I fight my way through a book, but is there to walk the dog on the coldest of Canadian mornings.

ABOUT THE AUTHOR

Hi, I'm **T.S. Valmond** the science fiction and fantasy author currently residing in Canada with my husband and dog in an undisclosed location. One can never be too careful when exposing the secrets of powerful governments, worlds, and illegal aliens.

(Yes, they're watching.)

I was into science fiction and fantasy long before Browncoats, Trekkies, and Jedi were cool. Like my readers, I long for the days when Reality TV didn't mean anything and entertainment was entertaining.

When I'm not writing I'm–

Nope. I'm always writing.

TSValmond.com/links